CENTER FOR HELLENIC STUDIES COLLOQUIA

Written Voices, Spoken Signs

Written Voices, Spoken Signs

Tradition, Performance, and the Epic Text

Edited by
EGBERT BAKKER & AHUVIA KAHANE

HARVARD UNIVERSITY PRESS

Cambridge, Massachusetts • London, England • 1997

Library of Congress Cataloging-in-Publication Data
Written voices, spoken signs : tradition, performance, and the epic
text / edited by Egbert Bakker and Ahuvia Kahane.
p.   cm. — (Center for Hellenic studies colloquia)
Papers originally presented at a colloquium held June 22–26, 1994
at the Center for Hellenic Studies in Washington, D.C.
Includes bibliographical references and index.
ISBN 0–674–96260–5 (cloth : alk. paper)
1. Homer—Criticism and interpretation—Congresses.
2. Epic poetry, Greek—History and criticism—Theory, etc.—Congresses.
3. Epic poetry, Medieval—History and criticism—Theory, etc.—Congresses.
4. Literature, Comparative—Greek and medieval—Congresses.
5. Literature, Comparative—Medieval and Greek—Congresses.
6. Oral interpretation of poetry—Congresses.
7. Written communication—Greece—Congresses.
8. Oral—formulaic analysis—Congresses.
9. Oral tradition—Greece—Congresses.
10. Oral tradition—Europe—Congresses.
I. Bakker, Egbert J. II. Kahane, Ahuvia. III. Series.
PA4037.A5W75   1997
883′.01—dc21
96–46776

The Center for Hellenic Studies, located on a wooded campus in Washington, D.C., is a privately endowed residential research institute affiliated with Harvard University. At its core is a specialized library devoted to ancient Greek literature, history, philosophy, and related fields. Each academic year the Center offers ten Junior Fellowships to an international group of Hellenists in the earlier stages of their careers, as well as a Summer Session for postdoctoral scholars who need ready access to a strong research library. In addition, the Center has recently begun an annual Colloquium series.

The CHS Colloquia are devoted to examining significant topics that will profit from extended interaction of experts in various fields within and outside of Ancient Greek studies. These projects have a distinctly collaborative character. The organizers first formulate their proposed topic in consultation with the Center's Directors and its academic advisory board of Senior Fellows. They then invite participants to prepare original papers that will address designated aspects of the topic. In addition to those who are writing papers, several experts are invited to contribute to the process as discussants. At the colloquium itself, in the relaxed and intimate atmosphere of the Center, participants present and discuss the papers over the course of four or five days. Each chapter is then rewritten in light of the discussion, again in collaboration with the organizers.

This volume represents the revised papers of the first CHS Colloquium, which was held in June 1994. The organizers, Egbert Bakker and Ahuvia Kahane, were Junior Fellows in 1992–93 and 1993–94 respectively. Both had worked on aspects of the performance of Homeric epic and were interested in studying such issues more broadly. They decided to organize a multiauthored, theoretically oriented book that would consider audience-performer interaction from the perspective not only of ancient Greek but also of later European oral epic traditions. At the same time, the Center was developing a new program of annual colloquia. Project and program matched perfectly, and the first colloquium was on its way.

We thank all who have contributed to the process: the organizers for their creative initiative and scholarly leadership, all participants for their cooperative spirit and intellectual energy, the Senior Fellows for their support and advice, the Press (in particular Margaretta Fulton) for its enthusiastic acceptance of the new series, and not least the entire CHS staff, who made the meeting a practical reality. We hope that this first volume in the series will convey to its readers some of the sense of excitement and mutual illumination that was experienced by all who participated.

Deborah Boedeker and Kurt Raaflaub
Directors, Center for Hellenic Studies

༄

CONTENTS

CONTENTS

Written Voices, Spoken Signs

Introduction

EGBERT BAKKER & AHUVIA KAHANE

A little more than two generations ago Milman Parry argued for the oral nature of Homeric verse. Parry's work started an intense debate that has irrevocably changed Homeric studies and that has provided valuable impulses for a wide variety of other disciplines.[1] In the last several years the study of oral poetry has itself received considerable impulse and has undergone a dramatic increase in the variety of approaches and points of view.

At the heart of Parry's original thesis was the notion of "formula,"[2] a term that has since been modified, extended, reapplied, reused, and rejected.[3] Although disagreement among scholars about "what is a formula" is notorious, it was widely assumed that "formulaic style" (in whatever understanding of the term) is the essence of orality. This assumption was fortunate, in that it provided focus to an otherwise heterogeneous discussion. But it was also restrictive. It led to increasingly narrowing technical and statistical studies of formulaic poetry. Many scholars, although they almost universally acknowledged some form of the oral-formulaic theory, nevertheless felt that such theory did not provide satisfactory answers to questions about social, political, religious, and poetic aspects of Homer and other oral poetry.[4] Thus, while very few scholars explicitly rejected the oral poetry theory, frontiers were drawn: "oral" came to be seen more and more as a matter of formulas per se, and so dissociated from "poetry." This dissatisfying and at times unproductive divide ultimately persuaded some scholars to seek more integrative solutions. Other fields, such as anthropology, philosophy, linguistics, and literary studies, provided methodological and theoretical frameworks. The resulting studies, including earlier work by contributors to this volume, suggest that the more narrow, technical features of oral poetry are but points of departure for our present and future understanding.

The papers contained in this volume are exploratory probes into the field of oral poetry as it widens and touches other disciplines. They have in common the basic assumption that the concept of formula, in and by itself, does not exhaust the richness, depth, and variety of orality as an object of interdisciplinary research. Their authors come from various directions—Homeric philology, medieval philology, linguistics—but their previous work transcended the boundaries of their proper fields, a line that is continued in the pages that follow. Indeed, an important goal of this volume is to bring together different historical disciplines and thus to allow homerists and medievalists to take advantage of recent developments made within each discipline.

The papers were originally presented at a colloquium held June 22–26, 1994, at the Center for Hellenic Studies in Washington, D.C. The vibrant discussions during the conference, and indeed the resulting volume as such, owe much to the general format of the colloquium as suggested by the Directors of the Center, Deborah Boedeker and Kurt Raaflaub: we turned the usual proportions upside down, with fewer papers and more time for informal discussion and exchange of ideas. This arrangement proved to be both happy and fruitful.

One of the most important features of the recent developments in oral poetry research is the move, whether or not explicitly, away from composition as the central element of the theory of oral poetry toward the notion of *performance*. For Milman Parry, and for many later students of orality, the formula was a device that made it easier for the bard to *make* hexameter verse without the use of writing. But in recent years more and more attention has been given to the complex interactions between the "makers" of discourse and their addressees: literary discourses and ordinary spoken utterances alike are increasingly seen as not exclusively composed by an author or generated by a speaker but as "jointly created" by the two parties in the communicative process.[5] These new developments are beginning to have an impact on the study of oral poetry, a direction to which the present volume intends to contribute.

This perspective is manifest in one way or another in all the papers in this volume. Some authors move away from tradition as the main factor in composition and versification to a more inter-active and "performative" understanding of tradition, for exam-ple, as the intention of the performer, rather than as an inherent property of the formulaic epic text (Bakker); or as the domain of signification and understanding for *both* performer and audience (Foley). For Nagy tradition is not so much a matter of composi-tion in performance as of *re*composition in performance, a dia-logue, as it were, between the performer and his or her forebears. Kahane draws meter out of the compositional and mnemonic sphere into the area of sense and interpretation, and the key term in Oesterreicher's presentation, "communicative strategy," speaks for itself in this regard: communication necessarily implies the two-way street of both composition/production and reception/interpretation. Ford's paper is concerned with the reception of Homer (or rather Homer's unity) in the sixth and fifth centuries B.C.E. Schaefer considers the reception question in a broad perspective, viewing it as part of a "paradigm shift" in the humanities; and Bäuml views the reality of "facts" in a writing culture as dependent on both production and reception.

It should nevertheless be pointed out that diminishing the importance of composition and production does not ipso facto imply a rejection of Parry, nor of the formula (whatever its definition). Nor is it a denial of work by the many researchers who came after Parry. Downplaying the importance of composition amounts to an admission that the field of study is more complex and less mechanical than previously recognized. It might even be suggested that Parry himself pointed in this direction. Attention to strategies, means, and modes, rather than simply to contents, is a central feature of many poststructuralist approaches to language and discourse. Parry did not speak of speech-acts, of reception theory, of discourse analysis, or of pragmatics; but at the heart of his enterprise was an attempt to uncover underlying poetic codes, to explain what we might describe in contemporary terms as basic communicative strategies. In this sense Parry's work should be recognized as pointing to the future. Consequently the use made by the papers in this volume of various poststructuralist approaches may be not so much an act of rebellion as an evolutionary development.

Such evolution, if that is what it is, may also be of value in a more general sense. It is today increasingly (although not unanimously) felt that there has been for too long an unproductive silence between more conservative philology and contemporary approaches to the study of language, literature, and society. It is not for us here to comment on this broad issue. It can, however, be pointed out that the study of orality in general and the study of Homer in particular may be an area where previously disparate methodologies can come together. Indeed, as we hope the papers in this volume show, not only can the study of oral poetry benefit from contemporary developments—it may also help to lead them forward.

If singing is more than singing by formulas, then the study of oral poetry must move beyond the formula. We must ask what it means for the signs that are so familiar to us on the written page (words, phrases, indeed formulas) to be spoken; or what it means for the voice of poets to be written. This question may require us to rethink and redefine basic assumptions that we would otherwise take for granted. Each of the chapters that follow suggests in its own way that our conceptual apparatus is heavily influenced by our writing culture and thus may hinder our understanding of the oral texts of the past, and of the mind that produced them.

Egbert Bakker's "Storytelling in the Future: Truth, Time, and Tense in Homeric Epic" questions conventional concepts of time and tense in narrative and suggests an alternative more appropriate to the reality of the epic performance. Instead of referring to past events by means of verbs in the past tense, Bakker argues, the epic performer is more concerned with reactivating a past that is as alive and present as the epic tradition itself. While other epic traditions express this "commemorative" nature of the past with present tense forms, the Homeric situation, Bakker suggests, is more complicated: a brief analysis of some specific features of Homeric Greek (the evidential particle *ara*, the modal verb *mellein*, and the so-called augment of the verb) shows that the Greek epic tradition betrays a complex, double vision of epic events as both now and not-now, both near and far. This vision leads to a conception in which the epic performance can be seen as the reexperience of an ever-present original event, with "truth" emerging from the crucial difference in understanding between the performer of *epos* and the characters in the original event.

The analysis of Homeric discourse is thus brought to bear on wider issues in archaic Greek poetics.

Bakker's argument against epic events as "historical" in our sense, independent from epic itself and its performance, fits in well with Franz Bäuml's thesis in "Writing the Emperor's Clothes On: Literacy and the Production of Facts." Bäuml defamiliarizes the notion of fact, arguing that this seemingly self-evident and innocuous concept is in reality the consequence of a writing culture and its concomitant mentality. He argues that our very notion of independent facts that are "out there" depends on literate modes of reasoning, and on texts, that are separate from any performer or performance. Without the literate apparatus, we have, according to Bäuml, only "truth," which is ever dependent on a performing mediator. Bäuml reminds us that performed discourse cannot take place without a context. He argues that unlike facts, which can be lifted out of context, what is performed is mute without a teller.

The notion of performance and its relation to the past is also central in John Miles Foley's "Traditional Signs and Homeric Art." Foley considers the scholarly tradition centering around the Parry-Lord approach. He argues that "the hypothesis of oral tradition in Homer was based on literate concepts and explicated via a textual mindset," formulas being originally treated as textual items that are *seen* on the page rather than heard in performance. Foley challenges our literate notion of the sign and the process of reference, arguing for an oral poetics that is characterized by a radically different conception of referentiality: "the art of traditional poetry is an *immanent* art, a process of composition and reception in which a simple concrete part stands for a complex, intangible reality. *Pars pro toto,* as it were." He proceeds then by examining some cases of this "traditional referentiality" within the epic tale: the way in which signs in the final recognition scenes of the *Odyssey* point "institutionally toward a metonymic reality."

6

In "The Inland Ship: Problems in the Performance and Reception of Homeric Epic" Andrew Ford tackles the question of the performance in full of the "monumental *Iliad*." This question again takes us away from composition as the central element of orality and considers instead the degree to which the *Iliad* was perceived as a coherent whole in the archaic age. Various quotations from the Homeric poems suggest that authority regardless of context is more important than the unity of so many modern discussions of Homeric epic: ". . . if a hexameter or so can be adduced and accepted as Homer's actual words, it becomes a self-standing utterance, a piece of wisdom that demands attention in itself because of its source. This kind of epic analysis was so widespread in archaic and early classical Greece . . . as to make one doubt whether our ideals of epics as literary wholes were equally important to the Greeks of the archaic age." Ford then suggests that the poem's magnitude is "an imitation of an oral performance." In other words, we are faced with the possibility that the poem is not oral as such, but oral once-removed. This necessarily challenges the dichotomy of "oral" versus "literate" in earlier studies.

Ahuvia Kahane in "Hexameter Progression and the Homeric Hero's Solitary State" puts forward the case for meter and rhythm as spoken signs. Kahane views the hexameter as a "distancing device," an artificial context that presents the events narrated as belonging to a different reality. Where one verse ends and another begins, at the boundaries between *coda* and *onset,* there exist, he suggests, "interstices of silence." Where there is silence there is no song. Where there is no song there is no past, only the present. Such an interstice of silence thus "momentarily alters the balance between the narrative reality 'out there' and the time-present reality of the performance, contrasting the past and the present in a more-vivid, concrete, experiential, rather than cerebral manner." This "stitching together" of fiction and reality, which is close to the "near" versus "far" of Bakker's paper, is then illustrated by a study of the allegedly synonymous words for "alone" (*oios* and *mounos*), defining the "solitary states" of the heroes of the past. The marked localization of these two words at the beginning and the end of the verse, respectively, strongly suggests that meter and sense cannot be separated.

Richard Martin's analysis in "Similes and Performance" suggests a completely new range of functions for the typically Homeric phenomenon of the simile. On the basis of an extensive survey of anthropological records of epic traditions around the world, Martin redirects our attention towards the function of the Homeric simile in the interaction between the performer and his audience. Martin suggests that similes are effectively "genre imports," swallowed up by the "ambitious supergenre" of epic. He uses internal evidence earlier adduced to prove the recent nature of the Homeric simile to propose affiliations of Homeric similes to other nonepic oral genres within Greek tradition. Martin argues that a major effect of similes, their "rhythmic" function, as he calls it, has thus far been neglected in Homeric studies. Martin's argument both implies a much more complex underlying performance context than hitherto assumed and releases a whole range of intriguing questions about orality: if the singer borrows from other performance genres, then what is the identity of the *singer's* performance?

Gregory Nagy in "Ellipsis in Homer" submits that a seemingly innocent feature of language, ellipsis, encapsulates the very essence of Homer and epic tradition. On the level of individual phrases, the concept of ellipsis as formulated by Nagy sheds light on a classic problem in Homer: the use of dual forms to describe a group of three characters in the text. The problem exists as long as we consider the text of Homer as a statement ("text") at a single point in time. Nagy, however, raises the possibility that in fact it is inappropriate to read Homer synchronically. On the level of the tradition as a whole, this leads to the idea of "recomposition in performance," implying the futility of looking for either an "original" or a "final" performance. Rather than misinterpretations of earlier versions, Nagy submits, the enigmatic duals in the *Iliad* reflect the systematic *re*interpretation that is inherent in an evolutionary model of Homeric poetry.

Whereas most papers in the volume focus on signs that are spoken, Wulf Oesterreicher in "Types of Orality in Text" presents a taxonomy of voices that are written. Oesterreicher considers the obvious but strangely neglected relations between orality and textuality: how can texts be "oral" if they are written? Oesterreicher's answer starts from a distinction between "medium" and "conception" in the study of orality: medium refers to spoken versus written, phonic versus graphic, whereas conception is a matter of the style or mode of expression of a given discourse. For Oesterreicher, "conception" is essentially a matter of the "distance" or the "immediacy" of a discourse. On this basis, orality can be defined as the degree of immediacy in a discourse, whether spoken or written. In the final part of the paper, Oesterreicher discusses the orality of oral poetry; he points out that most oral poetry presents a curious mix of "immediacy" and "distance" features (bringing the argument in line with Bakker's and Kahane's distinctions between "near" versus "far" and "real" versus "fictional").

Finally, Ursula Schaefer's "The Medial Approach: A Paradigm Shift in the Philologies?" is an explicit invitation to reconsider normally implicit perspectives of written and spoken media. Schaefer forces us to question the "philological approach," presenting the argument that "the media in which we communicate model our world." She submits that hermeneutics is dependent on writing and literacy (this indirectly corroborates Ford's thesis about quotations of Homer in the archaic age). In performed environments where "the human voice was still prevalent," a different critical paradigm is required, in which the *reuse* of a discourse and its authority is more important than its unity or textual constituency.

These, then, in alphabetical order, are the individual contributions in this volume, which we hope are a reflection of changing perspectives within our "interpretive community." We hope to contribute to an understanding of orality as something both different from our own direct, highly literate experience, and yet as something comprehensible to us in our present day world. Above all, we hope that this volume, as befits a study of orality, will form part of a living, open-ended dialogue, rather than present a fixed, finite, closed declaration of opinions and beliefs.

It remains for us to thank not only the contributors to this volume and the speakers in the colloquium, but also the select group of participants who did not present papers but who made substantial contributions to the discussion, among them Harry Barnes, Deborah Boedeker, Jenny Strauss Clay, Mark Edwards, Nicolai Kazanski, Vanda Kazanskiene, Françoise Létoublon, Deborah Lyons, Kurt Raaflaub, and Harvey Yunis. The colloquium and this volume would not have been possible but for the unique environment and facilities of the Center for Hellenic Studies and the enthusiastic support of its Directors and Senior Fellows. They have our deep gratitude for making the organization of this conference such an easy and enjoyable task.

CHAPTER 1

Storytelling in the Future:
Truth, Time, and Tense
in Homeric Epic

EGBERT BAKKER

"In living speech, the *ideal* sense of what is said turns towards the *real* reference, towards that 'about which' we speak. At the limit, this real reference tends to merge with an ostensive designation where speech rejoins the gesture of pointing. Sense fades into reference and the latter into the act of showing."

PAUL RICOEUR, "WHAT IS A TEXT?"

The question whether the Greek epic tradition is a matter of truth or of fiction remains a central issue in Homeric scholarship, and any answer to it betrays one's stance with regard to a host of other issues, such as text, tradition, and authorship. Opinions are divided as to whether the Homeric rendition of the heroic past is wholly traditional and so "objective," or allows of fictional, "original" admixture by an individual poet. What is less often asked is whether the notion of truth itself, in the sense of an acknowledged correspondence between a statement and a state of affairs referred to, is not something of our own making, a norm from which the poet whom we wish to be more than merely traditional and mechanical can depart at will.

The growing interest in *performance* as the crucial feature defining the orality of Homeric poetry bears directly on this issue.[1] When many features of Homeric poetry begin to be seen in terms of the special communicative conditions of the performance-context, the traditionality of Homer, too, is affected: it shifts from the poetic words and formulas themselves to their *utterance,* and so to the stance and intention of the speaker in the context of the performance event. Tradition, in other words, is a speech act, rather than a property of epic style.[2] And the truth of the epic tradition, even though it may be experienced by performers and their audiences as stable and "objective," may be more a matter of *belief,* a belief in the power of memory and of words to recreate the epic events in the context of the performance.

In this paper I explore some aspects of this dynamic conception of truth as opposed to our own more static understanding of that notion. We shall be concerned with linguistic reflections of a notion of truth in which the past is not so much an event referred to as a *state of mind in the present,* an act of remembering, not so much in the sense of a retrieval of a fact from memory as in the sense of a *reexperience* of an original experience that took place in another time. The tension between the idea of the past as something *near* and re-created in the context of the performance yet at the same time something *distant,* something with regard to which one can adopt an "objective" stance, defines, as I shall argue, the ontological status of the epic reality in the context of the Homeric performance.

TENSE AND REFERENCE

Our starting point is tense. What happens when we use a verb in the past tense? The question seems too obvious at first sight to lead to controversial answers. Tense, as most grammarians agree, locates events in time;[3] and past tense refers to a situation that held at some time prior to our moment of speaking. Such a reference may imply either the assertion of a state of affairs in the past or the denial of a state of affairs in the present. In the first case we may state, "objectively," a historical fact; or we may adopt, for the sake of a narrative, a point of view in the past, from which a given event in a story is perceived. In the second case, on the other hand, our point of view is in the present, in which we imply by our use of the past tense that something is not the case anymore.

What the two cases have in common is the distance in time between the event and our moment of speaking. Whether we speak objectively about the past; or create a fictional point of view other than our own; or speak in the past tense from our own point of view: the result is the reference to an event that occurred independently of the moment of speaking, at a moment in the past that *excludes* the present. It is to this conception of the past that I oppose the notion of the past in myth and epic tradition. The past here is not something recorded, reified, and subsequently referred to with sentences in the past tense. Such a separation of the knower from the known, the exclusion of the present from the past, has to yield, I believe, to a conception in which the past *includes* the present, in a way that is different from our sense of time and the past.

TENSE AND CONSCIOUSNESS

As a first step to this other notion of time, I suggest the possibility that tense has to do not so much with events as such, entities referred to, as with the *perception* or *remembrance* of events. After all, language can refer to the "real world" only insofar as this world is perceived by a consciousness that verbalizes its thought and that mediates between the world and a listener, whose consciousness perceives this representation of the real world as language.

In a recent discussion of language, time, and consciousness, the linguist Wallace Chafe suggests that consciousness, as far as speaking and language is concerned, can be in two "modes": "immediate" and "displaced."[4] In the first case a speaker receives input from the physical environment, and the speaker's consciousness can be called "extroverted," engaged in the perception of the surrounding reality. In the second case the speaker's consciousness is "introverted"; it receives its input not directly from the environment but from the perception of *another* consciousness, in practice a past consciousness that was once extroverted in a given environment. A first consequence of this distinction for the discussion of tense is that "immediacy," the coincidence of perceiving and speaking, has an affinity with present tense. "Displacement," on the other hand, the separation of perceiving and speaking, and the presentation of an event as not-now, is linked with nonpresent tense, in narrative virtually always past tense.

Thus when someone tells about what happened to him or her yesterday, there is a consciousness in the present that is engaged in verbalization, and this consciousness receives its input from a previous consciousness in the past that was engaged in perceiving or experiencing the events told. One may, and one frequently does, use present tense in such a story ("historical present"), pretending that the consciousness perceiving or experiencing the past event is actually perceiving in the present. This strategy to achieve the pseudoimmediacy that we call "vividness" is especially frequent in the case of the reporting of *speech events* ("direct discourse": "and he goes . . .," or "and he says . . ."), since it is this event, which coincides with what the verbalizing consciousness is doing in the present, that is best suited for drawing the remembered world into the here and now of the present.[5]

Yet whether one uses past or present tense for one's conversational stories, and whatever the nature of the event one calls to mind, the relation between the verbalizing consciousness in the present and the perceiving consciousness in the past is a matter of

remembering. And it is precisely the phenomenon of remembering as an experience linking past and present that is absent from
the abstract models of temporal deixis and reference in terms of
which tense is usually discussed.

STORYTELLING IN THE PRESENT

When we now move from ordinary conversational storytelling to
oral traditions, it is clear quite apart from the present discussion
that remembering plays an important role. Outside memory, in
fact, the past does not even exist in oral societies, and without the
"mind act" of remembering, the speech act of poetry would be
impossible.[6] With regard to this experience of the past as some-
thing-to-be-performed, our usual notion of past tense, geared as
it is to reference, the correspondence between language and facts
in the past, is particularly inappropriate. If the past is something
that is remembered, it does not exist in recorded form but owes
its existence to the verbalizing, introverted consciousness of the
performer that draws it into the present. The past, in fact, becomes "present," both in a temporal and in a spatial sense: it is
turned from "then" and "there" into "now" and "here" within the
context of a special social event and through the actions of a
special, authoritative speaker.

The natural and frequent consequence of this situation is that
the performer adopts the stance of an eyewitness or sportscast
reporter, one who verbalizes things seen, staging the participants
in the performance event as *spectators* of the epic events from
the past. Epic discourse strives to overcome the gap between the
natural, visual icon and the arbitrary sign that is language, producing a sustained attempt at *enargeia* (vividness).[7]

In terms of the discussion of consciousness just presented,
enargeia is pretended immediacy, doing as if one verbalizes what
one sees and pretending that the extroverted consciousness that

15

saw the epic events is actually seeing them in the present. It comes as no surprise, then, that epic traditions draw heavily on the linguistic means used by speakers whose consciousness is in the immediate mode, of which present tense is the most important for our present purposes. In other words, epic performers deploy strategies that are not unlike those used by conversational storytellers to achieve vividness of the discourse and thereby the *participation* and *involvement* of the audience.

The Romance linguist Suzanne Fleischman, for example, notes (like others before her) that medieval epic in Romance makes an abundant use of present tense, attaining a graphic and descriptive quality.[8] According to Fleischman, in the traditions that she studies events are not so much *narrated* (on the basis of causal sequential relationships) as *described* by way of visualization. Often the presentation of epic events has, as she notes, the effect of a slow-motion camera that freezes the action and breaks it down into its component parts.

The epic event verbalized by way of the pseudoimmediacy of present tense, then, is not historical in the sense that it is past; it belongs to the present just as much as it belongs to the past, and in fact the narrator makes an attempt at collapsing the *duality* that is inherent in referentiality, a duality between a referent and a referring sign. The past does not exist independently of the present; it is drawn into the present and comes alive at the moment of speaking, activated by the memory of the speaker and the participation of the audience. In epic storytelling, then, the epic event and the speech-event of the performance become in a real sense a unity.

But we now turn to Homer. The first thing we notice here is that even though the *enargeia* of Homeric discourse is beyond question, there is an important difference from many other epic traditions: the historical present does not occur in Homeric narrative.[9] Other narratives that are not related to performance may freely use the historical present, but this device does not belong to the arsenal of linguistic means of the Homeric narrator to create vividness. Why? In search of an answer to this question, we shall have occasion to observe that the Greek epic tradition aims at something other than mere vividness or pretended immediacy.

Recreating the past, reviving the crucial events of the epic world as models for the present, may be the concern of any tradition of epic poetry, but the Homeric tradition seems to go one step beyond this unreflective immediacy. What is recreated in the Homeric performance may be a very vivid affair, but the Homeric representation does not pretend to be a replica of the original event. In fact, as I will argue, the implicit poetics of the Homeric tradition reveal that the "true" poetic version of the epic events is better than the real thing: besides the urge to create the presence and nearness of the epic events, Homeric epic, I will suggest, is also concerned with duality and distance. In terms of time, this means that not *only* is the past turned into the present (as in the case of medieval Romance epic such as *Roland*) but *also* is the present turned into a *future*, a future from which the epic event is perceived with the knowledge and under-standing of the present. The epic event in its Homeric repre-sentation, then, is both close *and* distant, both here-and-now and "beyond." And the mutual expectancy of the near and the far can be gauged from the degree to which *linguistic signs* of the one presuppose the other, and vice versa.

EVIDENCE AND INTERPRETATION IN HOMERIC DISCOURSE

Two linguistic signs of "nearness" play a role in the present argument: the particle *ara* and the verb *mellein*. These two ele-ments have a strong semantic affinity to each other. They may be characterized, in their Homeric use, as markers of *visual evidence*

EGBERT BAKKER

in the here and now of the speaker; more precisely, they mark the *interpretation* of such visual evidence. This interpretation turns the visual evidence into a *sign* that points to a *previous experience or perception* in the past that in its turn transforms the experience/perception in the present into a *re-experience,* the interpretation and understanding of the past in the present. The best way to introduce this "evidential semantics" is to look at how *ara* and *mellein* are used by speakers within the epic tale, as they react, understand, and verbalize their experiences in speech revealing the implicit poetics of the *Iliad.*

Consider first the following passage as an illustration of the use of *ara* and the mental disposition that it reflects:[10]

ὦ πόποι, ἦ μέγα θαῦμα τόδ' ὀφθαλμοῖσιν ὁρῶμαι·
ἔγχος μὲν τόδε κεῖται ἐπὶ χθονός, οὐδέ τι φῶτα
λεύσσω, τῷ ἐφέηκα κατακτάμεναι μενεαίνων.
ἦ ῥα καὶ Αἰνείας φίλος ἀθανάτοισι θεοῖσιν
ἦεν· ἀτάρ μιν ἔφην μὰψ αὔτως εὐχετάασθαι.

(*Iliad* 20.344–348)

"Can this be? There is this big miracle that I see with my own eyes. His spear is lying here on the ground, but I can no longer see the man I was charging at in fury to kill. So Aineias was then dear to the immortal gods. But I said that his boasts were in vain."

The speaker here is Achilles. Somewhat earlier in the narrative he has met with the Trojan hero Aineias on the battlefield and they have exchanged a series of insults, boasts, and claims about their ancestry and genealogy. When Achilles is at the point of killing Aineias, the god Poseidon intervenes (20.291); he puts a mist before Achilles' eyes (20.321), drops Aineias' spear before Achilles' feet (20.324), and lifts Aineias from the scene (20.325). When the cloud is dispersed and Achilles regains his vision and consciousness (20.341), he begins to verbalize, spell out, what

18

goes on in his mind, characterizing what he sees as a "big miracle" *(mega thauma)*. The verb for "I see" that he uses *(horōmai)* is a verb in the middle voice, which means that Achilles is not a detached observer of an external fact, but that he is part of what he sees—in other words, the miracle takes place in his mind no less than in reality. The miracle, of course, is the spear-without-warrior that is lying there. Now in Achilles' mind this spear acquires the status of a sign pointing to the past and leading to a *correction* of an opinion that he held in the past: now he understands that Aineias' boasts and claims were not vain and that Aineias and his race are in fact under the protection of the gods.

This conclusion, verbalized in the phrase with *ara* (in the form of *rha*), is what is of interest here. The particle does not mark a fact so much as a mental disposition. Using Chafe's terminology as introduced earlier, we may say that Achilles' consciousness is in the immediate mode: being extroverted, it receives its input from the physical environment.[11] But since the perception is at the same time an interpretation, Achilles' consciousness is at the same time introverted, activating the previous consciousness of his memory. That previous consciousness is characterized by ignorance, just as the present consciousness is a matter of understanding, and the significance of the present speech-act derives precisely from this contrast. Achilles is quite explicit on this point: with *atar* (but, yet) he opposes the understanding of the present to the ignorance of the past. He might have characterized his ignorant previous self as *nēpios*, but that important Homeric word will not concern us until later.

For the moment we note that the *ara*-statement with which Achilles verbalizes his conclusion has *past* tense marking *(ēen:* "So Aineias, too, *was* loved by the immortal gods"). This past tense, however, is quite different from our notion of past tense discussed earlier: the past here is not an event located prior to the present, a "was" that excludes "is." Rather, this past is a past *consciousness* that is recognized as past but that *still* comes into the present. This is a past that is not separated from the present but that includes it; it owes its very existence to Achilles' sensory, mental, and verbal activity in the present. Achilles' mental situation may serve as a model for the poetics of the Homeric tradition, but before entering that topic, let us first turn to the second linguistic sign to be discussed, the verb *mellein*.

This verb is commonly seen as an auxiliary of future tense, a characterization that does not quite capture the meaning of this element in Homer. Homeric *mellein*, as Louis Basset has argued, may be conveniently dubbed a "probability verb": an instance of *mellein* with an infinitive X has as value: "it is highly probable that X," "tout porte à conclure que."[12] The "tout," we may observe, is in practice physical evidence observed by a speaker, so that the value of *mellein* lies in the semantic sphere of the evidential particle *ara* that we just discussed.[13] Consider the following example:

ἐξ αὖ νῦν ἔφυγες θάνατον κύον· ἦ τέ τοι ἄγχι
ἦλθε κακόν· νῦν αὖτέ σ᾽ ἐρύσατο Φοῖβος Ἀπόλλων
ᾧ <u>μέλλεις</u> εὔχεσθαι ἰὼν ἐς δοῦπον ἀκόντων.

(Iliad 11.362–364)

"Once again now you escaped death, dog. And yet the evil came near you, but now once more Phoibos Apollo has saved you, he to whom <u>you must</u> be praying when you go into the thunder of spears thrown."

The situation is not very different from that in the previous example. A Greek warrior, Diomedes in this case, has almost succeeded in killing a major opponent (the Trojan Hektor). The opponent escapes with difficulty, and Diomedes concludes from this physical evidence that his intended victim must be protected by Apollo (*hōi melleis eukhesthai*, "[Apollo], to whom you must be praying"), who has saved him once more. We see again that there is an interpretation based on physical evidence, the creation of a fact in the mind of the speaker. In this case the fact does not involve the past; it pertains to the present; both *mellein* itself and the infinitive it governs have present tense marking. But let us look at the next example:

> ἆ δειλοί, Δαναῶν ἡγήτορες ἠδὲ μέδοντες,
> ὣς ἄρ᾽ ἐμέλλετε τῆλε φίλων καὶ πατρίδος αἴης
> ἄσειν ἐν Τροίῃ ταχέας κύνας ἀργέτι δημῷ.   (*Iliad* 11.816–818)

"Oh you poor wretches, you leaders and men of counsel among the Danaans. So in <u>this</u> way you were going, far from your friends and the land of your fathers, to glut with your shining fat the swift dogs of Troy."

The speaker here is Patroklos, the dearest friend of the most important Greek hero, Achilles; Patroklos has just come from the tent of Nestor, who has given him the advice to enter the battle as a substitute for Achilles himself. On his way back to the tent of Achilles, Patroklos meets the badly wounded Eurupulos. He takes pity on the wounded man, and his exclamation that we see here is a striking co-occurrence of tenses that, I believe, has not yet been fully investigated or understood. First, the complement of *mellein,* the infinitive *asein* ("to glut") is not present, as in the previous example, but *future.* Furthermore, unlike the earlier example, *mellein* itself as used in the passage has not present but *past* tense. And most importantly, it co-occurs with *ara,* which was only to be expected when both the particle and the verb are in the semantic sphere of evidentiality and interpretation. Since *ara* applies to the immediate here and now, we have the past, present, and future coming together in one utterance.

Before proceeding with the analysis of Patroklos' words, we should look at the usual account of the use of *mellein* in this type of context. Both Basset and Ruijgh, who, as we saw, attributed to *mellein* in Homer a value that is close to the notion of interpretation of evidence proposed here, attribute to *this* and similar cases to be discussed later on, a value that is quite different. According to them, *mellein* here expresses "destiny in the past," a purely temporal meaning involving *relative tense* or future in the past: temporal deixis with respect to some reference point in the past. Now quite apart from the general methodological principle that it does not seem wise to multiply the meanings of linguistic elements when that is not absolutely necessary on independent grounds, I believe that notions like "destiny (future) in the past" are not entirely appropriate for this use of Homeric *mellein;* they imply a temporal relationship, whereas what seems to be the central feature is consciousness, present and past, with a crucial difference in knowledge between the two.

Let us first observe that Patroklos' exclamation is a speech-act that is uttered in a concrete situation, a physical here-and-now. He sees the wounded man before his eyes, and "points" to him verbally with the deictic element *hōs* ('in this way'). But with this adverbial demonstrative pronoun, Patroklos does much more than pointing in the present. The pronoun links the present with the past, for it presents the wounded Eurupulos as a sign that points to the past. In seeing Eurupulos, Patroklos constructs the past in his mind: a past *consciousness* that is, again, crucially different from the perceiving and verbalizing consciousness in the present, by its ignorance, opposed to the understanding of the present. Now it has become clear, in the mind of Patroklos, who will soon die himself, what the Greeks marching to Troy did not know: their corpses were going to feed the dogs of Troy. Again, just as in the case of Achilles and the spear of Aineias, we see that the past comes into being prompted by visual evidence in the present. And again, this is not a past that excludes the present; this is a past that merges with the present and that is constructed to verbalize and organize conscious experience in the present.

So far, Patroklos' exclamation is not very different from Achilles' words in seeing the spear of Aineias; a verb with past tense marking is used in combination with *ara* to mark the duality *and* unity of a past and a present consciousness. But the new example is more complex, for the infinitive complement of *mellein* is a future (*asein*, "to glut," fut.). The future character of the demise of the Greeks is, of course, intimately connected with the contrast between understanding and ignorance: the Greeks did not know, while Patroklos now knows, what the consequences would be of the campaign against Troy. Yet this same contrast in knowledge makes this future tense marking very different from an abstract temporal relation such as "future in the past." The future which Patroklos knows and which the Greek leaders in the past did not know *is in fact nothing other than the present moment of Patroklos' speech.* Patroklos' present not only gives him information about the past; more importantly, it makes him conscious of that past.

In Patroklos' discourse, then, the past comes alive in the present, whereas the present becomes a future from which the past that is now present is being seen. Insofar as the past intrudes into the present, the speech event of the present and the event of the past form a unity; but insofar as the present is conceived of as a future, the two consciousnesses form a duality, on the basis of a crucial difference in knowledge. It is this difference that defines the "truth" of Patroklos' statement, not as a referential relation between sign and referent, a word and its object, but as the verbalization of a consciousness that spans past and present.

EPIC DISCOURSE AS RECOGNITION

The step from Achilles' and Patroklos' discourse to that of the Homeric narrator and the voice of the Greek epic tradition presupposes a certain compatibility between the heroic discourse of Homeric characters and the poetic discourse that encapsulates this direct speech, a point that is gaining attention in current Homeric scholarship.[14] In the case of Patroklos' exclamation, which we have just studied, the blurring of differences between the speech of the narrator and that of the characters is particularly important, for what he says enacts as perhaps no other character's speech the central concern of Homeric epic: commemoration by way of lamentation.[15] Patroklos' compassionate outburst of commiseration, in fact, might perhaps be considered a reflection from *inside* the epic world on the terrible consequences of the wrath of Achilles and the plan of Zeus—could the idea of the dogs of Troy feeding on the Greek corpses be an echo of the very beginning of the *Iliad?* The deepest poetic insight on the wrath of Achilles voiced by a character who will be the most distinguished victim of that wrath, and who is as yet quite unaware of this future, constitutes a moment of the greatest and most sophisticated dramatic irony.

On a more general note, and apart from poetic irony, we may observe that the discourse of the narrator of the *Iliad* (the role of "Homer" in the performance) resembles the speech of Patroklos and Achilles in that memory and perception, past and present, merge, but do not form a complete unity.[16] A certain distance remains, in the form of an awareness that the experience that underlies the verbalization in the present, the event created in the performance, is a *re*experience of the original event, a reliving of the past, armed with the understanding of the present. And as a reexperience, the epic tale is also a repetition. We touch here upon the ritual aspects of performance as the discourse of what has been called *recognition*,[17] or as *restored, "twice behaved" behavior.*[18] Unlike written fiction, the activity of the performer does not draw the audience into the past; rather, the past is, conversely, drawn into the present through the nonfictional activity of the performer. However, it never fills the present entirely;

just as in other rituals and performances, such as theater, the performer and the public remain aware of a distance between themselves and the event, no matter how vividly it is represented or with how much abandonment one participates in it.[19] A striking case of this cooccurrence of immediacy and displacement, of the near and the far, is the description of the death of the speaker of the previous example, Patroklos:

> ἔνθ᾿ ἄρα τοι, Πάτροκλε, φάνη βιότοιο τελευτή·
> ἤντετο γὰρ τοι Φοῖβος ἐνὶ κρατερῇ ὑσμίνῃ
> δεινός· ὁ μὲν τὸν ἰόντα κατὰ κλόνον οὐκ ἐνόησεν·
> ἠέρι γὰρ πολλῇ κεκαλυμμένος ἀντεβόλησε·
> στῆ δ᾿ ὄπιθεν, πλῆξεν δὲ μετάφρενον εὐρέε τ᾿ ὤμω
> χειρὶ καταπρηνεῖ, στρεφεδίνηθεν δέ οἱ ὄσσε.

(*Iliad* 16.787–792)

"So, there then, Patroklos, the end of your life appeared. For Phoibos came against you in the strong encounter, terrible. And he did not see him as he was moving through the battle. For shrouded in deep mist he came in against him, and he stood behind him, and struck his back and broad shoulders with a flat stroke of the hand, and his eyes spun."

The poet directly addresses a major character from the epic tale;[20] but he does *not* use present tense. He does not address Patroklos as if the latter is involved in the action itself at the moment of speaking. It is as if the poet is watching a movie, together with the character, who is both "near," in the performance, and "distant," in the movie. But the very presence of the character in our here and now turns the narrative into "truth," a reexperience characterized by an understanding that was not available in the original experience. Thus the poet can announce the scene as the *biotoio teleutē*, "the end of (Patroklos') life," and add, in a series of phrases marked by the explicative particle *gar*, that the victim did not perceive (*ouk enoēsen*) how the dreadful god appeared. The recognition in the present, in fact, gives the narrative its significance; moreover, whereas other traditions may stage their performers as eyewitnesses, who verbalize what they see, in Homeric epic the performer is more like one who understands what he or she remembers, as a trustworthy interpreter, at the same time a proud master of truth and a humble servant of the Muses.

The evidence on which the epic tale is based is obviously pretended immediacy, but sometimes the context of Homeric discourse is just as concrete as the evidence that prompts the discourse of Achilles and Patroklos that was studied earlier. Just as does any meaningful discourse, Homeric narrative situates itself, producing the momentum for its own continuation. In other words, the *flow of discourse of the performance itself* may provide the evidence on which subsequent statements are based. The obvious example is character speech, direct discourse. At the end of these performances within the performance, in returning to the narrative proper, the poet/performer frequently uses the evidential-deictic phrase *hōs ar' ephē* (so in this way he spoke). Just as Patroklos did in his commiseration speech, he combines the evidential particle *ara* with the demonstrative adverb *hōs*. Again, the demonstrative is not merely deictic, pointing to something in the here and now; it also presents the object pointed at, the direct speech just finished, as a sign pointing to the past.[21]

NARRATIVE WITHOUT TENSE

So much for linguistic signs of the "near," a discussion that should not make us neglect the signs of the "far." After all, the original, extroverted consciousness perceiving or undergoing the real event is not the performer's own, and the verbalizing, introverted, and understanding consciousness that is active in the present is not the first one. The evidence presented to this consciousness, in fact, is not only the *present discourse* but also, and more so, the memory of *previous discourses,* the cumulative total of all the previous reexperiences, in short, the epic tradition. The tradition is, in effect, the only access route to a past of which the poetic speech act of the performance is the institutionalized invocation.

The observation that understanding and recognition of Homeric discourse is not only a matter of the present moment but also of previous reexperiences, may direct our attention for a moment to the formulaic nature of epic discourse, in its "postmodern" understanding: not—or not *only*—as a mechanism to facilitate oral composition but as a means to create *involvement,* to increase the understanding of the audience by familiar phraseology, to situate epic discourse in the physical here and now of the performance, and to locate that here and now in the diachronic space of the tradition.[22] Formulas, then, are not so much *inherently* traditional phrases as phrases with *traditional intent,* acknowledged elements of the performer's traditional strategies.

The fact that not all the meaning of the epic tale derives from the present discourse is also important for an account of tense and time in epic. Earlier I suggested that our usual conception of tense may be inappropriate for an account of time in Homer. If we now realize that epic discourse in the present has not so much the epic events themselves as referent as it is the actualization in the here and now of *previous* epic discourses, it becomes clear that the very foundation of the usual notion of tense, the location in time of the event referred to, has to be reconsidered, if not abandoned. What is located in time is not so much the event referred to as *the act of verbalization here and now,* whereas the

27

epic event itself is not referred to but instantiated, commemorated.

Even though an epic or mythical event is not generic or timeless by itself, its location in time is imprecise; temporal reference is in fact irrelevant for the epic singer, who is not concerned with how many years or centuries ago something happened, but with *that* it happened, in another time, not now. The epic singer is not concerned with *excluding* an event from the present, but with *including* the present statement in the accumulated mass of the tradition. The singer does not deal with what is distant for its own sake, referring "objectively" to it, but only insofar as it can be made "near."

Epic discourse, then, as the language of myth and ritual, is to a certain degree *tenseless,* and I believe that it is worthwhile to consider one peculiarity of the verb in Homeric Greek as textual evidence for this: the frequent absence of the so-called augment of the verb in Homer, in our Greek grammars the prime marker of pastness. In the description of the death of Patroklos, for example, we see verbs, such as *stē* (stood) or *plēkse* (hit) where Classical Greek would have had *e-stē* and *e-plēkse.* This phenomenon is usually dealt with as an optional *omission* of the augment in Homer, for the sake of meter.[23] That approach, however, amounts to taking the morphological situation of *classical* Greek as the norm for earlier stages of the language, a linguistically unwarranted elimination of the strangeness of epic discourse.

Without going into details here, I suggest that the *absence* of the augment is not so much an *omission* as the *presence* of the augment is an *addition* to the morphology of the verb, first optional, later obligatory, in the Eastern Indo-European dialects, including Greek. Being originally an independent element (comparable to a preverb), a temporal adverb,[24] the augment and its subsequent incorporation in the morphology of the verb testify to the rise of *tense* as the grammatical and morphological category that we know from Classical Greek, the point being that Proto-Indo-European was originally a language without an overt tense-system (as Chinese and some American Indian languages are today).[25]

On the supposition that present tense in Indo-European originates in the deictic suffix -i added to the personal endings of the verb (a suffix meaning "here and now," for example, es-m-i, I am),[26] we may now say that verbal forms *without* this suffix, and also without the augment, originally meant "*not* here-and-now," without the temporal connotation of "past" as we have it. Such forms are called *injunctives* in comparative-historical linguistics. When, finally, tense was established in the language as the grammatical category as we know it, these injunctives may have been preserved as a special, archaic category in the epic diction, suitable for epic storytelling and mythic and hymnic discourse deriving from a source that is different from, and larger than, the consciousness of the present speaker.[27] Such discourse is concerned not with the location of events in time but with their commemoration, the conjuring up of events and their participants into presence out of absence.

Augmented verbs, in their turn, may not be entirely compatible with our notion of past tense, either. They sometimes seem to be used in contrast with the injunctive forms, not to mark an event as "past" in our sense, but as "near," in the sense that a given idea derives not from the collective consciousness of the tradition but from the consciousness of the individual speaker here and now. The event is not presented as remembered or reenacted but as simply visualized or imagined. Thus, augmented forms are almost de rigueur in similes, the reality of which they mark as "near," and accessible to ordinary human perception, different from the distant reality to be reenacted in the surrounding narrative.[28] They are also several times more frequent in characters' speech than in narrative, a situation that is to be

expected given the different communicative goals of each dis-
course-type.[29]

STORYTELLING IN THE FUTURE

There is a broad difference, then, in terms of "near" and "far"
between the discourse of the epic poet and that of characters.
The former is based on a remote original consciousness and is
verbalized by an understanding consciousness in the present that
is the instantiation of a much larger, generic, collective consciousness. The discourse of characters, on the other hand, is a matter
of a particular consciousness that is not concerned with reenact-
ing. Yet in spite of these differences, there is an overlap between
the two types of discourse: the narrator may use the same linguistic elements as the characters, and in much the same way. This
usage brings us back to the verb *mellein*.[30] The following are
typical instances of the use of this verb by the epic narrator:

Ἔνθ᾽ ἄλλοι Τρῶες τηλεκλειτοί τ᾽ ἐπίκουροι
βουλῇ Πουλυδάμαντος ἀμωμήτοιο πίθοντο·
ἀλλ᾽ οὐχ Ὑρτακίδης ἔθελ᾽ Ἄσιος, ὄρχαμος ἀνδρῶν,
αὖθι λιπεῖν ἵππους τε καὶ ἡνίοχον θεράποντα,
ἀλλὰ σὺν αὐτοῖσιν πέλασεν νήεσσι θοῇσι,
νήπιος, οὐδ᾽ ἄρ᾽ ἔμελλε κακὰς ὑπὸ κῆρας ἀλύξας
ἵπποισιν καὶ ὄχεσφιν ἀγαλλόμενος παρὰ νηῶν
ἂψ ἀπονοστήσειν προτὶ Ἴλιον ἠνεμόεσσαν.

(*Iliad* 12.108–115)

"There the other Trojans and allies renowned in battle followed
the advice of blameless Poludamas. But not Asios son of
Hurtakos, leader of men: he did not want to leave his chariot
there and his charioteer. No, he kept them with him and drove
on to the fast-running ships, nēpios ["fool"]: in the pride of his
horses and chariot he was not going to return from the ships to
windy Ilion, after escaping the evil spirits of destruction."

Ὣς φάτο λισσόμενος μέγα νήπιος· ἦ γὰρ ἔμελλεν
οἷ αὐτῷ θάνατόν τε κακὸν καὶ κῆρα λιτέσθαι.

(*Iliad* 16.46–47)

"So he spoke pleading, greatly *nēpios* ("foolish"); for he was
imploring death and evil destruction for himself."

In the first example Asios, who is fighting on the side of the
Trojans, does not listen to the wise advice of Poludamas to leave
the chariots at the ditch, so that the chariots will not hamper
them in their attack on the Greek camp. This behavior provokes
the exclamation *nēpios* (commonly translated as "foolish") on the
part of the narrator, a word to which we shall return. The same
word is used in the second example to characterize Patroklos
when he begs Achilles to send him into the battle as his substitute, with Achilles' armor on. The usual explanation of *mellein* in
such cases, as we have seen, is destiny, fate in the past. On the
destiny-in-the-past reading, what happens in the two examples is
the reference to a future event that is still unknown to the
character, a future locked up in the past. To this reading I oppose
an account in which this future is the present, the moment of
truth and understanding in the performance.

Before we return to understanding and interpretation, it may
be worthwhile to stop momentarily and ask what the notion of
future or destiny in the past, or *fate,* actually means. Do epic
events have a destiny, in the sense of a future event with which
they contract a relationship of cause and effect?[31] In other words,
are events in the epic predetermined? Some events seem indeed
to be fated; for example, it is certain that Achilles will die young,
and that Sarpedon, king of the Lycians, will not return alive from
the battle. But even these preordained deaths are less a fixed
future than a certain constraint on the hero's life. When Sarpedon
actually dies, for example, in book 16 of the *Iliad* at the hands of
Patroklos, it is not at all clear who causes the event or who is

ultimately responsible for it: Patroklos who kills Sarpedon, or Zeus who does not rescue his son, or Sarpedon himself, because he recklessly engaged in a duel with a stronger hero?

However, this way of talking about a hero's fate, or his *moira* in Homeric parlance (meaning "portion" or "share"), does not seem to be a fruitful way of dealing with the problem; to conceive of the past in terms of events, their causes, and their consequences, is what the historian does in dealing with the events located in a past that is excluded from the present, events that exist as "facts" outside the historiographical discourse that seeks to explain them. For the epic poet, on the other hand, the situation is quite the reverse. Just as the historian, the poet deals with the past, but that past does not exist independently from discourse; on the contrary, it exists in and as a consequence of discourse, the poet's speech in the present. It is speech in an ever repeated present that results in *kleos aphthiton* (imperishable fame) of the epic events and their participants, *not* vice versa. Moreover, it is the certainty of the speech of the present that not only guarantees the truth of the epic event but also confirms it as fated. In fact, as Gregory Nagy has shown,[32] the word *moira,* commonly translated as "fate," is not easily distinguished from the *tradition* of a particular hero, especially in such phrases as *kata moiran* (according to destiny, according to the tradition) and *huper moiran* (beyond fate, in violation of the tradition). For example, in saving Aineias from a sure death at the hands of Achilles in the example discussed earlier, Poseidon saves not only Aineias but also the *tradition* of Aineias, and therefore he can say that Aineias' death at this point would have been *huper moiran,* not according to tradition.[33]

I conclude from this brief discussion of destiny that the fate of a hero is not some kind of fixed future, a future locked up in the past. Instead, the destiny of a hero is his tradition: if the memory of the tradition says that so and so happened, then it had to be that way. This view implies that the future of an event, instead of being something inherent in that event, is the *kleos* of that event, its representation in the poetry of the future. Such a future is not a fixed and definite future, consisting of causally generated events; rather, it is generic, for the *kleos* is a *kleos aphthiton,* a fame that will never die. The Greek epic tradition endows its characters with an acute awareness of this. Consider, for example, what Hektor says when he foresees the future, in other words, the *kleos,* of an envisaged act:

καί ποτέ τις εἴπῃσι καὶ ὀψιγόνων ἀνθρώπων
νηῒ πολυκλήϊδι πλέων ἐπὶ οἴνοπα πόντον·
'ἀνδρὸς μὲν τόδε σῆμα πάλαι κατατεθνηῶτος
ὅν ποτ' ἀριστεύοντα κατέκτανε φαίδιμος Ἕκτωρ.'
ὥς ποτέ τις ἐρέει· τὸ δ' ἐμὸν κλέος οὔ ποτ' ὀλεῖται.

(*Iliad* 7.87–91)

"And some day one of the men of the future will say, sailing by on the wine-colored sea in a well-benched ship: 'This is the tomb of a man who died long ago, who, being among the bravest, was killed by glorious Hektor.' So will someone speak some day. And my fame, it will never die."

The tomb (*sēma*) of his victim, Hektor thinks, will serve as sign pointing to the past. As a mortal he does not know what will happen in his life, but as a hero he does know that whatever he will do will lead its life in the memory of the future.[34] Somewhat different but equally relevant is what Odysseus says at the *moment suprême* when he reveals his identity to his hosts, the Phaeacians:

εἴμ' Ὀδυσεὺς Λαερτιάδης, ὃς πᾶσι δόλοισιν
ἀνθρώποισι μέλω καί μευ κλέος οὐρανὸν ἵκει.

(*Odyssey* 9.19–20)

"I am Odysseus, son of Laertes, who with my tricks <u>am in the mind</u> of all the people, and my <u>fame reaches into heaven.</u>"

Odysseus does not talk of his *kleos* in the future, as Hektor does, but, surprisingly, in the present tense. This means that Odysseus, as Charles Segal has argued,[35] is outside the heroic action. In terms of the present paper, he is *in the future,* listening to poetry that celebrates his own *kleos.* In addition to this remarkable piece of Odyssean poetics, there is the verb that Odysseus uses: *melō,* whose first meaning is given in LSJ as "to be an object of care or thought," and which I translate here as "I am on the mind of all the people." If Ruijgh[36] is right in his suggestion that the root of this verb, *mel-,* is connected with our verb *mellein* (**mel-y-ein*)—and given the mental nature of the meaning of both verbs, this seems plausible—then we have an interesting starting point for our return to *mellein* as used by the Homeric narrator.

To be on the mind of all the people, as Odysseus claims he is, is a matter of *kleos,* a generic state. In terms of the poetics of epic, it is the memory of the epic action *before* its concrete actualization in poetry. During this actualization the hero enters into the present of whoever is listening. This present is at the same time a future providing the performer and his audience with the understanding that comes with reexperience. What an etymological relation between *melein* and *mellein* could suggest in this connection is that actualization in the performance can be seen as a temporary transition of the *generic* state of *melein* (to be in the mind of all the people, in a "prepoetic" way) into the *concrete* state of *mellein* (to be in the mind of the performer here and now).[37]

The verb *mellein,* however, is not used for this instantiation and concretization as such. Instead, its use is reserved for those moments of truthful understanding at which the difference between the event as experienced for the first time and its reexperience during the performance is at its greatest. In this light, let us now return to Asios and Patroklos as they are presented in the examples previously quoted. In both these cases mention is made of the death of the character in question, an event that is as yet in the future in the scene depicted. Is it the temporal relation between the moment of the character's ignorance and his future death that is at stake in the semantics of *mellein?* My argument here suggests otherwise.

When we shift from epic events themselves to the *memory* of epic events, the epic tradition, the contrast is not any more between the event and its consequences in the future but between the *ignorance* of the original experience and the *understanding* of the present. In fact, it is the poet in the future who has the insight into the true nature of events, not the character himself. This way of understanding the two passages not only is more in line with the semantics of *mellein* as a marker of evidentiality and interpretation but also casts new light on another important and structural feature of these and similar passages, the adjective *nēpios.*

This word is usually understood in the sense "infant" or "child" (as in the frequent formula *nēpia tekna,* "infant children"), from which a sense "childish," "silly," "foolish" derives. This sense lies at the basis of the alleged moral qualification of Asios and Patroklos in the two examples discussed earlier. On the grounds that "infant" as the basic meaning in its *literal* sense of Latin *infans,* "nonspeaking"—*nēpios* being the negative derivative of *epos* 'speech'—is etymologically impossible, another solution has been recently proposed: "out of touch," "disconnected," with *nēpios* being the negative counterpart of *ēpios* and related to Latin *ineptus.*[38]

Yet whether "childish" or "out of touch" is the basic meaning, in the specialized poetic sense under study here, the word does not imply a qualification with respect to other characters in the tale: the *nēpios* is no more silly or out of touch than other humans. Rather, his fundamental condition is that he is out of touch with poetic truth. In the temporal terms introduced in this paper, this means that he is explicitly presented as *not in the future,* and since he is not in the future, *he is no poet.* His understanding of his situation is the experience of the real, original event, and as such conditioned by the inherent limits of human knowledge. It is with respect to this original experience that the Greek epic tradition can define itself as the reexperience of the epic event and the moment of truth. Only under the controlled circumstances of the epic performance can human nature overcome its limitations and rise to the level of the gods, but one needs the *nēpios* in his original situation to be aware of it.[39]

Such an experience of "truth" cuts across our artificial distinctions between "objective" and "subjective," "traditional" and "original." It is also, more importantly, in agreement with the well-known traditional Greek wisdom that human existence can be evaluated only *post mortem.*[40] But while it takes an outsider in the future to pronounce a life happy, it takes a poet in the future to make it come alive.

CHAPTER 2

Writing the Emperor's Clothes On: Literacy and the Production of Facts

FRANZ H. BÄUML

I shall propose the hypothesis that the development of literacy in the Middle Ages went hand in hand with the growing belief in the existence of "facts" as independent entities. Moreover, I shall maintain that this notion of "facts" is dependent on literacy and cannot arise in an oral culture, and I shall argue this using examples from medieval sources. Though I do not necessarily subscribe to a theory of two different "mentalities," one "oral" and one "literate," I do contend that the tools with which one thinks affect one's thinking, that the way in which one thinks has its social consequences, and that therefore control of the tools of thought is of the utmost importance for the maintenance of power.

In speaking of "facts," one is necessarily speaking of something called "reality." Because both are notions fraught with all kinds of difficulties, it will be well to clear at least some of these out of the way.

By "reality" I mean a world that we believe to be independent of our enquiries about it. I do not question its existence; I realize this raises many philosophical issues, but I am simply not concerned with these here, and shall not define "reality" beyond this statement of a widely held view. I am also well aware that we perceive by means of neural impulses sent by our sensory organs to the brain, which then distributes them to specific sensory domains, thus translating them into the brain's own language of "seeing," "hearing," "tasting," and so on, and that there is nothing to "see," "hear," or "taste" "out there." This is not to say that there is nothing "out there"; it is merely saying that everything thinkable and knowable is a construct. But this is a consequence of our physical existence, not of any social or cultural development in human history. This construct is the "reality" that determines human behavior. Therefore, this is what I shall call "reality": a form of existence thought to be independent of, but including, the thinker (Berger and Luckmann 1980:1). Of course, this "reality" can be interpreted in different ways, and "when a particular definition of reality comes to be attached to a concrete power interest, it may be called an ideology . . . The distinctiveness of ideology is . . . that the same overall universe is interpreted in different ways, depending upon concrete vested interests . . ." (ibid:113–114).

Now to "facts": Since our cognitive organisms, guided by experience, do not depict "reality," but rather a construct of it into which we may fit, "facts" are not items in an observer-independent world (von Glasersfeld 1989:438). Norwood Russell Hanson observed that a "fact" is created by its formulation (Hanson 1965:31–49). If one adds general acceptance of the formulation as a criterion, then Hanson's statement is true and forms the subject of this paper; though it is likewise true that socially accepted "facts" need not be "real." "Grass is green," as Hanson observes, is such an accepted "fact" that is not a "fact." Grass is not green, since its greenness depends on light; substitute a verb for the adjective, and "grass greens" produces a different "fact." *What is commonly meant by a fact is an entity that is understood, that is, socially accepted and agreed upon, as existing independently of its observation or any statement about it.* This view of a "fact" is contradicted by the linguistic analogy to Heisenberg's "uncertainty principle," that is, that naming things changes them by incorporating them in an existing, culturally determined lexicon. The question is, how does a circumstance or an occurrence come to be viewed as having an independent existence? Clearly, the view of an occurrence as a "fact" has nothing to do with whether it actually occurred: fictions are constantly viewed as "facts." Nor does it have anything to do with "truth." Truth requires a teller; being the alternative to falsehood, truth is the result of a choice made by someone. Even a "revealed Truth" requires a "revealer." In Greek, the notion of truth *(alētheia)* is related to the acts of remembering and forgetting. A "fact," if it is thought to have an independent existence, is not the alternative of anything; it either is or is not. There is no such thing as a "true fact"; either something is a fact, or it is not a fact. It is simply "out there," or it isn't.

It is only in the telling that "truth" and "fact" merge. The "truth" must be told about something, either a "fact" or some non-"fact," such as a fiction. Whether this telling is regarded as "true" or "false," or a "lie," or simply "correct" or "incorrect," depends on the intention imputed to the teller. "Facts" may be stated incorrectly, they may be falsified, and of course they may be replaced by other "facts"; but as long as they are thought of as existing independently, they cannot be altered.

One must differentiate here between "fact" and "reality." What "really" happens are not "facts." What "really" happens must first be known, and then seen as existing independently of any telling and be formulated as a "fact." Of course, as Wolfgang Iser has observed, no statement relates "to contingent reality as such, but to models or concepts of reality, in which contingencies and complexities are reduced to a meaningful structure" (Iser 1978:70; Blumenberg 1969:9–27; Luhmann 1970:73; de Rijk 1977:46–68).[1] What "really" happens may be that I observe, in the rich experiential context of a warm summer evening on the beach, first the smoke, then the smokestack, then the superstructure, then the hull of a ship emerging on the horizon, and I conclude from these sights the "facts" that the earth is indeed round, or that this is a ship, or that the thing is fouling the air and destroying my enjoyment of the sunset. Or I can convert my action of seeing the ship gradually emerge into a "fact," by saying that "it is a fact that I saw . . ." and so on. Thus I convert the "fact" of the emergence of the ship into the quite different "fact" of my observing the ship emerge.

It is easy, therefore, to yield to the temptation of calling a "fact" a statement of a certain kind and to let the matter rest there. But as we have seen, a "fact" is a notion of a circumstance existing independently of its observation or any statement made about it. Since this notion gives greater authority to "facts" than to statements, observations or tellings of "truth," a "fact" must be formulated in a special way to be used as such an authoritative concept. Of course, a "fact" is not unassailable. "Facts" may be denied. However, if a "fact" is conceived of as independent of any statement about it, then it can be invalidated only by another "fact"; what can be denied is merely the "truth" of a statement about it. "Truth" is not privileged in any way; it is the claim of a teller, who may or may not be believed. Though a fact is thought to exist apart from a statement about it, a statement about it must be made if the "fact" is to be thought about at all. And since it is thought to exist independently, it is worthwhile making statements about it. After all, it is incontrovertible except by another "fact," and it does not appear to depend on anyone's veracity for its existence; it appears to have its own built-in veracity. To state or to formulate a so-called fact, then, is to state or formulate a "truth" which is unassailable by the means with which one can question the mere "truth" of a statement: an allusion to the unreliability of the teller or his or her sources. "Facts," therefore, are potent weapons in the establishment and maintenance of power. But in order to be used to that end, "facts" must be stated in such a way that they are recognized as independently existing entities. In this sense one may speak of a "fact" as being created by its formulation.

As Dorothy E. Smith observes, "facts" are created in a radically purposeful way (Smith 1978:257–268). Whether a "fact" is accepted as such depends not on the accuracy with which its statement fits its referent but on the neatness with which it fits its purpose. Since its purpose as a "factual" statement determines the selection of what it includes, it will not concern itself with attempting to "make us believe that it conforms to reality and not to its own laws" by extensive attempts at verisimilitude (Todorov 1968:2–3; Culler 1975:139). Just the opposite: it will not conceal its own laws behind a mask of a "re-created actuality": the "fact" that the working conditions in nineteenth-century French mines were subhuman is constructed according to different laws from a description of those conditions in *Germinal*. What "happens" thus becomes an event, an episode, a state of affairs with its own structure, frozen in time, lifted from its context, deprived of teller or listener—the proverbial tree in the forest which falls whether anyone sees it or not.

How, then, is such a discourse formulated? Its chief characteristics are its purposeful, highly selective formulation, stripping an occurrence of its context as well as any context of telling and receiving, its conversion of processes into static events, and its consistency in this type of formulation. Any other kind of statement is to a statement of "fact" what a representational painting is to a diagram. The "fact" appears authorless, userless, independent. The ultimate form of a statement of "fact" is the statistic or the list (Koch 1990:139–155), or, for that matter, the traditional Jewish practice of placing pebbles on gravestones as a sign of visit and remembrance, or adding stones to a cairn, or, more to the point, the administrative use of Incan rope knots.[2] The Catalogue of Ships in Book II of the *Iliad* can be converted into an assembly of "facts" only by being lifted from its context. As long as it remains in its context, it is part of a performable "truth."

Clearly, no discourse requiring a performance can produce "facts." A performed discourse cannot take place without a context with which it is identified: the performance. Its content derives its force from its seat within a culture; it is mute without a teller to tell it as a "truth." What is told, whether true or false, depends on the teller and is identified with the teller, and it is judged on the basis of its tradition. Of course, it is not only in an oral culture that an utterance is viewed as an extension of the speaker. A disturbed reaction on the part of a speaker interrupted in mid-utterance is common in the most literate environments and testifies to the intimate linkage between speaker and utterance. But the notion of an utterance as separate from the speaker, as merely his or her product ("do as I do, and not as I say"), is distinctly literate, and is precisely the reason for the introduction of the term in modern linguistics specifically to indicate its linkage to a speaker. At any rate, when what is said is viewed as an extension of the speaker, it may be a "truth," it may be a correct statement of a "fact" in the sense that it is an acceptable restatement of a "bald" statement of "fact," but it can never be such a bald statement of "fact" itself, since the speaker is seen as present in his or her utterance. The requirement for a "bald" statement of "fact" is the type of "objectivity" best represented in writing. Writing eliminates the presence of an author from the public, the public from an author, and the consciousness of either on the part of the text. A "fact" in written form appears to be contextless, has no authorial voices or gestures, can be pruned to fit its purpose, and can retain its shape and independence. It is quite possible that between "truth" and "fact" some slippage may occur: a performed "truth" may conceivably become decontextualized, reified, and thus be converted into a "fact."[3] However, the most powerful device by which the creation of facts may be systematically accomplished is writing.

Under the year 749 the *Royal Frankish Annals* have the following entry: "Bishop Burchard of Würzburg and the chaplain Fulrad were sent to Pope Zacharias to inquire whether it was good or not that the kings of the Franks should wield no royal power, as was the case at the time. Pope Zacharias instructed Pepin that it was better to call him king who had the royal power than the one who did not. To avoid turning the country upside down, he commanded by virtue of his apostolic authority that Pepin should be made king" (transl. Scholz and Rogers 1972:39).

Actually these events occurred in the year 750 ("fact"!), but no matter. The formulation of this reference to the inquiry of Pepin III in preparation for his *coup d'état* against Childeric, the last Merovingian king, conforms to annalistic convention. Here the convention of official court records requires that the narrative to be recorded be limited to, and its formulation determined by, its function as justification for Pepin's planned action.[4] Pepin "inquires": he has not prejudged the situation; he inquires of the Pope: he turns to the preeminent moral authority; he inquires whether it was "good" that the kings don't have royal power, leaving unmentioned the fact that it is he, as major domo, who has it; it is left to Pope Zacharias to make the connection between Pepin as de facto possessor of royal power and the royal title as being "better"; it would be "better" because it would avoid chaos; therefore, he commands "by virtue of his apostolic authority" that Pepin be supported in his coup d'état.

The narrative of the *Annals* claims to state "facts." It is chronologically organized, it is entered under a certain year, its actors have "real" names and titles, and their performance is confined to their apparently "real" human powers and functions. But it leaves unmentioned a number of things that significantly constituted the context, the "reality," to which the narrative purports to refer: why choose, for instance, Bishop Burchard and Chaplain Fulrad? What specifically recommended them for this mission? How was the mission executed, orally or by letter? How did the Pope answer, orally or in writing? But the most glaring gap is the lack of connection between Pepin's question and the Pope's answer. Pepin is said to have asked whether it "was good or not" that the Frankish kings have no royal power, which requires merely a "yes" or "no" for an answer. The papal reply, however, is an instruction, and the apostolic command as stated by the *Annals* has nothing whatever to do with the question. The Pope's response follows from the question's purpose, i.e., the common interests of Pepin and the Pope.

All of these items that were part of the "reality" behind the narrative, and that played a role in its formulation by being left out, are now obliterated from the new "reality" created by the document. They are not treated as "unknowns," as things not remembered or not important, but as nonexistent. It is as if Burchard and Fulrad were interchangeable with all other bishops and chaplains, as if their mere appearance before the Pope posed the question, and as if the relationship between question and response were a bureaucratic formality. The *Annals* have replaced an actuality by an official ritual posing as "what happened." What "happens" happens in "document time": everything that has gone into its production is expunged; there are no notes, drafts, or comments. It is clearly marked off from all synchronic and diachronic context; its actors are figures, interchangeable with all other figures in the same category; its verbal interchanges are disjunctively formalistic; and its vocabulary is abstractly specialized: to "wield royal power" and to "command by virtue of

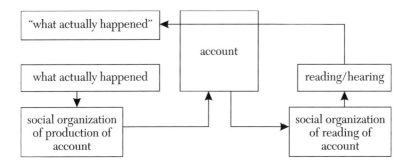

apostolic authority" are legalese abstractions used by, and aimed at, users of documents united by the production and use of certain types of "facts." It is this union of the social organization of the production of the account with that of its consumption that produces documentary "reality": the reading of the document is limited to the "reality" constituted by it.

Such "facts" now shape the "reality" of their producers and users. The document, rather than the occurrence, is now the source for "what happened," and any attempt to return to the occurrence by analyzing the report is inevitably an extrapolation from the "facts" produced by the report. The manner in which this happens has been illustrated by Dorothy Smith (1978:260) in the accompanying diagram.

The process begins with what actually happened, an account of which is produced in the context of a social organization with certain interests and purposes. The account, having been produced, is directed at, and read/heard in the context of, a social organization with certain interests and purposes. The receivers of the account, however, are to be distinguished from its producers, since much, if not all, of the actuality that gave rise to the account is obliterated by it, and therefore its receivers have access, not to the actuality, but to "what happened" in "document time." The formation of this "reality" is indicated by the arrow issuing from "reading/hearing," and penetrating the account. "What actually happened" is now interpreted on the basis of the account: it has entered "document time," and what actually happened must be supplied by quotation marks. Documentary "reality" is thus constituted by both ends of the process, the production as well as the reading of the account. Both result from and in a social organization. The social organization of its production formulates the "fact" for a specific purpose and directs it at a specific public for reception in a specific context, from which it is generally not separable (Smith 1978:260; Goetz 1993:242–243). The genre, Latinity, and content of the *Annals* indicate that they are produced by Carolingian officialdom for "official" use in "official" contexts. Even their use by a modern historian requires him or her to view these annals in their official Carolingian context if he or she is to make any sense of them at all. This limitation is guaranteed by the formulation of their "facts," the prior knowledge taken for granted, and the tacit assumption that these "facts" will remain unchanged regardless of different individual readings. The underlying regulatory process consists of a series of canons, of evaluative standards, which guarantee a type of knowledge which is itself an administrative construct. This construct becomes the substance of systematic collections of data for administrative purposes. The construct is knowledge that is prefabricated before it arrives at its point of application, before it reaches its "knowers" who use it, so that these "knowers" are interchangeable as "knowers."[5] Actualities have thus been transposed into the forms of "factual" accounts, and these "factual" accounts then become a "currency" within the organization that uses them (Smith 1978:261).[6]

Such a transposition of actualities into "factual" accounts results in "reality disjunctures" (Smith 1978:265). Every individual instance of anything is of course a coincidence, and the incoherent mass of coincidences, by being converted into data, becomes a system of "facts."[7] This system no longer has anything to do with the various "realities" that went into it: the hood ornament of a car has more to do with the reality of an auto accident than does the most carefully compiled statistic. These "reality disjunctures," moreover, do not remain in the realm of their origin. To the extent that the powers dependent on the manufacture of "facts" use them to identify and characterize persons, events and objects, society at large is drawn into an acceptance of the interpretive procedures of officialdom. The creation of "facts" and the attendant "reality disjunctures" are, of course, part and parcel of the development of institutions. The point is, however, that the creation of "facts" is impossible without writing, as well as necessary for the institutionalization of governance. It is thus more than a gradual shift of the means of communication and memorialization from orality to literacy and from personal to bureaucratic interaction; institutionalization requires, and writing enables, the manufacture of "facts" and their substitution for the "realities" that they erased.

In December 883 the Emperor Charles III ("the Fat"), on a journey back from Italy, stopped to rest for a few days at the monastery of St. Gall. On that occasion, the poet, teacher, and monk Notker Balbulus entertained him by telling him a series of tales, mainly about his ancestor Charles the Great (ed. P. Jaffé 1867; transl. Thorpe 1969:160). Among these tales is the following anecdote about Pepin:

> Pepin discovered that the leaders of his army were in the habit of speaking contemptuously of him in private. He ordered a bull of fantastic size and ferocious temper to be set free. Then a savage lion was set at the bull. With tremendous fury the lion charged at the bull, seized it by the neck and hurled it to the

ground. The king said to those standing round him: "Now drag the lion off the bull, or else kill it on top of its enemy." They looked at each other in terror, with their hearts frozen with fear, and just managed to gasp out an answer. "My lord," they muttered, "there is no man under heaven who would dare attempt such a thing." Pepin rose without hesitation from his throne, drew his sword, and cut through the lion's neck and severed the bull's head from its shoulders. Then he sheathed his sword and sat down once more on his throne. "Do you think I am worthy to be your master?" asked he. "Have you not heard what the diminutive David did to the huge Goliath? Or what tiny Alexander did to his noblemen?" They fell to the ground as if they had been struck by thunder. "Is there anyone so foolish that he would deny your right to rule over the whole of mankind?" they replied.

The purpose of this tale in its original form was obviously the same as that of the entry in the *Annals* for 749: a justification of Pepin's coup d'état. But this is a different matter altogether from the report in the *Annals*. The anecdote is made up entirely of action, speech, and concrete imagery. The entry in the *Annals* presupposes an acquaintance with the conventions of its text by a specialized community of users. The anecdote makes no such supposition necessary; indeed, it would be farfetched. However, despite its obvious oral-traditional characteristics—the sword as proof of strength and thus the competence to rule, the demonstration of this competence by a single blow, the test of wild beasts, the unquestioning submission of the doubters—we do not know whether the story was a true product of the oral tradition. It may have been "officially" produced for those nurtured by the oral tradition, for the knowers of "truth;" it certainly was not directed at the knowers of "facts" in the world of the *Annals*. It would be interesting to know whether Notker told the story to the Emperor in the vernacular before writing it down in Latin. He wrote it down, he says, to make up for the fact that about Pepin "very little has been recorded, thanks to the crass laziness of my contemporaries." But he also wrote it down because Charles commanded him to do so. It has now become a Latin tale about the father of Charlemagne in a sequence of tales about Charlemagne, a propagandistic glorification of the founder of the Carolingian dynasty, produced at the command of his great-great-grandson Charles III. It was addressed to a public who no longer questioned Carolingian legitimacy, but it looked back with admiration on Pepin's competence, which now was enshrined in a Latin narrative. Certainly, as such it had become directly accessible only to those who could read Latin. To some degree its written form acted as agent in the hierarchicalization of society, but one can say the same of anything written. If the tale was indeed the product of an oral tradition—and Notker's comment about the laziness of his contemporaries suggests that it was—its "truth" was collectively established and collectively transmitted. Not only was it hallowed by tradition and molded for the memory by traditional motifs, but also it was embedded in the life of its public by its ritual context, its telling. It is worth noting that Notker told it to Charles before it was written down, that is, he performed it for him. It was, thus, a present "truth," its verisimilitude emphasized in performance, a demonstration of the tradition as a social bond rather than a hierarchicalizing agent.

The production of "facts" in writing, on the other hand, with its elimination of context, supports an infinitely and institutionally rearrangeable fragmentation of the social distribution of knowledge by its establishment of communities of "knowers" and "not-knowers." In this sense, written "fact"-production is more flexible than the "truth"-reproduction of traditional oral societies.

Notker told his tale to Charles before it was written down, that is, he performed it for him. He performed it for him, not because he vocalized it, but because there was something to be performed. We know very well that until the later Middle Ages the acts of reading and writing were usually accompanied by the vocalization of what was being read and written, even if what was being read was not read to an audience other than the reader, and even if what was being written was not being dictated by one person to another. Vocalization was primary, the reception or the act of writing was secondary. But as Ursula Schaefer (1992:30–41, 128–130) has shown, there is a world of difference between vocalization and performance. A performance is possible only if that which is to be performed allows, as Egbert Bakker would say, for a recreation of past action in the present and thus the creation of "presence" (Bakker 1993:1–29). In short, there must be a possibility of enactment.

This is precisely what there is not in the formulation of a "fact." The item entered under the year 749 in the *Frankish Annals* can be vocalized, but it cannot be performed. That is, it cannot be given visual presence through a generous use of conventional gestures and stances, which are culture-bound and therefore a visual link between the message and "reality." In this respect, conventional gestures function much like oral formulae as binders to tradition, "reality," "truth" (Schaefer 1992:76–93 and passim). Moreover, gestures augment the linearity of verbal language, in which the parts form a whole, by the converse: the individual gestures and their parts derive meaning from the entire context; the analytic relationship of words to meanings is augmented by the synthetic relationship between many meanings and single gestures (McNeill 1992:19–20); and to the extent that they are recognized as gestures, that is, as meaningful, they are culturally shared. Since, under normal circumstances, there is no such thing as saying anything at all without gestures, for even the absence of gestures is a gesture, their function of supporting the "presence" of what is being said, their "Gestaltungsfunktion," is built into every utterance. Certainly the entry for 749 in the *Royal Frankish Annals* can be read aloud, and when it is, it is inevitably read with gestures; but they will be gestures rendering the reader "present," foregrounding the reader, rather than giving "presence" to the matter being read. Thus, the gestures of a reader of "facts" can only emphasize an "absence" of these "facts," resulting from their transcendence of context.

A "fact" cannot assume presence; it is thought to be present to begin with. It is the very essence of the notion of a "fact" as an "externalized object of knowledge" that it "transcends the primary intersubjective participation in and constitution of a world known in common" (Smith 1978:259). It is, thus, both present and absent: present as an externalized object of knowledge, and absent because it transcends the "constitution of a world known in common." Whether it is known or not, it is the same for everyone. However, by dividing society into "knowers" and "not knowers" of given facts, not only does this division subordinate knowing and not knowing to the "fact," which is simply "there;" but also its function is precisely the opportunity of a performance, which is a prime example of "intersubjective participation in and constitution of a world known in common." A world known as "true" is already known as such before any single performance because it is traditional, and it is recreated again and again in performance. As John Foley has recently put it: "Empowerment of the communicative act results from the keying of performance . . . and from the shared immersion in traditional context that is the performer's and audience's experiential heritage" (Foley 1992:275–301, esp. 294). It is that traditional context, the event of the performance as a whole, which empowers the utterances occurring in it (ibid.:285). It carries its values, its canons, within itself: what is canonic is the tradition, and the tradition defines what is canonic. It is self-controlling and therefore difficult to change. A preliterate tribal chieftain cannot significantly interfere with these "truths"; he himself is controlled by them. A "fact," on the other hand, as an "externalized object of knowledge," can be created as a "fact" by its statement, and as an "externalized object of knowledge" by depriving it of the attributes of performability, of a seat in its own world as an object, and in the world of those for whom it is an object. In short, a fact must be deprived of contextualization as an entity as well as in its reception. This deprivation is most effectively accomplished by writing and its institutionalization.

It is therefore no surprise that traditional "truths" clash with "facts" long before the Age of Discovery, to which the emergence of our notion of "fact" is usually ascribed: "A particular truth known by actual observation or authentic testimony," as the *Oxford English Dictionary*—itself a good example of decontextualized "fact"—defines it. Such clashes can result in a gradual absorption of the "truth" by "facts," and the accommodation of the social memory to this absorption. A case in point may be the absorption of the *chanson*-material on Charlemagne by such "facts" as are implied by his canonization by Barbarossa in 1165, in the ceremony of which it probably played a role. In any case, the *chanson*-material certainly was absorbed into Latin chronicle-writing (Fentress and Wickham 1992:154–162).[8] The clash of "truth" and "facts" can also lead to the failure of such an absorption, as in the case of Etzel (Attila) of the *Nibelungenlied*. The process of historicization, of situating an event, text, person, or notion historically, transforms its object into a "fact"; conversely, a view of "facts" as discourse-produced deprives them of their authoritative "historical" status (Spiegel 1990:59–86, esp. 62). In its attempt to historicize, "factualize" the story of the epic (Wehrli 1972:96–112; Curschmann 1979:85–119), the so-called *Klage*, which accompanies the epic in all important manuscripts, fails in respect to Etzel. Instead of secularizing his life completely in terms of the epic, the epic demonizes him, placing him outside of history. In attempting to account for what happened to Etzel, the narrator confesses his ignorance:

> Some say that he was murdered; others say "no," . . . whether he got lost, or vanished into thin air, or was buried alive, or ascended to heaven, or slipped out of his skin, or crept into holes in stone walls, or just how he left his body, or just what has taken him away, whether he went to hell, or whether the devil devoured him, or whether he disappeared in some other way no one has found out yet. The poet who tells us this story says that nothing else remains of him; he would gladly have written it down, so that one would know what had happened to him, if he had somehow found out or heard from someone. Consequently no one yet knows where King Etzel got to, or what kind of an end he had.

If the poet had known the "facts" of the case, he "would gladly have written . . . [them] down," but of course, of someone who might have "slipped out of his skin, or crept into holes in stone walls," there are no "facts" to be known, and so they are deferred to an indefinite future. Since the "courtly" Etzel of the *Nibelungenlied,* unlike the Charlemagne of the *Chanson de Roland,* was not useful as a political or social symbol, he dropped out of social memory just as he dropped out of existence at the end of the *Klage.* He survives solely as the *flagellum Dei* of the chronicles. Indeed, the eventual victory of the "evil" Attila in social memory over the "courtly" Etzel is already announced at the end of the *Klage,* where, for no internal reason at all, it is considered possible that the devil devoured him.

There is, of course, no shortage of cases in which the opposition of the learned to the vernacular narrative tradition becomes explicit. Usually this is based on the claimed superiority of Latin literacy to the oral tradition, of the learned to the peasant, and commonly takes the form of labeling the oral tradition a pack of lies. In at least one instance, though, an appeal is made *by a vernacular text* to the superiority of "fact" to traditional "truth." The most popular and influential of Middle High German chronicles, the *Kaiserchronik* (ca 1130–1147), denounces the oral epic not only because it lacks written proof but also because it violates chronology:[9] the songs of Dietrich von Bern are lies, since they make him a contemporary of Attila, whereas he wasn't born until forty-three years after Attila's burial. Precisely because the *Kaiserchronik* itself is anything but a good example of a "factual" account, this belligerent use of a "fact" against traditional "truths" argues for a faith in the tactical deployment of "facts" as weapons superior to the "truths" of tradition.

Nothing points to the link between the notion of "facts" as independent, a priori entities and writing as clearly as the metaphor of the "book of nature." For St. Augustine it is the companion to Holy Scripture: from the one, those who can read may hear; in the other, those who cannot read may see. And according to Bonaventura, Scripture interprets the Book of Nature (Scholz 1993:52–74; Olson 1986:115). From Augustine to seventeenth-century emblems and beyond, Nature is to be read, by *litterati* and *illitterati* alike, like a book. Here are the "bare facts," "written" by God, unperformable and inescapably valid for all. Their interpretation is Scripture—the performable "Truth." The notion of "fact," as we have seen, requires writing for its formulation so that it may be read as independent and universally valid. For those who cannot read, one must invent a "book" that they *can* read—the Book of Nature—and that "book" will present them with "facts" to justify the "Truth" they have heard. Moreover, the very notion of a commentary on, or an interpretation of, "facts" is dependent on a view of "facts" as transcendent entities, separate from the commentary or interpretation. This distinction between the given and the interpretation was "invited by literacy because writing, . . . split the comprehension process into two parts, . . . the given, and . . . the interpretation" (Olson 1986:120). This split, conceived of as a split between text and commentary, with its implication that hermeneutics is a creation of literacy (Olson 1986:113), is analogous to our separation of "facts" from the rest of contingent "reality."

Traditional Signs
and Homeric Art

JOHN MILES FOLEY

houtō toi tode sēma piphauskomai
"Thus I expound to you this *sēma*"
(*ODYSSEY* 23.202)

The present contribution will focus on the roots of Homeric epic in an ancient Greek oral tradition, exploring Homeric art not as a literary triumph over that heritage but as the direct product of its unique, empowering agency. That is, it will consider how the bard and his tradition employed a dedicated medium for expression to achieve a more-than-literary art.[1] Our exordium for the exercise is the unassuming word *sēma*—not as in the contemporary linguistic and literary approach called "semiotics" but as a trope and a term in the native poetics of ancient Greek epic poetry. To indicate where we are headed, I take *sēma* as a sign that points not so much to a specific situation, text, or performance as toward the ambient tradition, which serves as the key to an emergent reality. *Sēma* both names and is the tangible, concrete part that stands by contractual agreement for a larger, immanent whole, and as such it mimics a central algorithm or strategy of Homeric poetry: representation by metonymic reference.[2] Within the marked idiom of the *epos,* and of other traditional oral works as well, many such signs or units—whether actually labeled as *sēmata* or not—are specially licensed to bear more than their individual, unmarked lexical or semantic burdens. Enriched within the augmented discourse, these "bytes" of phraseology and narrative pattern index traditional ideas, characters, and situations, standing by prior negotiation for much more than a literary reading can decode.[3]

BACKGROUND: OPPORTUNITIES AND LIMITATIONS

In order to come to terms with what I take as a current and demanding version of the Homeric Question, in which we are asked to move from structure to meaning, we first need some understanding of a few important moments in the history of studies in oral tradition. The following remarks briefly summarize some turning points in the evolution of this approach, with emphasis not so much on the well-known sequence of events as on the entrenched perspectives they engendered. As we shall see, it has in fact been the rediscovery of ancient Greek oral tradition that has, paradoxically, both enhanced and diminished our capacity to hear what Homer was saying.[4]

When Milman Parry began his epochal research with his M.A. (1925) and doctoral theses (1928a, b), he was seeking to demonstrate the *traditional* character of Homeric style. Thus his elaborate analyses of noun-epithet formulas such as *podas ōkus Achilleus* (swift-footed Achilles) or *glaukōpis Athēnē* (grey-eyed Athena) were intended to establish that the *Iliad* and *Odyssey,* far from being the creation of a single person or the composite result of a massive editing project, had roots sunk deep in a poetic tradition, an inherited craft of which Homer was presumably the latest and finest practitioner. For Parry everything derived from

utility, and the traditional poet was one who dextrously manipu-
lated a ready-made language, the bequest of generations who had
gradually evolved and polished it to the highest degree.

The hypothesis of *orality,* it should be stressed, came only
later, after Parry was exposed to accounts of oral traditions from
various lands, especially to Matija Murko's writings on the South
Slavic epic and V. V. Radlov's reports on central Asian epic.[5]
Eventually, in the company of Albert Lord, Parry would under-
take a full-scale collecting expedition to then-Yugoslavia, recording more than 1,500 epic poems from chiefly nonliterate *guslari*
either acoustically or by dictation. On the basis of this analogy, he
and Lord seemed to confirm an oral as well as traditional Homer,
a poet who composed under the continuous pressure of performance, a poet for whom a ready-made, useful idiom was thus of the
greatest importance.

Upon this foundation Lord built a comparative edifice of im-
posing proportions, a construction project eventually involving
many hands that is still very much underway.[6] From the *formula,*
or phraseological "word," he enlarged the oral poet's repertoire of
ready-made compositional units to include *themes*—"words" at
the level of recurrent scenes—and *story-patterns* or tale-types.[7]
He also illustrated how multiformity, or variation within limits,
informed the recurrence of all of these units, which maintained
some measure of stability at the same time that they adapted,
according to their lights, to different situations. This critical program, drawn up from the reasonably close fit between Homeric
Greek and Moslem South Slavic epic, was then applied to both
living and manuscript-based traditions in a multitude of genres
across the board, and the Parry-Lord theory of traditional oral
composition gained widespread currency.[8]

Moreover, not only did these initial steps blaze an exciting new
path in Homeric studies but also they set the agenda for sub-

sequent discussion, foregrounding certain concerns while necessarily deemphasizing or even submerging others. First and foremost, the early theory privileged composition over reception, placing almost exclusive emphasis on explaining how the oral poet managed the apparent miracle of composition in performance. The audience was credited as a shaping force, to be sure, but the stress was placed on the ways in which the audience influenced the composer and not on their role in completing the communicative circuit. Another hidden problem, and one closely linked to the privileging of composition, lay in the very nature of the evidence brought forward on Homer's style. Parry began his demonstration by isolating what he named "formulas," at first only noun-epithet phrases but later less rigid phraseology, characterizing them initially as traditional and later as oral elements of the poet's inherited diction. But the most telling feature of his witnesses to the existence of an ancient Greek *oral* tradition is that they were in fact *seen*, that is, they were visually culled out as discrete items according to their *textual* identity. Although Lord also described a grammar of formulaic composition in *The Singer of Tales*, he and most other scholars spoke more often of self-contained, separable items or elements in lieu of the language they constituted, of isolated integers rather than a composite mathematics of expression. The hypothesis of oral tradition in Homer was based on literate concepts and explicated via a textual mindset.

This contradiction in terms—a textually conceived and defined orality—exposes a third shortcoming of the early Parry-Lord theory, or "strong thesis." At the heart of this approach from the beginning had been the untested assumption that "oral" could always and everywhere be distinguished from "written," that the two modes were typologically opposite, mutually exclusive.[9] Given this assumption, the scholarly task amounted simply to sorting ancient and medieval texts, which of course could be known only via the manuscripts that survive, into one of two possible categories.[10] The hypothesis of a transitional text, situated midway between the two perceived poles, was therefore unacceptable: if there were no real difference in kind (as opposed to degree) between types of documents, then the hard-won explanations of composition-in-performance and of the role of constituent building blocks would founder.[11] Assimilation to the conventional literary model would be only too ready, especially given the pressure applied by scholars who felt that the Oral Theory sacrificed Homer's art on the altar of tectonics and mechanism.

There have been a number of liberating responses to these challenges to the "strong thesis." For example, the initial impulse to unearth archetypal similarities has been balanced in succeeding years by the need to distinguish among different traditions, genres, and media. Reports from the field and from the study have fractured universalist assumptions, revealing the palette of worldwide oral traditions to be at least as various as the wonderfully heterogeneous (but finally much smaller and narrower) collection of verbal art we call "literature." Put simply, different traditions—with their diverse performers, languages, prosodies, expressive units, and social contexts—work differently, as do the various genres within them. There can be no better example of this need to distinguish as well as to compare than the fact that the initial and still primary analogy for Homeric and other oral traditions is the Moslem South Slavic epic—a single subgenre of epic from a single tradition that matches the *Iliad* and *Odyssey* in several important dimensions.[12] But the same subgenre proves less congruent with many other texts and performances, and the definitions and concepts based on Moslem epic deserve to be pluralized—a goal quite possible of achievement even elsewhere within the same oral tradition.[13] Likewise, the media through which we come to know traditional oral forms—from actual experience of a performance through audio and video facsimiles and on to textual transcriptions—have an enormous impact on just how we "read."[14] Making and becoming fully aware of these distinctions can only improve our grasp of verbal art in and from oral tradition.

Second is the matter of *language*. Whatever the tradition, genre, or medium, we must view its "words" not as detachable, isolatable items but as elements that collectively make up a coherent, idiomatic "way of speaking."[15] Instead of seizing upon formulas as playing cards to be shuffled and reshuffled, we need to understand their emergence under the aegis of grammatical and syntactic rules governing that particular variety or register of language. These rules for the structure and texture of phraseology will of course vary from one tradition and genre to the next, and even within a single genre there will be room for idiolectal and dialectal species of the poetic language. But the point is that the poet composes not so much by manipulation of ready-made building blocks as through fluent command of an idiom dedicated to a single purpose.[16] The situation is similar for those larger "words" not so immediately dependent on linguistic principles, that is, for the typical scenes and story-patterns that inform many narrative works.[17] They too are part of the specialized, dedicated idiom through which poet and audience communicate in a highly focused transaction, as are any other linguistic, paralinguistic, or nonlinguistic features licensed for usage within the given speech-act.

A third major development in recent years has to do with the exposure of the Great Divide of orality versus literacy as a false dichotomy, and with its replacement by a more realistic model. Just as evidence has accumulated on the variety of oral traditional performances that can still be attended in our time, so numerous witnesses from ancient, medieval, and modern traditions have stepped forward to testify against this once unquestioned typology.[18] To put the matter positively, these witnesses have together described a *spectrum of expressive forms,* all the way from living oral traditions experienced in the field to highly textual works that nonetheless betray roots in oral tradition. And instead of muddying the waters, thereby destroying our ability to discriminate meaningfully among categories, these witnesses have in fact pointed the way toward understanding how and why traditional forms can so stubbornly survive the advent of writing and texts, at least for a time.[19] Since these forms constitute a real and singularly expressive language, rather than a standard kit of handy compositional tools, there is no reason why they should immediately cede place to an entirely new, unrelated mode of expression. To an important extent language and poetics persist, and *sēmata* will continue to function as *sēmata,* at least for a while and with certain qualifications, whether spoken as "winged words" or scratched on a tablet. Just as an airtight typology of oral versus written now seems an unsupportable imposition on the complexity of cultural activity, so an overnight abandonment of mother tongue in favor of foreign language is much too tidy an explanation for the many voices of traditional verbal art.

THE RIDDLE OF REFERENTIALITY

How then are we to read Homer's traditional signs? An effective response to this formidable challenge depends on rebalancing the equation of composition and reception by focusing on the special dynamics of Homer's (and his tradition's) language or way of speaking. In pursuing this goal we should of course be under no illusion that we can simply assume the role of the original audience for these and other traditional poems; indeed, such a goal may not even be desirable as we seek to read Homer in and for our own time as well as on its own terms. However, some attention to reception of the *epos* within its native idiom will solve cruces generated by the double myopia of privileging composition and assuming congruency with literary, posttraditional poetics. By recovering something of what the *sēmata* imply, our reading experience will be uniquely enriched.

The core of our inquiry thus depends on the nature of referentiality in traditional oral works in general, and in the Homeric texts in particular. As demonstrated elsewhere, the art of traditional poetry is an *immanent* art, a process of composition and reception in which a simple, concrete part stands for a complex, intangible reality. *Pars pro toto,* as it were.[20] "Grey-eyed Athena" or "wise Penelope" are thus neither brilliant attributions in unrelated situations nor metrical fillers of last resort. Rather they index their respective referents, in all their complexity, not merely in one given situation or even poem but against the enormously larger traditional backdrop. Likewise, singular instances of feasting scenes, guest-host encounters, or Return songs naturally engage plural contexts, with their implied wholes brought into play under the agreed-upon code and dynamics of Homeric idiom.

An unassuming line from South Slavic epic offers a simple example of how traditional meaning can be encoded, and of how it must be figured into the reception of such works. Ubiquitous throughout the Moslem songs, "San usnila, pa se prepanula" (You've dreamed a dream, so you're frightened) regularly occurs as a response to a report of a battle about to begin or some other dire event on the near horizon, and is customarily spoken by someone apparently in charge to the supposedly less qualified reporter. Its proverbial nature marks a gently chiding, perhaps patronizing attitude on the part of the person who seeks to dismiss the threat as merely a dream and therefore not to be taken seriously. The metonymic meaning of this South Slavic *sēma,* however, mandates something that cannot be predicted without the immanent contribution of the poetic tradition: to wit, the "dream" will very soon become a reality, and ignoring the warning will cost many lives. Clearly, the brutal irony of the unfolding drama depends crucially upon apprehending the formula in traditional context, on being aware of the prolepsis onto which the sign institutionally opens.

Viewed plainly, this property of *metonymy* amounts to nothing more than a special case of a fundamental linguistic principle: the essentially arbitrary relationship between sign and meaning. A brief parable will illustrate the point. We know that ultimately there is nothing inherent in the morphemes "ship," *bateau,* or *nēus* to convey the idea of a vehicle particularly well suited for travel on water. These English, French, or Greek words—or ultimately their Indo-European precursors—come to signify as they do on the basis of continued usage in social context. Additionally, any such item can take on more than lexical significance in certain cases, as for example when a landlubber unschooled in nautical jargon divulges his or her amateur status by calling an elegant seagoing craft not a "ship" but a "boat." All such idiomatic changes rung on the semantics of standard meanings are, like their apparently more basic etymologies, absolutely arbitrary impositions on the morphemes that bear them. They have no claim to innate signification, but serve their institutionalized expressive functions under the continuing social contract of language.

Metonymy in traditional oral art is no different. The special valences assigned to certain phrases or other units within the Homeric register emerge not from some primeval license but from the demands of fluent, economical communication in a traditional context. Far from constraining poetic expression, these recurrent metonyms provide a dedicated avenue to traditional meaning above and beyond the usual literary repertoire of communicative channels, collectively yielding more than the sum of their parts and uniquely enabling both composition and reception. Thus noun-epithet phrases like "grey-eyed Athena" or "purple-cheeked ships" refer not just—or even principally—to the goddess's eyes or the ships' hue, but rather the phrases use those characteristic yet nominal details to project holistic traditional concepts. Such synecdoche extends the fundamental arbitrariness of language at the same time that it extends its significative "reach," with the phrase indexing a character or object in its extrasituational, extratextual wholeness. While there is certainly nothing literal in the grey eyes or purple cheeks that lexically projects such complexity, these phrases engage their referents institutionally through metonymy. By traditional usage the simple part projects a complex and immanent richness.

Other kinds of phrases, as well as the "larger words" of narrative, work similarly. Upon the nominal meaning of "intimate word" *(pukinon epos)* is projected the idea of "a message or communication of great importance, one that if properly delivered and received would change the present course of events profoundly."[21] As James Holoka has pointed out, the simple phrase *hupodra idōn* (looking darkly) also bears a complex implication; it "conveys anger on the part of a speaker who takes umbrage at what he judges to be rude or inconsiderate words spoken by the addressee" (1983:4). In these and other cases, the extra layer of meaning is not the singular creation of a particular event or context but rather a traditional harmonic that deepens the resonance of each of its occurrences. If we move to a larger unit, we note the same phenomenon. When a woman enters upon a formal lament in the *Iliad,* she will regularly observe a three-part structure that consists of (1) a statement that "you have fallen," (2) a summary of personal history and the dire consequences for those left behind and (3) a final intimacy.[22] This matrix is not a constraint under which the poet labors but is the traditional form that drives reception. At the most expansive level, it is the very *nostos* pattern itself—the well-worn path of the returning hero blazed in numerous Indo-European traditions[23]—that informs the narrative by indexing its contents according to familiar, evocative actions. In all of these cases and at all of these levels, the referent for the concrete "words" of performance or text lies outside the immediate performance or text. Referentiality is immanent and traditional.

Of course, not all phrases, scenes, or story-patterns function with identical force, any more than all traditions, genres, or media obey precisely the same rules for the structure of phraseology or of larger levels of discourse. Because certain formulas or narrative patterns resound more deeply than others, it would be a mistake to assume absolute congruency of signification among them.[24] At any level, whether in an unmarked standard version or in a highly dedicated traditional dialect, language cannot and does not work in so lockstep a manner. We will do better to conceive of the value-added meaning of the Homeric and other traditional idioms as a quality that manifests itself in different ways and to different extents: some phrases and scenes serve a chiefly workaday function, some are imbued with rich and complex associative meanings, and most fall somewhere in between those extremes.

With this qualification in mind, we can explain the workings of metonymy by invoking the model of a network of instances or nodes that extends far beyond the present performance or text. In effect, the immediate context, always an artificially limited horizon for the play of this kind of verbal art, opens onto the more realistic "text" of the ambient tradition. Individual occurrences of "words"—whether phrases, scenes, or larger patterns—contribute to what will always be an only partially textualized network, but nonetheless one that will just as certainly be present to each of its components. We can thus observe that the singular instance derives its signification not only from the usual lexical resources but also by participation in the grander design of traditional referentiality. These signs defer primarily neither to contiguous "echoes" nor to particular instances in other performances or texts,[25] but to the immanent implication that each instance is licensed to bear by traditional fiat.

In this respect we can see how the mechanism versus aesthetics impasse arose. If one perceives such metonyms as merely useful and repetitive rather than resonant and constitutive, there are indeed only two choices one can make: either to impute to every recurrence a catchall generic meaning or to struggle to discover something genuinely unique about each iteration. By sensing how "words" project a different kind of referentiality, however, we can aspire to the best from both worlds. Alongside the natural fecundity of metonymic expression, the bequest of tradition, stands the differentiating or diversifying context of the individual situation. Reading Homer's signs finally means discounting neither traditional nor situation-specific meaning: the essential and liberating point is that even the most singular action or event is naturally suspended within a network of implication.[26]

EMPOWERED SPEECH:
THE ROLE OF REGISTER

In explicating this network of implication, let us concentrate on one aspect of traditional oral referentiality and metonymy: the nature of the special language in which the artistic transaction takes place. As noted earlier, the history of studies in oral tradition shows time and again that the "words"—the cognitive units of traditional expression—resist universal definition; phraseology and narrative structure must be ascertained on their own terms from one tradition, genre, and medium to the next. In short, one needs to learn each language, or each variety of language, for to attempt a uniform definition of "words" across this remarkable diversity of forms is to resort to reductionism.

Within such heterogeneity, however, metonymy as an expressive strategy stands as an enabling feature of *composition* and should thus figure just as prominently in the decoding process of *reception*. At both ends of the circuit, arbitrary yet institutionalized meanings are keyed by performance (real or rhetorical) and evoked by reference to tradition. To put it aphoristically, *performance is the enabling event and tradition is the enabling referent.*

This hermeneutical proverb moves reception into the foreground, along with composition, and effaces the false boundary between living oral traditions and texts that derive from oral tradition. Instead of categorizing works by what are finally impertinent criteria, this proverb directs our attention to two factors of primary importance. First is the matter of *performance,* which, as the anthropologist Richard Bauman observes, "represents a transformation of the basic referential . . . uses of language," and "which says to the auditor, 'interpret what I say in some special sense; do not take it to mean what the words alone, taken literally, would convey'" (1977:9; compare Bauman and Briggs 1990). When performance is keyed, the audience is signalled to receive via a designated channel and according to specific rules. Even when the performance must be rhetorically invoked in a text meant for readers, the keying strategies and their dedicated responses will still be available to any author and reader who share fluency in the idiom. The empowering aspect of performance, real or rhetorical, is its identity as an event, which mandates a modulation in the communicative exchange. The very phenomenon of performance offers a context for the utterance and its reception, and likewise with *tradition,* which constitutes the field of reference to which performance adverts. As we have seen, value-added phrases, scenes, and other patterns resonate in a network of signification, with the singular instance dwarfed—but implicitly informed—by the whole. All that is required for the transaction to succeed is fluency at both ends of the transmission.

Such fluency depends on three aspects of traditional oral art:

performance arena, register, and communicative economy. *Performance arena* designates the "place" that performer/author and audience go to make and receive the work. In living traditions, this arena amounts to a series or collection of actual sites, at which the oral narrators and their audiences accomplish the exchange; it is the many Ottoman courts and later the *kafane* (coffeehouses) of Moslem South Slavic epic, or the less well defined but equally numerous special occasions (weddings, family gatherings, evening assemblies) of its Christian counterpart. But even when we can stipulate a geographical location, it is fundamentally the speech-act that defines the physical place (and not vice versa), that indexes it along with all other such sites as a place that promotes and sustains a special kind of communication. Thus there is no wholesale dislocation when the performance arena changes from an actual site to a rhetorically induced forum in a text. Although the performer-audience relationship is no longer face-to-face, it rhetorically recalls the same arena because it mirrors the same speech-act. It may do so with varying degrees of success, depending above all on the fluency shared by composer and audience. Whatever the case, entering the performance arena means opening a specific channel for communication and participating in a focused kind of exchange. Whether face-to-face or at one textual remove, this much is prescribed simply by the "locus" where the performance takes place.

When poets and audiences enter the arena, they must converse in the local vernacular. Anthropological linguists refer to such speech varieties, selected by "recurrent types of situations" (Hymes 1989:440), as *registers*. It is characteristic of such idiosyncratic idioms that they offer a somewhat unusual version of the contemporary language, perhaps maintaining archaisms and different dialect forms alongside more current, streamlined speech, as in the case with Homer's own register.[27] Here are the first few lines of the South Slavic *guslar* Halil Bajgorić's *Ženidba*

Bećirbega Mustajbegova (The Wedding of Mustajbeg's Son Bećir-beg) as an example:[28]

Oj! Rano rani Djerdjelez Alija,
*v*Ej! Alija, careva gazija,
Na Visoko više Sarajeva,
Prije zore *v*i bijela dana . . .
*v*A *v*ovako momak govoraše:

"Oj! Djerdjelez Alija arose early,   1
Ej! Alija, the tsar's hero,
At Visoko above Sarajevo,
Before dawn and the white day . . .
And in this way the young man spoke:"   131

The exclamations *Oj!* and *Ej!* are features of the singer's idiom and may constitute part of the decasyllable (as in line 2) or stand as extrametrical (as in line 1). The italicized phones (*v* in lines 2, 4, and 5) are hiatus bridges peculiar to this sung genre. These five lines also exhibit a metrical biform (*prije* for *pre* [before] in line 4); a Turkish loanword (*gazija* [hero] in line 2); an ijekavian dialect expansion made *metri causa* (*bijela* [white] in line 4); and an aorist verb inflection (*govoraše* [spoke] in line 131), a tense that continues in the epic singer's register but has not been a part of the standard, unmarked language for more than a century.

Alternatively, in other genres these specialized, marked idioms may supplement what can be preserved in a text with important constitutive dimensions of loudness, pitch, gesture, or other performative characteristics, as in the case of South Slavic charms, for example.[29] But specific tradition-dependent and genre-dependent features are much less important for our purposes than the given register's identity as a dedicated, unified language exclusively devoted to communication in the performance arena. Neither Homer nor the epic *guslari* turn to their curious forms of ancient Greek and South Slavic in an attempt at antiquarianism, but rather because over time these poetic dialects have come to serve as finely tuned instruments for the expression of their target narratives. By definition, no other medium could do as well. Furthermore, the very efficacy of the register is the best reason for continuing its use into the early stages of textuality. The method and medium are wholly dedicated to a specific goal, marked for the accomplishment of this purpose to the exclusion of all other purposes; why, then, would the poet and audience immediately forsake such unique expressivity when textuality is just entering the world of discourse, an infant technology merely taking its first few steps? Why suddenly introduce an unintelligible language into the performance arena?[30]

The answer, of course, must be that a highly developed, mutually intelligible language is far preferable to the alternative, especially in the early stages of the new medium. To reroute the exchange from a dedicated, marked idiom to any other tongue is to shortcircuit the remarkable *communicative economy* of the traditional oral register. To avoid confusion, let me stipulate immediately that this quality of economy in composition and reception is not at all the same phenomenon as the "thrift" studied by Parry and Lord, which apparently is a tradition-dependent property of ancient Greek *epos* that does not translate well, if at all, to either South Slavic or Anglo-Saxon traditional verse.[31] I speak here not of the thrifty surface of the phraseology, the integers themselves, but rather of the economy of expression, the mathematics of the process. If a short phrase such as *pukinon epos* or *hupodra idōn* can index a complex traditional idea, then the phrase offers evidence of a significative economy in certain dimensions of that idiom. The poet is not constrained at the level of diction because the poet's phraseology naturally reaches beyond the present moment or situation to the immanent traditional network; in fact, this uniquely reverberative method makes available an automatic context that is available only via the dedicated register. To simulate this context outside the register would require an enormous commitment of textual supplementation and apparatus, and even then the experience of the work of verbal art would be very different: nontraditional and thoroughgoingly textual. However, the poetics I have been describing supplements the most immediate performance or text extremely economically by referral to the performance arena and the appropriate idiomatic way of speaking. Instead of introductions, appendices, footnotes, or other strategies, Homer depends upon traditional signs.

SĒMATA AND THE POETICS OF RECOGNITION

Let us now turn directly to these traditional signs, or *sēmata*. First, here is a bare minimum of statistical background. The word and term *sēma* occurs a total of 58 times in Homer: 33 in the *Iliad,* 20 in the *Odyssey,* and 5 in the Hymns.[32] It will perhaps surprise no one that in the martial context of the *Iliad* the greater number of instances apply to burial mounds. Yet while fully 19 of the 33 occurrences name the "final signifier" in this world of *klea andrōn* [glories of men], in the adjacent cosmos of the *Odyssey* only 3 of the 20 mark the last tangible sign of heroic enterprise, and the Hymns have no such signs. Leaving aside these mortuary *sēmata,* which nonetheless exhibit a distinct kinship of meaning,[33] let us recall a few of the other occurrences.

Although their particular application ranges widely from Zeus' relatively frequent portents, the identifying marks on Aias' lot and Dolon's spoils, and Orion's Dog (the brightest of all stars that also forebodes evil), to signs measuring achievement in athletic contests, Teiresias' prophecy of the oar and winnowing shovel,[34] and especially the famous scar that projects Odysseus' identity, these 36 other *sēmata* all share a common thrust: they signal an emergent reality. As keys to what is to happen, each of them marks a prolepsis, a connection from what is present and explicit to what is immanent and implied, and each of them is uniquely effective because it charts a unique revelatory pathway. For example, Zeus' portents often provide a predictive basis for action or conclusion, as when Nestor urges the Achaeans to remain in *Iliad* 2, or when, seven books later, Odysseus tells the withdrawn Achilles of Zeus' propitious signs for the Trojans. The marks on Aias' lot and Dolon's spoils determine priority and action, and the comparison to the traditionally resonant *sēma* of Orion's Dog makes Achilles' advance toward Hektor only that much more ominous. Even when the sign indicates only the length of a *solos-* or a discus-throw, it portends the direction of the narrative, whether of Aias' victory in the Funeral Games or the disguised Odysseus' setting himself apart in the Phaeacian competition.

Of all Homeric *sēmata,* however, I choose to concentrate here on the metonymic sign-language employed by Penelope and Odysseus in the self-fashioning that constitutes their final recognition. In considering the implications of this remarkable series in particular and of metonymic cues in general, we naturally must be willing to admit our less than optimal preparation for entry into the performance arena and our less than perfect fluency in the Homeric register. But we should also resist the temptation to "throw out the baby with the bathwater." Not being able to hear with the clarity and responsiveness of an ancient Greek audience does not necessarily amount to mishearing. Some of the resonance of language and narrative structure can be recovered, and with patience their metonymic force can be at least partially reconstructed.

This is the case, to take a persuasive parallel, with Laura Slatkin's rebuilding of Thetis from a bit player in the Iliadic drama to a goddess whose covert power is sufficient to shake Olympian foundations. Not that Homer explicitly "inscribes" her larger mythic character in any episode comprising our *Iliad;* quite the contrary. Still, Slatkin is able to recover Thetis because she understands the special nature of spoken and unspoken in Homeric epic. As she puts it (1991:xv): "The mythological corpus on which the poet draws, taken together, constitutes an internally logical and coherent system, accessible as such to the audience. The poet inherits as his repertory a system, extensive and flexible, whose components are familiar, in their manifold variant forms, to his listeners. For an audience that knows the mythological range of each character, divine or human—not only through this epic song but through other songs epic and nonepic—the poet does not spell out the myth in its entirety but locates a character within through allusion or oblique reference." This is a principle that operates in traditional oral art around the world, frustrating outside researchers at the same time that it enables a highly economical discourse among insiders who "speak the register." The more highly coded the particular idiom, the further removed it must be from the contemporary unmarked standard—whether at the level of phraseology or of mythic pattern.[35] Indeed, even the distancing terminology of "allusion," "oblique reference," and "partial," to which we as textually trained scholars are driven, bespeaks our lack of acquaintance with the mode of signification made possible by traditional signs. Whether they are specifically labeled as *sēmata* or not, we need to read Homer's "words"—the formulas, narrative patterns, and other units of utterance—not as textual ciphers but as signals potentially rife with implication, as keys to an emergent reality. The metonymic signs are by their nature prolepses—expandable in some way during the process of reception—and we must give ourselves a chance to understand how and what they mean.

It is just such a chance that Penelope provides Odysseus during the final stages of their rapprochement. Consider first the longer view over books 19–24, as Penelope recognizes the *sēmata* that the stranger has offered (19.250), as the mill woman speaks a portent before Odysseus that the suitors should feast their last (20.111), and as the returning hero reveals his telltale scar to Eumaios and Philoitios (21.231). Portending the slaughter, Zeus then thunders *sēmata* as Odysseus strings the bow (21.413); afterward, Eurukleia chastises her mistress for refusing to believe her report of the longed-for revenge, citing the *sēma* of the scar as proof (23.73). Then we reach the heart of the sequence, as Penelope responds to Telemakhos' complaint about her obstinacy that she and Odysseus share *sēmata* that are *kekrummena* (hidden) to others, known only to themselves (23.110). The ruse involving the olive-tree bed follows, with Penelope suggesting that the immovable bed be transplanted outside her chamber and with Odysseus announcing that there is a great *sēma* built into the bed (23.188) and that he will now expound it (23.202)—a signal that effectively restores his identity as no other signal could, mimicking the function of the Homeric trope of metonymy at the same time that it undeniably establishes the completion of his *nostos* or return. Notice that the relationship between bed and identity, between metonym and meaning, is essentially arbitrary: the bed need not signify Odysseus' return, but tradition certifies that it does. What is more, like all *sēmata* the olive-tree bed provides a unique pathway to knowledge outside the immediate moment. Penelope says as much when, having recognized the *sēmata* (23.206), she stipulates their necessary *traditional* meaning (23.225). Odysseus then tells her of Teiresias' prophecy, which involves another *sēma* (23.273); with the scar as *sēma* recognized by Laertes (24.329, 346) this dense, reverberative sequence of signs comes to a close.

In order to gain a sense of the more immediate narrative progression as against its punctuation by metonymic reference, let us narrow the focus to the skein of *sēmata* between lines 70–230 of Book 23. There are in fact six clustered occurrences in the space of about 150 lines, far the highest concentration any-

JOHN MILES FOLEY

where in Homer, and they reveal much about the deepest concerns of the poem as the *Odyssey* draws toward what the ancient
critics called its *telos*.

First, we encounter Eurukleia chastising her mistress Penelope for refusing to believe her report of the slaughter and
Odysseus' homecoming (70–79):[36]

τέκνον ἐμόν, ποῖόν σε ἔπος φύγεν ἕρκος ὀδόντων,
ἦ πόσιν ἔνδον ἐόντα παρ' ἐσχάρῃ οὔ ποτ' ἔφησθα
οἴκαδ' ἐλεύσεσθαι· θυμὸς δέ τοι αἰὲν ἄπιστος.
ἀλλ' ἄγε τοι καὶ <u>σῆμα</u> ἀριφραδὲς ἄλλο τι εἴπω·
οὐλήν, τήν ποτέ μιν σῦς ἤλασε λευκῷ ὀδόντι,
τὴν ἀπονίζουσα φρασάμην, ἔθελον δὲ σοὶ αὐτῇ
εἰπέμεν· ἀλλά με κεῖνος ἑλὼν ἐπὶ μάστακα χερσὶν
οὐκ ἔα εἰπέμεναι πολυκερδείῃσι νόοιο.
ἀλλ' ἕπευ· αὐτὰρ ἐγὼν ἐμέθεν περιδώσομαι αὐτῆς,
αἴ κέν σ' ἐξαπάφω, κτεῖναί μ' οἰκτίστῳ ὀλέθρῳ.

"My child, what sort of word escaped your teeth's barrier?   70
Though your husband is here beside the hearth, you would
     never
say he would come home. Your heart was always mistrustful.
But here is another <u>sēma</u> that is very clear. I will tell you.
That scar, which once the boar with his white teeth inflicted,
I recognized it while I was washing his feet, and I wanted   75
to tell you about it, but he stopped my mouth with his hands,
     would not
let me speak, for his mind sought every advantage. Come then,
follow me, and I will hazard my life upon it.
Kill me by the most pitiful death, if I am deceiving you."

Eurukleia's traditional rhetoric lies mostly below the textual
surface in this rejoinder to Penelope's intransigence. She opens
the speech with a highly resonant metonymic question: namely,
"poion se epos phugen herkos odontōn?" (What sort of word
escaped your teeth's barrier?). This query appears six times in the

Odyssey, indexing a situation in which an older, wiser, or otherwise more authoritative person chastises another for not knowing
better, for not trusting him or her. Additionally, the phrase im-
putes a rashness on the part of the person addressed, suggesting
that something needs to be set right.[37] Thus Zeus begins his
promise to help the wanderer by so chastising Odysseus' champion Athena (1.64; doubled at 5.22), Athena as pseudo-Mentor
scolds Telemakhos for distrusting the gods' power to intervene
(3.230), Eurukleia herself chides her still disguised master for
thinking she would not be strong enough to conceal his identity
(19.492), and Antinoos derides the minor suitor Leodes for suggesting they stop their attempts to string the bow.[38] These quite
separate moments are metonymically aligned by the "teeth's barrier" exclamation, which provides an implicit traditional context
in which to place a variety of different moments. Like other
reverberative phrases in the Homeric register, it furnishes a guide
for negotiation of the narrative landscape.

Another such cue—this one marked by actually calling it a
sēma—is the famous *oulē* or scar that unambiguously identifies
Odysseus. Like other such signs, it reaches outside the present,
immediate situation to an event that precedes the period covered
by our *Odyssey;* that is, its meaning lies not in the mere fact of
the scar, but in its unique testimony, as verified by implicit,
institutionalized referral to the prior episode of the young Odysseus' wounding by the boar. The sign thus keys an emergent
reality—namely, that this is indeed the returned hero—and it is a
reality that cannot be gainsaid.[39] The bridge between the *oulē* and
the man is as strong and durable as the relation between any
sēma and its traditional referent. We may observe that in warning Penelope as she does, Eurukleia is both employing and citing an absolutely fundamental trope of Homeric representation.
She pinpoints the scar, which has an obvious traditional referent;
and she terms it a *sēma*, to the traditional force and meaning of

which there can be no appeal. Together with the "teeth's barrier" phrase, this second metonym lends enormous power and authority to what the old nurse says, all of the power and authority that conventionally reside in the only partially textualized network of tradition.

A short while after this episode Penelope must face another rebuke of her obstinacy, this time from her son Telemakhos, who complains of her "heart harder than stone" *(kradiē stereōterē . . . lithoio,* 103). She responds that she is much at a loss to determine what to do, and perhaps we cannot blame her for that confusion, but she closes her speech to Telemakhos by assuring him that she and Odysseus have *sēmath'* (110) hidden from others, known only to the two of them. In avowing the existence of these signs, Penelope is of course pointing toward the olive-tree bed, but she also provides a working definition of a *sēma* in the process. To all others, the bed will be simply a bed: its nominal identity as a functional human artifact, nothing more and nothing less, will exhaust its meaning. Yet to those "in the know," the bed also harbors an institutionalized signification as the uniquely fashioned union of nature and culture to which only Penelope, Odysseus, and a single serving-maid are privy. These three alone can expand metonym to extrasituational reality, they alone can project immanent meaning from the concreteness of the *sēma.* They alone are the competent audience versed in the traditional implications of the bed and therefore able to "read" it. It is with some confidence, then, that Penelope assures her son that she has the means to identify her husband quite unequivocally, for, with the sole exception of the serving-maid, she and Odysseus are in effect the only fit audience for this particular *sēma.*

The test of the bed in effect becomes a test of the poetic efficacy of the traditional register, as Penelope begins the gambit with an intentional and provocative *mis*reading: she asks the old nurse to make up Odysseus' own bed outside their chamber.

When Odysseus objects, it is with the fervor of one who possesses special and disqualifying evidence, that is, one who calls into question Penelope's abrogation of traditional referentiality. Only if the bed has been torn from its living trunk, he complains, could it be moved from its rooted place—and, we may add, from its rooted signification. In explicating how he created the bed, and thereby making evident its traditional metonymic character, he begins explicitly by announcing that there is a great *sēma* built into the bed (188) that will have prevented anyone from dislocating it. Just as with all of Homer's traditional signs, the permanence of the sign's meaning cannot be compromised except by the most radical of misconstruals—severing the vessel that links metonym to tradition.

Via the familiar Homeric strategy of ring composition, Odysseus frames his account of the bed's making with the phrase that stands as the epigraph to this essay: "*houtō toi tode sēma piphauskomai*" (Thus I expound to you this *sēma*, 23.202). In both of these framing instances, the sign points away from the immediacy of the here and now and toward a time and set of actions outside the scope of our *Odyssey*. It recalls an origin, a source of meaning that lies far beyond the reach of explicit textual signification. This same sign also serves as the key that unlocks an emergent event, the climactic and unifying event of Odysseus' long-awaited apotheosis toward which the epic has been working for more than 22 books. *Sēma* specifies the involved poetic trope, marking this particular nexus as one of those moments that must be placed against the backdrop of an implied reality, so that the audience is set, as Slatkin puts it, "the apparently paradoxical task of listening for what is unspoken" (1991:xvi). In short, Odysseus here refutes the literal in favor of the metonymic,[40] affirming both his own emergent identity and the overall strategy of traditional implication. Penelope, it turns out, was absolutely right: by a *sēma* she shall know him.

And so she does. The poet tells us that this final stage in her *anagnōrisis,* marked as well by the indexical formulaic description of her knees and heart going slack, stems directly and unambiguously from his explication of the *sēmat'* (23.205–6). As before with the "teeth's barrier" label, the slackness phrase meshes harmoniously with the instance of *sēma* to enrich our sense of the unfolding drama. Surveying the eight additional occurrences of knees and hearts being loosed provides a map for reading all of the different situations in a single general context: abject helplessness in the face of an inexorable power or event.[41] As a result, we come to realize by implication how deeply Penelope is affected, how her stubborn, self-preserving refusal to believe in Odysseus' return has finally melted away. Her recognition, we are told, and told traditionally, is both disabling and enabling—the slackness phrase indicates by convention its overwhelming and irresistible force, while the *sēma* citation effectively re-creates Odysseus before her. She goes on to ask him not to be angry with her, explaining that she was guarding against any possible deception and invoking the example of Helen, whom she likewise exculpates through drawing a parallel to her own situation. All that remains, then, is her stipulation, again via the marked idiom, that he has convinced her by "reading" the bed, something no other mortal man could have done (23.225–30):

. . . νῦν δ᾽, ἐπεὶ ἤδη <u>σήματ᾽</u> ἀριφραδέα κατέλεξας
εὐνῆς ἡμετέρης, τὴν οὐ βροτὸς ἄλλος ὀπώπει,
ἀλλ᾽ οἶοι σύ τ᾽ ἐγώ τε καὶ ἀμφίπολος μία μούνη,
Ἀκτορίς, ἥν μοι δῶκε πατὴρ ἔτι δεῦρο κιούσῃ,
ἣ νῶϊν εἴρυτο θύρας πυκινοῦ θαλάμοιο,
πείθεις δή μευ θυμόν, ἀπηνέα περ μάλ᾽ ἐόντα.

". . . But now, since you have recounted clear <u>sēmata</u>   225
of our bed, which no other mortal man beside has ever seen,
but only you and I, and there is one serving-woman,

Aktor's daughter, whom my father gave me when I came here,
who used to guard the doors for us in our well-built chamber;
so you persuade my heart, though it has been very
stubborn."   230

CONCLUSION

Citing *sēmata* has persuaded other hearts as well. Zeus' portents,
Odysseus' scar, Orion's Dog, the prophecy of the oar-become-
winnowing shovel—all of these and more constitute signs that
mimic a fundamental trope of representation in Homeric epic
and in many oral and oral-derived traditions: a concrete signal
pointing institutionally toward a metonymic reality. Those phenomena and objects named as *sēmata* of course have a special
force: in these cases traditional referentiality is not simply realized but explicitly stipulated with what I take as a term in the
native Homeric poetics. But we should also remember that metonymic projection, the part standing for the whole, is a quality of
the idiom or register at large, and that far the greater number of
its occurrences are unmarked by the term *sēma.* Thus the noun-
epithet formulas and myriad other aspects of phraseology, the
typical scenes, and the story-patterns all participate in driving
reception: in addition to their nominal surfaces, they are responsible for providing access to an extrasituational, extratextual, and
finally untextualizable context. Naturally, each of them will project a different traditional reality, with some less heavily and some
more densely coded,[42] but the *pars pro toto* principle will operate
throughout as a basic algorithm linking composition and reception. From this fundamental trope emerges the mandate for any
audience, ancient or modern: to speak and hear the Homeric
register with as much fluency as they (and we) can muster.

Learning to communicate in this way would deepen our understanding of verbal art from oral tradition, be it Homeric epic or

any other form, simply because it would increase our fluency in the highly specialized and focused idioms that performers and audiences use to transact their exchanges. Does such an approach demand a wholly new poetics, entirely distinct from the various literary, text-based brands of poetics that now dominate critical discourse? No, it does not, since as suggested earlier, the perspectives that derive from considering the role of oral tradition are very often complementary to or even resonant with what we (perhaps too readily) take as literary perspectives. What is needed is not an "either/or" but a holistic approach, one that gives full voice to the newer discoveries about traditional oral works without discarding whatever aspects of the text-based program may be applicable and apposite. Homer's traditional art deserves no less.

CHAPTER 4

The Inland Ship:
Problems in the Performance
and Reception of Homeric Epic

ANDREW FORD

> For the older analysts the place and manner of Homer's
> recitation did not arise. Any occasion was improbable and
> the full performance impossible; the extant poems were
> concocted for a festival. But for the unitarian the ques-
> tion is grave. It is also embarrassing. Urgent as the ques-
> tion is, there is in fact not a scrap of real evidence for the
> occasion or manner of the original performances.
>
> BRYAN HAINSWORTH, *HOMER*

The time seems to be passing when the Parry-Lord theory that
Homer's epics were composed in oral performances was thought
to be incompatible with the high artistic quality of our *Iliad* and
Odyssey. Recent studies of oral formulaic language, as represented elsewhere in this volume, have shown it to be capable of
many subtly expressive effects and structural patternings.[1] But if
we are approaching a time when it will make little difference
whether the Homeric poems were composed orally or not (Martin 1989:1), another, and older, question becomes more pressing:
how could such large-scale poems as the Homeric epics ever have
been presented to an audience? Indeed, it was not so much
Homer's probable illiteracy as the difficulty of conceiving of the
Iliad being performed in its entirety that led Wolf to "cast the

die" in Chapter 26 of his *Prolegomena* and to claim that our texts are late compilations, since no archaic "Homer" would even have conceived of such large epics: "If as the only man of his time to have [writing materials] he had completed the *Iliad* and the *Odyssey* in their uninterrupted sequence, they would in their want of all other favorable circumstances have resembled an enormous ship, constructed somewhere inland in the first beginnings of navigation: its maker would have had no access to winches and wooden rollers to push it forward, and indeed no access to the sea itself upon which to make some trial of his skill . . . [I]f Homer lacked readers, then I certainly do not understand what in the world could have impelled him to conceive and plot out poems which were so long and so unified in the close interconnection of their parts" (Wolf 1795:112/1963:85–86; Eng. trans., p. 116, adapted). Even scholars who insist that Homer must have used writing will concede that Greek epic, like almost all archaic poetry, was normally presented and received in oral performances, and thus it is very hard to see how their overall coherence and design might have been exhibited to an audience. Hence, whether one believes in an oral or a literate Homer, the question of performance may rightfully be termed the "most troublesome" problem in Homeric studies (Notopolous 1964:18; Lesky 1967:18).

Such evidence as we have is inconclusive: it is like that early epic was performed in the agora, the palace, or the men's club, and that occasional recitations or contests were held in connection with funerals and religious festivals (Kirk 1962:274–281). But it is very doubtful that on any of these occasions an *Iliad* could have been performed all the way through. Nor is this unthinkable: just because a city or a singer may possess an "authoritative" text does not mean that the full and continuous presentation of that text is the work's ideal mode of presentation.[2] Indeed, there may be advantages in partial disclosure for keepers of certain texts, as can be seen from a story about an oracle-expert in late sixth-century Athens. Onomacritus was expelled from Athens by the Peisistratids when he was caught interpolating prophecies into a collection of the oracles of Musaeus; yet later when the Peisistratids themselves were expelled, they brought Onomacritus to the court of Xerxes in Susa and called on his skills with a text: Herodotus (7.6.4) tells us that when he recited *(katelege)* prophecies to Xerxes, he picked out *(eklegomenos)* what was encouraging and omitted ominous news for Persia in his performance. Of course, an oracle collection more easily invites selective performance than does a good epic, but esoterism is no respecter of generic boundaries: even in Plato's day certain rhapsodic guilds found it useful to claim that they were in possession of uncirculating verses of the master (*Phaedrus* 252B–C).

But the question of whether Homer's epics could be performed in full may be moot if one assumes that the poems were performed in relatively short pieces (as is suggested by the representations of bards in the *Odyssey*), but with such regularity that audiences acquired a thorough knowledge of each epic through repeated performances of its parts. Certainly epic singing was very popular in the archaic period, and certain themes doubtless became very familiar through repeated performance; it is also likely that audiences related particular themes being performed to a larger cycle of epic stories (see Slatkin 1991 for a recent reading of the *Iliad* in these terms). However, to go further and assume that audiences acquired a distinct sense of individual poems as complete, self-contained, and unified works may be to project a literate mode of aesthetic reception onto the archaic period. In a comparative study of the special ways that traditional epics may encode meaning, John Miles Foley has argued that structural elements in oral works can have meanings that transcend immediate reference and metrical utility but finds that this "traditional referentiality" intends "fields of reference much larger than the single line, passage, *or even text in which they occur.*"³ Hence, the "whole" to which an oral epic performance belonged may not have been confined to even an ideal single text. It is at any rate clear that organic unity and completeness are not timeless and universal properties of literature, and the processes by which they have been elevated into hallmarks of great art may be independent of the processes by which their subject texts came into being (Ford 1991).

Reconstructing the mechanics of epic performance thus involves questions of audience reception, and in the second section I will consider this aspect of the problem, examining early references to Homeric poetry and asking how far a coherent and complete poem is hypostasized in each case. Considering those passages in which Homer is explicitly cited or quoted will suggest that it is not only improbable but distorting to posit a full performance of a complete epic as the normative presentation against which all partial (or eccentric) presentations were measured. If this consideration is accepted, it then becomes difficult to define the precise status and function of a long poetic text in archaic Greece; accordingly, I will suggest some uses for such an "inland ship" in conclusion.

In the twentieth century, Gilbert Murray first raised and answered the question of how and where large-scale epics could have been performed in archaic Greece. Estimating reasonably enough that the *Iliad* would occupy twenty to twenty-four hours of continuous recitation, he concluded that only the great international religious festivals of archaic Greece would have provided the incentive to create and the opportunity to display monumental poems (1934:187–192). The suggestion has been taken up more than once, some relieving the vocal strain by distributing the task among a team of rhapsodes (references and critique in Notopolous 1964:1–18). It has been claimed that the text of our *Iliad* falls naturally into large performable sections, but there is no consensus on what these are: some suggest three large pieces (1–9, 10–18.353, 18.354-end) were given over three days (Wade-Gery 1952:14–16, 69); or that cantos of four books were performed in three double sessions (Davison 1965:23–25); or that four books a day were sung over six days (Thornton 1984:46–63).

Uncertainty also attends the search for actual festival occasions at which the Ionians could have gathered to hear poetry over several days. The Panionia at Mycale (referred to at *Iliad* 20.403–405) or some early form of the Delia (*Homeric hymn to Apollo* 146–164 refers to singing contests) are most often mentioned, but we know nothing of the program of these events. More recently, attention has fallen on the rhapsodic performances at a later but better attested festival, the quadrennial Greater Panathenaea of Athens, begun or enlarged in 566–565 B.C.E. We have evidence from as early as the fourth century that Solon (Dieuchidas *apud* Diogenes Laertius 1.57) or Hipparchus, son of the Athenian tyrant Peisistratus ([Plato] *Hipparchus* 228B) established a rule requiring that performers of Homeric poetry at this festival go through the songs in order, each singer picking up where the previous one had left off. Many now accept this tradition, considering the most likely instigator to be Hipparchus, around 520 (Jensen 1980:128–171; S. West 1988:36–38; Janko 1992:29–32).

But if epics were presented in organized fashion at this festival, we are still short of proof that any epic was performed there in its entirety. The sources say that performers had to go through the stories in order (*ephexēs*), but not that they had to be performed in full. The rule implies following a fixed plot-structure, but not necessarily completing a text (Janko 1992:30), and could have been enforced on the basis of nothing more than an ordered list of epic themes (Sealy 1957:349). Moreover, there are considerable difficulties in imagining complete presentations. In the first place, it seems that down through the fifth century "Homer" was credited with most heroic epics, including the *Thebaid, Cypria* and *Epigonoi;* his corpus was winnowed down to the *Iliad* and *Odyssey* (plus the *Margites*) only during the fourth century (Pfeiffer 1968:11, 43–44, 73, 117, 204). It is thus far from clear that performing "Homer" in the sixth century would have meant performing only the *Iliad* or the *Odyssey.* While the Panathenaic rule may have amounted to this by the fourth century (Lycurgus, *Against Lecorates* 103; Murray 1934:300), Hipparchus would have been well ahead of his time in having such a discriminating sense of which epics were really by Homer. In addition, the full recitation of an *Iliad* or *Odyssey,* taking up the bulk of three days, would have competed with many other distractions, such as processions, athletics, and contests in other musical forms: rhapsodic contests never dominated the program of the Panathenea in the way that drama held center stage at the Dionysia, or Wagner at Beyreuth (Notopolous 1964:13–14; pace Wade-Gery 1952:14). Such considerations might seem to justify Walter Burkert's peremptory dismissal: "There never could be a question of performing the complete text of the *Iliad* at a rhapsodic contest: the attested length of the Panathenaea is 4 days" (1987:49; but see Stanley 1993:402–36).

Some of these difficulties have been met in two recent unitarian readings of the *Iliad* by Oliver Taplin and Keith Stanley, who attempt to show how the epic might have been presented as a whole so that its unity and architectonic design could have been appreciated. Logistical problems are met more or less satisfactorily, for example by hypothesizing that individual epics were performed in rotation at the lesser Panathenaea (Stanley 1993:402n36; but Lycurgus mentions only the quadrennial Greater Panathenaea), or by suggesting that rhapsodic performance took place at night (Taplin 1992:29; presumably, one does not need to be caught up on sleep to enjoy the other festivities). Taplin (1992:22–44) situates full performance at some noncompetitive eighth-century panegyris, where he envisions a single singer giving out the *Iliad* (minus book ten) in three installments of roughly ten, nine, and eight hours. Stanley (1993:279–281) would place the fixing of the text at the sixth-century Panathenaea where a team of reciters could have given out seven, ten, and seven books over three days, with a double session on day two. The two also disagree on whether the traditional book divisions represent early performance-divisions (Stanley 1993:249–261) or are later artificial impositions on the text (Taplin 1992:285–293; on this issue, see S. West 1967:18–25 and Pfeiffer 1968:115–116).

These scenarios are inevitably hypothetical, though none is physically impossible.[4] But for me a decisive refutation comes, paradoxically enough, from the Greek who first championed epic unity, Aristotle. In the *Poetics,* Aristotle demanded of epic an ideal of organic form that he had developed in connection with tragedy, whose actions should have a unity and completeness that is "easy to take in at one glance" (*eusunoptos,* 7.1451a4). Allowing that epic must remain "less unified" than tragedy by virtue of its length and use of episodes, he singled out the *Iliad* and *Odyssey* as more unified than others (23.1459a31ff.). But Aristotle also recommended that, because of the greater magnitude that belongs to epic (24.1459b17), to ensure that its beginning and end can be taken in together *(sunhorasthai),* an ideal epic would have to be "shorter than the old epics," about the size of the number of tragedies put on at one sitting (24.1459b17–22). Although Aristotle seems to have been a perceptive enough reader to appreciate the high quality of our Homeric texts, he was also enough of a realist to see that they were about three times too long for successful oral presentation in full.

It is therefore far from easy to assume that the Homeric poems were ever presented in full to an audience. Whether Homer's epics were nevertheless seen as artistic wholes in the archaic period then becomes a question of epic reception.[5] To pursue

this question, I propose to consider the earliest instances of a
Greek writer's quoting Homer's words and assigning them to
Homer, asking what account is taken of the whole in each case.
Although the whole of post-Homeric literature must be sifted
for the immensely complicated problem of reconstructing the
early state of the text (on which, Davison 1962, S. West 1988,
Janko 1992:20–38), I focus on passages of explicit quotation because only they implicitly point to an idea of a Homeric text in
the sense of a fixed and definite source of his words. Brief poetic phrases found in lyric that also appear in Homer attest only
to the wide currency of traditional poetic language (Fowler
1987:20–39). More extensive but general similarities between
passages of epic and lyric (for example, *Iliad* 22.71–76 and Tyrtaeus 10.21–30 *IEG*) are unreliable because they may be independent realizations of prototypes (Richardson 1993:113). Nor
can ancient reports that an early poet alluded to Homer be
trusted in the absence of specific citations (Davison 1968:70–84;
compare West (1988) on Archilochus 303 *IEG*). To be sure, there
are passages of sixth-century lyric—most notable Stesichorus'
Geryoneis (Fowler 1987:36–39; Burkert 1987:51) and Alcaeus Fr.
44 (Fowler 1987:37; West 1988:151n.5)—which strongly suggest
that at least the major episodes of the Homeric poems were
already being performed in a form very like that which we now
read. But these texts are not decisive for this investigation, since
the lyric poets are shown thereby only to be treating well-known
epic episodes and tales rather than wholes.[6] For our purposes the
most useful texts will be those in which specific words do not
simply resemble Homeric passages but are assigned to Homer as
words he has been able to put his mark on and claim out of a
more general epic tradition.

Because this is an admittedly small parcel of evidence, we
cannot expect it to rise above the generally low level of pre-Alex-
andrian treatments of Homer's text. Yet a close examination of

this apparently "slipshod, arbitrary and dogmatic" (Kirk 1985:39) treatment of Homer at least shows that long heroic songs could have other uses than to be contemplated as aesthetic wholes.

The first certain instance of a Greek's quoting a specific phrase as Homer's is from Simonides in the later sixth century.[7] In what appears to be a sympotic elegy (19 *IEG*), he quotes a hexameter spoken by Glaukos to Diomedes in *Iliad* 6.146 as a fine saying of "the man from Chios":

ἓν δὲ τὸ κάλλιστον Χῖος ἔειπεν ἀνήρ·
οἵη περ φύλλων γενεή, τοίη δὲ καὶ ἀνδρῶν·
παῦροί μιν θνητῶν οὔασι δεξάμενοι
στέρνοις ἐγκατέθεντο· πάρεστι γὰρ ἐλπὶς ἑκάστωι
ἀνδρῶν, ἥ τε νέων στήθεσιν ἐμφύεται

"One very fine thing the Chian man said:
'as the generation of leaves, such is the generation of man';
    but few among mortal men, although they have taken this in
        with their ears,
have laid it in their breasts; for hope remains in each—
    hope which is planted in the breasts of the young.'"

It is typical of the looseness of ancient habits of quotation that these words are assigned to Homer, though they are spoken by one of his characters: the epic poet is assumed to endorse everything said in his poem. Typical too is the fact that the line is cited for what it may be taken to say in itself, without any reference to or consideration of its function in context. Mimnermus (2 *IEG*) had already appropriated the image of leaves with similar freedom to describe the fleetingness of youth and not, as in Homer, the transitoriness of life; and later poets like Bacchylides (5.65) and Aristophanes (*Birds* 685) put the image to their own uses without mentioning Homer. In fact, Homer's Glaukos himself is already adapting a gnomic commonplace, for the comparison between leaves and generations is also used by Apollo when he refuses to fight with Poseidon over wretched mortals, "who like leaves sometimes/bloom and blaze with life while they eat the fruit of the field/and then fall away lifeless" (*Iliad* 21.464–466; compare Musaeus 2 B 5 DK).

But Simonides' text is distinctive in two respects. First, he quotes a particular version of the idea rather than adopting the image in his own words as Mimnermus had. One reason for quoting might be that in *Iliad* 6 the commonplace is neatly embodied in a single hexameter line and so suits the metrical game of incorporating a hexameter into an elegiac poem while playing on it.[8] Secondly, Simonides ascribes this hexameter to a particular author, and among the Greek lyric poets Simonides quotes or cites earlier figures most often. When he quotes and corrects a saying of Pittacus (541 *PMG*) or paraphrases some verses of Cleoboulus in order to contradict him (581 *PMG*), his motive seems to be that assigned to him by Plato: "by overthrowing a wise saying of a wise man, Simonides will get a reputation for wisdom himself" (*Protag.* 343b–c) Yet even when Simonides agrees with the earlier saying, as with Homer, he still manages to exhibit a singular wisdom *(sophia)* that is both moral and poetic: for in the poem at hand not only does Simonides claim to have a deeper appreciation of the often-imitated line than others (perhaps with a glance at Mimnermus, whose lugubrious expatiation on the image yet allowed a brief space for the joys of youth), but also he exhibits *sophia* in the act of quoting itself: he is able to identify and isolate a particularly fine piece of wisdom in Homer, to take the measure of the wise poet in a single line.

If selecting itself is a form of *sophia,* we may perhaps take the *kalliston* of line one as a real superlative and assign this text to that subgenre of lyric and elegiac skolia that debated what was the finest thing in life. Simonides' poem (the opening of which would admit of many different setups) could well be performed when battling with another poet over what is finest *(kalliston)* in

Homer. (It is suggestive that both Homer's Apollo and Glaukos speak the proverb in a scene of confrontation). Often enough, the archaic setting for such philosophizing was drinking with one's friends (890 *PMG*), and perhaps the prototypic example comes from an after-dinner speech in Homer. At *Odyssey* 9.6–11 Odysseus declares to his host Alkinous and the company that, when a house is merry with plenteous food, wine, and music, "This seems the finest thing to my mind" (*Odyssey* 9.11): *touto ti moi kalliston eni phresin eidetai einai*. This same speech of Odysseus is quoted in the *Contest of Homer and Hesiod* in another scene of competitive poeticizing:[9] his judgment on what is "finest" is there recited by the character Homer in response to a challenge from Hesiod to say, "What do you think is the finest thing for mortals?" (*Certamen* p. 228.82: *ti thnētois kalliston oieai en phresin einai*). Indeed, the contest had started with Hesiod challenging Homer, "Come tell me this first of all, what is best for mortal men?" (*Certamen* p. 228.76: *ti phertaton esti brotoisin*), and it ends on a similar note with King Panedes bidding each one to recite "the finest passage from his own poems" (*Certamen* p.232.178: *to kalliston ek tōn idiōn poiēmatōn*). The *Contest* is a late text which incorporates some early material, and I suggest that its competition to pick out what is "finest," in life or in poetry, shows us the context in which we should place the text of Simonides: he displays his wisdom in being able to pick out the very finest thing in all the wisdom Homer has to offer, and to have a deeper appreciation of it than the common run of men.

In this game, a run of narrative hexameters is broken down in search of compact, ethical pronouncements, despite the fact that in Homer they express the thoughts of particular characters in particular situations. The epic poem as a structured and dramatic whole thus disappears as it becomes a mine of useful one-liners and parables. Its author is taken not as a designing narrator but as a Sage in whose treasured words all kinds of advice may be found.

This same distorting selectiveness, along with the same wisdom in selecting, seems to be at play in a different context in Heraclitus.

Heraclitus' general hostility to early poetic traditions is well known (22 B 42,104), but we have only slight traces of his critiques of specific epic passages. Of Homer he is said to have "rebuked the poet who said 'would that strife perish both from gods and from men,'" (A 22 DK), since he regarded strife among opposites as the very basis of existence. Like Simonides, Heraclitus reads this impossible wish from Achilles' complaint to his mother in *Iliad* 18.107 without distinguishing what a poet says from what his characters say, and he wholly disregards the tone of the passage. Moreover, he does even more violence to the original context, for in order for Heraclitus' critique to work, he must cut his quotation off at the end of the hexameter when in fact the syntax runs on into the following lines: "would that strife perish both from gods and from men,/and anger, which drives even a prudent man to rage" (18.107–108). This suite of lines on how sweet anger can be were not forgotten by Plato (*Philebus* 47E) or Aristotle (*Rhetoric* 1370b10) when they quoted Homer; but Heraclitus must stop short because anger, unlike strife, has no role as a cosmic principle in his system.

The procedure seems hardly fair. If any sentence, indeed any hexameter which appears to be end-stopped, can be wrenched from context and taken as a general proposition about the state of the world, Heraclitus might as well have approved Homer for saying "for always strife is dear to you and wars and battles" (*Iliad* 1.177, 5.891). If a substantive discussion of *eris* is wanted, Hesiod's *Works and Days* is surely the text to take on; but Heraclitus cites that poet only on trivial matters, such as making Day the offspring of Night, when the two are in fact identical (B 57, with reference to *Theogony* 123, 748–749).

It is hard to gauge the tone of all this, but I agree with Rösler (who offers other examples of Heraclitus' *Auslegungspraxis*,

1980:288) that Heraclitus is not simply joking. There can be no doubt that Heraclitus is serious about the ignorance of poets and the credulity of audiences; he is just not interested in giving the poems a full hearing. He seems indifferent not only to local context but also to the tenor of the *Iliad* as a whole; for, taken all in all, the world of the *Iliad* seems rather close to Heraclitus' cosmos, as Plato playfully but perceptively suggested when he called Homer the leader of Heraclitus and all flux theorists (*Theaetetus* 152E, 180D, with a "Heraclitean" interpretation of *Iliad* 14.201). It seems that with Heraclitus, as with Simonides, the point is not to grapple with the whole of Homer's or Hesiod's work but rather to be able to produce a line for discussion and then to have the wit to discern in it something not generally appreciated, such as a cosmic proposition underlying a Homeric hero's complaint. He chastises another wise man (B 129 DK), Pythagoras, for having contented himself with extensive research *(historiē)* into texts and then just passing off the results as wisdom: "having made a selection [*eklexamenos*] of these writings he contrived a wisdom of his own, his polymathy a cheater's art" (B 129). Heraclitus' wisdom, by contrast, lets him see more deeply not only into the nature of the cosmos but also into revered texts. In this he works like Simonides, this time assimilating the narrative poet to the role of gnomic philosopher, a role in which he himself was unsurpassed.

Given the widespread notion at this time that poets provide information and instruction, it seems inevitable that those offering new moral or scientific wisdom should confront Homer and critique him. But when these savants come down to cases, one repeatedly detects an indifference to giving any adequate account of the overall structure of the original combined with a search for novel applications of bits of the poems. Even when Homer is approved, as by Diogenes of Apollonia (64 A 8) for recognizing that Zeus is all-knowing air, this approval appears to be based on a misconstrual or misremembering of a half line such as "Zeus who knows counsels that never fail" (*Iliad* 24.88). The prodigious writer on Homer, Democritus (68 A 101), reads amazingly much into a single Homeric epithet. He argues that Homer divined the identity of mind *(nous)* with soul *(psukhē)* because Hektor, dazed by a blow, is called *allophroneōn*, apparently etymologized as "thinking other thoughts." The etymology is dubious and the citation apparently misremembered.[10] Nevertheless, in his scrutiny of, so to speak, an atom of the epic, Democritus is able to find an anticipation of his own psychological views. Something of the same trivializing use of epic appears in the Hippocratic *On the Sevens* (§8) which cites an unplaced epic hexameter saying "as when spring comes welcome to shambling cows" to show how "finely Homer knew that of all domestic animals cows are most eager for spring." And Herodotus (on whose Homeric researches more later) supports his opinion that cold climates retard the growth of horns on cattle by quoting (4.29) *Odyssey* 4.85, "and Libuē where lambs grow horned quickly," which in context only means they grow up quickly (see S. West *ad loc*).

The ability to quote and put to new use a telling line of old epic appealed not only to those wishing to demonstrate their *sophia* but also to the educated aristocracy who patronized them. Pindar assumes that his patron shares this educated taste in the only place he quotes Homer by name, *Pythian* 4.277–79:

τῶν δ᾽ Ὁμήρου καὶ τόδε συνθέμενος
ῥῆμα πόρσυν᾽· ἄγγελον ἐσλὸν ἔφα τιμὰν μεγίσταν
  πράγματι παντὶ φέρειν·
αὔξεται καὶ Μοῖσα δι᾽ ἀγγελίας ὀρθᾶς

"Of the sayings of Homer that you understand, take this one to
heart as well: 'A good messenger brings great honor to any
enterprise.' The Muse herself is exalted through a message
rightly phrased."

In this case it is Homer's very words and not simply the original context that mean next to nothing, for I can find little in common between this passage and its presumed source in Homer *Iliad* 15.207. There Poseidon praises the messenger Iris for trying to dissuade him from issuing a too brusque response to Zeus:

ἐσθλὸν καὶ τὸ τέτυκται, ὅτ᾽ ἄγγελος αἴσιμα εἰδῇ.

"This too is good, when a messenger knows the right thing."

It may be that Pindar has an obscure purpose in changing, or "exalting," the Homeric Muse; but perhaps he simply misreads Homer here, as he elsewhere muddles another choice part *(korupha)* of wisdom to be found in Homer, the great allegory of the jars of Zeus (*Pythian* 3:80–82):

εἰ δὲ λόγων συνέμεν κορυφάν, Ἱέρων, ὀρθὰν ἐπίστᾳ,
    μανθάνων οἶσθα προτέρων
ἓν παρ᾽ ἐσλὸν πήματα σύνδυο δαίονται βροτοῖς
    ἀθάνατοι.

"But since you, Hiero, know how to discern the choice part of
right speech, you know the lesson from earlier men that the
immortals apportion two pains to man for every good they
grant."

Although Pindar adduces this saying as proverbial, there is a definite reference to *Iliad* 24:527–528:

δοιοὶ γάρ τε πίθοι κατακείαται ἐν Διὸς οὔδει
δώρων οἷα δίδωσι κακῶν, ἕτερος δὲ ἑάων·

"Twin jars lie on the threshold of Zeus
filled with the gifts he gives, evils, and the other with goods."

The grammar of this couplet is not perfectly smooth, but in context it is clear that Zeus has not three jars but two, one of evil and one of good. In the lines following 24.528 Zeus gives some people mixed evil and good, and some only evil, thus necessitating only two jars. So Plato understood (*Republic* 379D), but he cites the couplet with a different, decisively clearer text of 528. It is possible that Pindar's misreading stems from his general reluctance to speak ill of the immortals, for in his version Zeus is never responsible for unmixed evils but only for the mixed good and bad of human fate. As his following lines say, such a dispensation at least has the advantage of making clear the difference between fools who cannot bear ills with good grace and the noble who can. Pindar's piety is not so strong as Plato's—who rejects the couplet outright because god can never be the cause of evil—but one that sits well with the poet's aristocratic outlook.

Such high-handedness might be explained either as the primitive practice of people working in a milieu in which they do not expect to be challenged on points of textual detail or as the whimsy of decadents who know the text so well that they delight in twisting it into unexpected new meanings. I suggest that it was the pragmatic practice (a long poem is more widely useful in small pieces) of people for whom Homer was more important as an authority than as an author of an aesthetically unified text.[11] In this vein, it is a short step from quoting Homer as a source of wisdom or guide to right behavior to quoting him as a badge of the speaker's education and values. The ability to come up with an appropriate Homeric verse for a given situation said something about the speaker's cultural position. The "encomiasts of Homer" of Socrates' day, the rhapsodes and their satellites making a living off the texts, used to say that the poet was worth taking up and learning by heart not only for the conduct of life but also find its refinement (*Republic* 606E). As cultural refinement was progressively democratized in the fifth century, especially at Athens, the distinctive thing became not simply being able to quote from esteemed poets but being able to deploy these texts with sophistication or "cleverly" (*dexiōs*). The kind of games in which this attainment was displayed can be seen often in Plato, whose Socrates can come up with and ring ingenious changes on Homeric lines or familiar proverbs in certain social situations, as when he takes Aristodemos to Agathon's dinner party uninvited by playing upon an old proverb and Homer together (*Symposium* 174B–D). Aristophanes too was an adroit quoter of poetry in his plays, and maladroit epic quotation is a comic theme in *Peace* (1265–1297) when the son of general Lamakhos can offer the party only the most bellicose lines from Homer and the cycle, despite the comic hero's countering with epic lines describing feasts and food.

To meet the increasingly widespread demand for *dexiotēs*, sophists and teachers of the later fifth century began to supply anthologies which conveniently "selected from all the poets the key sayings *(kephalaia)* and whole speeches *(rhēseis)* which had to be learned by heart if one is to become good and wise" (Plato *Laws* 810E–811A). The sophist Hippias advertised one such volume as containing "some things said by Orpheus, others by Musaeus, in short, by this poet here and that poet there, some things by Hesiod and some by Homer, and by many others of the poets, and by prose writers, some Greek and some foreign" (86 B 6 DK). The *Frogs* flatters its audience by saying that everyone will follow its poetry-context because each has a book from which to learn the clever passages of the poets *(ta dexia:* 1114). Of course, some of the old aristocracy, like Nicias' son Niceratus, learned the entire *Iliad* and *Odyssey* by heart (Xenophon, *Symposium* 3.5); but thumbing through a papyrus was good enough for Socrates, who, Xenophon says (*Memorabilia* 1.6.14), used to go through the "treasuries *(thēsauroi)* of wise men of old" with friends, picking out *(eklegometha)* what was good and "unraveling" or "explicating" *(anelittōn)* it in hopes of becoming distinguished for wisdom.

In these cases, readers make Homer an aphorist and thereby

ANDREW FORD

create a new use of his poetry for a select audience who could distinguish themselves by their subtle understanding. But I do not think this use was restricted to elite or competitive commentators. A similar exploitation of Homer through selective quotation can be found in a public Athenian inscription of about 476–475. Kimon's victory over the Persians at Eeion in 479 was commemorated on three inscriptions in the Agora, one of which began with an allusion to the *Iliad:*[12]

> Ἔκ ποτε τῆσδε πόληος ἅμ᾽ Ἀτρείδῃσι Μενεσθεὺς
> ἡγεῖτο ζάθεον Τρωικὸν ἐς πεδίον
> ὅν ποθ᾽ Ὅμηρος ἔφη Δαναῶν πύκα θωρηκτάων
> κοσμητῆρα μάχης ἔξοχον ὄντα μολεῖν

> "Once from this city with the Atreidae Menestheus
> set out as leader to the holy field of Troy,
> who Homer once said was the outstanding
> leader of the close-armored Danaans."

A paraphrase refers the public to *Iliad* 2.552–554, where Menestheus is indeed described as a nonpareil leader:

> Μενεσθεύς
> τῷ δ᾽ οὔ πώ τις ὁμοῖος ἐπιχθόνιος γένετ᾽ ἀνὴρ
> κοσμῆσαι ἵππους τε καὶ ἀνέρας ἀσπιδιώτας.

> "Menestheus,
> who was unmatched among mortal men
> at marshalling cavalry and spear-bearing men."

But the patriotic invocation of Homer loses force to the extent that one appreciates what an "inconspicuous, even undistinguished" role Menestheus plays in the *Iliad* as a whole (Kirk 1985:206). This fact, however, weighed little in comparison with the potent praise embodied in the couplet: Herodotus reports (7.161.3) that the Athenians quoted the same tag to Gelo of Syracuse as evidence that they deserved to lead the Greeks against Persia. That these apparent games with Homer's text should have played a role in international politics seems odd, but there are parallels in stories that Solon or Peisistratus claimed Salamis from Megara by quoting or interpolating a couplet in the catalogue of ships (*Iliad* 2.557–558) that placed Salaminian Ajax' ships next to those of the Athenians (Merkelbach 1952.27–29; Jensen 1980:137–142; Janko 1992:29–30).

Taken as a whole, early quotations of Homer, on the one hand, hypostasize a Homeric corpus: they draw their authority from being accepted as words said by Homer himself and not by another; they draw their validity by being his precise words and not a paraphrase. On the other hand, the lines are not treated as if they demanded explication in terms of their context in the corpus but more like formulae of wisdom or ancient lore. The idea seems to be that if a hexameter or so can be adduced and accepted as Homer's actual words, it becomes a self-standing utterance, a piece of wisdom that demands attention in itself because of its source. This kind of epic analysis was so widespread in archaic and early classical Greece—including its most brilliant *littérateurs*—as to make one doubt whether our ideals of epics as literary wholes were equally important to the Greeks of the archaic age.

Of course, other Homerizing was going on all this time, of which we know little more than that it existed. We may suppose that a Democritus treated the poet more responsibly and synoptically in his lost treatises on aspects of Homer's poetry. In addition, rhapsodes had early accompanied their performances of epic poetry with "interpretative" comments or at least ancillary information (Pfeiffer 1968:12), and by the fourth century vied with each other in discoursing about the fine "thoughts" to be found in Homer (*dianoiai*, Plato, *Ion* 530c–d). In such contexts it is conceivable that rhapsodes considered the larger meanings of the poems they performed, but what form this comment may have taken is hard to know. The sixth-century Theagenes of Rhegium, recorded as the first to write about the life and poetry of Homer, was remembered as allegorizing the battle of the gods in *Iliad* 20 and 21 in terms of the opposition between cosmic elements (8.1–2 DK). I would not combine this with a variant reading from a line in *Iliad* 1 attributable to him (8.3 DK) and infer that Theagenes wrote a detailed and extensive commentary on the whole of the *Iliad.* Such a philological work would have been unexampled for at least two centuries, and if there had been one it seems we should know a good deal more about Theagenes than we do. It is furthermore hard to imagine that he had a ready allegorization for every appearance of the gods through the whole poem: an allegorist has an easier time making his case if he can concentrate on favored passages, as Plato suggests they did (*Republic* 378D). No doubt he would be expected to meet audience challenges on any well-loved episode, but especially on those passages he chose to bring forth.

Too much remains unknown to prove the negative thesis that Homer was never sung, heard, or read all the way through in archaic Greece. But the evidence reviewed above, if it cannot demonstrate the absence of unitary conceptions of epic, at least shows that apparently purposeful distortions of small pieces of epics had important uses.[13] It is also worth noting that the literary, aesthetic appreciation of epics as coherent texts is indeed to be found among the Greeks, but neither so early nor so generally as is often assumed. And when it does appear, around the middle of the fifth century, the wholeness and integrity of Homeric poetry often seems only conceptual or notional.

I begin with a heuristic question: who is the first Greek—a performer, listener, or critic—to conceive of an epic text as a whole and not just as a long string of episodes or as a storehouse of wise sayings? Who, in other words, is the first Greek we can say with certainty went through any epic text from start to finish and knew he had done so? My candidate for this role is Herodotus based on a little remark from Book 2. Herodotus is partial to what he calls the Egyptian version of Paris' flight with Helen in which they were driven by a storm to Egypt where Helen remained while Paris went on to Troy. To show that Homer was aware of this story even though he chose not to use it, Herodotus quotes (2.116) four hexameters describing "beautiful robes woven by the women of Sidon" in Paris' bed-chamber whom he "brought from that land when he took Helen to his home" (*Iliad* 6.289–292). Herodotus knows that the Phoenicians, to whom Sidon belongs, live in Syria, and that Syria borders on Egypt. But what sews up the case is the striking further observation, that "nowhere else does Homer contradict himself over this point" (*anepodise heōuton*, 116.2). This (correct) claim is based on the notion of the *Iliad* as a definite and delimited text quite distinct from other epics. I say "notion" of the text, since it may be doubted whether Herodotus commanded the same text we call the *Iliad* because he attributes this passage (from book six in our texts) to "The Aristeia of Diomedes," which occupies book five in our texts (Diomedes has left the narrative after 6.236). Be that as it may, his sense of epics as coherent and consistent texts is well developed: he also argues (2.117) that the *Cypria* is not Homer's because it has Paris make it back to Troy in three days. Again, there is a disturbing conflict with what is known of the plot of the *Cypria* (see Lloyd 1988:51), but individual epics are clearly being read through by Herodotus as distinct entities, assumed to be coherent and internally consistent.

It may not be surprising to find thorough and careful reading of Homer, and indeed a certain sophistication, among historians whose business is examining sources. Thucydides exhibits the same close but skeptical (1.10.3) knowledge of Homer's text in search of revealing tidbits. He has pored over the "catalogue of ships" (as he identifies the passage) to estimate the size of

Agamemnon's expeditionary force. He also commands the entire text, for he infers the relative disunity of the Greeks at this time from the subtle and true observation that Homer never uses *Hellenes* for all the Greeks, but only for those living around Phthia (1.3.2). In this, historians may have benefited from sophistic interest in poetry, which seems sometimes to have regarded its larger structures. Protagoras' quotation of the opening to the *Iliad* to show that both *mēnin* and *aeide* may be faulted for grammatical incorrectness (80 A 29 = Aristotle, *Poetics* 1456b15) uses the text as little more than a stalking horse in a bravura performance. Its tone was likely bantering, much like the moment in the *Frogs* (1128–1131) when Aeschylus has recited the first three lines of the *Choeophoroi* and Euripides finds "more than a dozen" faults in them. (When Dionysus objects that they are only three lines, Euripides retorts and each one has twenty mistakes.) But on one occasion Protagoras (80 A 30 DK) said that the episode of the fight between Xanthos and Achilles was intended to provide a break *(dialabein)* in the battle, in order that the poet might make a transition *(metabēi)* to the battle of the gods, an observation that has found favor with modern critics (Richardson 1993:70) Hippias the sophist offers a scrap of learning that resembles Thucydides' remark on *Hellene* in Homer (86 B 9 DK). He made the nice surmise that the word "tyrant" *(turranos)* entered Greek at the time of Archilochus, and apparently he backed this up with the thesis that Homer's word was "Ekheton" (as in *Odyssey* 18.85, 116, 21.308). Unfortunately, Ekheton appears to be a Homeric person, "Holder," but Hippias' negative thesis on *turranos* exhibits a command of the epic lexicon.

Other thinkers of this time also appear to be taking their Homer whole. Among Homer's champions, Metrodorus of Lampsacus in the time of Cimon and Pericles may have extended allegorical exegesis to the whole text. The recoverable details of his system indicate that his allegoresis was not focused on isolated lines or passages but was based on interrelations among gods and heroes through the whole poem. "[I]n a class by himself for his extremism" (Richardson 1975:69), Metrodorus is criticized by Tatian for "facilely dragging everything into allegory" (61 Fr. 3 DK). A comparable mix of philology and madness may be found in the Derveni commentator who reads Orphic texts wildly yet can find and appositely quote *Iliad* 24.527–528 and *Odyssey* 8.335 to illustrate the meaning of an archaic word (col. 22).

One thing that might be changing in the middle fifth century is that copies of Homer's poems are moving out of the hands of rhapsodes, schoolteachers, and state archives and into the audience. The well-educated Euthydemus collected as many writings of the poets and sophists as possible, including "all the *epē* of Homer" (Xenophon, *Memorabilia* 4.2.1: *Symposium* 3.5), and Niceratus took his verbatim knowledge of the *Iliad* and *Odyssey* into the agora where he loved to listen to rhapsodes (Xenophon, *Symposium* 3.6). Antimachus of Colophon, the first person recorded to have edited Homer, worked around this time (Pfeiffer 1968:72, 94–95). All this would have made new demands on performers, who may have responded like Plato's Ion in knowing their Homer with complete thoroughness. More importantly, reading the poems as integral wholes also would have offered Homerists new resources of signification, just as close reading revealed to historians new truths about Homer's world. As an example, I give my final instance of reading Homer, from the Socratic Antisthenes.

Antisthenes despised rhapsodes who could only recite the Homeric poems (Xenophon, *Symposium* 3.6), and excelled them by closely studying and reasoning about the texts. This can be seen in a remarkable résumé of one of his interpretative sallies treating the meaning of the word *polutropos*, "of many turns," in the first line of the *Odyssey:*

Antisthenes says that Homer is not praising Odysseus in calling him *polutropon* any more than he is blaming him. Now he has not represented Agamemnon or Achilles as *polutropos*, but as straightforward and noble. Nor is even wise Nestor tricky and shifty in his character, but is straightforward in his associations with Agamemnon and the rest of the army, not holding back if he has anything good to advise. Achilles was so far from this quality as to say that he hates like death "the man who says one thing and keeps another hidden in his heart" [*Iliad* 9.313].

Now Antisthenes solves the problem thus: "What? Is it to be supposed that Odysseus is wicked because he was called *polutropos,* and not rather that it is as being skillful [*sophos*] that he is so designated? Well, perhaps 'turn' [*tropos*] refers both to character and to the use of language. For a 'well-turned' [*eutropos*] man is one disposed to do well: and 'turns' of speech are its various shapings [*plasai*]. Indeed, Homer uses *tropos* in connection with the voice, that is of the modulations of songs, as in the case of the nightingale: 'she pours out her many sounding voice with quick turns [*trōpōsa*]' [*Odyssey* 19.521]. If the skillful are very clever at conversation, they also understand how to say the same thought in many ways [*tropoi*], and, understanding the many 'turns' of speech, they would be 'of many turns.' And the skilled are good. For this reason Homer calls Odysseus skilled in saying he is *polutropon,* because he knew how to get along with people.'"[14]

Whether *polutropos* is a bad or good quality seems to have been a sophistic debating topic (a comparable discussion is in Plato *Hippias minor* 364c), but Antisthenes' reasoning exploits the text in remarkable ways. Like a Thucydides or a Hippias, he knows that the epithet (occurring only twice in extant epic) is restricted to Odysseus: unlike a Simonides or a Heraclitus, he knows that "I hate like the gates of Hades . . ." is spoken by Achilles, Odysseus' antitype; like Democritus, he appeals to etymology to uncover the true sense of *polutropos* and finds a suggestive passage in which *trepein* is used figuratively of the voice. In Antisthenes all the basic tools for literary analysis are in place, and his reading is not at all far from what may be found in the most sophisticated of present-day readers of Homer (see Pucci 1987:16–17, 24, 243).

When age-old songs are appearing increasingly in the form of palpable texts that may be read and reread as wholes, new forms of analysis become available and may be rewarded if they offer valuably different perspectives on the poems. When technology, economy, and society put these cultural heirlooms in more and more hands, they also made it possible to distill a new set of meanings from them, a new way of interpretation that exploits the fixity of words and their stable interrelations. Not before the time of Antisthenes do we clearly see Greeks basing interpretations of Homeric epic in the play of whole texts, notionally true and stable, rather than excerpting them ad lib. or vesting authority in the lore of the performer. From this time formalisms become facilitated, and all formalisms of Homer, from unitarian readings to deconstructions, rely on a postulated whole text. That this way of construing the *Iliad* may not be old or original need not make it inauthentic. Only a Romantic idealization of origins would consider it a refutation of a particular interpretation to say that it derives from a particular kind of reception of a work made possible by particular developments in technology and the social uses of poetry. I should put it that formalistic readings were and are a new way of reperforming epic, a successor to early oral reperformances but exploiting written texts to discover and value new things "in" the poetry.

Although the minute and scrupulous examination of whole epic texts seems no earlier than the middle of the fifth century, I do not suggest that an archaic epic performance was a mindless theatrical orgy. Performative context always includes audience expectations, canons by which the performer's skill and effectiveness are judged (Bauman 1977). The traditions about the Panathenaic rule point to one occasion on which such expectations were adjusted, favoring knowledgeable and versatile singers, professionals in a word. A command of a fixed text and an ability to demonstrate its unity may also come to be features of epic performance required of a performer wishing to be recognized as competent, but it is far from clear that early singers of Homer were expected to show this.

Whatever significance we attach to the history of Homeric reception and interpretation, the function of such a long, well-designed text as the *Iliad* remains enigmatic in a society accustomed to hearing epic in oral performance, whether one places this composition in the eighth century or the sixth. Accordingly, some scholars have spoken of the earliest Homeric texts as collector's editions (Lord 1962:196), never to be completed in a single performance (Goold 1977:7, 34). This is possible, but the analogy may fail to do justice to the oddity of such an object, an oddity that Wolf expressed in his analogy with an inland ship and which Gilbert Murray expanded on in often-quoted words: "Every work of art that was ever created was intended in some way to be used. No picture was painted for blind men: no ship built where there was no water. What was to be the use of the *Iliad?*" (1934:187). Both scholars ask an important question, even as both leave out a particular kind of making. While it is true that no landlocked people ever built ships, not every ship is built to sail, nor is every painting to be publicly displayed. As an analogy, I return once more to the Greater Panathenaea: for this festival the Greeks built a wagon fitted out with a mast to resemble a ship: this ship/wagon carried a very large robe, exquisitely embroidered with Athena's heroic deeds, and proceeded overland to bestow this too-large and ornamented robe on an unseeing statue. This inland ship may offer the best way of thinking about the peculiar place that any epic text would have held in an oral society. That is, whatever form Homer's texts may have had in the archaic period, a written *Iliad* can only have been an imitation of an oral performance, an artifact with its own uses and symbolic values, but not quite identical with an epic song. Such a perspective is the reverse of literary approaches that would see oral performances as partial, contingent, or imperfect realizations of the complete and unified text. However, at least from the fourth century, the imitation of innumerable oral performances by a single text was reused as an integral work of art in its own right, and served as the basis of a new kind of reperformance that is literary appreciation. But when we try to think it back into its earlier phases, a written Greek epic becomes again an inland ship for us, no doubt made as well as possible, though, perhaps like any text, yawing here and there. Thanks to the creation and dissemination of available written texts, the *Iliad* is present and can be viewed in full and reviewed at leisure; but it is worth remembering that we have very few early sightings of the full, proud sail of Homer's verse.

CHAPTER 5

Hexameter Progression
and the Homeric Hero's
Solitary State

AHUVIA KAHANE

TEXTUAL AND NONTEXTUAL PROPERTIES

The poetry of Homer as we have it today is a highly *textualized* verbal artifact. In other words, we come into immediate contact with the *Iliad* and *Odyssey* as fixed sets of graphic symbols that are independent of any particular performance event, rather than as time-bound sequences of sounds that are unique to their performance context. Many aspects of this *text* are indeed unchanging regardless of whether we speak out, or hear the poems, or read them silently. At the same time, we are increasingly aware of what we might call the *nontextual* aspects of Homer, that is, of the *Iliad* and *Odyssey* not as fixed texts, but as reflections of a broad repository of themes, motifs, scenes, word-groups, and so on, as the manifestation of a potential that we sometimes refer to as an *oral tradition*. As a consequence, we are also increasingly aware that a simple dichotomy between "oral" and "literate" is somewhat restrictive.[1]

But perhaps the most immediately obvious *nontextual* element of Homer's poetry is its meter, or what is better called its rhythm.[2] Paradoxically, writing seems to preserve perfectly the hexameter's *dum-da-da-dum-da-da-dum-da-da-dum-da-da-dum-da-da-dum-dum*. Furthermore, even in writing this rhythm remains an event: it calls for a speaker/reader/hearer; it is not a hexameter unless complete (sequential, unbroken) and in the right order; it is a time-bound, linear "beginning-movement-end" sequence, and as such it is a performance.

THE FUNCTION OF RHYTHM

Let us now ask, what is the function of rhythm in Homer?[3] Does it facilitate memorization of the poems? Perhaps not. Or at least not directly. Oral traditions normally display a degree of *mouvance*, as Paul Zumthor has called it: each performance is one manifestation of an otherwise flexible tradition.[4] But if the very thing we call "oral poetry" is flexible, that is, if full verbatim repetition (in our literate sense) is not in fact achieved, what is the purpose of rigid metrical/rhythmic form, of formulae, type-scenes, and other "oral" devices? Would such devices not thus be a burden on memory, rather than, as is commonly assumed, an aide-mémoire? Would it not have been more convenient to transmit the "contents" or "message" of the tradition, for example, as nonmetrical folktales? Why, then, the use of metrical/rhythmic structure?

One possible answer is that the hexameter rhythm and its technical apparatus, the metrical structure, formulae, and perhaps also type-scenes, are *symbols of fixity and "sameness,"* and hence *symbols of cultural continuity*.[5]

In literate cultures the written *text* ("the Book"; the Bible, the Koran) is the most common symbol of fixity and "sameness."[6] However, a society that knows no writing, or that knows writing only in a very limited sense, will by definition not know this symbol. Oral societies must rely on other means to satisfy their need for fixity and continuity.

To those who know no writing, our literate notion of verbatim, *object*-ive "sameness" over thousands of lines is meaningless. Indeed, no two performances can ever be fully coextensive. However, if during different performances an identical rhythm is used, and if diction is inseparable from rhythm, then a *semblance of fixity* is achieved.

It is easy to identify the fixed entity we call hexameter. If a particular proper name, for example that of Odysseus or Achilles, is used repeatedly at different times during a performance and/or during different performances but always "under the same metrical conditions" (as Milman Parry would have it), then a "sameness" is easily and immediately affected, even though there may be many real differences between the verbatim contents of one version and another; this is what I mean by "a semblance of fixity." In manifestations of traditional poetry like the *Iliad* and the *Odyssey,* whose stated purpose is to preserve the *kleos* "fame," "glory," "hearsay" (a manifestation of fixity and continuity) of the past, such fixity is essential. Let me, however, stress again that this version of fixity does not restrict the inherent flexibility of the tradition.

Two other features of hexameter rhythm should be noted here: first, the rhythm's ability to mark epic as "special" discourse, and second, its ability to indicate that the tradition is always broader than any individual performance.

The hexameter progresses regularly for six feet, then pauses at the verse-end,[7] then repeats itself, then pauses, and repeats itself again more or less regularly for many lines. This manner of controlled, cyclic progression contrasts hexameter discourse to ordinary parlance and hence to our "ordinary" everyday verbal experiences. While all discourse has rhythmic features, almost no form of everyday parlance displays such extended, cyclic regularity. The hexameter rhythm is thus a performative act: its very utterance is the making of "special" discourse.[8]

Furthermore, each hexameter verse/unit is by definition not unique; it is but one of many similar units within larger poems. However, the size of these poems themselves is *not* regarded as a fixed unit.[9] The implication is that each utterance of a hexameter is a manifestation of a body of hexameter discourse of undetermined scope that is, as it were, "out there."

The point is this: Homeric poetry sharply distinguishes between the heroes of the past and the men of today.[10] By speaking of such special characters in "special discourse," their special nature is thus enhanced. By allowing each line to represent a broader body of hexameter discourse, we allow the shorter, performed utterance to function as an elliptic representation of the greater tradition.[11]

THE SEMANTICS OF RHYTHM

Let us try to apply the preceding to a concrete example. Perhaps the most widely recognized manifestations of rhythmicized regularity in Homer are noun-epithet formulae describing the heroes, such as *polumētis Odusseus*, "many-minded Odysseus," or *podas ōkus Achilleus*, "swift-footed Achilles." As John Foley suggests, such formulae invoke "a context that is enormously larger and more echoic than the text or work itself, that brings the lifeblood of generations of poems and performances to the individual performance or text."[12]

These common formulae are concrete "symbols of fixity." They are easily recognized as words that are "the same" as those uttered in other places, at other times, in other performances, by other poets singing about Achilles and Odysseus in hexameter, hence they are "traditional," hence they are also far more "echoic."

Noun-epithet formulae do not simply refer to a character. Rather, they invoke an epic theme, creating what we might call "an epiphany." As one scholar has recently put it, "If an epithet is a miniature-scale myth, a theme summoned to the narrative present of the performance, then, like any myth, it needs a proper (one could say, 'ritual') environment for its reenactment."[13]

The ritual summoning of a hero is a very practical matter: in order to reenact "Odysseus" we must, literally, *say the right words,* that is, repeat the *same* words that we know have been used before for the same purpose, for example, *polumētis Odusseus,* "many-minded Odysseus." But of course this, and most of the other formulae invoking the central characters of epic, are also fixed metrical sequences, for example *da-da-dum-da da-dum-dum (po-lu-mē-tis O-dus-seus).* Furthermore, this sequence is not a freestanding semantic-rhythmic unit. *It is meaningful only when embedded and localized in the proper rhythmic/metric context, at the end of a line of hexameter.* Odysseus is thus "recognized" and invoked not just by the words but also by the rhythm—which is a distinctly hexametric, distinctly epic and heroic medium.

LOCALIZATION, SILENCE, AND REALITY

It can hardly be unimportant that common formulae such as *polumētis Odusseus* and the very idea of the epic hero are localized at the end of the verse,[14] or that others, such as the emotional *nēpios* ("fool," "wretch"), the speech introductory *ton d' apameibomenos* ("to him answered . . ."), *hōs phato* ("thus he spoke . . ."), and many others are anchored to the beginning of the verse. The beginning and the end of the hexameter are its most distinct points, the points at which the flow/pause opposition and the cyclic nature of the rhythm are most clearly marked. As we have suggested above, this cyclic rhythm can mark epic as "special," "extra-ordinary" discourse. The hexameter, like other contexts of *mimetic* activity such as the stage and amphitheater, like the darkness of a cinema-hall, creates a "distancing" effect; it is an artificial context that indicates to us that what happens "out there," the events described/presented, are an imitation, that they are part of a different reality, and not directly a part of our own here-and-now. No matter how elaborate the tale, the modulations of gesture and voice, or for that matter the animatronics (as they are known in Hollywood), we know that epic heroes, tragic personae, Jurassic dinosaurs, and the like, are not real. No self-respecting Greek ever rushed down from his seat to prevent murder onstage. No hearer of epic, no matter how enchanted or moved by the song, ever mistook the poet's imitation for the real thing.[15] As we hear, say, a speech by Odysseus, we are never fully allowed to forget that this is an imitation, an artificial reconstruction of "Odysseus" and specifically of "what Odysseus said." The most immediate reason for this, of course, is that no character in real life, except poets who are by definition the mouthpieces for "other worlds," ever speaks in hexameters.

The conclusion to be drawn from this is as inevitable as it is central to our argument: as we hear the rhythm of epic, it must be that we are both "here" and "there." We are ever conscious of two (paradoxically) overlapping realities or planes: on the one hand, the plane of our own time-present and of the here-and-now performance, and on the other hand the plane of the fiction and of heroic *temps perdu*.[16]

But now briefly consider cinema again: our sense of the reality on-screen depends heavily on a continuous, rapid flow of what are otherwise still images. Stopping the projector means "stopping the show." Slowing down the projector may produce a flickering sequence in which the world of the narrative is still "out there," but now more markedly "punctuated" by split-second interstices of real-life cinema-hall darkness. Such interstices (as in early, particularly silent, cinema) bring "fiction" and "reality" into a sharper contrast. They have the power to affect what we might call the *deictic* balance between the reality of the narrative and the real world.

The case of cinema and the flow of images is a useful (if somewhat contrastive) analogy when considering the flow of words, and in our case, the flow of epic. A pause in the performance of discourse, if it is long enough, affects the balance between our perception of the fiction "out there" and of the here-and-now reality around us.[17] At the same time, as Wallace Chafe says: "The focus of consciousness is restless, moving constantly from one item of information to the next. In language this restlessness is reflected in the fact that, with few exceptions, each intonation unit expresses something different from the intonation unit immediately preceding and following it. Since each focus is a discrete segment of information, the sequencing of foci resembles a series of snapshots more than a movie."[18]

While the hexameter has several conventional points at which a pause in the rhythmic flow can occur (for example, caesurae),[19] the pause at the end of the line, and consequently at the beginning of the next, is the one that is most clearly marked.[20] It coincides with a word-end without fail, and it coincides with sense breaks more often than any other pause in the verse.[21] It is affirmed by special prosodic features, such as the license of the final *anceps* syllable,[22] the lack of hiatus, of correption, of lengthening by position, and it is in the most immediate sense the boundary of the hexameter (the very name "hexameter" defines this boundary). I would suggest, therefore, that the beginnings and ends of the verse, its *onset* and *coda*,[23] are those points where the potential for "interstices of silence," and hence for creating ripples in the flow of epic fiction is greatest. They are the points at which the poet can begin or end his song, hence affecting a full *deictic shift*.[24] More significantly, they are the most convenient (although not necessarily the only) points where, in the midst of song, a poet may pause for an instant, affecting what we might term as *deictic fluctuations*, situations that contrast more sharply the heroic reality of the past, and the (arguably more humble) here-and-now reality of the performance.

Although I would not hazard a more precise definition of this mechanism without considerable further research, the general function of the hexameter's pause/flow nature is, I believe, sensible to most readers and audiences of Homer. As the poet says the much repeated hexameter line ending with the name of Odysseus *ton d'apameibomenos prospehē polumētis Odusseus* (answering him, said in reply many-minded Odysseus), he pauses, as surely he must, not only because the hexameter unit has come to an end, but also because a sense unit (the grammatical sentence) has terminated, and because a discourse unit (the narrative section) has ended, and we are about to begin a different type of discourse (direct-speech), which requires the poet notionally to change his person (from "narrator" to "Odysseus," and, of course, no physical change takes place in the here-and-now). An epiphany of Odysseus, the hero of the past, is thus invoked at the end of the speech introductory line, but immediately there follows a pause. This interstice of silence, brief as it may be, does not break the "flow of fiction"; but I would suggest that it momentarily alters the balance between the narrative reality "out there" and the time-present reality of the performance, contrasting the past and the present in a more vivid, concrete, experiential, rather than cerebral manner.[25] And of course, this is more or less what ritual is meant to do: it summons something from "out there" to the reality of the here-and-now, creating, as it were, a complex warp. This effect is also a practical manifestation of *kleos aphthithon*, "undying fame," a process of preserving events outside of their "normal" spatio-temporal boundaries. Furthermore, *kleos aphthiton* is precisely what epic strives to generate. We may thus describe our poems as a type of event that stitches together the past and the present, as an *enactment* of *kleos,* as a special type of *performative* speech-act.[26]

What follows is a specific example of the workings of this mechanism, centering on the verbal presentation of the epic hero's solitary state.

OIOS, MOUNOS, AND THE EPIC HERO

The hero is a basic paradigm of epic, and one of the hero's most important properties is his state of being alone, that is to say, his existence as a heroic one-of-a-kind. Achilles, for example, is unique both in his military prowess and in his greatness of heart. This idea of isolation, of being unique and/or alone, is implicitly embedded in many Homeric scenes. However, it is most directly expressed by the use of two words, *oios* and *mounos.* These words have different roots, in that *oios* is probably a numeral,[27] and *mounos* an adjective describing a state, but our lexicons do not suggest any difference in the functional semantics of the terms,[28] which raises the question of why two words are used.[29]

In *Iliad* 24.453–456 we find the following lines:

. . . θύρην δ' ἔχε μοῦνος ἐπιβλὴς
εἰλάτινος, τὸν τρεῖς μὲν ἐπιρρήσσεσκον Ἀχαιοί,
τρεῖς δ' ἀναοίγεσκον μεγάλην κληῖδα θυράων,
τῶν ἄλλων· Ἀχιλεὺς δ' ἄρ' ἐπιρρήσσεσκε καὶ <u>οῖος</u>·

". . .the gate was secured by a single beam
of pine, and three Achaeans would close (<u>epirrēsseskon</u>)
and three would open (<u>anaoigeskon</u>) the huge door-bolt; three
other Achaeans, that is, but Achilles could close (<u>epirrēsseske</u>) it,
    alone (<u>oios</u>)."

This important description of a mechanism for opening *(anaoigeskon)* and closing *(epirrēsseskon/-ske)* the door of Achilles' hut is very significantly positioned: it opens the closing scene of the *Iliad*. The lines are also a situational definition[30] of Achilles as a hero separate from all others. The three long iterative verb-forms emphasize that this is not a one-time event but instead a matter of long-term significance.

The passage commenting on Achilles and the door is a digression, a form of narratorial comment not strictly required for the flow of narrative time.[31] The climax of this digression, both in "meaning" and in "form" is the verse-terminal word *oios* "alone," "on his own" in 456.[32] *Oios* is emphatically positioned at the end of the line, the end of the long sentence (453–456), the end of the passage, and the end of the whole narrative unit that is the introduction to the concluding section of the *Iliad*. It is thus the verbal focus of the narrator's amazed admiration for his hero's singular, larger-than-life abilities. In addition, as we have suggested, line-ends, especially those that are likely to have longer pauses (interstices of silence) after them, are points of potential *deictic fluctuation*, where the narrative reality can be contrasted with the reality of the performance. This, I suggest, is what actually happens here. Through the use of the localized, verse-terminal word *oios*, Achilles in his capacity as a hero of singular ability has been brought as close as possible to the surface of our own "here and now." Rhythm has generated a situation in which we, through the poet, are most sensible to the contrast between Achilles, the singular hero of the past, and ordinary men.

This reading of the *nontextual* function of *oios* cannot, of course, be based on a single example. In fact it relies on a tightly woven rhythmic-semantic network comprising many other examples of the word, the usage of *mounos*, and ultimately, the usage of other words and types of words, and thousands of individual examples.

Consider three further passages that present us with prom-

inent situational definitions of an Iliadic hero as existentially
"alone." In all, *oios* is positioned at the end of the verse (this is
linked, of course, to the use of formulae, on which see further
below), at the end of the sentence (which is usually long), the end
of the passage, and at the end of the narrative unit. In *Iliad*
5.302–304 the poet describes the larger-than-life (as in *mega
ergon* "a great deed") abilities of Diomedes:

> ὁ δὲ χερμάδιον λάβε χειρὶ
> Τυδεΐδης, μέγα ἔργον, ὃ δ᾽ οὐ δύο γ᾽ ἄνδρε φέροιεν
> <u>οἷοι</u> νῦν βροτοί εἰσ᾽. ὁ δέ μιν ῥέα πάλλε καὶ <u>οἶος.</u>

> ". . . But Tudeus' son in his hand caught
> up a boulder, a great deed, which no two men could carry
> such as (<u>hoioi</u>) men are now, but he lightly hefted it, alone
> (<u>oios</u>)."

These lines are repeated word for word in *Iliad* 20.285–287, except that the name of Aineias is substituted for that of Diomedes.
Terminal *oios* is the focus of the narrator's amazement, or, shall
we say, of his emotionally charged awareness of the sharp opposition between the qualities of the heroic past and the humble
present.

Consider further the example of *oios* in *Iliad* 12.445–451:

> Ἕκτωρ δ᾽ ἁρπάξας λᾶαν φέρεν, ὅς ῥα πυλάων
> ἑστήκει πρόσθε, πρυμνὸς παχύς, αὐτὰρ ὕπερθεν
> ὀξὺς ἔην. τὸν δ᾽ οὔ κε δύ᾽ ἀνέρε δήμου ἀρίστω
> ῥηϊδίως ἐπ᾽ ἄμαξαν ἀπ᾽ οὔδεος ὀχλίσσειαν,
> <u>οἷοι</u> νῦν βροτοί εἰσ᾽· ὃ δέ μιν ῥέα πάλλε καὶ <u>οἶος.</u>
> τόν οἱ ἐλαφρὸν ἔθηκε Κρόνου πάϊς ἀγκυλομήτεω.
> ὡς δ᾽ ὅτε ποιμὴν ῥεῖα φέρει πόκον ἄρσενος <u>οἰὸς.</u> . .

> "Hektor snatched up a boulder that stood before the gates
> and carried it along; it was broad at the base, but the upper

end was sharp; two men, the best in all a community,
could not easily hoist it up from the ground to a wagon,
such as (hoioi) men are now, but he lightly hefted it alone (oios).
The son of devious Kronos made it light for him.
As when a shepherd lifts up with ease the fleece of a wether
  (oios)."

These examples allow rhythmic functions to generate yet more complex effects. In 5.302–304, 20.285–287, and 12.445–451, not only is *oios* verse-terminal, but in fact, at the beginning of the verse, just after the preceding interstice of silence, a word highly similar in sound occurs, *hoioi*, which is the plural of *hoios*, "such a . . ./what a . . ." Furthermore, if we recall expressions such as *eu de su oistha, (. . .) hoios ekeinos deinos anēr,* "for you know well, what a mighty man he is . . ." (*Iliad* 11.653–654, Patroklos to Nestor about Achilles), we shall realize that the word *hoios* is a key element of Homeric expressions of amazement. Indeed, its function, on many occasions, is *expressive,* not *directive* (in speech-act terms). The common phrase *hoion eeipes,* for example in Zeus' words to Poseidon *o popoi, ennosigai' eurusthenes, hoion eeipes* (*Iliad* 7.455) is best translated "o my, o mighty lord of the earth, I am amazed by your words!" (literally "what kind of thing have you said?").[33] Once we accept this, the alliteration of "o-o-o" sounds in 7.455 takes on special significance: it replicates and extends the archetypal exclamatory Greek utterance *"o,"*[34] whose meaning, or rather whose *function,* is central to the verse as a whole.[35]

I am suggesting that within the specific discourse of Homeric hexameter there are significant pragmatic links between the word *oios* (alone, on his own) and the word *hoios* (such a . . ./what a, as an expression of emotion), and that these links are strongly marked by basic rhythmic properties (that is, by prominent localization).[36] This idea need not surprise us. What Milman Parry termed *calembour* (more serious than a "pun") is a recurrent feature of Homeric poetry: *aütmē* // and *aütē* //; *omphē* // and *odmē* //; *dēmos* // (fat) and *dēmos* // (people) are some well known examples, all localized (like the rhyme in later poetry) at the end of the verse.[37] Finally, if any further emphasis on this phonetic and rhythmic marking is needed, we may note the verse-terminal *oïos* (of a wether) in our last example (12.451), which echoes yet again the link between *oios* and *hoios*.

Like 24.453–456, these passages are not, strictly speaking, narrative; rather they provide narrator comments. In our very first passage, 24.453–456, the narrator comments on Achilles' abilities without openly acknowledging the reality of the perform- ance. In the stone-lifting passages the normally reticent narrator makes unambiguous verbal reference to the present, to the per- formance and the audience *hoioi nun* "[the men] such as they are today." Regardless, in all passages, the contrast between past and present is the very essence of the words. And it is precisely this contrast that the extremities of the verse bear out, indeed *enact* so well.

To sum up my point so far: the preceding examples are con- densed, highly memorable concrete images, effective situational "definitions" of the epic hero, in which the word *oios* in verse terminal position is a codified element of ritual, an enactment of the epic hero as the possessor of singular abilities unmatched by the men of today, and a marker of the narrator's amazed reaction to these abilities, and his consciousness of the wide breach be- tween past and present.[38] Terminal position, being a point at which the world of fiction and the real world can be effec- tively contrasted, allows the contents of the definition—the con- trast between the epic hero and the men of today—to be en- hanced by the cognitive features of performance mechanics. In the three stone-throwing passages we saw how terminal *oios* is further emphasized by the contrastive *calembour,* using verse-initial *hoios,* a word close in phonetic value to *oios* and having an exclamatory force.

It is widely recognized that "unmarked" terms are semantically more general, or even "neutral," compared to their "marked" counterparts.[39] Terminal *oios* is clearly a "marked" term. Almost two thirds of the nominative masculine singular are localized at the end of the verse;[40] other grammatical case-forms are hardly ever used at the verse-end;[41] usage of the apparent synonym *mounos* at the verse-end would have provided a convenient metrical alternative (and hence formulaic "extension" in the Parryan sense), but in fact it is all but avoided.[42] Unmarked (non-terminal) *oios* does seem to be used in a less focused manner,[43] but virtually all other examples of terminal, nominative usage of *oios* can be read, sung, heard, or in general, *enacted* in accordance with the interpretation suggested here.

Here are a few more examples: first, passages that convey the essential idea of "walking alone" and that employ the terminal, nominative singular *oios.*[44]

In *Iliad* 10.82 the surprised Nestor demands to know the identity of an addressee who is walking about the camp at night (10.82–83):

τίς δ᾽ οὗτος κατὰ νῆας ἀνὰ στρατὸν ἔρχεαι <u>οἶος</u>
νύκτα δι᾽ ὀρφναίην, ὅτε θ᾽ εὕδουσι βροτοὶ ἄλλοι,

"Who are you, who walk through the ships and the army alone (<u>oios</u>)
and through the darkness of night when other mortals are sleeping?"

In *Iliad* 10.385 Odysseus interrogates Dolon about the latter's nocturnal perambulation (10.385–386):

πῇ δὴ οὕτως ἐπὶ νῆας ἀπὸ στρατοῦ ἔρχεαι <u>οἶος</u>
νύκτα δι᾽ ὀρφναίην, ὅτε θ᾽ εὕδουσι βροτοὶ ἄλλοι;

"Why is it that you walk to the ships, away from the army, alone
(<u>oios</u>)
through the darkness of night when other mortals are sleeping?"

Comparable use of *oios* may be found also in *Iliad* 24.203
(Hecuba to Priam about his visit to the Greek camp; in *Iliad*
24.519 (Achilles to Priam about the visit); and in *Odyssey* 10.281
(Hermes to Odysseus on Kirke's island). These five passages are
another node in the nexus of exclamatory, heroic, verse-terminal
oios.[45] All imply that the addressee is doing something exceed-
ingly bold, something that we would have called heroic but for
the fact that the addressee is, or is assumed by the speaker to be,
a nonhero. The speaker construes the actions as reckless and/or
abnormal, indicating his awareness of the discrepancy between
character and circumstances.[46] In each one of these examples,
heroic isolation is enacted in an inappropriate context, with the
result being that it is construed as "madness." The speaker's
understanding of the situation, and no less our own, relies on a
contrast between "heroic" activities and "ordinary" abilities. And
this, of course, is precisely the kind of contrast that can be
marked by the interstice of silence at the end of the verse, where
oios is positioned.

The last example is *Iliad* 1.118: Agamemnon, having heard
Kalkhas' explanation of the plague, agrees to send Khruseis
home, but adds (118–120):

αὐτὰρ ἐμοὶ γέρας αὐτίχ᾽ ἑτοιμάσατ᾽, ὄφρα <u>μὴ οἶος</u>
Ἀργείων ἀγέραστος ἔω, ἐπεὶ οὐδὲ ἔοικε.
λεύσσετε γὰρ τό γε πάντες, ὅ μοι γέρας ἔρχεται ἄλλῃ.

"Give out to me forthwith some prize, so that I shall not (<u>mē</u>) be
alone (<u>oios</u>)
among the Argives without a prize, since that is unseemly;
for as you can all see, my prize goes elsewhere."

This passage of direct discourse is an emotive request. If my interpretation is correct, then here too *oios* is marked as an exclamatory echo and may be enhanced by the effects of a *deictic fluctuation.*

The king's speech is preceded by a long and intensely visual display of anger (a "heroic" emotion . . .). Agamemnon is the *far* ruling (102) raging (103) *black* hearted (103) *burning eyed* (104) evil *staring* (105) overlord. Remarkably, over the course of just fifteen lines his rage simmers down to a whimper: "Give out to me forthwith some prize so that I shall not be alone among the Argives without a prize, since that is not seemly. For, *as you can all see,* my prize goes elsewhere." And yet, as the assembled Greek host can *see,* the person speaking is not a feeble priest begging for his child or an ancient king begging for a corpse. Indeed, the speaker is not anyone resembling men as they are "now," but a mighty hero and far-ruling king, a point stressed by the repeated visual vocabulary.

But there is more. We the audience also see the raging Agamemnon in our mind's eye (the reality within the narrative), but we no less see in front of us, with our real eyes (in the reality of the performance) a humble bard (helpless? blind . . . like the poet Demodokos in the *Odyssey?* Like "Homer" himself?). To the assembled Greeks the discrepancy between sight and sound to Agamemnon's audience spells out a message: the humbler the plea, the bigger the threat. The contrastive falsity of Agamemnon's words is also, I suggest, directly reflected by the mimesis itself, and no less by verse-terminal *oios* (indeed *mē oios,* "not" *oios*), a word that pretends to speak of a uniquely wretched and dependent state (as are the men of today . . .) but that enacts, at the point of *deictic fluctuation,* the violent, larger-than-life hero who does not depend on the consent of their peers but who acts "alone."

Consider now more closely the use of *mounos*. First let us note
that although *mounos* itself contains the *"o"* vowel (the word
derives from *monwos*) there is in our extant text far less alliter-
ative play on the exclamatory sounds, and, of course, *mounos*
cannot echo the exclamatory *hoios* ("such a . . ."). In the one
example of *mounos* we have seen so far (our first passage, *Iliad*
24.453–456 above) *mounos* was used to describe the beam secur-
ing the door of Achilles' hut, but the word was verse-internal.

The beam, we assume, is unique in size among door-bolts, and
as such is an important matching accessory for the great hero. It
is not, however, a discreet element of the lost, heroic past. Neither ritual song, nor a singer are essential for its reenactment. An
ax, a steady arm, and a big tree might easily produce a real object
that is "bigger and better" than door-bolts of the past . . . By
contrast, no amount of woodwork will summon Achilles to the
present. My point is that *mounos* in 24.453 is an important word
in the context, but it is not rhythmically marked in the manner of
oios in line 456, and it is not the focus of a verbal reenactment
ritual.

It is, nevertheless, easy to find examples of *mounos* that are
formally marked and that relate significantly to examples of terminal *oios*, both in terms of their localization and in terms of their
discourse functions. By far the most prominent cluster of attestations of *mounos* in Homer appears in *Odyssey* 16.113–125, where
Telemakhos is speaking to the disguised stranger, who is his
father:

τοιγὰρ ἐγώ τοι, ξεῖνε, μάλ᾽ ἀτρεκέως ἀγορεύσω.
οὔτε τί μοι πᾶς δῆμος ἀπεχθόμενος χαλεπαίνει,
οὔτε κασιγνήτοις ἐπιμέμφομαι, οἷσί περ ἀνὴρ
μαρναμένοισι πέποιθε, καὶ εἰ μέγα νεῖκος ὄρηται.
ὧδε γὰρ ἡμετέρην γενεὴν <u>μούνωσε</u> Κρονίων.
<u>μοῦνον</u> Λαέρτην Ἀρκείσιος υἱὸν ἔτικτε,
<u>μοῦνον</u> δ᾽ αὖτ᾽ Ὀδυσῆα πατὴρ τέκεν. αὐτὰρ Ὀδυσσεὺς

μοῦνον ἔμ᾽ ἐν μεγάροισι τεκὼν λίπεν οὐδ᾽ ἀπόνητο.
τῷ νῦν δυσμενέες μάλα μυρίοι εἴσ᾽ ἐνὶ οἴκῳ.
ὅσσοι γὰρ νήσοισιν ἐπικρατέουσιν ἄριστοι,
Δουλιχίῳ τε Σάμῃ τε καὶ ὑλήεντι Ζακύνθῳ,
ἠδ᾽ ὅσσοι κραναὴν Ἰθάκην κάτα κοιρανέουσι,
τόσσοι μητέρ᾽ ἐμὴν μνῶνται, τρύχουσι δὲ οἶκον.

"So, my friend, I will tell you plainly the whole truth of it.
It is not that all the people hate me, nor are they angry,
nor is it that I find brothers wanting, whom a man trusts for
help in the fighting, whenever a great quarrel arises.
For so it is that the son of Kronos made ours a line of only sons
(mounōse). Arkeisios had
only one (mounon) son, Laertes. And Laertes had
only one (mounon) son, Odysseus. And Odysseus in turn left
only one (mounon) son, myself, in the halls, and got no profit of me,
and my enemies are here in my house, beyond numbering."

The idea of *mounos,* of being alone, here in the sense of "an
only son" is repeated four times in as many verses. In three consecutive lines *mounos,* or rather the accusative masculine singular
form *mounon,* is verse-initial.[47] As in the case of Achilles and the
beam, and also the stone-throwing passages, these lines too are a
situational definition. They too describe not one particular moment in time but a permanent attribute of the main characters of
the *Odyssey.* Previously, this permanence was effected by iterative verbs; here it is effected by (rhetorical) anaphora and by the
idea of a genealogical chain put together by Zeus.[48]

The word *mounos* here is not uttered in amazement and admiration for the abilities of some singularly great character ("what a
. . .!") as in the case of terminal *oios.* And as just stated before,
it carries none of the phonetic echoes of exclamation. Being
mounos as Telemakhos clearly explains, is the state of having no
brothers *hoisi per anēr // marnamenoisi pepoisthe* "whom a man
trusts for help in the fighting" (115–116), that is, it is a state of

helplessness. He speaks of Laertes, an old man, of Odysseus, a great hero but presumed dead, and of himself, a boy too young to resist his enemies. Furthermore, this hereditary helplessness has been ordained by the most powerful of the gods, the son (. . .) of Kronos, whose will is supreme. So *mounos* here does not mark amazement at the larger-than-life heroic abilities of a hero but rather the very opposite, a reaction to isolation as a state of weakness that is beyond mortal control.

Mounos in this passage is an element of exposition. This, says Telemakhos, is how Zeus decided that our family should be: [interstice of silence] "*mounos* my grandfather" [interstice of silence] "*mounos* my father" [interstice of silence] "*mounos* I myself . . ." The word *mounos* is physically the first word of each verse. It may be difficult to determine the precise length of the pauses (which in any case are likely to differ from performance to performance), but such precision is not needed. The threefold repetition of *mounos* at the beginning of the hexameter unit stresses the cyclic nature of the utterance. To reject a pause at the beginning of these lines is to reject the very rhythmic essence of epic, which is impossible. Three times we face a member of the family at the point of the *deictic fluctuation.* Each time we meet not an epic hero who is *oios,* not "bigger and better" than ourselves, but a supposedly helpless *mounos,* someone more like "the men of today." Our empathy and pity almost fully overlap Telemakhos' anguish. This, I suggest, is where epic is *enacted,* as the past and the present are placed side by side. And of course *mounos* is localized in a position that is formally the opposite of *oios: after* the pause, not *before* it.

Many examples of verse-initial, "emphatic," "weak" *mounos* can be found in Homer. They suggest that *mounos* and *oios* function as complementary/opposing rhythmic-semantic terms. At the same time, several important clues indicate that among the two words, *oios* is the more-specific, marked term, while usage of *mounos* covers a broader, more loose range. We have noted how distinctly *oios* is used at the verse-end, how *mounos* is excluded from the verse end, and how *mounos* does not replicate the exclamatory sound "o." Furthermore, judging by the extant remains of ancient Greek literature, usage of the word *oios,* and especially in the nominative masculine singular, is commonplace only in Homer and ancient commentaries on the *Iliad* and *Odyssey* (!).[49] Usage of *mounos* in authors other than Homer is much wider,[50] and in Homer verse initial usage varies between nominative *mounos* and accusative *mounon.* All this makes good sense: conceptually *oios* is the more "special" term (describing "special" heroic abilities), *mounos* the more "ordinary." Inasmuch as these two are a pair, *oios* is the marked term.[51]

In *Odyssey* 2.361–365 Telemakhos' plans to sail in quest of information upset the nursemaid Eurukleia:

ὣς φάτο, κώκυσεν δὲ φίλη τροφὸς Εὐρύκλεια,
καὶ ῥ' ὀλοφυρομένη ἔπεα πτερόεντα προσηύδα·
"Τίπτε δέ τοι, φίλε τέκνον, ἐνὶ φρεσὶ τοῦτο νόημα
ἔπλετο; πῇ δ' ἐθέλεις ἰέναι πολλὴν ἐπὶ γαῖαν
<u>μοῦνος</u> ἐὼν ἀγαπητός;"

"So he spoke, and the dear nurse Eurukleia cried out,
and bitterly lamenting she addressed him in winged words:
'Why, my beloved child, has this intention come into
your mind? Why do you wish to wander over much country, you,
an only (<u>mounos</u>) and loved son?'"

The *deictic fluctuation* at the beginning of the verse has the potential to provide concrete illustration to the contrast between a weak Telemakhos, who is more like the men of the present, and the dangerous reality in which he is situated, that calls rather for the unique abilities of a hero.

In *Odyssey* 16 the poet breaks the narrative in order to comment on Eumaios' greeting of Telemakhos by use of a simile (16.19):

ὡς δὲ πατὴρ ὃν παῖδα φίλα φρονέων ἀγαπάζῃ
ἐλθόντ᾽ ἐξ ἀπίης γαίης δεκάτῳ ἐνιαυτῷ
<u>μοῦνον</u> τηλύγετον, τῷ ἔπ᾽ ἄλγεα πολλὰ μογήσῃ,
ὡς τότε Τηλέμαχον θεοειδέα δῖος ὑφορβὸς
πάντα κύσεν περιφύς, ὡς ἐκ θανάτοιο φυγόντα.

"And as a father, with heart full of love, welcomes his son
when he comes back in the tenth year from a distant country, his
only (<u>mounon</u>) and grown son, for whose sake he has undergone
    many hardships
so now the noble swineherd clinging fast to godlike
Telemakhos, kissed him even as if he had escaped dying."

Closely related is the example of *Iliad* 9.481–482, within Phoinix' speech to Achilles:

καί μ᾽ ἐφίλησ᾽ ὡς εἴ τε πατὴρ ὃν παῖδα φιλήσῃ
<u>μοῦνον</u> τηλύγετον, πολλοῖσιν ἐπὶ κτεάτεσσι,

"and [Peleus] gave me his love, even as a father loves his
only (<u>mounon</u>) son who is brought up among many possessions."

The love of fathers for their ("only") sons in the reality of the present and in the world of the narrated heroic past is doubtless identical; here we encounter this emotion, centered on the word *mounos,* precisely at a point that itself allows the poet to enhance our consciousness of *both* realities.

In *Odyssey* 20.30 the narrator describes the thoughts of Odysseus as he wonders how he should take revenge on the suitors (*Odyssey* 20.28–30):

ὡς ἄρ᾽ ὅ γ᾽ ἔνθα καὶ ἔνθα ἑλίσσετο μερμηρίζων
ὅππως δὴ μνηστῆρσιν ἀναιδέσι χεῖρας ἐφήσει
<u>μοῦνος</u> ἐὼν πολέσι.

"So he was twisting and turning back and forth, meditating
how he could lay his hands on the shameless suitors, though he
was alone (mounos) against many."

The beginning of book 20 describes Odysseus' deliberations.
The passage kicks off with the active, wild and reckless thoughts
("let's jump and kill them all at once!" 11–13) of a barking heart
(14–16), through a transitory stage of rational reflection and re-
straint (17–18), to a simile, in which Odysseus tossing to-and-fro
is likened to entrails roasting in the fire—a powerful image, but
one of passivity and helplessness, not of singular heroic ability
and resolve. The dog imagery and entrails simile are externalized
representations of an internal transition: from "that which bites/
kills/threatens" to "that which has been killed/is screaming in
agony/is about to be bitten." By the end of the transition the
polytropic hero is hardly feeling ready to perform astonishing
deeds.

Again we have no means of measuring the precise duration of
the interstice of silence preceding *mounos,* but its potential as a
concrete enhancement of the contents of the situation is clear.
Verse-initial *mounos* presents us with the hero at his weakest, at a
moment when he is least like the *oios* hero. Interesting comparable usage may be found, in fact, in *Odyssey* 20.40 and in *Iliad*
11.406.

In our next passage the poet describes the death of the unsus-
pecting Antinoos at the hands of Odysseus (*Odyssey* 22.9–14):

ἦ τοι ὁ καλὸν ἄλεισον ἀναιρήσεσθαι ἔμελλε,
χρύσεον ἄμφωτερον, καὶ δὴ μετὰ χερσὶν ἐνώμα,
ὄφρα πίοι οἴνοιο. φόνος δέ οἱ οὐκ ἐνὶ θυμῷ
μέμβλετο. τίς κ᾽ οἴοιτο μετ᾽ ἀνδράσι δαιτυμόνεσσι
μοῦνον ἐνὶ πλεόνεσσι, καὶ εἰ μάλα καρτερὸς εἴη,
οἷ τεύξειν θάνατόν τε κακὸν καὶ κῆρα μέλαιναν;

"He was on the point of lifting up a fine two-handled
goblet of gold, and had it in his hands, and was moving it
so as to drink of the wine, and in his heart there was no thought
of death. For who would think that a man in the company of
    feasting men,
alone (<u>mounon</u>) among many, though he were very strong,
would ever inflict death upon him and dark doom?"

The omniscient narrator is here voicing the thoughts of one who
is oblivious to impending doom: Antinoos has no grasp of reality.[52]
Indeed, the whole section relies on the tension between heroic
characters who *can* stand up to the many (more or less) alone,
and helpless characters, marked by the word *mounos,* who *cannot.* This, again, is also the essence of the distinction between the
heroic reality and the weaker reality of the performance (the
"men of today") which interstices of silence bear out.

Finally, consider the case of *Iliad* 17.469–473. Alkimedon is
here wondering that Automedon is about to enter battle alone:

Αὐτόμεδον, τίς τοί νυ θεῶν νηκερδέα βουλὴν
ἐν στήθεσσιν ἔθηκε, καὶ ἐξέλετο φρένας ἐσθλάς;
<u>οἷον</u> πρὸς Τρῶας μάχεαι πρώτῳ ἐν ὁμίλῳ
<u>μοῦνος</u>. ἀτάρ τοι ἑταῖρος ἀπέκτατο, τεύχεα δ᾽ Ἕκτωρ
αὐτὸς ἔχων ὤμοισιν ἀγάλλεται Αἰακίδαο.

"Automedon, what god put this unprofitable purpose
into your heart, and has taken away the better wits,
so that (<u>hoion</u>) you are trying to fight the Trojans in the first
    shock of encounter
alone (<u>mounos</u>), since your companion has been killed, and
    Hektor
glories in wearing Aiakides' armour on his own shoulders?"

Automedon is charioteer to both Achilles and Patroklos (a man
professionally inclined to fighting in pairs, not "alone"), and not
thus of equal heroic rank to the great warriors. He has just been

deprived of his companion Patroklos, is thus in a passive state of isolation, but has also chosen to fight alone. *Mounos* is used in its familiar verse-initial position, but the very preceding line speaks of insane, valorous action, perhaps reminiscent of the *oios*-type hero.[53] Indeed, line 471 begins with the word *hoion* (in this case adverbial) and thus immediately contrasts, both semantically and thematically, with the following *mounos*. Two lines later, Automedon in his reply to Alkimedon says (17.475–480):

'Αλκίμεδον, τίς γάρ τοι 'Αχαιῶν ἄλλος <u>ὁμοῖος</u>
εἰ μὴ Πάτροκλος θεόφιν μήστωρ ἀτάλαντος,
ζωὸς ἐών; νῦν αὖ θάνατος καὶ μοῖρα κιχάνει.
ἀλλὰ σὺ μὲν μάστιγα καὶ ἡνία σιγαλόεντα
δέξαι, ἐγὼ δ᾽ ἵππων ἀποβήσομαι, ὄφρα μάχωμαι.

"Alkimedon, which other of the Achaeans was your match
    (homoios)
in the management and the strength of immortal horses,
were it not Patroklos, the equal of the immortals in counsel,
while he lived? Now death and fate have closed in upon him.
Therefore take over from me the whip and the glittering guide
    reins
while I dismount from behind the horses, so I may do battle."

Automedon the charioteer, the man whose fighting role is "incomplete" without a partner, a *mounos* type character, undergoes a transition and becomes more of an *oios* type hero who can and does fight successfully alone (cf. 17.516–542). The passages are rich in echoes and melodies. And yet part of their complexity is set within an ordered rhythmic, hexametric framework. The central poetic opposition of this section—the contrast between helplessness and heroic abilities, between pity and amazement, is firmly linked to usage at the extremities of the verse *(hoion, mounos, homoios)*, which, we have seen elsewhere, mark important examples of *mounos* and *oios,* and which can emphasize the contrast between the larger-than-life past and the present. How far do these echoes extend? This is a difficult, if not impossible, question to answer. But to assume that so many repeated attestations of such significant words at such prominent positions in the verse are due to mere chance or to mere technicalities, is to assume a poet whose indifference to the sounds of his words is almost complete. And of course, soundless words, if they exist at all, exist only on a written page.

THE EXTENT OF RHYTHMICIZED SEMANTICS

We have seen some examples of a system of rhythmicized semantics/poetics in Homer that relies on the basic pause/flow nature of the hexameter. Two types of solitary states were noted: isolation as the mark of larger-than-life heroic abilities, which is the "special" attribute of Homer's heroes, and isolation as the mark of "ordinary" mortal helplessness. The two opposing notions were formally marked by use of two otherwise synonymous words, *oios* and *mounos,* employed in notable examples with repeated localization at opposing verse extremities. This formal opposition helped mark the contrastive, but perhaps no less the complementary, nature of the two terms. The relationship between the two terms was made even more significant by the fact that they correspond to a conceptual opposition central to Homeric epic: the contrast between the larger than life reality of epic past, and the more humble reality of the present and the performance. I have tried to argue that the very cognitive functions of the pause/flow rhythm at the points where these two words are prominently localized embody this contrast. Localized usage of *oios* and *mounos* at the extremities of the verse allows an almost literal *enactment* of *kleos,* "fame": a juxtapositioning of past and present.

But have we been using a sledgehammer to crack a nut? After all, *oios* and *mounos* are but two words in the Homeric lexicon, and in order to explain their usage, we have argued for the existence of a mechanism that endows every verse with the potential for emphasizing *deictic fluctuations.* How often, then, is this potential realized?

I have elsewhere argued for statistically significant and hence also semantically significant localization tendencies of lexical/semantic/grammatical items, largely single words, at the ends of the verse, for example theme words of the epic, such as *andra* (man), *mēnin* (wrath), and *noston* (return), vocative proper names, nominative proper names.[54] These tendencies apply to thousands of individual examples, and there are other obvious candidates for the further study of rhythmical semantics (for example, *nēpios* "wretch!" at the beginning of the verse[55]). While the localization of many words, grammatical types, and so on, clearly relates to, indeed overlaps, "formulaic" usage, it extends well beyond the use of formulae, as they are presently defined, and it cannot be explained in terms of simple metrical convenience. Now, the mediation between past and present is not simply one among many motifs in the poetry of Homer. It is arguably the most important aspect of the poems, their very raison d'être: the poems are exercises in the preservation of *kleos.* Any device that can emphasize the contrasts and/or similarities between the realities of past and present could be of use in a very wide range of Homeric contexts and would have the ability to imbue many epic words with specifically hexametric, "performed" significance.[56]

ONE MORE WORD, AT THE END

In worlds such as our own, that rely so heavily on texts, and especially in the even more highly textualized world of scholarship, vocality risks being construed as a flourish. Many will admire the voices of an Auden, an Eliot, or an Angelou, and still feel that the performance is in essence a fleeting thing, an ornament to the "real" artifact, an object that "does not change in time," an object that can be held in our hands and possessed.

Auden, Eliot, Angelou, and many other "literate" poets rely heavily on voice, but a full understanding of their poetry always assumes a book. They require a close, leisurely (that is, not monodirectional, time-bound) contemplation of the *text*. But if access to a *text* is limited or even nonexistent (either in the production or in the reception process), if words must flow at a constant pace, how can there be contemplation? Approaching Homer with this problem in mind has lead on the one hand to implicitly (or explicitly) *textual* readings, and on the other to various degrees of denial of precise shades of meaning (for example in formulaic discourse). More recently, phonology, discourse analysis, pragmatics, and the study of orality (indeed, the work of many of the contributors to this volume) have shown that epic words *do* allow us to reflect. Epic words relate to and recall, not so much this or that fixed point elsewhere in a *text,* rather they activate a whole "theme," a "myth," a "node" in the tradition.

Thus, essentially, one line of "ritual" of epic verse opens the same kind of window to the epic world as do a hundred lines. "The Movie" of a television series and the shorter network "episodes" are in a deep sense "the same." Likewise, it is "the same" if we are shown the world of epic heroes "out there" either for part of an evening or for three whole days. A thousand-line epic poem about Achilles is in this sense "the same" as a poem fifteen times in size.[57] Paradoxically, writing, the very medium that seeks to preserve "sameness," converts a long and a short version of "the same" song into two "different" *texts:* writing results in two objects that can be placed side by side at a single point in time and hence shown, in a literate sense, to be "not the same." But if two poems are nothing but fleeting streams of words and if each is performed at a different time, how would we ever know that they do belong together, that they are both parts of "the same" world?

It is because key elements of this world are repeated, again, and again, and again: *po-lu-mē-tis-O-dus-seus, po-das-ō-kus-A-chil-leus,* chanted ever in a fixed position within a short, repetitive pattern we call the hexameter.

At this point vocal, rhythmic properties become the key to sameness, to continuity, to "authority," to "*nontextual* contemplation." We can transcode vocal similarities in two hexameter sequences using graphic signs, but the moment we do so, we have produced two *different* verses, and in a concrete sense two *different* texts! Inasmuch as the poetry of Homer is traditional, and inasmuch as traditional implies "sameness," Homer's poetry is not, nor can it ever be, *textual.* However, this does not mean that it cannot be written down. It can, it has (how, and when, I dare not here say), and furthermore, as I have tried to show, the written voice does "sound" the same.

Similes and Performance

RICHARD P. MARTIN

The linguist Michel Bréal, better known as a semanticist than Homerist, had been a teacher of Antoine Meillet, the great comparatist who succeeded him in the chair in comparative grammar of the Collège de France.[1] Bréal's little book *Pour mieux connaître Homère* is actually cited once by Meillet's student Milman Parry in *L'Épithète traditionnelle*, to the effect that the fixed epithet provides not only a rest to the singer but also a pause for the audience.[2] It is not his view on the formula, however, that seems to me an appropriate introduction to this paper, but rather Bréal's remarks on the simile: "These comparisons, which the poet draws out pleasantly, where he often adds several verses not at all necessary, are completely the opposite of popular poetry, which, if it sees a resemblance, says it in a word without dwelling on it. To enjoy these models of descriptive style would require an audience with time to spare, and, moreover, one with a taste for little tableaux."

Similes, he continues, are "pieces which are apparently out of place, which have the look of borrowings from another literary genre."[3] This pronouncement will serve nicely to summarize my argument: in short, I will suggest that Bréal is wrong when it comes to similes in oral poetry but quite right in speculating on another genre as their source. I want to show that similes in Homeric poetry play a role that we can fully appreciate only after examining living oral performances from a range of cultures, performances that feature a number of compositional devices, including similes. I will argue that a major effect of similes in performance has been neglected thus far in Homeric studies but that this effect is in fact analogous to the one achieved in non-Western performances by other genres interacting with epic. Finally, I will attempt to show through linguistic analyses that similes are affiliated with, and may be taken from, the epic performers' prior knowledge of *nonepic* Greek poetic genres. In the end, I believe we can come away from such an exploration with a new appreciation for the component arts which went into the complex craft of Homeric verse-making.

As in any comparative enterprise, we must begin with an internal analysis. What do similes accomplish *within* the Homeric poems? Given the tendency in Classics for interpretive modes to drop from sight and return generations later unchanged by subsequent advances in literary theory, it will be more efficient to sketch out the three basic modes of answering this question, rather than attempt a chronological history of critical stances. These modes can be characterized as *rhetorical, thematic, and rhythmic.* It is not surprising that there is a correlation between these modes and varying historically conditioned views on the nature of Homeric poetry. When the text is still imagined, in some dim way, as a sort of performance, the rhetorical interpretation of similes prevails; once the poems are taken up as artifacts rather than as enactment, especially in the early part of the twentieth century, thematic and ultimately structural criticism holds sway.

The rhetorical critique of similes permeates the ancient hermeneutic tradition, in which similes are primarily interpreted as affective devices. Our sources for this mode comprise mainly the scholia to the poems, themselves deriving in turn largely from Peripatetic treatments both of Homeric *cruces* (such as Aristotle's *Homeric Problems*) and more generally of discourse (such as his *Rhetoric* and *Poetics*).[4] Using Erbse's index to the *Iliad* scholia, one can survey the words *homoiōsis* "likening" and *parabolē* "comparison" to gain some idea of this rhetorical mode.[5]

Most noticeable in such a survey of the scholia is the concern of the commentator with the appropriateness of the comparison to the specific narrative moment. For example, at *Iliad* 5.487, when Sarpedon uses a simile in his rebuke to Hektor and says, "Watch out that you do not become prey and a find for the enemy, like ones caught in the mesh of an all-catching net," the scholiast remarks, "The *homoiōsis* is apt *(oikeia)* as of many different men being surrounded and caught like fish."[6] Equally important for the ancient commentators are the ways in which similes bring a scene vividly before the eyes.[7] Of the simile that compares the Trojan onrush at 15.381 to waves swamping a boat, the scholiast says, "The poet always surpasses himself in comparisons—for what could be more vivid, more emphatic, or altogether more concordant *(sumphonōteron)*?"[8]

The usefulness of the simile for heightening emotion and for creating *pathos* is commonly noted by the scholiasts.[9] We should realize also what the scholiasts *do not* do: there are no attempts at "symbolic" interpretation or cross-referencing to similes in other books of the poems, no attempt to treat these devices as part of a larger pattern. The mode can be called rhetorical because the interpreter is mainly concerned with the immediate role that a particular trope plays in persuading an audience of the reality of the narrative. Richardson remarks that it is easy to disparage the scholiasts' approach to similes, but more valuable to see "how often the scholia do in fact appreciate more fully than we do the way which the similes enhance the poem."[10] One could expand on this to observe that the ancient interpretive tradition even in its late "scholiastic" form preserves in this rhetorical mode more of a sense of the poem as performance—albeit something more akin to oratory—than do subsequent interpretive modes. Though Richardson does not make much of the fact, he points out that the Townleian scholiast to *Iliad* 16.131 even comments on how this section of the *Iliad*, the arming of Patroklos, should be performed: "It is necessary to recite *(propheresthai)* these verses in a rush *(speudonta)* expressing the yearning for the end." The phrasing, *"epipothēsin tēs exodou mimoumenon,"* could be translated as well "representing" or "imitating" the "desire for the end." Of course, we might think first of all of rhapsodic performance, which, in Plato's *Ion,* resembles a kind of dramatic representation. But the further point to make here is that the representation involved is actually triplicate: the performer's desire to bring about an effective *exodos;* the desire of Patroklos, the character he represents, to achieve an end to battle; and finally, the *audience's* desire to see and feel the most satisfying conclusion. "Miming a desire" is a beautifully apt way of describing what we know happens in interactive oral performances of epic, in which performers enact what audiences want, using all the poetic and musical resources at their disposal.[11] It is stunning that the scholiast preserves a sense of this interaction.

The scholiasts do in fact consider Homer to be thus engaged with his narrative, almost in the manner of a participant on one side. On 11.558–562, the bT scholia notice the simile comparing Aias to a stubborn donkey whom the Trojans, like boys with sticks, try to dislodge from a field. "The *parabolē* is to show contempt of the Trojans *(pros kataphronēsin tōn Trōōn)* because he (Aias) flees Zeus not them." By means of the simile Homer scores a point against the adversary. This agonistic language appears in an explicit reference to poetics, in the bT scholia to 12.278–286, a simile comparing flying weapons to a snowfall. The poet had used a more compact version of the image earlier in the book, at line 156:

> They threw as they defended themselves and the huts and the swift ships.
> They flew like snowflakes (niphades . . . hōs) to the ground, which the blowing wind, whirling the dark clouds, sheds thick on the nourishing earth.

When the poet expands the image and applies it to a shower of rocks at lines 278–286, the scholiast says "The poet seems to hold a contest with himself regarding the comparison. He elaborates it more magnificently." To sum up, the ancient mode of interpreting similes in the scholia imagines something like the conditions of oral performance, even down to the milieu of contest and poetic heroics.

In describing the more familiar, second mode, the thematic, I want to focus on a paradox. We might have imagined that the study of similes would change radically after Parry's and Lord's work became assimilated by a generation of classicists. Instead, what happened shows how a dominant intellectual paradigm redirects new advances, for the work of Moulton, published in 1977, can be seen to rely essentially on the same interpretive strategies as the well-known book by Hermann Fränkel brought out by the same press fifty-six years before. This, despite the publication in 1974 of William Scott's book, a reworking of the dissertation he completed at Princeton ten years before.[12]

Scott had shown that the style of repetition-plus-variation visible in the similes marked it as an oral art form parallel in its workings to the deployment of epithets and the construction of type-scenes. However, his useful lists and typologies seem not to have produced new work specifically focused on the *implications* of an orally generated simile.[13] Moulton in his introduction, after acknowledging Scott's approach, argues for subtle patterning of similes in relation to narrative structure, characterization, and themes. In this project, Moulton is largely successful. But he is also simply returning to the path that Fränkel trod. In both, the interpretive strategy is to group together similes by content and then analyze each as the expression of a larger theme. Fränkel, discussing the snow similes in Book 12, first finds all the other examples of the image and contrasts the somber, threatening mood of these (as far as can be determined from the contexts) with the modern reader's responses, our *Schneegefühle*.[14] Where Moulton makes an advance over Fränkel is in his demonstration that the *succession* of similes forms a running commentary on the action within the narrative. Similes are "synergetic" with narrative. Of course, this interpretation depends on a prior assumption about the mood of an individual simile, sometimes, for instance, at the level of a diffuse fire and light imagery.[15] The strategy is static because it insists on the text as a closed set of tropes, balanced against or connected to one another, but appreciated fully only in retrospect, not at the moment of performance but in the leisure of rereading. If the discussion of fire imagery in such a framework reminds us of Cedric Whitman's brilliant chapter on the same topic and if Moulton's charts begin to resemble the famous outline of the Geometric *Iliad*, it is not, I think, coincidental.[16] The resemblance goes to the heart of the critical method shared by most Anglo-American literary critics, especially classicists, until recently.[17] The dominant mode of close (and closed) reading directs these critics away from the full implications of oral poetics. Their shared method can be characterized by the summing-up statement in the chapter on image in Wellek and

Warren's *Theory of Literature,* that vade mecum of New Criticism: "Like meter, imagery is one component structure of a poem. In terms of our scheme, it is part of the syntactical, or stylistic, stratum. It must be studied, finally, not in isolation from the other strata, but as an element in the totality, the integrity, of the literary work."[18]

Rather than denigrating either rhetorical or thematic approaches, I am urging a marriage of the two. We have to consider for any given simile both the local immediate affective strategies at work and the wider-reaching thematic purposes. But these are not the whole story. There is room for, and I would hold, a need for, a third approach, which we might call the "rhythmic." Let us imagine the similes as they would come to the ear of an audience during the performance of Homeric epic. When we do this, the most noticeable feature of similes is the way in which they punctuate the narrative, giving it an almost musical rhythm and providing episodic definition. In fact, in the midst of the *Iliad's* battle books, we begin to expect similes; Tilman Krischer has shown that they are an intimate part of the technique, not simply a relief from what modern readers consider tediously boring slaughter.[19]

To illustrate the rhythmic function of the similes and explain why we come to expect them, there follows my sample analysis of one of the *Iliad's* longer books, with similes marked in relation to episodes. I have done the same for a number of other books, with similar results. A look at the breakdown here will show what I consider to be the key performance factor in the uses of similes—namely, the way in which they demarcate narrative segments:

    1–14   Zeus sends Eris, who rouses Achaeans
    15–46   Agamemnon arms
    47–61   Both sides prepare for battle

62–66	*Hektor = star, his armor = lightning*
67–73	*Troops = rows of reapers, wolves*
73–83	Disposition of the gods (om. Zen., ath. Aristoph, Ar.)
84–90	*Timing of conflict = woodcutter's day*
91–112	Killings by Agamemnon
113–121	*Agamemnon = lion, Trojans = deer*
122–129	Agamemnon pursues two Trojans until they stop
129–130	*Agamemnon stands against them like a lion*
131–155	Speech of suppliant warriors
136–142	Agamemnon refuses them
143–146	Agamemnon kills them
147	*He rolls one like a holmos*
148–154	General chase
155–158	*Agamemnon = fire in forest*
159–162	Description of aftermath
162–171	Chase goes to Skaian gates
172–178	*Fleeing ones = cows, pursuers = lions*
179–217	Aftermath and Zeus' promise to Hektor
218–263	Agamemnon's opponents
264–268	Agamemnon's pain worsens
269–272	*His pain = woman's in labor*
273–283	Agamemnon leaves battle
284–291	Hektor urges on the Trojans
292–298	*Hektor = hunter, gust of wind*
299–304	Hektor's opponents
305–309	*Hektor = west wind*
310–323	Diomedes and Odysseus begin killings
324–327	*The heroes = boars among dogs*
328–335	They take sons of Merops
336–367	Hektor versus Diomedes
368–395	Diomedes versus Paris
396–400	Diomedes retreats wounded
400–410	Odysseus' soliloquy
411–413	Trojan ranks close in
414–419	*Trojans = dogs around boar*

420–455	Odysseus' killings, fight with Sokos
456–473	Odysseus calls for help, Aias and Menelaos respond
474–484	*Trojans = jackals*
485–491	Aias attacks Trojans
492–497	*Aias = rushing river*
498–509	Hektor battles near the river
510–520	Nestor leads away Makhaon
521–542	Kebriones urges Hektor to aid others; he does
543–547	Aias in fear
548–557	*Aias in retreat = lion from cattle*
558–565	*Aias = donkey beset by boys*
566–574	Aias slowly retreats under attack
575–595	Eurupulos going to help is wounded
596	*All fight like fire*
597–618	Achilles sees Nestor coming back and summons Patroklos
619–644	Nestor refreshes Makhaon
645–803	Nestor welcomes Patroklos with story and advice
804–848	Patroklos returns, treats Eurupulos

Another way to describe the principle governing the use of similes can now be ventured: similes do not occur in the middle of an action: they draw attention either to the start of an action or to its finish. Put another way, similes are not like freeze-frames or slow-motion sequences in film, but like transition shots, often accompanied by theme music. To point out that the similes are devices to regulate the flow of narrative is not to deny that they also mark emotional peaks; it happens that, as in most dramatic narratives, these two, the episodic boundary and the emotional peak, occur together. The underlying principle, in its respect for the integrity of the narrated episode, might be compared with what has been called Zielinski's Law, the tendency for Homeric epic to present, as sequential, events which are actually imagined as happening simultaneously.[20] Both the placing of similes at boundaries and the narrating of simultaneous events as if they were consecutive, work to focus the audience on one event as they propel the narrative forward.

I am not suggesting that the similes came first and that Greek epic poets built a narrative around them, although techniques of this kind are not unheard of in oral art: Harold Scheub's book on the *ntsomi* of the Xhosa people of South Africa shows how the technique of "core-images" allows experienced women who narrate this genre to compose in performance.[21] A closer poetic parallel to the combined rhythmic/thematic function of similes in narrative might be the function of the chorus in Athenian drama. If we go somewhat farther afield, however, it turns out that there are even more relevant comparanda to this episode-framing function of the simile. The comparative material I shall cite comes from a wide range of cultures, but from specifically *heroic* traditions within each culture, thus from traditions parallel in content to the Greek epic. In each of the traditions episodic boundaries and emotional peaks are emphasized, this being done by a shift in performance mode, either from prose to verse, from chant to melodic song, or from one type of song to another. In a number of cases, the songs are the locus for simile and metaphor, though this is not obligatory in all the traditions that I shall mention. The main point is that we must recognize in living oral performances the feature of performance shifts and layerings: rarely if ever is a performance "text" uniform in its texture. My argument is that these shifts are functionally akin to the rhythmic function played by similes in Homer.

Within the past decade or so, we have gained from folklorists and anthropologists excellent transcriptions of complex oral performances. For instance, in her book *Dried Millet Breaking*, Ruth Stone shows how in the highly interactive Woi epic of the Kpelle people of Liberia three levels of performance exist simultaneously.[22] First, there is epic framing, in which metatextual comments are made by the performer, either casual asides to the audience ("my kneecaps are hurting") or stylized phrases. An example of the latter category is the formulaic calls by the performer to the chorus and to the designated audience member who is "answer-giver."[23] With a very demanding audience, interested in "vividness" and "trustworthiness," the metatextual can include such exchanges as that which occurs after a rather strange episode—when the hero rubs newly forged iron on his buttocks and flys off. The designated audience spokesperson asks "Were you there?" to which the narrator answers "Very near."[24] Sometimes this sort of exchange is actually built into the next performance level, the storytelling that takes place in normal prose: the audience/questioner will say "Don't lie to me" to which the narrator might report the speech of the hero by way of proof.

These first two levels are of course completely absent from our Homeric texts. The third level of performance in the Woi epic is that of song produced by the narrator. In Stone's words, "Here we find the most esoteric and abstract ideas. Proverbial phrases and formulas, some that are found in other Kpelle music, lace this text." She goes on to observe that, in the tunes, sung by the narrator and then repeated by a chorus, the narrator "inserts the heart and soul of the epic, the proverbs and other nuggets of 'deep' Kpelle."[25]

In the Woi epic, one item regularly associated with song is proverbs: these play a generalizing role, placing the situation in terms of larger cultural entities, while also highly developed in terms of set diction and useful in placing characters in relation to one another. A sung phrase like "the large large rooster, the hen's voice is sweet, the rooster crows the dawn" emphasizes the paradox of a lesser character trying to outdo a superior, while it also restates a general cultural maxim.[26] Although these are not similes, it has been remarked by many that similes in Homer perform just such functions as generalizing experience and incorporating acknowledged cultural views of both the civilized and natural worlds. Less often noticed about Homeric similes is their frequent concentration on the *sound* of an action (for example, *Iliad* 3.1–9), another performance feature over and above the rhythmic which the Woi epic brings to light.[27]

Turning to other cultures in Africa, we can note that Igbo epic performance (Southeast Nigeria) features four distinct and shifting styles: (1) narrative in ordinary voice; (2) three kinds of lyric song, used respectively to comment on emotional states of characters, make appeals to a hero as if he were present, and give a hero's own lyrical outburst at peak moments; (3) invocative style to declaim hero lists and praise epithets; and (4) oratorical style, in the singer's own voice, giving the audience moralizing or prophetic advice.[28] Once again, I do not claim that similes are found exclusively in one of these voices but rather that the epic shows *functionally conditioned performance shifts.* The Igbo tradition has formalized and made distinctive in performance a pragmatic feature which has caused considerable discussion in Homeric studies, the direct address of characters in the poems.[29]

For epic in Central Asia, we are lucky to have Karl Reichl's recent guide to Turkic oral poetry, giving an expert collection of techniques and tales. From his rich material, I select just one example: the use of verse in the *Book of Dede Qorqut* to contrast with usual epic prose.[30] One function of the verse is in "catalogue of beauty" passages. "My wife with the body of a cypress, my wife with joining eyebrows like a drawn bow—with red cheeks which are like autumn apples" runs one passage that continues in this lyrical mode to make a number of other comparisons. Praise and lament are done in a similar style, also in verse. Here we can see not only a contrastive device (verse *versus* prose) to highlight peaks in the narrative; in addition, we see how the tradition, dating back to the thirteenth century, also employs similes in lyric portions.

In Sumatra, Nigel Phillips has recorded performances of *sijobang*, the singing of a narrative about the hero Anggun Nan Tungga, which can be performed either by soloists with musical accompaniment or by dramatic troupes of fifteen to twenty male actors who mime the story as the narrator sings.[31] *Sijobang* features a prose story line that is framed and interrupted by a verse form called *pantun*, in which the singer can introduce comic touches, refer to love stories, or even talk about audience members. In the metaphorical system of the performers, these verse segments are known as "flowers," and the song is said to blossom most fully in certain social situations (for example, when the audience is not well known to the performer, thus allowing him to expatiate on topics otherwise prohibited). Not only do *pantun* verses have a rhythmic function, punctuating episodes, but also they play the role of metaperformance comment, of deixis pointing to the *hic et nunc* of the song's production. Interestingly, it is in these "flowers" of song-segments that one also finds simile, as occurs in Philips' transcript B: "I tried to tell it but I could not, it is like felling a *sampie* tree . . . I tried to stop you but I could not, it is like stopping water flowing downstream: what is the good of suffering."[32] Admittedly, there is nothing here as detailed or as rich in narrative elements as the Homeric simile, but the *sijobang* similes can, like the Homeric, be readily extended in length, mainly through the use of parallelism.

My final examples are from Southeast Asia. Even greater varieties of textural elaboration occur here in traditions I have sampled. In the Tamil performances of the Palavecamcervaikkarar story, Stuart Blackburn identifies no fewer than five musical and song styles above and beyond the ordinary speech style that is used to represent the narrative line.[33] A first style is reserved for marking dramatic tension at births, marriages, and deaths in the story; a second performance marker, involving the addition of a particle *"e"* to key words, is used for most crucial events.[34] A third marker consists of audience ululation at certain moments. Again, there is an extraepic dimension to this stylistic variation: the same behavior occurs ritually at births and marriages, yet it is not reserved for these events in the epic performance. Finally, two musical and rhythmic effects exclusively mark such events as the imminent death of the hero. I will return shortly to the analogue within Greek epic for the sort of genre-embedding one sees in the Tamil tradition.

Let me conclude this rough survey by singling out the work of Susan Wadley, who set out to find the significance of performance shifts within the North Indian *Dhola* epic. She shows, first, that scenes or episodes are demarcated by "verbal strategies that involve the use or nonuse of music"—that is to say, one cannot disentangle text from performance in this tradition.[35] One of these strategies, called *dhola dhar,* is a long song-run used for ending episodes. It can be filled with simile: "When destruction comes to man, first lightning falls on the brain, one's own mother is like a lion, and father seems like Yamraj."[36] Using speech-act terms, Wadley differentiates informing talk (the prose narrative) from situating talk—the song-sections, of which she finds at least six styles. These in turn are associated with song genres, often employing similes. For instance, the *alha* section—"and he rose immediately from his room, think of a lion moving in the forest, as he went his boots thumped loudly and his shield clanked on his shoulder"—is done in a performance style associated by its tune and rhythm with martial epic, but embedded here in the larger narrative text to create characterization. From her field work Wadley concludes, ". . . In Indian epic singing, the moods and characters of events and persona are conveyed by changing voices and situations through shifts in song genres." Narratives, and especially character development, is achieved "through the conscious choice of symbolically-charged melodies, textures, and rhythms borrowed from the regional pool of genres."[37]

Now we shall take the comparative evidence and make a hypothesis that can be tested in terms of Greek poetry. Given that similes in Homer have a rhythmic performance function and that this function is filled by song or other genre shifts in *actual* oral epic, we should allow for the possibility that similes develop from or are related to a separate performance style within Greek. From the comparative and typological viewpoint, similes in fact belong with the elevated "song" portions of performance, whereas the narrative functions like the lower-register, explanatory "prose" sections of performance.

Having suggested this possibility of a distinct genre origin for similes on the basis of typology, I note now that a supporting argument is available from a completely independent study of Homeric language.

Starting with work published in 1953, and more fully in the second edition of his *Studies in the Language of Homer,* G. P. Shipp found that linguistic features that had independently been established by Pierre Chantraine as "late" developments, appear in similes in a much greater proportion than in the rest of Homer's text.[38] More than half the similes include late forms, according to Shipp. The implications of his finding have been taken two ways. Shipp himself thought that this meant similes were either composed later than the narrative of the poems or interpolated.[39] Meanwhile, T. B. L. Webster and Geoffrey Kirk saved the integrity of the poems by assuming that the monumental composition of the epics was as late as the time of composition of the similes. Of course, "late" is a relative term in this discussion; no absolute dating is possible.[40]

Logically, the "lateness" of the similes could be interpreted on the surface as a simple reflection of the performer's situation. Those portions, which one can imagine must change from year to year or even from one performance to the next—the asides, digressions, and similes—since they refer to the "real" world of the audience, are more likely to be in less standardized, "later" language of a form more contemporary with the poet. Hainsworth puts it this way: "It is certainly the case that contemporary language was freely admitted to the less traditional parts of the diction, such as similes, comments by the poet, and anecdotes."[41] There is, however, further complication to be considered. The rediscovery of the work of Mikhail Bakhtin, for one thing, has helped us remember that there is really no such thing as unmediated "natural" language in texts.[42] The same might be said a fortiori for traditional performance media. If indeed the language of similes was simply an example of a poet's contemporary, later Ionic dialect intruding on a poem expressed in an earlier, delimited *Kunstsprache,* we would have no problem agreeing with those who see in the "late" similes a simple sign of recent composition. As it is, however, the similes contain features *not* to be identified with any one dialect and moreover, some that are definitely *not* Ionic as we know it.

To test my hypothesis, let us make use of Shipp's extensive analysis, in which he matched items throughout Chantraine's grammar to their occurrence in specific Homeric narrative segments. My analysis of this material compares the "late" and rare items that Shipp found in similes with the other surviving Greek song traditions, especially those of Pindar's choral lyric and of Theognidean elegy. We can conclude that there is a relation between the subgenre of similes, on the one hand, and the genres of lyric performance, on the other. Notice that the correlation of many of Shipp's "late" features with Pindaric choral art tells against the simple solution of making similes "contemporary" Ionic, because Pindar's quite specialized medium is almost exclusively Doric and Aeolic in its makeup.[43]

I have listed more than a dozen places, hitherto unremarked, where Pindar or Theognis and Hesiod use the "late" features that Shipp and critics before him found problematic in Homeric similes. Although a full-scale analysis would no doubt produce many more, these examples will suffice to show the range of phenomena involved in the correlation.

At the least complex level, that of morphology, we can see that a word for "milk" takes an unusual form only once, in a repeated simile. The other Homeric instances of the word show a *t*-suffix (compare *Odyssey* 4.88, 9.246), as does the Latin cognate *lac, lact-is*. But in the simile there appears the nominative of a neuter-*s*-stem (*Iliad* 16.643 = 2.471):[44] "In spring when milk (*glágos*) moistens the pails." In a Pindaric hyporcheme (fr.106.4 SM) the genitive of this *s*-stem form is incorporated in a longer poetic trope, a priamel, in which goats from Skuros are said to be best for milking.[45]

Still on the level of morphology, let us consider two words that are apparently later formations competing with earlier forms even within Homeric diction. At *Iliad* 4.424–426 the battle lines of the Achaeans are compared with relentless waves cresting about the headlands:

> On the deep, first, it rises to a crest (korussetai) but then
> broken on the land it roars greatly, and around the cliffs
> curling, it comes to a head (koruphoutai) and spits sea spume.

The verb *koruphoutai* stands out as one of a handful of present stems of its kind derived from nominal stems other than *o*-stems.[46] Pindar uses the same word in the figurative phrase "the farthest point forms a peak (*koruphoutai*) for kings" (*Olympian* 1.113).[47] Pindar and Homer also share *korussetai*, a denominative verb of commoner morphological type which seems to have developed a similar meaning, "rise to a crest," but primarily means "put a crest (of helmet) on," and by extension, "arm."[48] This latter verb (ultimately from the same root) is used in the same simile at *Iliad* 4.426, where we can read a metaphorical force, and thus perhaps detect a locus of diffusion for the secondary denotation. If *korussetai* means primarily "arms itself" (like a hero—compare *Iliad* 19.364, 7.206), the application to a wave—which "gets its crest up"—in this line brilliantly elides two aggressive phenomena characterized by high threatening "crests" and destructive encounters with whatever stands in their way. Notice that even though the overt point of comparison within this simile turns on the *frequency* of waves whipped up by Zephuros and the movement of multiple lines of Greek troops (compare 423 and 427), the immediately preceding object of the poet's gaze, nevertheless, has been an armed hero, Diomedes, leaping into action with a crash of bronze (420–421), and the simile begins by sounding as if it is meant to elaborate on *this* movement rather than the general troop advance (compare 422–423 *Hōs d'ot' . . . ornut'*). Therefore, the choice of *korussetai* to describe the wave is even more apt in context.

In addition, we may note that the use of the verbal metaphor in the simile does what good poetry always does, recovering the radical vividness of the language itself. *Korussetai* here takes us back to the original metonymy underlying the semantic extension of the verb; that is to say, the etymological sense "put on a helmet" has already been watered down elsewhere in Homeric diction to mean "put on arms" in a more general sense (thus even spears can be "helmeted"—compare *Iliad* 3.18 *kekoruthmena*). The formulaic quality of expressions with the broader semantic range shows that this use is already traditional. But in the simile, the wave/warrior comparison is most exact if we assume the verb means literally "put on a crest" rather than the more extended "arm oneself." In short, the simile (an allegedly "late" feature) seems to preserve an *earlier* state of the language in this case. At the same time, it could be argued that the odd shift in comparison—from what first appears to be a description of Diomedes to a general characterization of waves of troops—occurs because this radical meaning of *korussetai* has by this time become obscure to both poet and audience, though the motif of waves in a martial comparison remains important.

In the next example of shared diction, we find an adjective meaning "powerful," with a distinctive formation, used in the simile at *Iliad* 11.119: "rushing, covered with sweat, under attack from the powerful beast [krataiou thēros]." As Shipp points out, the masculine *krataios* is secondary to the inherited *u*-stem adjective *kratus,* having been formed by analogy to the inherited feminine *krataiē.*[49]

Pindar used this later-formed masculine in describing Telamon, father of Aias, who once took Troy (*Nemean* 4.25–26). The Pindar passage shows no sign elsewhere in its context of borrowing a strange word from Homer; this is not allusion.[50] The most we can say is that Pindar and Homer share diction that is unusual from the Homeric standpoint. Although the masculine *kratus* is not common in Homer, the usual adjective form in epic is *krateros.*

"Late" or rare features found by Shipp in similes can be detected in the diction of Theognidean poetry as well as Pindaric. For example, the word *smikros* for "little" (instead of the more common *oligos* and *tutthos*) occurs in Homer only in the simile at *Iliad* 17.755–757:[51]

> As a cloud of starlings or daws comes
> shrieking destruction when they catch sight of a hawk
> on its way, that brings the little (smikrēisi) birds death . . .

The phrase "little bird," with the nonepic adjective, recurs at Theognis 579–582:

> I hate a bad man, and having veiled myself I pass by
> with the empty mind of a little bird (smikrēs ornithos).

And I hate a woman who runs around and a greedy man
    who wants to plow someone else's field.

This intriguing small dialogue seems to use the phrase in question within lines spoken by a female (as the participle shows), with a reply spoken by a male.[52] The whole exchange has the sound of a traditional insult duel: the exactly structured pair of couplets is formally equivalent to modern-day Cretan *mandinadhes,* which are also used extensively in negotiating male-female relations.[53] It could be that the word *smikros* for "little" enters epic through a preexisting lyric tradition that features encounters involving gender clashes. In this connection I observe that in the Homeric simile we are examining, the *kirkos* is masculine, and the little birds (like the first speaker in Theognis), feminine. A further stylization of the lyric *topos* that I am postulating might be the bird-to-bird talk we find in Hesiod's fable of the hawk and nightingale (*Works and Days* 202–212), where the clash is also along gender lines, but where one bird, the nightingale, also clearly represents the poet. Finally, it is not impossible that Pindar, in *Pythian* 3, combines this set of poetic associations (bird = small, female, opposed to male) with the other well-known *topos,* of poet as bird, when he asserts towards the poem's end (107–109):

I will be little among the little <u>(smikros en smikrois)</u>, big with
    the big,
and the divinity ever at my mind I shall honor,
doing service according to my own device.[54]

Of course, I am not claiming that any of the lyric associations of this trope affect the simile in the *Iliad,* but I note that the nonepic adjective does fit comfortably into a *systematic* series of related themes outside epic, another indication perhaps that this is where the generic origin of the diction is to be sought.

Still on the lexical level, we find several substantives, uncommon in Homeric diction but used in similes, deployed within a more fully articulated set of themes in lyric poetry. The following simile (*Iliad* 15.410–413) contains the only occurrence in Homer of the word *sophiē*, "wisdom," the only abstract noun formation of this type in Homer.[55]

> But as a chalkline makes straight ship's wood
> in the hands of a skilled carpenter, one who knows
> all wisdom (sophiēs) well, by Athena's suggestions,
> Thus was their war and battle made evenly taut.

Pindar uses the word twenty times, and Theognis ten, but most interesting is the further context in Theognis 1003–1009:

> This virtue, this prize is best among men
> and fairest for a wise man (sophōi) to bear;
> A common good is this, for the polis and all the people:
> The man who stays firmly standing at the front.
> In general for men I shall advise (hypothēsomai): with youth's
> glorious flower he who thinks noble thoughts
> should enjoy his own possessions well . . .

The speaker's promised advice to the wise man here comprises an elegiac imperative contrasted with the martial poetic ideal.[56] The *Iliad* passage in a similar manner mentions the advice of Athena (*hypothēmosunēisin*) alongside the recipient's own wisdom. But whereas wisdom is touched on only briefly in epic, it is unmistakably a topic appropriate to lyric and epinician advising; poetic direction on how to obtain it constituted a recognizable genre distinct from epic but interacting with that form.[57]

In the simile at *Iliad* 15.381–384, the word *toikhos*, which elsewhere in Homer means "wall of a house," is applied to the sides of a ship that waves are swamping:

> As a great wave of the broad-wayed sea
> goes down above the ship's side (toikhōn) whenever the force

of the wind drives it on—for that's what most swells waves—
the Trojans with a great shout went down upon the wall.

This shift from "wall" to "hull" has been thought to represent a
later semantic development; in the absence of other attestations
we cannot be sure.[58] I note only that, within this simile, there is a
contrast between the ship's "walls" and the famous Achaean wall
(compare the related word, *teikhos,* at line 384). This is followed
by a sort of reification of the simile, as the Trojans pour over the
defensive wall and threaten the *actual* Achaean ships: the simile
of the waves describes a flood of men, yet the objects of both
metaphorical and real inundations are the same. Rather than
representing a catachresis of the regular meaning of *toikhos,* I
suggest further that the simile at *Iliad* 15.381–384 taps into an
independent series of tropes visible in such lyric forms as Theognis' lines (673–676) on the "ship of state":

> They do not care to bail, and the sea dashes over
>   both sides (toikhōn). With difficulty, to be sure,
> Is any one saved, such things do they do. They stopped
>   The good helmsman, who kept watch knowledgeably.

We could say that these lines are reminiscent of the Homeric
simile. But, put the other way, it could be that the simile makes
use of an emotionally intense song-moment in which one can
lament the total loss of civil order in a *polis.* It is easier to believe
that Homeric art redeploys traditional diction (including the nautical meaning of the otherwise unusual *toikhos*) in this way, just as
the Dhola epic borrows freely from a regional genre pool. At the
moment of describing the worst disorder in the Achaean camp,
the poet would then be eliciting in his audience all the associations entailed by an allegory of the Theognidean type. The alternative is to think that Theognis borrowed specifically from the
one Homeric simile where the word *toikhos* meant ship hulls and
developed his own allegory from there. That the elegiac lines

embody a carefully elaborated, enigmatic utterance, artful in the extreme, is made clear from lines 681–682, characterizing the verses as an *ainigma,* hidden from all but those of an in-group skilled in poetic wisdom.[59] This sort of characterization applies more to a complex reworking of a traditional extended poetic metaphor than to a random borrowing from Homeric hexameters. If anyone "borrows" here, it is the Homeric composer.

Sometimes, the least obvious word leads one onto a rich vein of shared diction and motif indicating lyric/epic interaction in similes. The adverb *exaiphnēs* "suddenly" is a "late" rarity in a simile that compares fighting to a fire that rises up suddenly (*Iliad* 17.738):[60]

> Thus they speedily bore the corpse from the war
> to the hollowed ships. But war was tense for them
> like a wild fire that starting up suddenly (exaiphnēs), attacks
> and burns a city of men, and houses get ruined.

Pindar (*Olympian* 9.52) uses the same adverb once, precisely in a scene of natural disaster, when speaking of a primordial flood:

> They say that water's strength had flooded the black earth but then,
> by Zeus' devisings,
> an ebb-tide suddenly (exaiphnas) took the bilge.

The phrase *ormenon exaiphnēs,* "starting up suddenly," occurs in another simile (*Iliad* 21.14) that describes the Trojans fleeing Achilles as locusts flee to a river when they are set aflutter by flames. The contrast is ironic: although the river is relief for the locusts, in this case it will be death for the Trojans, and in fact the river is about to flood the plain, in this poetic rendition of a clash of the elements outside Troy. If we imagine that the primordial flood scene alluded to in Pindar recapitulates some mythic narrative, and does so with a conventional signal (the adverb *exaiphnēs*), then we can speculate that the similes about sudden fire key the Homeric audience to similar mythic descriptions of cosmic disaster, over and above the explicit martial conflict in the similes. At any rate, it is worth noting the closeness and specificity of contexts surrounding this seemingly banal adverb.

A simile at *Iliad* 16.384–388 presents a similarly complex case of intertextual (or, as I now prefer, metaperformative) poetics:

> As the whole black earth is pressed hard by hurricane
> on an autumn day, when Zeus pours torrential rain
> the time he is angered at men who by violence
> render crooked judgements in the agora
> and drive out justice,
> not respecting the regard of the gods <u>(theōn opin ouk alegontes)</u>.

Shipp, citing Chantraine, observes that the verb *alegō* takes an accusative rather than the usual genitive object only when used in the simile line *theōn opin ouk alegontes,* "not respecting the regard of the gods." Meanwhile, it has long been seen that this simile resembles a motif in Hesiod (*Works and Days* 248–251):[61]

> O kings, you yourselves take notice of this justice,
> for close by, among men, immortals note
> how many grind down one another with crooked judgements
> not respecting the regard of the gods <u>(theōn opin ouk alegontes)</u>.

The Homeric simile containing this line thus apparently recasts as an allusion the juridical and theological message of the Hesiodic lines, adding to them the meteorological details of Zeus' wrath but omitting the reference to kings, while the Hesiodic passage fails to mention the signs of the gods' displeasure. We should not assume borrowing in either direction; both passages partially articulate a larger shared complex of ideas and images.[62] Even more interesting is Pindar's use of the verb *alegō*, again with the unusual accusative, as he explains his motives for praise (*Olympian* 11.11–15):

Child, Hagesidamos, for your boxing
I shall sing a sweetsung ornament upon your crown of gold olive
respecting the race of the Zephurian Lokrians (genean alegōn).

It is worth noticing that the grand opening priamel of Pindar's poem foregrounds his choice of sweet-sounding hymns by contrasting it with other human needs, specifically for wind and rain—exactly the two cosmic threats in the Homeric simile about Zeus' justice (*Olympian* 11.1–3):

Sometimes men need winds the most, sometimes waters
from the heavens, watery children of cloud.

Pindar's respect for the victor's homeland, embodied in the form of this choral song, will by implication reinforce the cosmic order (*dikē*) so conspicuously absent in the world described by Homer and Hesiod. The choral poet by his song ensures that the injustice imagined in the Iliadic vignette (16.384–392) never happens. The verb *alegō* with its rare accusative object is a dictional peculiarity specifically associated with this theme, a theme embedded in turn, and independently, in the poems of Hesiod, Homer, and Pindar.[63]

The place of Pindaric poetry in these examples needs to be put into perspective. We are really talking about two phenomena. First, there is the diachronic priority that praise poetry of the type represented by Pindar, seems to have over epic, of the type represented by Homer.[64] Second, Pindaric art may appear diachronically "older" than Homer because, for its own compositional reasons, it preserves ideologies either forgotten, suppressed, or barely alluded to by Homeric epic. We have seen one such case in the motif of Zeus' justice and the flood. Another such topic may have been life after death, on which Pindar has been thought to preserve traces of Orphic ideas.[65] In that case, it is significant that one proof-text for Pindar's "Orphic" view of the afterlife contains the adjective *apalamnos* "helpless; hard to deal with" (*Olympian* 2.57). The word appears once in Homer, in a simile at *Iliad* 5.597, describing a traveler who stands helpless before an impassable river. The expected form of the adjective, *apalamos,* is found in Hesiod, *Works and Days* 20.[66] Shipp's comment on the word reveals much about his assumptions: "As *apalamnos* and also *palamnaios* are common in early poetry including Doric and tragedy, it is more likely that the simile has the word from such a source than that it has an epic origin." He therefore imagines a very late stage of composition for this simile, because it contains a word found otherwise in later poetry.[67] But if we take into account the way in which living oral poetic traditions function, we can reformulate the solution without recourse to problematic late datings and interpolations: given its context in Pindar, it is likely that the word comes from another genre of poetry, of the Orphic-hymnic type. Part of that tradition made its way down into the work of Pindar and other lyric poets, while Homeric poetry independently made contact with Orphic themes and diction.[68]

In this case, and in others, of course, it is not the actual words of the fifth century Boeotian poet, but the art of his lyric forebears, which has been deployed by the epic composer. Most of that earlier lyric tradition is lost to us. When we do have it, interesting questions of mutual shared themes and diction arise. A centerpiece for the investigation must remain two similar passages about the effects of midsummer, Hesiod *Works and Days* 582–588 and Alcaeus 347 LP. Recently, J. C. B. Petropoulos has convincingly explicated the link between these two in terms of their recasting of functional, local song traditions still attested in modern rural Greece. The two passages, long considered in standard literary terms as the result of "borrowing" by one poet of another's work, "may well be independent manifestations derived from the same stock of thematic material," Petropoulos concludes.[69]

I want to extend this finding in terms of Homeric poetry and the relationship that I have been outlining between lyric traditions and similes. The well-known passage describing the Trojan elders on the walls of their city compares them to cicadas (*Iliad* 3.150–152):

> . . . γήραϊ δὴ πολέμοιο πεπαυμένοι, ἀλλ᾽ ἀγορηταὶ
> ἐσθλοί, <u>τεττίγεσσιν ἐοικότες</u> οἵ τε καθ᾽ ὕλην
> δενδρέῳ ἐφεζόμενοι ὄπα λειριόεσσαν ἱεῖσι·

"Stopped from warring by old age, but talkers,
good ones, like cicadas which in the wood
sitting on a tree emit a slender voice."

The late feature noted by Chantraine and Shipp is at line 152: *dendreōi ephezomenoi* has a rare synizesis reflecting the loss of an original intervocalic digamma (**dendrewōi*).[70] Shipp believes the synizesis is produced under pressure from an Attic form *dendros* (dative *dendrōi*) that is itself a reinterpretation backformed from the plural *dendrea,* by analogy. If the Homeric simile, as well as the Hesiodic scene (which has the same phrase, at *Works and Days* 583), compresses a traditional poetic motif found expanded in the Alcaeus song, the traditional *type* represented by Alcaeus 347 could be the source for the hexameter treatments. Furthermore, if the phrase *dendreōi ephezomenoi* was originally in a different generic context, it may not have been metrically intractable—as it appears to be in Homer and Hesiod.[71] I leave for another time further exploration of the thematic implications of *Iliad* 3.150–152 in the light of the passage's apparent relationship to traditional lyric motifs.

Following up the notion that lyric forms may have affected the diction of similes, we might attribute some other metrical irregularities within Homeric verse to the differing demands of lyric meter; seemingly aberrant diction may have been precut to fit another mold. This seems to be the case in *Iliad* 23.226–228:

When the Dawnstar (Heōsphoros) goes to utter light upon the
  earth
After whom saffron-robed Dawn spreads over the sea
Then the fire was dying down and the flame stopped.

Shipp notices the harsh synizesis in the initial syllable of the word
for Dawnstar, *Heōsphoros*.[72] We can add that a similar synizesis
must occur at Pindar *Isthmian* 4.24 (also a simile):[73]

But, awakened, has a sheen on its skin
Like the wondrous Dawnstar (⟨Hao⟩sphoros) among other stars.

The Pindaric form might in fact be restored as *Hasphoros,* a form
featuring the expected West Greek contraction instead of
synizesis.[74] In sum, the poet of *Iliad* 23.226 uses this word metrically as if it had its Doric contracted form and may do so under
the influence of local western Greek nonepic lyric.

Finally, a similar argument might help explain at least one
"acephalic" line, which occurs in a simile at *Iliad* 9.4–7:

As two winds stir up the fish-filled sea,
Boreas and Zephyrus which blow from Thrace
coming on suddenly, and the black wave gathers
in a crest, and spreads much seaweed alongside the sea.

The short initial vowel of *Boreēs* causes the irregularity.[75] As it
happens, in Pindar there is a context in which these two wind
names are fitted with other dictional elements in such a way that
the syllables retain their natural quantity (*Parthen.* 2 [fr. 94b SM]
16–18):

κεῖνον ὅς Ζεφύρου τε σιγάζει πνοάς
  αἰψηρὰς ὁπόταν τε χειμῶνος σθένει
φρίσσων βορέας ἐπι-
  σπέρχησ'. . .

"That one, that calms the quick winds of Zephyr
And when Boreas bristling with storm's strength rushes . . ."

If Homeric poetry is here assimilating a nonhexameter poetic motif, one perhaps appropriate to seasonal or hymnic material, then it acquires along with the motif the diction and meter of the source tradition. In this connection, then, it is a pleasant surprise to find in the same Pindar passage another peculiarity of the language of Homeric similes, namely the unusual deployment (from a Homeric standpoint) of a compound of *sperkhō* in the active, rather than middle, form, used intransitively to mean "rush."[76]

In sum: starting from the internal evidence of the rhythmic punctuation provided by similes within the *Iliad,* we then find by comparison that this corresponds *functionally* to that of distinctive song-genres in the performance of epics in a number of cultures. Returning to nonepic song-texts from ancient Greek tradition, we further find a number of formal congruences between similes and lyric poetry, at the level of diction and even meter. An analogy to the process would be the way that Homeric speeches stylize elements of actual "sociopoetic" performance genres.[77] As with those embedded speech-acts, the "lyric" similes are "subgenres" only if we take the viewpoint of the all-encompassing Homeric performer; but we know that even as late as the fifth century a poet like Pindar, as Gregory Nagy has elegantly shown, can hold a quite different view about the priority and value of Homeric art.[78]

We shall probably never know whether similes were ever perceived by an ancient audience as having a different performance register. But one thing this investigation of Homeric epic can tell us: once more, the genius of this ambitious supergenre appears to be its inclusion of every other form of song-making. Like the art of the *Hymn to Apollo's* Delian maidens, which they learned from the man of Chios, it is polyphonic and therefore marvelous.[79]

CHAPTER 7

Ellipsis in Homer

GREGORY NAGY

This preparation concentrates on four questions: (1) What is ellipsis? (2) How does ellipsis work in Homeric song-making? (3) How does ellipsis typify Homeric song-making? (4) How does Homeric song-making use ellipsis to typify itself?

(1) A WORKING DEFINITION

In the dictionary of Liddell and Scott, the verb *elleipō* is defined as (1) leave in, leave behind; (2) leave out, leave undone; (3) fall short, fail.[1] The abstract noun *elleipsis*, derived from this verb, designates a "leaving out" of something, as we see from the use of the word in a grammatical sense: in Athenaeus 644b, for example, the term *elleipsis* is applied to explain the word *plakous* "flat-bread" as consisting of an adjective "flat" plus substantive *artos* "bread" understood. That is, the substantive can be inferred *kata elleipsin* "by ellipsis." Where we would say "adjective with substantive understood," Athenaeus is saying "adjective with substantive by way of ellipsis."

Let us pursue the idea of "understood" elements in a given combination by highlighting the principle of the elliptic plural in ancient Greek. Ordinarily, the plural of a given entity, let us say A, will designate A + A + A + . . . On the other hand, the *elliptic* plural of an entity A will designate A + B + C + . . . Here are two examples:

a. *toxon* "bow" (as in *Iliad* 4.124) versus *toxa* "bow and arrows" (as in *Iliad* 21.502) = "bow + arrow + arrow + arrow + . . ."[2]
b. *patēr* "father" vs. *pateres* "ancestors" = "father + *his* father + *his* father + *his* father + . . ."[3]

Similarly, the elliptic dual will designate A + B, unlike the A + A of the "normal" dual. For example, Sanskrit singular *pitā* is "father" but dual *pitarau* is not "two fathers" but rather "father and mother."

What is "left out" by way of ellipsis need not be left out "for good," as it were. It may be a matter of shading over; what is shaded over in one place may be highlighted in another. In other words, the location of the ellipsis may vary: it can be at the ending, at the middle, or at the beginning of a sequence.

So far, we have seen examples of ellipsis at the beginning plus the middle or at the middle plus the ending. In the case of *patēr* "father" vs. *pateres* "ancestors" = "father + *his* father + *his* father + *his* father + . . .," for example, the father concludes a sequence of an unspecified number of ancestors, potentially starting with a first father.[4] Here I surmise that the beginning and middle are shaded over, while the ending—one's own father—is highlighted as an instance of all preceding fathers. In the case of *toxon* "bow" vs. *toxa* "bow and arrows" = "bow + arrow + arrow + arrow + . . .," on the other hand, the bow initiates a sequence of an unspecified number of arrows, potentially ending with a last arrow. Here I surmise that the middle and ending are shaded over, while the beginning is highlighted.

Ellipsis can highlight even what is being said at the very end of a given sequence for the purpose of referring to the very beginning. For example, the ending of the first sentence of Herodotus' *History* signals the point of departure for the history: . . . *ta te alla kai di hēn aitiēn epolemēsan allēloisi* "including all the other things *alla* but especially the cause for their entering into war with each other." Each of the *alla* "other things" is in effect an *allo* "other thing": thus we have a sequence of *alla* = *allo* + *allo* + *allo* + . . ., with the last element of the sequence referring back to the first element that had logically started the sequence of events—and which is yet to be stated by the *History*—that is, the original cause of the war about to be narrated.[5]

There is also ellipsis of the middle, the leaving out of the middle man or men, as it were. An example is the figure of the *merism,* in the sense of "a bipartite, commonly asyndetic noun phrase serving to designate globally an immediately higher taxon."[6] That is, the combination of two words can express a totality that is merely framed rather than filled by the two individual referents that match these two individual words. Thus for example the Hittite expression *ḫalkiš* ZÍZ-*tar,* literally "barley (and) wheat," designates *all* cereals, not just barley and wheat.[7] It is as if Hittite "barley and wheat" were barley and wheat and every other kind of grain in between.

(2) ELLIPTIC CONSTRUCTIONS IN HOMER

We turn to actual cases of ellipsis in Homeric composition. It is important to concede, from the start, that all discourse is to some extent elliptic. Still, keeping the focus on the formal mechanisms

that make ellipsis possible, even explicit, I propose to offer a
sample of some specific mechanisms, as attested in the *Iliad* and
Odyssey.

It is instructive to begin with a striking example of a singular of
a given noun where we might have expected the plural:

1a. ὣς ἄρα φωνήσασ᾽ ἀπέβη γλαυκῶπις <u>Ἀθήνη</u>   78
    πόντον ἐπ᾽ ἀτρύγετον, λίπε δὲ Σχερίην ἐρατεινήν,   79
    ἵκετο δ᾽ ἐς Μαραθῶνα καὶ <u>εὐρυάγυιαν Ἀθήνην</u>,   80
    δῦνε δ᾽ <u>Ἐρεχθῆος</u> πυκινὸν <u>δόμον</u>, αὐτὰρ Ὀδυσσεὺς   81
    Ἀλκινόου πρὸς δώματ᾽ ἴε κλυτά· . . .   82

"Speaking thus, [epithet] <u>Athena [*Athēnē*]</u> went off   78
over the [epithet] sea, and she left behind lovely
    Skheria,   79
and she came to Marathon and to <u>Athens [Athēnē]</u>,   80
and she entered the well-built <u>house</u> of <u>Erekhtheus</u>.
    But Odysseus   81
went toward the renowned house of Alkinoos"
    Odyssey 7.78–82   82

We see here at verse 80 an exceptional attestation of the word for
"Athens" in the singular, *Athēnē*. Elsewhere "Athens" is *Athēnai*,
in the plural. We see the plural form as we look ahead at text 1d
below, verse 546, and we see it in general everywhere in ancient
Greek literature.

As we look back at verse 80 of text 1a, we notice that this form
Athēnē, meaning "Athens," is identical with the form that means
"the goddess Athene"—or Athena, in the Latinized spelling—as
attested at verse 78 of text 1a and at verse 547 of text 1d. Why,
then, is "Athens" in the singular at verse 80 of text 1a? Second,
can we even say that this is the same Athens that we know from
later sources? Third, can we say that the plural *Athēnai* in the
sense of "Athens" is a *functionally* elliptic construction?

Let us start with the first question, why is Athens in the singular here? On the level of surface metrical structure, we can justify the combination of singular substantive and singular epithet on the grounds that it *scans,* that is, on the grounds that it fits the metrical requirements of the dactylic hexameter, whereas the plural of this combination would clash with these requirements. If we look at text 1b, we can see what would happen if the plural of "Athens" were slotted into the same metrical position within the dactylic hexameter and if it kept the same epithet assigned to the singular form as attested at verse 80 of text 1a:

1b. *. . . εὐρυαγυίας Ἀθήνας [option canceled]

This combination is purely hypothetical (hence the prefixed asterisk) and in fact untenable for three mechanical reasons: (1) we expect the last syllable of the epithet εὐρυαγυίας to be long;[8] (2) the first syllable of the word for "Athens" in this position has to be short; (3) the second syllable of the word for "Athens" has to be long. These three specific reasons add up to one overriding general reason: such a hypothetical combination of words would produce a rhythmical sequence of long + short + long (the criterion of measure is syllabic length), and this sequence is systematically shunned in Homeric diction.[9] I should add that the same idea, as expressed by this hypothetical epithet + noun combination, could indeed be expressed, *within the same metrical framework,* by another epithet + noun combination:

1c. . . . εὐρυχόρους ἐς Ἀθήνας

". . . to Athens, with its spacious areas for song and dance"
Herodotean *Life of Homer,* par. 28

Moving to the second question, we may ask this: can we even say that this "Athens" in *Odyssey* 7.80 is the same "Athens" that we know from the historical period? The answer emerges from the next major relevant passage:

1d. οἱ δ' ἄρ' Ἀθήνας εἶχον, ἐυκτίμενον πτολίεθρον,   546
δῆμον Ἐρεχθῆος μεγαλήτορος, ὅν ποτ' Ἀθήνη   547
θρέψε Διὸς θυγάτηρ, τέκε δὲ ζείδωρος ἄρουρα,   548
κὰδ δ' ἐν Ἀθήνῃς εἷσεν, ἑῷ ἐν πίονι νηῷ·   549
ἔνθα δέ μιν ταύροισι καὶ ἀρνειοῖς ἱλάονται   550
κοῦροι Ἀθηναίων περιτελλομένων ἐνιαυτῶν·   551
τῶν αὖθ' ἡγεμόνευ' υἱὸς Πετεῶο Μενεσθεύς.   552

"And those who held Athens [Athēnai], well-founded
city   546
the dēmos of stout-hearted Erekhtheus, whom once
Athena [Athēnē]   547
nourished,[10] daughter of Zeus, but the grain-giving
earth gave birth to him.   548
And she established him in Athens [Athēnai], in her
own rich temple.   549
And there he is supplicated, with sacrifices of bulls and
rams,   550
by the young men of Athens, each time the seasonal
moment comes round.[11]   551
And their leader was Menestheus, son of Peteoos."   552
Iliad 2.546–552

The "Athens" of text 1d must surely be the same place as the "Athens" of text 1a, as we see from the reference at verse 549 to the temple of Athena as the home of the goddess. At verse 547, we see that the temple is also home for the hero Erekhtheus, whom Athena establishes inside her temple, much as the goddess Aphrodite establishes the hero Phaethon inside her own temple in Hesiod, *Theogony* 990–991.[12] Similarly in text 1a, the singular "Athens" is the home of the hero Erekhtheus at verse 81, and it *seems* to be the home of the goddess Athena, who is described as going to the palace of Erekhtheus, situated in a place that has a name identical to the name of the goddess. While Odysseus proceeds to the *palace* of Alkinoos, Athena flies off to the *palace* of Erekhtheus. So Athena's city par excellence is presumably Athens.

It remains to determine, to be sure, how far back in time we may apply this formulation. Already in the era of the Linear B tablets, we find a distinct goddess named *Athāna* (spelled a-ta-na- in the syllabary), equivalent of Homeric *Athēnē:*

> 1e. a-ta-na-po-ti-ni-ja = *Athānāi potniāi* (dative) "to the Lady
> Athena"   Linear B tablet V 52 from Knossos
>
> πότνι᾽ Ἀθηναίη "lady Athena"   *Iliad* 6.305

The Linear B tablets provide no direct information, however, about the name for the city of Athens. We need not assume that the goddess worshipped at Knossos in the second millennium B.C.E. was known as the goddess of Athens. Still, the city of Athens was perhaps already then understood as belonging to the goddess.

Putting such questions aside, let us return to what seems more certain: that *Athēnē* the goddess and *Athēnē* the city in text 1a are the same as *Athēnē* the goddess and *Athēnai* the city in text 1d. True, *Athēnē* and *Athēnai* may be the appropriate designations of the same place at different times. The exceptional instance of singular *Athēnē* in text 1a may reflect a relatively earlier context. According to Martin P. Nilsson, the relationship between goddess (Athene) and king (Erekhtheus) is here still in a "Mycenaean" stage in their relationship.[13] We see here the goddess as a patron-ess of the king in power and as a resident in his palace. She is his ultimate tenant, Mycenaean style, occupying as her abode a shrine-room within the palace. By contrast, the instances of plural *Athēnai* as in text 1d reflect a later stage in the relationship of Athena and Erekhtheus, when the palace of the king has been transformed into the temple of the goddess. What we now see, from the perspective of a palace-turned-temple, is a hero who is worshipped within the sacred precinct of a goddess. From the viewpoint of the there-and-then identified with heroic times, Erekhtheus is a king empowered by Athena. From the viewpoint of the narrator's here-and-now, by contrast, he is the protégé of the goddess, a cult-figure sharing in her overall cult.

In sum, the perspective of the distant past allows a residual situation, where Athens is in the singular, whereas the narrator's perspective of his own here-and-now requires Athens to be in the plural. We have yet to refine, to be sure, what it means to say "the narrator's perspective of his own here-and-now."

In fact, many questions remain about the semantics of any contrast between singular *Athēnē* and plural *Athēnai*. Even when the singular is used to designate the whole city, is that usage not in itself an implicit ellipsis, as distinct from the explicit ellipsis of the plural? Does the identification of the name of the goddess with the name of the city imply that the concept of the goddess subsumes the concept of the city? Or, to put it another way, does the essence of the goddess lead into the essence of her population? Here is a list of some possible parallels:

1f. *Thēbē* = Thebe the Nymph, versus *Thēbai* = Thebes[14]
1g. *Mukēnē* = Mycene the Nymph, versus *Mukēnai* = Mycenae[15]
1h. *Messēnē* = Messene the heroine;[16] compare Linear B me-za-na[17]
1i. *Philippos* = Philip, versus *Philippoi* = Philippi[18]
1j. Modern Greek example, from the Island of Ikaria, where the town name in the plural designates the town and its environs[19]

Of all available traces of residual ellipsis, the most striking example is this one:

2a. ἐκ μὲν <u>Κρητάων</u> γένος εὔχομαι <u>εὐρειάων</u>,
    ἀνέρος ἀφνειοῖο πάις· . . .

> "I proclaim that I am by birth from <u>Crete [plural]</u>, the
> far-and-wide,
> the son of a rich man . . ."   *Odyssey* 14.199–200

2b. ἐκ μὲν <u>Κρητάων</u> γένος εὔχεται <u>εὐρειάων</u>,
    φησὶ δὲ πολλὰ βροτῶν ἐπὶ ἄστεα δινηθῆναι
    πλαζόμενος . . .

> "He proclaims that he is by birth from <u>Crete [plural]</u>,
> the far-and-wide,
> and he says that he has wandered around over many
> cities of mortals,
> veering from his path."[20]   *Odyssey* 16.62–64

There is of course only one island of Crete, and we may readily conclude that the plural usage reflects the idea of "Crete and everything that belongs to it." Such an idea corresponds to the historical construct of a "Minoan thalassocracy," as already intuited by Thucydides (1.4), who speaks of King Minos of Crete as the founder of a prototypical naval empire extending throughout the Cyclades Islands and beyond.[21]

So far, we have looked at elliptic constructions in Homer from a diachronic viewpoint. But what are the implications of ellipsis from the synchronic viewpoint of composition-in-performance? A case in point is the problem of the dual of the heroic name *Aias*, that is, *Aiante*. I will summarize the key Homeric contexts of the dual Aias by quoting from a 1959 book on the *Iliad* by Denys Page, representing what he himself calls an "analyst" as opposed to "unitarian" interpretation of the epic.[22] Words emphasized by Page himself are left italicized, while those highlighted by me are underlined. At key moments, I will interrupt Page's words by noting salient opportunities for alternative explanations.[23]

Page's central argument is that the "original" meaning of

Aiante is not *the greater Aias (son of Telamon) and the lesser Aias (son of Oïleus)* but *Aias and his half-brother Teukros.* He speaks of a place "where the *original* meaning of Aiante, 'Ajax and his brother,' is deeply embedded in the *Iliad.*"[24] The passage is *Iliad* 13.177 and following:

> Ajax [= Aias] and his brother Teucer [= Teukros] are fighting side by side. Teucer kills Imbrios: he therefore has the right to strip the body of its armour; and he sets out to do so. Hector intervenes, but is repelled by Ajax; *and the Aiante proceed to drag and despoil the body of Imbrios.* Here it is very obvious that Aiante means "Ajax and Teucer"; nobody else took part in the killing of Imbrios; nobody else has any interest in, or claim to, the spoils. It is indeed so obvious, that the later poets were inspired to correct what they thought to be a mistake. If the term Aiante was used, the smaller Ajax *must* have been engaged in the action; let us proceed at once to say "that the head of Imbrios was now cut off *by Ajax the son of Oileus*" [line 203]. This we shall certainly not tolerate: what, we shall ask this bounding intruder, are you doing with a head which belongs to us? Imbrios was our victim, not yours: Teucer killed him, Ajax helped to secure the body; you had nothing whatever to do with him. The smaller Ajax pops into the scene suddenly, and out of it again immediately, having done his simple duty; which was, to bring the term Aiante into line with modern opinion.[25]

In the case of a similar problem, the use of the duals where we expect plurals in the "Embassy" passage of *Iliad* 9, Page again resorts to the rhetorical device of an apostrophe addressed to a Homeric character: "Unhappy Phoenix [Phoinix], Achilles' oldest friend, not one single word of you; and if that were not enough, your leadership is instantly and silently taken from you."[26] In this case, Page thinks that Phoinix is the odd man out in the dual references to what seems to be a trio composed of Phoinix, Aias, and Odysseus.[27]

Let us return to the problem of the meaning of Aiante, as Page sees it:

> The trouble began in [12] 343 ff.: Menestheus sent a herald[28] to fetch Ajax [Aias], *"both,* if possible, otherwise Telamonian Ajax alone."* In order that "both" might signify "both Ajaxes" instead of "Ajax and Teucer," a line was added, 350, *"and let Teucer come with him"* (repeated 363); the addition was properly athetized by Aristarchus as wanting in MS authority.[29] When he hears the message, Telamonian Ajax tells Oilean Ajax to stay where he is; he himself and Teucer go to help Menestheus. Thus in [12] 400 ff. Telamonian Ajax and Teucer fight side by side, having left Oilean Ajax in another quarter. And now Poseidon ([13] 46 ff.) speaks to the Aiante: who are they? Obviously Ajax and Teucer, for the poet has just gone out of his way to tell us that the two Ajaxes are *not* together. But once again the occurrence of the term Aiante leads to a jack-in-the-box intrusion by Oilean Ajax ([13] 66 ff.), just as it does in the later passage (197 ff.); in this case the confusion is great and obvious, since we were told a moment ago in so much detail that the one Ajax had separated himself from the other.[30]

I suggest, however, that there is no "confusion," and that it is inaccurate to speak of "intrusions." Instead, if we adopt an evolutionary model for the making of Homeric poetry, there are simply different levels of recomposition-in-performance, which are traces of an evolving fixity or textualization—and I use this term without implying the presence of written texts.[31]

(3) ELLIPTIC MEANING IN HOMER

Here we reach the next question to be asked: how does ellipsis typify Homeric song-making? A related question has just been raised as we contemplated the shift in the meaning of Aiante, from Aias and Aias to Aias and Teukros: what are the implications of ellipsis from the synchronic viewpoint of composition-in-performance? Another related question is this: is it even possible to speak of a synchronic analysis of Homer? The evidence of ellipsis suggests that the answer has to be a complex one.

A case in point is the reference at *Iliad* 12.335–336 to *Aiante duō . . . Teukron te* "the two Aiante . . . and Teukros." According to the commentaries, the explicit mention of Teukros here means that "the two Aiante" must have been understood as Telamonian Aias and Oïlean Aias.[32] And yet, from a diachronic point of view, this kind of syntactic construction actually retains the elliptic function in the dual, thereafter highlighting what was initially shaded over by the ellipsis. That is, the implicit Teukros in the expression "the two Aiante" is joined to an explicit naming of Teukros. We see parallels in other Indo-European languages, as, for example, in the Indic expression *Mitrā . . . Váruṇo yáś ca* in *Rig-Veda* 8.25.2, meaning "dual-Mitra [= Mitra and Varuṇa] and he who is Varuṇa" = "Mitra and Varuṇa"; similarly in French, *nous deux Paul* means "I and Paul" = "the two of us, one of whom is Paul," not "I and you (or he/she/it) and Paul."[33] It is only if Paul gets stranded, as it were, from the two of us that the two of us—*nous deux*—could default to "I and you (or he/she/it)."

It is an elusive task, then, to establish the synchrony of the elliptic dual *Aiante* in the *Iliad,* or of the singular *Athēnē* as opposed to the elliptic plural *Athēnai* in the *Odyssey.* And yet, surely there are synchronic mechanisms in Homeric diction—and surely there must have been at any given historical time and place a synchronic system for generating the language of epic in general. But the question remains: is there a synchronic reality to the world of the epic? My own answer is that there is no such thing. We may perhaps agree that the pattern or system of epic discourse has been for the most part set by, say, the middle of the eighth century B.C.E., an era of general cultural consolidation in the Greek-speaking world.[34] And yet, this epic discourse may continue to communicate different levels of perspective, even different levels of meaning. We outsiders looking in, as it were, on this system can reconstruct a diachronic dimension in order to highlight some of these different levels of perspective, but there seems to be no level playing field for producing a single perspective. I once said that Homeric diction defies synchronic analysis.[35] This is not to advocate any abandonment of the search for synchronic—or let us say "working"—mechanisms. Rather, it is to emphasize that there are different levels of meaning that cannot be reduced to any one single synchrony.

These considerations can be brought to bear on the specific problem of duals that seem to be used in the place of plurals in Homeric diction. While some experts have dismissed even the possibility that the dual can be used for the plural,[36] we now know for a fact that the Alexandrian scholars and poets not only admitted the possibility in their Homeric exegesis but also used the device of dual-for-plural in their own poetry when they wished to make specific "citations" of Homer.[37] It can be argued in general that *citation,* not *allusion,* is a more accurate term for references to Homeric poetry in Alexandrian poetry: for the Alexandrians, Homer was the absolute *source,* not only the unsurpassable *model.*[38]

In the Alexandrian poetics of figures like Apollonius of Rhodes and Callimachus, *citation* is a matter of reusing: a given archaic usage, no longer current in the spoken language, becomes reused as a mark of the poetic language. In the oral poetics of the Homeric tradition, by contrast, there is no reusing, only *reactivation.* A case in point is Egbert Bakker's demonstration that Homeric diction can reactivate the use of verbs without augment as a newly active mechanism in expressing "epic tense."[39] Another case, I suggest, is the "Embassy Scene" of *Iliad* 9, where the use of the dual becomes reactivated to serve the special purpose of expressing an archaic situation where there *should* be only two ambassadors even though there are now three.[40] Thus the language of Achilles, in addressing two instead of three ambassadors, can develop the side-effect of effectively snubbing one of the three ambassadors in the context of a newer situation that is recreated out of an older one.[41] In both these cases, then, reactivation of older forms results in newer meanings.

If indeed there exist different levels of meaning that cannot be smoothed over as one single synchrony, then the elusiveness of a synchronic perspective in Homeric discourse may well be a mark of its essential fluidity. Here we may turn to the perceptive formulation of Albert Lord: "Our real difficulty arises from the fact that, unlike the oral poet, we are not accustomed to thinking in terms of fluidity. We find it difficult to grasp something that is multiform. It seems to us necessary to construct an ideal text or to seek an original, and we remain dissatisfied with an ever-changing phenomenon. I believe that once we know the facts of oral composition we must cease trying to find an original of any traditional song. From one point of view each performance is an original."[42]

I might add that we must cease trying to find an absolutely *final* version of any traditional song.

Concluding that we cannot speak of a single "world of Homer" or a single "age of Homer," I have proposed an evolutionary model for the making of Homeric poetry.[43] Following such a model, I have also proposed that there were at least "Five Ages of Homer," five distinct consecutive periods of Homeric transmission, with each period showing progressively less fluidity and more rigidity:

1. a relatively most fluid period, with no written texts, extending from the second millennium B.C.E. into the later part of the eighth century in the first millennium;
2. a more formative or "pan-Hellenic" period, still with no writ-

ten texts, from the later part of the eighth century B.C.E. to
the middle of the sixth;

3. a definitive period, centralized in Athens, with potential texts
   in the sense of *transcripts,* at any or several points from the
   middle of the sixth century B.C.E. to the later part of the
   fourth; this period starts with the reform of Homeric performance traditions in Athens during the regime of the Peisistratidai;

4. a standardizing period, with texts in the sense of transcripts or
   even *scripts,* from the later part of the fourth century B.C.E.
   to the middle of the second; this period starts with the reform
   of Homeric performance traditions in Athens during the regime of Demetrius of Phaleron, which lasted from 317 to 307
   B.C.E.;

5. a relatively most rigid period, with texts as *scripture,* from the
   middle of the second century onward; this period starts with
   the completion of Aristarchus' editorial work on the Homeric
   texts, not long after 150 B.C.E. or so, which is a date that also
   marks the general disappearance of the so-called "eccentric"
   papyri.[44]

Such an evolutionary model differs radically from some other
explanations. Here I give two examples, formulated by two of the
contributors to *The Iliad: A Commentary,* produced under the
general editorship of Geoffrey Kirk. Kirk himself posits a "big
bang" genesis of Homeric poetry. He argues for a one-time "oral"
composition achieved by a so-called "monumental composer"
sometime in the eighth century B.C.E., which then continues to
be reperformed "orally" by rhapsodes for around two hundred
years.[45] A second kind of "big bang" theory is offered by Richard
Janko, another of the contributors to this *Iliad* commentary. He
thinks that the *Iliad* and *Odyssey* were dictated by Homer himself around the second half of the eighth century B.C.E.[46]

In contrast to an evolutionary perspective on the dual-Aias

usages of the *Iliad*, let us examine the "big bang" perspectives of Kirk and Janko.[47] To start with Kirk, he says that the Aiante were understood as Telamonian Aias and Oïlean Aias "by the monumental composer himself."[48] But then he adds: "Despite that association, the Locrian Aias was not greatly admired in the heroic tradition, a reflection perhaps of his light-armed, unheroic and provincial . . . side."[49] He recounts the reprehensible or "stupid" things done by this Aias;[50] later on, commenting on *Iliad* 4.272–273, he says that "there can be little doubt that here [the Aiante] are the greater Aias *and Teukros*, since the Locrian Aias' light-armed contingent . . . would hardly be described as "bristling with shields and spears" as at 282 here."[51]

As for Janko, he says that the form of Aiante "was reinterpreted to mean two men called Aias, but Teukros is always nearby; at [13] 202ff. the same hypothesis explains Oïlean Aias' unexpected intrusion in a killing by Teukros and his brother [177–178]."[52] He goes on to say: "This verse [13.46] originally denoted Teukros and Aias, who clearly derives from Mycenaean epic . . ., but the dual led Homer to insert Oïlean Aias and then add Teukros (66f., 92)."[53] Commenting on 13.177–178, Janko says that "the poet has momentarily confused Teukros with Aias 'son of Telamon,' because he was unsure who was meant by 'the two Aiantes' (46)."[54] In considering the mutually contradictory references to the positioning of the Aiante at the ships of the Achaeans, he says: "The contradiction over the Aiantes' position surely derives from Homer's pervasive and creative misunderstanding of Aiante, originally 'Aias and Teukros' (46n.)."[55] Commenting on 14.460, he says: "The unusual sense of Aiante in earlier stages of the tradition caused confusion over the Aiantes and Teukros (13.46n); all three are present in this battle."[56]

We may have expected both these representatives of "big bang" models of composition in the eighth century to devise a corresponding set of "big-bang" explanations for the complexities of the dual-Aias constructions. Instead, they seem to be resorting to explanations based on assumptions of mostly random misinterpretations on the part of the poet.

From an evolutionary perspective, on the other hand, it is a question of systematic reinterpretations instead of unsystematic misinterpretations, and I find that the views of an old-fashioned "analyst" like Page are more useful for analyzing the complexities of reinterpretation.[57] I should stress at the outset, however, that I distance myself from Page's assumptions about older and newer poets, about original poets and later redactors, and, especially, about earlier texts and later texts. Still, his wording is replete with suggestive possibilities, as when he says

> Certainly the poet, if asked, would say that Aiante means "the two Ajaxes"; and would admit that he has made a mistake. But he has not made a mistake, except in his <u>interpretation</u> of Aiante; he has preserved an almost obliterated truth, the usage of Aiante in the sense "Ajax and his brother." Tradition supplied him with a formula for addressing Ajax, *Aiante Argeiōn hēgē-tore,* in which Ajax's brother was included; in the early Epic this formula had been employed <u>correctly; and the force of imme-morial tradition has preserved it in a few contexts up to the end</u>. It is very natural that the later poet should fail to notice the occasional confusion which is caused by the difference between the old and the new meanings of a word or formula; but no poet would of his own free will, <u>as a positive and creative act</u>, describe the two Ajaxes as joint commanders of an army comprising the regular Salaminians and the highly irregular Locrians.[58]

The notion of systematic reinterpretation may be described as a process of *mouvance.* For Paul Zumthor, who pioneered the term, *mouvance* is a widespread phenomenon in medieval manuscript transmission. He defines it as a "quasi-abstraction" that becomes a reality in the interplay of variant readings in different

GREGORY NAGY

manuscripts of a given work; he pictures *mouvance* as a kind of "incessant vibration," a fundamental process of instability.[59] In another work, I have written extensively about this term, pointing out that there has been a great deal of *mouvance* even in the concept of *mouvance*.[60] Moreover, I suggest that the association of *mouvance* with "instability" may be misleading if it implies unsystematic change. To the extent that *mouvance* is the process of recomposition-in-performance in oral poetics, it is a stabilizing rather than destabilizing force.

It is pertinent here to consider the semantics of the word *mimēsis* (henceforth spelled "mimesis") in the older sense of "reenactment."[61] A driving idea behind this word is the ideal of stability in the reenactment of the "same" thing by a succession of different performers.[62] It is as if the composition remained always the same, even though the performers kept changing.[63] It is as if there were no change in the process of recomposition-in-performance.[64]

There are numerous examples in which the process of change in recomposition-in-performance is *not* recognized by a living oral tradition *as change*. A case in point is the following passage from Theognis:

Κύρνε σοφιζομένῳ μὲν ἐμοὶ σφρηγὶς ἐπικείσθω
  τοῖσδ' ἔπεσιν, λήσει δ' οὔποτε κλεπτόμενα
οὐδέ τις ἀλλάξει κάκιον τοὐσθλοῦ παρεόντος,
  ὧδε δὲ πᾶς τις ἐρεῖ· Θεύγνιδός ἐστιν ἔπη
τοῦ Μεγαρέως· πάντας δὲ κατ' ἀνθρώπους ὀνομαστός,
  ἀστοῖσιν δ' οὔπω πᾶσιν ἁδεῖν δύναμαι

"Kyrnos, let a _seal [sphrāgis]_ be placed by me, as I practice my
    skill [sophia],
upon these my words. This way, it will never be undetected if
    they are stolen,

184

and no one can substitute something inferior for the genuine
   thing that is there.
And this is what everyone will say: 'These are the words of
   Theognis
of Megara, whose name is known among all mortals.'
But I am not yet able to please [= verb handanō] all the
   townspeople [astoi]."   Theognis 19–24

I have written the following about this passage: "Like the code of
[a] lawgiver, the poetry of Theognis presents itself as static, un-
changeable. In fact, the *sphragis* "seal" of Theognis is pictured as
a guarantee that no one will ever tamper with the poet's words.
Outside this ideology and in reality, however, the poetry of
Theognis is dynamic, subject [like the law code of Lycurgus] to
modifications and accretions that are occasioned by an evolving
social order. And the poet is always there, observing it all—despite the fact that the events being observed span an era that goes
well beyond a single lifetime."[65]

With his "seal," the figure of Theognis is authorizing himself,
making himself the author. There is an explicit self-description of
this author as one who succeeds in *sophia,* the "skill" of decoding
or encoding poetry.[66] On the basis of this success, the author lays
claim to a timeless authority, *which resists the necessity of changing* just to please the audience of the here and now, who are
described as the *astoi* "townspeople."[67] The author must risk
alienation with the audience of the here and now in order to
attain the supposedly universal acceptance of the ultimate audience, which is the cumulative response of Panhellenic fame:[68]

οὐ δύναμαι γνῶναι νόον ἀστῶν ὅντιν᾽ ἔχουσιν·
οὔτε γὰρ εὖ ἔρδων ἁνδάνω οὔτε κακῶς·
μωμεῦνται δέ με πολλοί, ὁμῶς κακοὶ ἠδὲ καὶ ἐσθλοί·
μιμεῖσθαι δ᾽ οὐδεὶς τῶν ἀσόφων δύναται.

> I am unable to decide what disposition it is that the <u>townspeople</u>
>   [*astoi*] have towards me.
> For I do not <u>please [= verb *handanō*]</u> them, either when I do
>   for them things that are advantageous or when I do things
>   that are disadvantageous.[69]
> There are many who find blame with me, base and noble men
>   alike.
> But no one who is not <u>skilled [*sophos*]</u> can <u>reenact [*mimeisthai*]</u>
>   me.   Theognis 367–370

Here the notion of mimesis becomes an implicit promise that no change shall ever occur to accommodate the interests of any local audience in the here and now, that is, of the *astoi* "townspeople." The authorized reperformance of a composition, if it is a true reenactment or mimesis, can guarantee the authenticity of the "original" composition. The author is saying about himself, "But no one who is not skilled [*sophos*] can reenact my identity."[70]

Here we see an ultimate ellipsis, formulated by poetry about poetry, where an entire succession of performers is being shaded over in order to highlight a single "original" composition-in-performance, executed by a prototypical poet who eclipses all his successors.

(4) ELLIPTIC HOMER

We come now to the fourth and last question: how does Homeric songmaking use ellipsis to typify itself? A prime case in point is the Homeric "I," which highlights the prototypical singer of tales, elliptically shading over an open-ended succession of rhapsodes in the lengthy evolutionary process of countless recompositions-in-performance over time.

There is an Iliadic passage that reveals a symbolic reference to such a diachrony of rhapsodes. While Achilles, becoming the

ultimate paradigm for singers, is represented as actually performing the epic songs of heroes, *klea andrōn* "glories of men," at *Iliad*
9.189, Patroklos is waiting for his own turn, in order to take up
the song precisely where Achilles will have left off:

Τὸν δ᾽ εὗρον φρένα τερπόμενον φόρμιγγι λιγείῃ
καλῇ δαιδαλέῃ, ἐπὶ δ᾽ ἀργύρεον ζυγὸν ἦεν,
τὴν ἄρετ᾽ ἐξ ἐνάρων πόλιν Ἠετίωνος ὀλέσσας·
τῇ ὅ γε θυμὸν ἔτερπεν, ἄειδε δ᾽ ἄρα κλέα ἀνδρῶν,
Πάτροκλος δέ οἱ οἶος ἐναντίος ἧστο σιωπῇ,
δέγμενος Αἰακίδην ὁπότε λήξειεν ἀείδων

And they [the members of the embassy] found him [Achilles]
    delighting his spirit with a clear-sounding lyre,
beautiful and well-wrought, and there was a silver bridge on it.
He won it out of the spoils after he destroyed the city of Eetion.
Now he was delighting his spirit with it, and he sang the glories
    of men [*klea andrōn*].
But Patroklos, all alone, was sitting, facing him, in silence,
waiting for whatever moment the Aiakid would leave off singing.
                                                      Iliad 9.186–191

I have argued that both the plural usage here of *klea andrōn*
"glories of men" (as opposed to singular *kleos* "glory") and the
meaning of the name *Patrokleēs* are pertinent to the rhapsodic
implications of this passage: "it is only through *Patrokleēs* 'he who
has the *klea* [glories] of the ancestors' that the plurality of performance, that is, the activation of tradition, can happen."[71] So
long as Achilles alone sings the *klea andrōn* "glories of men,"
these heroic glories cannot be heard by anyone but Patroklos
alone. Once Achilles leaves off and Patroklos starts singing, however, the continuum that is the *klea andrōn*—the Homeric tradition itself—can at long last become activated. This is the moment
awaited by *Patrokleēs* "he who has the *klea* [glories] of the ances-

tors."[72] In this Homeric image of Patroklos waiting for his turn to sing, then, we have in capsule form the esthetics of rhapsodic sequencing.[73]

By contrast, the "I" of Homer, as in the first verse of the *Odyssey*, implies that it will always be Homer who is told the tale by the Muse and who will in turn continue to tell it each time he invokes her:

ἄνδρα μοι ἔννεπε Μοῦσα . . .

Narrate to me, Muse, . . .   *Odyssey* 1.1

Still, this "I" of Homer is interchangeable with a "we," as in the ἡμεῖς "we" of *Iliad* 2.486 or in the καὶ ἡμῖν "us too" of *Odyssey* 1.10, and I propose that such a "we" can refer elliptically to a whole vertical succession of performers.[74]

Still, no ellipsis can ultimately overshadow the lonely uniqueness of the performer when the vertical succession at long last reaches *him,* when *his* moment comes in the here-and-now of his own performance.[75] Though the present of performance, as Egbert Bakker notes, must be included into the "accumulated mass of the tradition,"[76] there must remain nevertheless "a certain distance" between the countless performances of the past and the unique performance of the present.[77] What must happen is a "reexperience."[78] The singer is just about to have such a reexperience when he says

πληθὺν δ᾽ οὐκ ἂν ἐγὼ μυθήσομαι οὐδ᾽ ὀνομήνω,	488
οὐδ᾽ εἴ μοι δέκα μὲν γλῶσσαι, δέκα δὲ στόματ᾽ εἶεν	489
φωνὴ δ᾽ ἄρρηκτος, χάλκεον δέ μοι ἦτορ ἐνείη,	490
εἰ μὴ Ὀλυμπιάδες Μοῦσαι, Διὸς αἰγιόχοιο	491
θυγατέρες, μνησαίαθ᾽ ὅσοι ὑπὸ Ἴλιον ἦλθον·	492
ἀρχοὺς αὖ νηῶν ἐρέω νῆάς τε προπάσας	493
But their number I could not tell nor name	488
(not even if I had ten tongues and ten mouths	489

and a voice that was unbreaking, and if a heart of bronze
    were within me)   490
<u>if</u> the Muses of Olumpos, of Zeus the aegis-bearer   491
the daughters, <u>did</u> not <u>remind</u> me,[79] how many came
    to Troy.   492
But *now* I will say the leaders [*arkhoi*] of the ships, and
    all the ships.   493

Iliad 2.488–493

All of a sudden, the singer steps out of the elliptic shade, and he
starts to sing . . .

Types of Orality in Text

WULF OESTERREICHER

The subject of the following article is orality in text. Although this term may seem paradoxical at first, the formulation reflects a fundamental distinction, which is discussed at some length in the first part of the article. In the second part, some examples from the field of Romance philology are given to show not only the applicability but also the importance of this distinction and the concepts associated with it. In the main part of my argument, a typology of orality in written texts is presented. This typology is illustrated by Latin documents, because these are easily accessible and generally well-known. Finally, the status of oral poetry and specific types of literacy with respect to orality in text phenomena are assessed.

I would like to emphasize that the problems of this topic are examined mainly from the point of view of variational linguistics and pragmatics. Nevertheless, the findings of anthropological research, arguments from the theory of communication, discourse analysis, and other disciplines have also been taken into consideration.

The juxtaposition of orality and text points to a crucial issue in the current orality/literacy debate. It is quite obvious that I am not using the term text in the sense of modern text linguistics, including all kinds of spoken and written discourses. Particularly when dealing with questions of orality and literacy, I find it mandatory to distinguish carefully between written texts on the one hand and spoken utterances on the other hand and thus to indicate whether a discourse is represented either in the graphic medium or in the phonic medium. Consequently, the term orality in the title of this article has nothing to do with the phonic realization of language. Rather, it is used to characterize the style or the mode of expression. Orality refers to the linguistic conception of discourse, as I prefer to call it. As we shall see, this conceptional aspect of language must be strictly differentiated from the medium aspect of language.

The overall distinction between linguistic medium and linguistic conception has been made by several linguists, although their definitions vary to some degree. Nevertheless, they all insist that the conceptional profiles of any discourse are, as a matter of principle, independent of the medium of discourse. Unfortunately, this fundamental insight has not been applied consistently; otherwise, a great deal of confusion in discussing orality/literacy problems could have been avoided. However, in French linguistics Ludwig Söll has made this distinction explicit by introducing two sets of terminological pairs: *code phonique* and *code graphique* to refer to the medium, and *langue parlée* and *langue écrite* to refer to the linguistic conception.[1] Similar distinctions are made by M.A.K. Halliday, Wallace Chafe, Elinor Ochs, Deborah Tannen, and other scholars. They use—more or less systematically—the terms spoken versus written to mark the medium-opposition, and terms like oral versus literate, informal versus formal, or unplanned versus planned to denote aspects of the linguistic conception.[2] In addition, Basil Bernstein's distinction between restricted and elaborated code reflects differences in linguistic conception, too.[3]

The necessity of making a distinction between medium and conception becomes evident when scholars play with the ambiguity of the generic terms oral and literate. In Italian and German linguistics this deliberate ambiguity is perfectly possible and currently employed.[4] Following the example of Giovanni Nencioni[5] a double combination of the terms *parlato* "spoken" and *scritto* "written" can be used to characterize, for example, an everyday conversation of two friends as *parlato parlato* and a legal document as *scritto scritto*. On the other hand, the delivery of a prepared paper would be a case of *scritto parlato,* and a letter to an intimate friend in an informal style could be classified, then, as *parlato scritto*. Without employing ambiguous terms, Niyi Akinnaso[6] maps out a similar two-by-two matrix with the following four categories: informal spoken, informal written, formal spoken, and formal written.

As these examples show, there is an awareness of the difference between medium and conception and even of mixed phenomena, which somehow resist a simple oral/literate classification. In this article I am concerned precisely with those phenomena which correspond to Akinnaso's class of informal written discourse or Nencioni's parlato scritto type. Although these double terms are quite helpful for identifying such mixed phenomena, the labels are nevertheless too simplistic. Because the interplay between medium and linguistic conception is even more complex than it may seem at first sight, I would argue that we need to discriminate further between different degrees or forms of parlato scritto—these I have called types of orality in text.

At this point it is important to note that the medial opposition between the phonic and graphic code represents a clear-cut dichotomy. The differences in linguistic conception, on the other hand, cover a whole continuous spectrum, ranging from extremely informal oral-type expressions to extremely elaborate, formal literate-type language. Between these two poles, innumerable intermediate degrees of linguistic conception are possible.[7] That is to say, the informal-formal distinction can be considered as no more than a first step in the right direction.

Although it must by now be obvious, I would like to stress again that in evaluating any particular utterance or text, we must treat the aspects of medium and conception independently, because the medium-distinction is a dichotomy and cannot reflect the scalar differentiations of linguistic conception. Furthermore, it will be shown that medium and conception are by no means of equal importance in determining the oral/literate status of discourse.

The last point can best be illustrated by looking at the example of primary oral cultures.[8] It should be noted that what is being dealt with here is a third field of reference to which the terms oral and literate have been applied.[9] With societies that have no recourse to writing, the medial dichotomy collapses, because the written dimension remains empty. Nevertheless, members of such communities do employ different conceptional strategies in different types of situations and utterances, such as familiar conversation, practical explanations, reports, riddles and proverbs, tales and poetry, political oratory, funeral dirges, religious and legal discourse.[10] Thus, even in oral societies we necessarily find a complete spectrum of linguistic conception, ranging from informal to formal utterances, although this spectrum is certainly not as extensive as in literate societies.

In order to avoid confusion of the terms orality/literacy denoting medial and cultural discussions, I prefer to rename the poles of the conceptional continuum by using the term language of immediacy *(Sprache der Nähe)* to designate the informal/oral type of linguistic conception and language of distance *(Sprache der Distanz)* to designate the elaborate/formal/literate type.[11] The choice of these metaphoric terms is further justified because they also shed light on the communicative conditions and the resulting strategies of verbalization that determine linguistic conception.

Although the following list is by no means exhaustive, it should indicate the parameters that characterize communicative conditions of immediacy and distance respectively. Except for the first one, they are all of a scalar nature:

1. face-to-face-interaction of partners versus distance in space and time
2. private versus public setting of the communicative event
3. familiarity versus unfamiliarity of the partners
4. context embeddedness versus contextual dissociation of a discourse
5. dialogue versus monologue
6. maximum versus minimum cooperation of partners
7. spontaneity versus reflexion
8. involvement versus detachment
9. free topic versus fixed topic[12]

Depending on the degree of immediacy or distance of these parameters, a speaker or writer will choose his or her communicative strategies. These strategies will again be marked by differing degrees of information density, integration, compactness, explicitness, complexity, elaboration, and discourse planning.[13] The linguistic conception is thus determined by a whole set of features, which make up the conceptional profile of discourse.

In addition, it should be observed that any particular utterance or text will necessarily conform with certain discourse traditions.[14] They function as historical models for discourse production and reception and thus always reflect a specific configuration of com-

municative conditions and strategies. Discourse traditions, in this
sense, have a distinctive conceptional profile. A list with examples
of idealized and stereotyped communicative events and discourse
traditions ranging from immediacy types to distance types may be
ordered as follows:[15]

  intimate conversation
  telephone conversation with a friend
  private letter
  counselling
  interview with a politician
  sermon
  university lecture
  editorial
  scientific article
  legal contract

There is great affinity between conceptional immediacy and
speech, on the one hand, and conceptional distance and script, on
the other. By no means, though, does this affinity invalidate the
fundamental rule: that medium and conception are independent
of each other. As such examples as the informal letter (conceptional immediacy and script) and the university lecture (conceptional distance and speech) show, there are also discourse
traditions that override systematically this affinity and constitute
"asymmetrical" forms, that is, the mentioned parlato scritto/infor-
mal written or the scritto parlato/formal spoken types.[16]

At this point a brief remark on the possibility of transcoding
discourse seems appropriate. As John Lyons has pointed out: "It
is possible to read aloud what is written and, conversely, to write
down what is spoken. In so far as language is independent, in this
sense, of the medium in which language-signals are realized, we
will say that language has the property of *medium-transferability*.
This is a most important property—one to which far too little

attention has been paid in general discussions of the nature of language." (1981:11) Simple medium-transcoding does not affect the conceptional content of discourse. As a matter of fact, it is precisely this property of language to undergo such processes of medium-transfer or transcoding that is the very condition of the existence of our orality in text problem.

This problem—and we can say now more precisely, the problem of immediacy in text—is of course not altogether new. But so far, either it has been widely neglected, or it has been dealt with—if at all—only in a most unsatisfactory way. Three examples from the field of Romance linguistics will serve to support this complaint. The discussion of these examples should also bring us closer to an understanding of what actually constitutes orality or immediacy in text phenomena.

The first example concerns the status of so-called vulgar Latin,[17] which is also referred to as popular Latin, spontaneous Latin, or spoken Latin *(Volkslatein, Spontanlatein, Sprechlatein)*. Some varieties of this nonstandard Latin also appear under the heading *sermo vulgaris, sermo cotidianus, sermo familiaris, sermo castrensis* (Latin spoken in the army), or *sermo piscatorius* (Christian Latin). It should be noted here that these terms are already used by Latin authors, who show by this use a clear perception of Latin varieties.

The knowledge of vulgar Latin is a central issue in Romance linguistics, for the Romance languages have developed out of this form of Latin and not out of literary or classical Latin. From a methodological point of view, the main question that still needs to be answered is this: "How can we recognize in the written documents the typical oral phenomena and the features of Latin varieties that represent communicative immediacy?" This recognition is an extremely difficult task because, as a matter of principle, we have to determine the totality of linguistic elements and procedures that are not written down, that normally do not appear in written texts. These elements differ, by definition, from what we know as classical or literary or written Latin (*klassisches Latein, literarisches Latein, Schriftlatein*).[18]

For the second example, not only in the case of vulgar Latin are more systematic analyses of conceptional profiles needed, but also there is the same need with respect to the first documents and the early *monumenta* of the Romance vernaculars.[19] The problem here is that the diglossic situation during the early Middle Ages prevented for a long time the emergence of texts written in Romance. Whenever such texts are available, they have almost inevitably been modeled on Latin texts and text traditions, and they exhibit the same characteristics of communicative distance. However, there is limited evidence of Romance forms and constructions of the immediacy type in the famous cartoonlike "speaking inscriptions," in legal documents that contain nonformulaic testimonies of witnesses, in spontaneous glosses in the margins of manuscripts (so-called *Federproben* "testing of the pen"), in lists and registers, and so on. Occasionally we can find traces of linguistic immediacy even in texts that belong to strictly distance-oriented discourse traditions such as parody.

What these examples are meant to show is that when an originally spoken discourse is written down and conserved graphically, this process does not in itself constitute a case of orality in text, since the mere process of medium-transcoding does not affect the conceptional profile of discourse; such written versions of spoken discourse cannot automatically be identified with language of immediacy.

It is rather conspicuous—and this is my third point—that linguistic manifestations of communicative immediacy have always been presented in a very derogative way by the authors of histories of the Romance languages. It appears that these authors are concerned with linguistic variation and communicative immediacy only with respect to the early stages of writing in the vernacular, when dialects with a limited communicative radius begin to enter the domain of Latin literacy. For the subsequent periods, these authors ignore the nonstandard varieties that show communicative immediacy and discuss almost exclusively the rise and elaboration of the language in question. The descriptions focus on the high variety that will function as national language, literary language, and standard written language. Only when the selection, elaboration, and normalization of a language variety remains problematic because of competing varieties does the discussion of these varieties remain important.[20]

We must conclude from this that the existing language histories are not histories of French, Spanish, Portuguese, Romanian, and so on but are very biased and partial historical descriptions of the elaborate and distance-oriented variety that develops or has developed into the standard form of the respective languages. As a consequence, examples of written texts that could serve as examples of discourses of immediacy are neither analyzed nor collected.

From the discussion of these examples, the following conclusions can be drawn: in every linguistic community we can recognize a series of descriptive linguistic norms that regulate dialectal (diatopic), social (diastratic), and situational (diaphasic) differences. The totality of these different varieties constitute what I call the variational space of a historical language.[21] However, only one of these varieties—as a rule—is used systematically in the domain of script and used to express communicative distance. This standardized form of the language, with high prestige and a wide geographical acceptance (communicative radius), is produced precisely by the historical process of selection, elaboration, and normalization, as I have indicated before. The use of this standard form, in fact, is inappropriate by definition in informal communication and discourse traditions of the immediacy type.

Now, the paradox of the formula orality in text is even more manifest: the only material available for a historical study of linguistic immediacy consists of written records, from which we can glean only indications, because in written communication—and this point is crucial—fully authentic renderings of linguistic immediacy will never appear. That is to say, texts of a strict immediacy type cannot exist. The reason for this situation lies quite simply in those communicative conditions that are potentially concomitant with the use of the graphic medium and are thus conducive to specific verbalization strategies. As indicated earlier, writing easily allows for a spatial and temporal separation of text production and reception, and it enhances planning, offers the possibility of correction and editing, including recourse to supplementary information; there is also a quasi-exclusive use of cotextual, that is, digitized information.[22] All these factors produce a filter that causes immediate forms of expression to be altered or eliminated from texts in the process of writing. Thus, it should not be surprising that all we can hope to find in written texts is merely indirect evidence: traces or indications of conceptional orality, the *disiecta membra* of the language of immediacy.

However, what can be encountered are, on the one hand, the features of linguistic immediacy resulting from the specific communicative conditions and strategies that do not appear in communicative distance; and, on the other hand, there are examples of the despised or prohibited diatopic, diastratic, or diaphasic varieties of the language.[23] In the section of this article that follows, I hope to show that the occurrence in text of phenomena corresponding to the immediacy type must be motivated quite differently. In fact, it is my conviction that not only in linguistics but also in all disciplines dealing with texts the following question is long overdue: "Why do linguistic elements, constructions, and procedures of the immediacy type occur in texts?" Any adequate appreciation of the relevance and the status of what I have called the orality in text phenomena will depend on the answer to this question.

EIGHT TYPES OF ORALITY IN TEXT

There are three points to start with. First, there follows a rough framework of eight types of orality in text and some relevant examples, whereby their respective communicative conditions and specific verbalization strategies will not be dealt with in detail. Such a substantiation would, however, be perfectly possible if we employed combinations of categories such as "linguistic competence of the writing person," "mastery of the norms of discourse traditions," "type of discourse tradition," "involvement of the writer," "planning intensity," and "aesthetic intention," as well as corresponding categories for the reception. Secondly, I want to emphasize from the outset that the phenomena under consideration cannot be deduced from discourse traditions. Nor is it sufficient simply to classify the linguistic features, because what may seem like the same oral phenomena on the surface have to be seen and interpreted differently with respect to the original motivations and the specific contexts. What is being proposed here, therefore, is not a collection and classification either of linguistic phenomena or of discourse traditions of the immediacy type. Instead, the focus is on a description of the underlying communicative constellations that control the production of such texts or text groups of the type labelled orality in text. Finally, it is not to be expected that the different types that are being introduced will present clear-cut limits; there are even overlapping phenomena and combinations of several types.

1. Writing by Semiliterate Persons

This type of orality in text would be produced by persons not familiar with the possibilities and the requirements of written communication. Such persons would not have mastered the linguistic variety appropriate for the intended text types, nor would they be acquainted with the required standards of text organization, the thematical and argumentative structures, and so on. The texts written by these semiliterate individuals—or the texts dictated by them in case they are unable to write personally—generally display linguistic elements and procedures that are, as a rule, alien to written communication: on the one hand, they show us the universal characteristics of the language of immediacy, for instance, anacoluthons, repetitions, and vagueness of referentialization or inconsistencies in deictic orientation; on the other hand, in these texts we find grammatical and lexical features of diatopic, diastratic, and diaphasic varieties that generally violate the norms of written communication. Moreover, it must not be forgotten that the notorious lack of certainty of such inexperienced writers concerning the linguistic and textual norms frequently leads, as a matter of course, to exaggerations, overadjustments, and ill-conceived imitation of higher stylistic norms, in short, to the known phenomena of hypercorrection.

Impressive examples of this type of orality in text (and of hypercorrections!) can be found in Latin inscriptions, especially in the famous inscriptions of Pompeii, and in the *defixionum tabellae* (spell tablets) of the different *provinciae* or in texts like the fourth century *Peregrinatio Egeriae ad Loca Sancta,* an account of a Spanish nun's journey to Palestine.[24]

2. Writing by Bilingual Persons in a Diglossic Situation

I am using here the term *diglossia* in the sense of Fishman[25] and not in the strict definition proposed by Ferguson in 1959. This second type of orality in text can be found in the writings of bilingual persons in a situation in which one language dominates the other. In those instances in which writers are not acquainted with the high variety of the dominant language, they tend to use nonexemplary varieties that are the only means available for them to express themselves linguistically. In those cases, too, the textual material requires cautious interpretation because we must expect linguistic interferences or even a mixing of languages.

The most interesting documentation of this type can likely be encountered in the private letters of Roman soldiers and veterans of second century C.E. Egypt, who lived in a diglossic situation, with Greek as the dominant language and Latin reduced to the area of private and familiar communication. The letters of two bilingual soldiers, Claudius Terentianus and Rustius Barbarus, who were stationed in the South of Alexandria, serve as an illustration.[26]

3. Relaxed Writing

Persons who are well trained and thus perfectly able to conform to all linguistic and textual norms need not, in all circumstances, write according to the prescriptions of written style. It is obvious that familiarity with the receiver as well as hurried or spontaneous writing processes are conducive to the use of elements of the language of immediacy. This style is most likely to occur in strictly private texts, for instance, personal notes and records or letters to close friends.

Such letters and certain types of Latin inscriptions, which show grammatical and lexical evidence of the colloquial, informal diaphasic register type, are examples of this type of orality in text.[27] It is important to note that simple errors and mistakes are *not* relevant indicators of immediacy. The phenomena must be significant either in the universal perspective or in the variational perspective of the language under consideration.

4. Records of Spoken Transactions

It should be noted first that records as such have no specific conceptional profile. As we have seen, medial transcoding makes it possible to represent phonic utterance of any type in script. Therefore, we must look for particular conditions that produce linguistic immediacy in texts. In the history of our languages there are, in fact, certain types of records with a high degree of the required features. I will mention only the word-by-word citations of curses that were transmitted as direct speech and legal texts that recorded insults and offenses of defamation. In addition to the other phenomena, these records are especially interesting because of the lexical material they display, such as diatopic and low diastratic examples of socially stigmatized expressive forms of coarseness and vulgarity.[28]

5. Writing Adjusted to Lower Competence of Readers

This type of orality in text refers to select cases in which the writer tries to adjust the linguistic expression to the intellectual capacities of his or her readers. Here, a writer who possesses the high competence and skill needed to formulate a precise and elaborate linguistic style is opting for expressions of the immediacy type for the sake of easier comprehension by the reader or in order to create a certain intimacy. This quasi-pedagogic strategy is frequently employed in written communication with children, simple-minded people, and also foreigners.[29]

6. Writing Subjected to "Simple" Discourse
Traditions or Genres

In the previous type, the decision of the writer to adjust his or her writing to the lower competence of the reader is a matter of individual choice. But such an orientation can also be a defining characteristic of a discourse tradition or text type. In this case, orality in text refers to communicative strategies that result from a strict orientation at conceptional simplicity of language and composition.

Here seem relevant the texts written by Christian authors[30] who, in order to reach the lowest social strata of the Roman Empire, frequently employed the so-called *sermo piscatorius* and other nonstandard varieties, following the advice of Saint Augustin: *Melius reprehendant nos grammatici quam non intellegant populi* (It is better that the grammarians should find us at fault, than that the masses should fail to understand us). Another example of this type are the numerous treatises by the so-called *scriptores rei rusticae,* authors dealing with practical matters such as agriculture, cattle breeding, veterinary medicine, or housekeeping.[31] Of special interest here are the cookbooks. In this context we may even adduce a passage from *De architectura* by Vitruvius, in which he urges his colleagues to use a linguistic expression near the *sermo cotidianus.* Otherwise, such highly specialized texts—because they use a lot of terminology and require a certain spatial imagination—would be incomprehensible: *non enim de architectura sic scribitur uti historia aut poemata* (one does not write about architecture as one writes history or poetry).[32]

7. Writing According to Plain Style Rhetoric

This is the first of two types of orality in text that are manifest mainly in the field of literature. In certain literary genres, authors employ intentionally a markedly simple language in opposition to what may be called linguistic mannerism, or rhetorical bombast. In general, this option is a reaction to rhetorical exaggeration and excessive artificiality. In other words, the *stilus humilis/stilus planus* is necessarily defined in a rhetorical and stylistic dimension, as is illustrated already in the *rota Vergilii.* In this sense it always represents a relative style,[33] and by this very condition it must never be simply identified with the expression of linguistic immediacy. It is characteristic of this style to draw on a number of features that have been conventionalized in a certain literary tradition in order to create the impression of naturalness, spontaneity, simplicity, and ease. This style is therefore aesthetically motivated and is not intended fundamentally as an imitation of the language of immediacy.[34] In Renaissance Europe this stylistic advice was condensed in the imperative formula "Write like you speak!"[35]

8. Mimesis of Immediacy or Simulated Orality

This second type of orality in text in the field of literature is sometimes referred to as "quotation of orality." As opposed to the "plain style" imperative that does not aim at imitation of concrete oral utterances but aspires to the linguistic expression of naturalness and simplicity, simulated orality incorporates linguistic material that is taken over directly from the language of immediacy. Such imitations of casual speech function as literary devices, that is, in a novel or a stage play, and feature the characteristics of people and their affective dispositions and mark communicative and dramatic constellations.[36] But the mimesis of immediacy can also be used in nonliterary writing, for instance, in pragmatic texts, in private letters, or in advertising, to provoke attention.

The evidence of the Latin texts is again striking. The comedies of Plautus are well-known; and the *Satyricon* of Petronius is a most remarkable instance of the mimesis of immediacy; especially the *Cena Trimalchionis,* which contains a caustic parody of the manners of uneducated, nouveau-riche people and a realistic evocation of the bilingual Latin-Greek environment in the South of Italy.[37]

It is important to note, however, that such a mimesis of the language of immediacy can never match *authentic immediacy.* The essential point is that we have to accept that it is always a matter of *simulation.* The author of the text, actually the linguistic consciousness of the author, will select specific linguistic elements, forms, and constructions of the universal or idiomatic type that are considered particularly characteristic of conceptional orality.

As a conclusion to this part of the article, I would like to emphasize the following points:

The eight types of orality in text just presented are based only on Latin examples, but, of course, the distinctions apply also to other literate communities or societies;

an adequate analysis of orality in text phenomena requires a precise description of the specific historical contexts of the communicative events;

diachronic research on linguistic immediacy should be based on these eight types; the results, however, must be checked against possible metalinguistic statements of grammarians;

it is necessary to distinguish whether linguistic and other textual features are universals or whether they result from contingent historical processes;

in diachronic studies, the classification of linguistic features as nonstandard varieties depends on a prior identification of the type of text in which they occur: thus, a phenomenon appearing in a text of a semiliterate or even illiterate soldier is more likely to be diastratically relevant than a feature appearing in relaxed writing;

this variational perspective demands that linguistic data have to be evaluated with respect to both the underlying discourse traditions and the relevant communicative constellations;

phenomena of orality in poetic or literary texts—and this is the central part of this article—must be examined with caution because they normally do not reflect spontaneous or natural language but functionalize select features of linguistic immediacy.[38]

STATUS OF ORAL POETRY

The theoretical framework having been established, a discussion of the status of oral poetry is now in order.[39] The eight types of orality in text will contribute considerably to our understanding of certain aspects of oral poetry. The central question that needs to be addressed in this context is, "What exactly is the oral in oral poetry?" Or more precisely, "What do the terms orality or oral features signify with respect to written epic poems?" As a first step to an answer to this problem, the conceptional profiles of epics in the framework outlined must be evaluated, that is to say, we have to assess the different parameters of communicative conditions and communicative strategies. All in all, there are at least five points that must directly or indirectly be considered:

1. production or composition of an epic poem;
2. linguistic and textual structure of epics;
3. modalities of communication of an epic discourse;
4. aspects of reception and audience interaction;
5. conditions of conservation and transmission of an epic poem.

Let us first examine the communicative conditions of oral poetry. Although epic poems can be composed either orally or in writing, their enactment or mise en scène typically occurs in a face-to-face-situation. It is this new concept of *communication-in-performance*—which differs from Parry's and Lord's *composition-in-performance*—that our analysis of oral epics has to start from; all other modes of transmission or conservation are only secondary or derivative. We must be aware, however, that this kind of face-to-face communication is markedly different from everyday conversation: in his performance the singer is speaking not as an individual to an individual but is addressing a whole audience in a public and formal setting.

Basically, this constellation conditions communicative distance.

Nevertheless, the communicative profile of such an oral performance is not fully defined by these dimensions. The actual degree of distance is determined by other factors, which can vary from performance to performance or can even change during the performance.

In illustrating his concept of time of integration *(temps d'intégration)*, Paul Zumthor has mapped out the scenario of two quite different performances of the Chanson de Roland, to show how the factors occasion, time, location, mood, and type of audience interact to generate a unique setting for any particular performance: he imagines, on the one hand, the singer standing up in front of the champions of the Battle of Hastings; and on the other hand, he envisions the singer in a castle, addressing the knights, unarmed, sitting by the fire, with their dogs at their feet, eating and drinking and merrymaking . . .[40]

The audience may or may not know the particular singer. We can, however, safely assume that they are familiar with the stories told on such occasions, because the poems performed were *never* narratives of some insignificant event but had to be sanctified by tradition. The performance of such known stories and themes was a fundamental means to establish and reaffirm group identity and thus was likely to arouse strong feelings and involvement on the part of the audience. The singers themselves usually insisted that they told their stories in the right order and in the right way. The topic of any given poem may thus be considered a fixed topic.

The performance itself is strictly monologic, although there is of course cooperation by the audience in that they pay attention, make comments, show emotional reactions, and give encouragement. They are, however, not involved in the actual discourse production, since there is no intentional turn-taking.

The singer, who is of course a *routinier,* a specialist, a professional, can and will react to signals by the audience or other circumstances at the time of integration and modify his tale to meet the demands of the momentary situation. This presence of mind that is tangible in all artistic improvisation is not to be confounded with the kind of spontaneity we meet in conversational dialogue. Thus, as far as the dimension of spontaneity versus reflexion is concerned, there is no significant difference between the oral and written composition of a poem, because the singer has memorized the poem, and the repertoire includes not only a number of variations but also rules for producing them.

If we consider the totality of the individual parameters defining the communicative conditions of an epic performance, we must conclude that this communicative event is clearly of a distance type, although not of extreme distance: it is a monologic discourse, a formal rendition of a fixed topic in a public setting. These factors outbalance the impact of cooperation and involvement in the epic face-to-face communication. However, this second set of features, which normally tend towards immediacy, weakens the degree of distance of an epic performance. These findings are corroborated by the analysis of the communicative strategies.[41]

For the sake of brevity the focus will be only on that aspect of communicative strategies that I consider most important: the creation and employment of contexts. As pointed out earlier, written communication is most successful when all relevant information is stated explicitly, that is to say: when it is transformed into linguistic cotext.[42] However, in oral communication a speaker may draw on various semiotic codes and situational contexts simultaneously to complement the linguistic message. And al though the performance of an epic is a distance-type discourse, these additional communicative channels are of course available to both the singer and the audience, who can so interpret, accentuate, or even modify what is being said. I am thinking here particularly of paralinguistic features such as intonation, rhythm, flow, speed, and pauses but also of nonlinguistic but communica-

tive contexts such as gestures, facial expressions, costumes, deco-
ration, or musical accompaniment. All these factors affect what
Zumthor has called *integrated time (temps intégré)*.[43] In addition,
the singer can rely on historical knowledge, convictions, and
values that he or she shares with the audience. These sociocultural contexts which are firmly rooted in the epic tradition, are
a prerequisite for an adequate understanding of the epic performance.

The parametrical values of communicative conditions and
strategies do not necessarily remain constant during any performance. As the singer proceeds, his or her familiarity with the
audience is likely to increase; the audience will show their approval or dislike of the rendition by changing degrees of cooperation and involvement, to which the singer in turn will react by
adjusting the tale or the mode of telling.

These adjustments and the resulting variations constitute the
mouvance of the epic discourse.[44] It would be wrong, however, to
consider this *mouvance* as a sign of deficient or low discourse
planning or of incomplete memorization. As we have seen, *mouvance* is produced by changes in the communicative conditions
during performance. Thus, *mouvance* is better understood as a
dynamic potential that the singer can activate, depending on the
singer's sensitivity, skill, creativity, and range of repertoire. In
order to do this successfully, the singer needs to be endowed with
a high communicative competence such as is required for master-
ing distance-type discourse. This is still true even if under certain
circumstances a singer consciously opts for communicative strategies of immediacy, for example, to achieve a greater emotional
impact on the audience.

Heinrich Lausberg has coined the two terms *Verbrauchs-Rede*
and *Wiedergebrauchs-Rede*,[45] which may also be quite helpful in
assessing the status of immediacy in an oral epic performance.

Roughly translated, these terms mean something like "self-consuming discourse" and "reusable discourse." The language of immediacy as it is used in a casual conversation would belong to the first category. The types of linguistic immediacy which we find in epic *mouvance,* however, are forms of reusable discourse, because any variations in the treatment of themes or formulations are not purely accidental but a matter of choice. Tradition has limited these choices and incorporated them as part of the repertoire. In addition, there are formal constraints, such as meter, rhythm, rhyme, and assonance that demand communicative strategies of distance.[46]

Because of their *mouvance,* oral epics or orally derived epics will never show the same degree of definiteness and reification that is characteristic of written or literate texts. However, although epic discourses are not fixed to the last word, the range of variation is quite limited. Thus, the *mouvance* of the epic discourse represents a mitigation of extreme distance, although it must never be identified with the provisionality of immediacy in colloquial or informal speech.

The next points to be considered are the so-called oral features in epic discourse and the question of in what sense they could be considered as examples of our orality in text types. The linguistic and discursive features in epic poems that are generally related to orality are the following:

use of formula and repetitions of narrative elements;[47]
use of *hic-et-nunc* deictic scenarios for the narrated episodes
     (*demonstratio ad oculos: here, there, now,* etc.);[48]
introduction of ego-based deictic relations in the narrative (*I/my,
     we/our;* personal pronouns and possessives);
use of present tense or nonmarked and relational forms;[49]
addresses of the audience and exclamations of the singer;
use of direct speech;

emotional expressions (similes, metaphors, etc.);[50]
syntactic phenomena such as segmentation, anacoluthon, ellipsis, and preference for paratactic construction.

Even at first glance it is clear that it would be difficult to identify these features with our types of orality. The respective difficulties in brief are as follows:

neither the author nor the singer of epic poems shows the type of deficiencies that we find in our semiliterate individuals, and this point is readily comprehensible because author and singer both produce highly artistic works;

the type bilingual persons in a diglossic situation may be discarded without discussion;

the communicative conditions of epics as poetry and reenactment of a performance-oriented discourse do not allow the relaxed verbalization type;

direct speech of epic characters has no affinity to the kind of natural speech that we find in records and transcripts of casual speech; it should be noted that epic characters speak normally with gravity and solemnity;[51]

the epic discourse is an elevated genre and does not correspond to our sketch of such discourse traditions that have as addressee the illiterate lower strata of society;

whatever types of stylistic simplicity we find in oral epics are not determined by antirhetorical plain style postulates;

the only type that may have some bearing on the problem is the last type, but even this type of simulation or mimesis of orality must be handled with care.

This result is not at all surprising if it is recalled that both oral epics and orally derived epics reflect communicative conditions of distance. On the other hand, they display features that are reminiscent of conceptional orality, such as casual conversation. But what does the existence of these so-called oral features in epic verse actually signify?

Contrary to current views in research, I believe that these features in oral epics are not intended as imitation or quotation of orality; they do not serve to increase verisimilitude. These poems functionalize differently the linguistic and discourse material that *may* correspond to features that are used in oral narratives or casual speech. That is to say, we have to accept a difference in theoretical status of the respective data.

An example from another field may serve as an illustration: for a long time scholars held that in medieval Spanish historiographic texts, asyndetic constructions and paratactic *et-et*-series in clause-combining reflected popular and oral origins and would thus be a reflex of linguistic immediacy. However, closer analysis has shown that these elements simply form part of the specific historio-graphic style of the period and have no conceptional implications of immediacy at all.[52]

From these observations we can deduce an important meth-odological rule: the previously mentioned linguistic phenomena are not sufficient to turn the scales in evaluating the complete conceptional profile of an utterance or text; immediacy-orienta-tion of a discourse or discourse type can be determined only by considering all the linguistic and textual dimensions. Such an examination shows that there is an overall functional principle organizing epics: repetitions and other intratextual references weave a dense network of shared knowledge, convictions, and beliefs. The presentation of the already known of tradition and group identity is further enhanced by the staged epic discourse and the strategies of highlighting the moment of the *we-now-here* in the performative act. The use of so-called oral formulaic style and of the features mentioned is here a very effective device to influence people by creating the impression of traditionality and authenticity. Epic performance thus proves itself a vital means for the social construction of reality and for controlling social dynamics.

However, we cannot conclude that writing epic poems is a

simple continuation of prior discourse traditions. There is also a strong possibility that epic poems were written not only for the preservation of tradition but also with a deliberate intent to modify or even manipulate existing traditions for new purposes. I see an analogon in the two versions in German and French of the Strasbourg Oaths that were composed to provide a linguistic basis for social identification and to reflect a new self-consciousness in the new post-Carolingian kingdoms.[53] Even if we do not take seriously the proposal to localize the *Cantar de mio Cid* in the early thirteenth century and accept that the author(s) were from a clerical or legal milieu in Burgos, there are strong indications that the *Cantar* was used for massive political purposes, especially religious propaganda for monasteries along the Santiago pilgrim's route and for "national" exaltation in the context of the Castilian *reconquista* of Arabic territories in the South.[54] Similar interpretations of the *Chanson de Roland* and other medieval epic texts are possible.[55]

It seems safe to conclude here that the epic word conserved in texts and put into action is not imitating conceptional orality or linguistic immediacy but instead is following oral derived formulaic traditions or is an imitation of such a style.[56] It is characterized by a series of specific linguistic features that create, by allusion to immediacy in the authentic performance, an atmosphere of confidence and solidarity. Determining exactly the varying functionalizations of epic form and poetic craft in specific historical contexts—that is the task that needs to be completed.

And my contribution—as a linguist—to this demanding task was, so to speak, "negative." The critical overview of the orality-problem and the examination of the applicability of the types of orality in text to epics were pursued with only one aim in mind: to prevent purely linguistic concepts from being overestimated and to encourage further investigation of the specific historical, sociocultural forms and the poetic effects of the epic word.

CHAPTER 9

The Medial Approach:
A Paradigm Shift
in the Philologies?

URSULA SCHAEFER

In their introductory essay to a collection of articles by Eric H. Havelock, Aleida and Jan Assmann speak of "the new paradigm 'Communication and Media.'"[1] Assmann and Assmann credit Eric Havelock with having given to the formula *From Mythos to Logos* the empirical basis of media science:[2] "The new idea which Havelock has elaborated on and varied in all of his works is that of the media dependence of thinking. Sense [*Sinn*], experience, reality—these are all variables of the media that we avail ourselves of. Anything that may be known, thought and said about the world is only knowable [*wissbar*], thinkable and utterable in dependence on the media which communicate this knowledge."[3] Assmann and Assmann see in Havelock's work the transformation of the "Relativity Theory of Language" as it had first been phrased by Wilhelm von Humboldt in the earlier nineteenth century and as it was further developed by Whorf and Sapir in the twentieth century into the "Relativity Theory of the Media": "Not the language in which we think, but the media in which we communicate, model our world. Media revolutions are sense revolutions, they re-model reality and create a new universe."[4] Havelock's achievements are thus characterized as being (1) based on a *new idea:* the media dependence of thinking. This "new idea" subsequently has led (2) to the *Relativity Theory of the Media.* With regard to further research, this theory has, moreover, provided the academic community with a new approach to a variety of problems, an approach that Assmann and Assmann have dubbed (3) the *"new paradigm:* communication and medium."

As is well known, the concept of the (scientific) *paradigm* and in particular that of *shifts* from one (scientific) *paradigm* to another as the result of a "(scientific) revolution" was first introduced by Thomas S. Kuhn over thirty years ago in his monograph *The Structure of Scientific Revolutions* (1962). However, in search of a firm and stable working definition of what Kuhn means by "paradigm" we find ourselves at a loss with the first edition. Kuhn himself provided a terminological clarification in the postscript to the second edition of 1969: "The term 'paradigm' is used in two different senses. On the one hand, it stands for the entire constellation of beliefs, values, techniques, and so on, shared by the members of a given [scientific] community. On the other, it denotes one sort of element in that constellation, the concrete puzzle-solutions which, employed as models or examples, can replace explicit rules as a basis for the solution of the remaining puzzles of normal science."[5] The central question that has often been advanced is whether it is legitimate to transfer this notion or concept developed in and for the natural sciences to the humanities.[6] And in view of the postulated new paradigm "Media and Communication" the question is all the more intriguing, as this very paradigm intends to account for that questionability itself.

The basic cognitive difference between the ways and means of the natural sciences *(Naturwissenschaften)* and the humanities *(Geisteswissenschaften)* was formulated by Wilhelm Dilthey around the turn of this century in the discussion of the systematization of the academic disciplines that the nineteenth century had produced. Dilthey characterized the endeavor of the sciences as that of *explaining,* while the arts aim at *understanding.*[7] As Jürgen Habermas has rephrased it in *Erkenntnis und Interesse* (1968): "we can *explain* given events with the help of law hypotheses on the basis of extrapolated primary conditions, while symbolic correlations are *understood* by reproductive explication."[8] What Dilthey furnished was the systematization of a cognitive diversification that started centuries earlier. Historically the first steps toward a problematization of textual understanding were made in the Reformation with the claim that the Bible may, as it were, speak for itself: *scriptura sui interpres,* "the Scripture is its own interpreter." In the present context it is particularly interesting to note that within the Medial Approach itself we may account for these beginnings of *hermeneutics.* David Olson has done so and thus provides an apt illustration of the explanatory power of this paradigm.

As David Olson has convincingly argued, the Reformation "rested . . . on a new conceptional distinction . . . [that] derived from writing and literacy":[9] "A written text preserves only part of language. What is preserved is the form, and the meaning has to be regenerated from that form by the reader."[10] More generally, Olson states: "Literacy created hermeneutics. The development of a distinction between statements and texts on one hand and their interpretation on the other was a consequence of literacy."[11] This has then resulted in a new set for the "reading of the *Book of Nature.*" As Olson delineates, "modern science was the product of applying the distinctions needed for understanding the book of Scripture, namely that between the given and the interpreted, to the book of nature," resulting in the distinctions "observation versus interference, fact versus theory," and so on.[12] Recast in Habermas' words, Olson gives an example of "explaining a given event"—here: the realization of the difference between reading and interpreting—"with the help of (law) hypotheses"—here: that of conceptual change (which Olson explicitly labels *a hypothesis*)—"on the basis of extrapolated primary conditions"—here: literacy (reinforced by print).

In claiming that the Medial Approach has caused a paradigm shift, however, not only do we cross the border whose delineation seems to have begun at the threshold of Modern Times, but also we imply that this shift may be regarded as a *revolution*. For reasons that would take further scrutiny, it is not this Medial Approach that has spread the sense of revolution in the humanities in general and literary studies in particular. The spectacular revolution in the last two decades or so was brought about by Deconstruction, this temporally concomitant, yet—at best—*faux ami* of the Medial Approach. It is Deconstruction that has, by now, epidemically put in question our established ideas as to how to conceive of processes of linguistic understanding. And so has the Medial Approach, which, however, has attracted little notice, one reason being that the Medial Approach has been of interest mainly to historical disciplines. Nevertheless, the Medial Approach and Deconstruction alike pose a threat to the "philological establishment," and this is so because both have—in their own ways—severely shaken the grounds on which philology and all other disciplines whose main material are texts have proceeded—or run in circles. Suffice it to stress here that what the two have methodologically in common is that they thematize how understanding and the media relate. Yet, in other ways the two approaches differ considerably.

Deconstruction tells us that any search for a "better" understanding of understanding (other than the "best understanding" that there is no such thing as "*ultimately* understanding") is a futile endeavor in the first place. As Stierle has put it: ". . . understanding has become the understanding that understanding has no bottom and no subject."[13] In other words, Deconstruction has radicalized the hermeneutic problem of "understanding under-standing" by trapping *what* we understand within the realm of language: *il n'y a pas de hors-texte*, the referent or transcendental signified is absent.[14] The Medial Approach, in its turn, does not ask so much *what* we understand but *how* we understand. It does so by insisting on the working hypothesis of the "media depend-ence of thinking," adducing good evidence that the "concepts basic to . . . our understanding of language are by-products of alphabetic literacy."[15]

In concentrating more on the cognitive *how* than on the *what,* the Medial Approach has an interface with—or may even be a part of—what has recently been termed *New Philology.* New Philology in its turn, R. Howard Bloch argues, overlaps with "the original spirit of philology in that both presuppose . . . the privi-leging of language over its referent in the production of meaning, which means that some attention is paid not only to *what* words mean but to *how* they mean. . . ."[16]

With this in mind, it might appear that our question of whether the Medial Approach is a new paradigm in the Kuhnian sense turns out to be immaterial to begin with. But I do not think so! We may, for the time being, have to concede that—in case we stick to the cognitive difference between the sciences and the humanities as delineated by Dilthey—our use of the notions *paradigm* and *paradigm shift* can only be metaphorical. Yet, whether the Medial Approach is only metaphorically a Kuhnian paradigm or not, its rise and further application have all the traits that Kuhn has named for scientific revolutions: "Led by a new paradigm, scientists adopt new instruments and look in new places. Even more important, during revolutions scientists see new and different things then looking with familiar instruments in places they have looked before."[17] The scandal for established philologists when they began to see those media-oriented "revolutionaries" at work was just this: the "revolutionaries" were still engaged in the familiar concern of understanding, and they were still doing so with the same texts; however; they were indeed seeing *new and different things.* To characterize these activities in more detail, I will delineate some of the heuristic consequences as they have arisen for medieval philological studies and then substantiate this with some examples from Old English studies.

MEDIAL HEURISTICS AND MEDIEVAL LITERARY STUDIES

It is not necessary to review here in greater detail the contributions that various disciplines have made with regard to findings on and insights into orality and literacy, both as ways of media-dependent types of communication and as cultural states dominated by these types of communication. Rather, I want to concentrate on heuristic consequences that some medievalists who have engaged themselves in the Medial Approach have drawn for their dealing with medieval poetry.

First and foremost is that these medievalists assume that the Middle Ages' transition from a prevalently oral culture at their beginning to a considerably more literate culture must have left traces in medieval verbal artifacts. Second, these medievalists share in the hypothesis that linguistic understanding and hence also linguistic encoding are functionally corollary to the respective cognitive conditions of orality and literacy. Third, they infer from this that their—*our*—own linguistic understanding, trained in and for fully developed literacy, is not necessarily identical to linguistic understanding in the "less literate" Middle Ages.

With these heuristic premises spelled out, we are still facing one basic problem: the philological medievalists' investigations have as their object *written* material. And this written material is, in itself, always a *primary* piece of evidence for literacy. In order to save the idea that this material may also contain "traces of orality," it suggests itself to take recourse to the concept of *transitionality*. I myself find nothing wrong with this concept as long as we make a difference between the physical medium and the encoding/decoding concept.[18] As far as the graphic and the phonic medium are concerned, we are dealing with an exclusive opposition. Things are different if we posit that orality and literacy gear different linguistic *en*coding and *de*coding processes. Then we must be prepared to find in the graphic medium, for example, poetry that leans more to the one or the other side for a period in which literacy has not (yet) completely effaced oral en-/decoding modes.

In medieval literary studies the discussion of "transitional texts" has referred particularly to the pervading formulaicness of vernacular poetry. Here the philologies have suffered for some time from a methodological fallacy. Because of an all too ready adoption of Parry's and Lord's empirically gained insight that oral heroic tales are highly formulaic, high formula density in medieval texts had, for quite some time, been taken as evidence for oral composition. By now, this claim has been thoroughly relativized, and we need not reiterate here the pros and cons that have been advanced in the discussion of the so-called Oral Formulaic Theory.[19] In the meantime it has proven much more useful to turn away from the question of text production to that of text reception. Thus, for medieval German poetry Franz H. Bäuml has, from a receptional stance, newly appreciated formulaicness in evidently "literate" poetry.[20] Moreover, many valuable insights have been furnished by John Foley for traditional epic narrative in Ancient Greek, in Old English, and in modern South Slavic.[21] I myself have attempted to examine Old English poetry from a receptional viewpoint, positioned within a cultural realm where the human voice was still prevalent.[22]

In view of the question of *how* oral-based poetic discourse functions semiotically, John Foley has introduced the useful notion of *traditional referentiality*. This notion has made us sensitive to a basic difference between the way meaning is encoded in traditional epic and in conceptionally written texts: "The key difference lies in the nature of tradition itself: structural elements are not simply compositionally useful, nor are they doomed to a 'limited' area of designation; rather they command fields of reference much larger than the single line, passage, or even text in which they occur."[23] Certainly from the point of view of Poststructuralism this "traditional referentiality" works the same way as does signification in a literate text: it ties one signifier only to yet another signifier. However, this does not invalidate Foley's point. Moreover, it is basically due to this *traditional* referentiality (albeit from signifier to signifier) that—once literacy had taken over in medieval poetry—this traditional language may be assigned the new function that Franz H. Bäuml has illustrated with regard to Middle High German poetry. In oral epic, "formulism" serves, among other things, according to Bäuml, "the cultural memory by providing culturally essential links to the tradition which it formulates."[24] Bäuml continues: "In written composition thematic and lexical stereotypes . . . *necessarily* serve a referential function: they refer to a specific type of text, the oral text, and thus represent, without being part of, the convention which lies behind the written text."[25] Both referentialities, the traditional oral (or oral-based) one, and the one constituted in written texts, are "ultimately" intertextual. Yet with the second type the "distinction between the intelligible and the sensible"[26] comes to the fore and may thus be semiotically functionalized.

In the following I want to turn to a very specific type of "traditional language"; gnomic diction as it occurs in Old English poetry. Gnomic diction may be regarded as a specific type of formulaicness that has persisted to the present day, and whose occurrence in Old English poetry may be taken as an indication of a way of encoding and decoding meaning that is not of the literate, the *textual* sort (nor in *our* continued use of gnomic diction). I suggest that the use of gnomic diction is the most extreme case of formulaic language being most idiomatic and least free in terms of syntactic construction.[27]

I think that the use of gnomic diction in Old English poetry is particularly amenable to an application of the Medial Approach to medieval vernacular texts. Gnomic diction highlights the social function of language, a function that seems, as we may note in passing, not of great interest to Poststructuralism. I fully agree with Gabrielle Spiegel who, along with John E. Toews, has made the following observation concerning the contemporary methodological discussion: "What gets lost in the concentration on meaning in place of experience is the sense of social agency, of men and women struggling with the contingencies and complexities of their lives in terms of the fates that history deals out to them and transforming the worlds they inherit and pass on to future generations."[28] An integral part of this "social agency" *is* language, "doing things with words" (despite the detrimental judgment Deconstruction has passed on Speech Act Theory[29]), and one very specific way of linguistic social agency is the use of gnomic diction.

As regards the social aspect of linguistic communication Egbert Bakker has made the following general observation: "As far as involvement and rapport are concerned, anything is permitted, even saying things that have to be categorized in the conceptual system of Western informational semantics as 'old' information and therefore dull . . . What matters to speakers . . . is the establishment of a common ground . . ."[30] Formulaic diction may be regarded as linguistically congealed "old information" that, by its quality of being formulaic, reiterated, carries the (positive) mark of being just this: "old," "traditional" information. As Deborah

Tannen has pointed out, formulaic expressions "signal knowledge that is already shared," they are "a convenient tool to signal already shared *social* meaning."[31]

GNOMIC DICTION IN OLD ENGLISH POETRY

There have been numerous attempts to define gnomic expression.[32] I adopt a description by Harald Thun that focuses on the proverb in context and may be considered to hold for all gnomic diction: "Generally speaking, the function of proverbs in their concrete use in texts and situations may be characterized as that of *commenting*. Proverbs are not integrated into the description or presentation as are other, ordinary text segments. They rather interrupt the descriptive sequence with a meta-statement, and that is: with a comment."[33] With this in mind it is interesting to look at how gnomic passages are situated in Old English poetry.

For one thing we find a number of gnomic or proverbial passages in the epic *Beowulf*.[34] They are uttered either by the narrator or by the characters within the epic. Secondly, *gnomai* occur at prominent places in the so-called Old English Elegies, that is, in those seven rather short poems that have a first-person speaker lamenting about past joys and present hardships. And thirdly, we have two collections of *gnomai,* or maxims. The larger collection (205 lines), usually referred to as *Maxims I,* has come down to us in the Exeter Book, the codex in which also the seven "elegies" have been preserved. The smaller collection (66 lines), *Maxims II,* has come down to us in MS Cotton Tiberius B.i. I will, however, leave these collections out of consideration because they do not contribute much to the point I want to make here.

Let us first look at a frequently discussed gnomic passage from *Beowulf,* the so-called "Christian Excursus."[35] This passage has drawn the attention of critics because it explicitly refers to the Christian God. This fact is remarkable because the epic may otherwise be characterized as rather a-Christian. The preceding context of the "Excursus" is the following: the Danish king Hrothgar has built a beautiful hall which is named Heorot ("Hart"). This building and the resounding joy and feasting cause the rage of the monster Grendel that attacks the hall and kills many of Hrothgar's retainers. In their grief the survivors worship their "heathen" idols because[36]

> Swylc wæs þeaw hyra,
> hæþenra hyht; helle gemundon
> in modsefan, Metod hie ne cuþon,
> dæda Demend, ne wiston hie Drihten God,
> ne hie huru heofena Helm herian ne cuþon,
> wuldres Waldend.   *Beowulf* 178b–183a

> "Such was their custom,
> the hope of the heathen; they remembered Hell
> in their deepest thoughts. They knew not the Lord,
> the Judge of our deeds, were ignorant of God,
> knew not how to worship our Protector above,
> the King of Glory."

The "Christian Excursus" immediately follows:

> Wa bið þæm ðe sceal
> þurh sliðne nið sawle bescufan
> in fyres fæþm, frofre ne wenan,
> wihte gewendan! Wel bið þæm þe mot
> æfter deaðdæge Drihten secean
> ond to Fæder fæþmum freoðo wilnian!   *Beowulf* 183b–188

> "Woe unto him
> who in violent affliction has to thrust his soul
> in the fire's embrace, expects no help,
> no change in his fate! Well is it with him
> who after his death-day is allowed to seek
> the Father's welcome, ask His protection!"

Evidently the *woe*-part (183b–186a) is a general comment on the eschatologically desolate situation of the heathen Danes. It is a narrator's comment in which he steps, as it were, out of the narrative flow and looks at those Danes from a commenting distance. It is the same distance from which the narrator implicitly comments on his Christian audience, that may find itself, in the *well*-part, reassured of the Father's welcome and His protection. Thus narrator and audience may meet in the gnomic "common place."[37] As the late Paul Zumthor has generally remarked with regard to formulaic diction in medieval poetry:

> Formulaicness embraces the [poetic] discourse as such, even more so than its linguistic organisation, and, in its putting into practice, it concerns the performance rather than the composition: this is the function of the *places* or *topoi*, which originally belonged to the rhetorical *memoria* and the *actio* . . . The *common place* has the function of bringing closer to the listener the *materia remota* of the discourse, making a content more concrete, avoiding, nevertheless, all particularisation . . .[38]

The very same observation holds for the occurrence of *gnomai* in the Old English Elegies. As one example I take the shortest but also most obscure of these poems, usually entitled *Wulf and Eadwacer.* Here a female persona laments over her being separated from a man by the name of Wulf. Towards the end of the poem the woman persona addresses another man by the name of Eadwacer (who may be her husband, whereas Wulf is her lover—or vice versa). Most critics agree that the "wretched cub" of line 16 is the speaker's and Eadwacer's child:[39]

> wulf min wulf wena me þine
> seoce gedydon þine seldcymas
> murnende mod nales meteliste
> gehyrest þu eadwacer uncerne ear[g]ne hwelp
> bireð wulf to wuda   *Wulf and Eadwacer* 13–17

"Wulf, my Wulf, it was my hopes of thee,
thy constant absence and my mourning heart,
that made me sick—not from lack of food.
Dost thou hear, Eadwacer? Our wretched cub
Wulf will bear to the forest."

And immediately following we get the laconic closing lines:

þæt mon eaþe tosliteð þætte næfre gesomnad wæs
uncer giedd geador.   *Wulf and Eadwacer* 18–19

"What never was united is easily torn asunder—
our song together."

There is a touching ring about these lines as they seem to resound an anthropological constant of deeply emotional relationships between women and men. So do the closing lines of the other elegy with a female persona, called *The Wife's Lament,* where the persona bewails the separation from and/or loss of a man (two men? three men?):[40]

wa bið þam þe sceal
of langoþe leofes abidan.   *Wife's Lament* 52b–53

"Woe befalls him who must
wait with sad longing for his beloved."

In both poems these concluding lines also touch the modern reader. In any case, they are poignant generalizations—literally—"bottom lines."[41] Just by their occurring at the very end, they—by contiguity to what precedes—sum up what is in the respective poems, or rather, what the poems are about.[42] They do, as such commenting *gnomai* always do, not *interpret* the poems, they do not unfold, explicate their meaning, but rather wrap up the poems in a concise—gnomic and hence socially relevant—general formula.

If we can agree on the assumption that proverbial diction is a transcultural phenomenon of linguistic encoding availing itself of preconceived significance, we may draw from these few examples the conclusion that they represent a clue to how meaning was conveyed and meant to be retrieved in these poems.[43] This way of conveying and retrieving meaning cuts across the way with which we are familiar in our literate world: *we* are trained to encode the meaning *in* the text and are hence wont to retrieve the meaning *from* the text.[44] This method is—with all that we know now—the literate way, the way of literacy. The abundant number of explications of both *Wulf and Eadwacer* and *The Wife's Lament* are excellent illustrations of the failure of this method with verbal artifacts whose organization is not textual, where the meaning is not encoded in the text to begin with.[45]

In his discussion of the "Dimensions of Understanding,"[46] Karlheinz Stierle has remarked that one "can *only understand* a [literary] work, but one can *never have understood* it."[47] This is why Lausberg ([2]1973) speaks of such discourses as *Wiedergebrauchs-Rede,* "reusable discourse."[48] We may surmise that once the contemporaneous recipients have come to the bottom lines of the two Old English Elegies that I have briefly presented here, they *have understood* the poems' messages, and that they would yet "reuse" these poems—exempla that they are—as much as they would "re-use," say, the epic *Beowulf.* This amounts to postulating that the classification of these texts as aesthetic, literary texts does not apply.

Here we appear to come close again to Deconstruction. Is not the categorical differentiation of literary and nonliterary texts denied by Deconstruction all the way along? Yes, but Deconstruction abolishes the distinction for *all* periods and cultures. I want to do nothing of this sort. In saying that texts such as the ones we have looked at may be "understood," "consumed," "used up," and, at the same time, "be reused" again, I want to argue only that the distinction literary/fictional versus nonliterary/nonfictional is not a relevant one for each and every culture and period. And it will not be surprising if I further claim that the rise of fictionality correlates with the expansion of literacy.[49]

CONCLUSIONS

A fundamental difference between philologists who accept that the production of any discourse is medium-conditioned (including all the consequences accompanying this conditioning), and those who do not accept this, is that the former are able to spell out their working hypotheses and that they can make these hypotheses intersubjectively accessible. In my initial glance at the epistemological separation of the sciences and the humanities at the turn of the nineteenth to the twentieth century, it may be noted that when the philologies were first established as academic disciplines in the nineteenth century, they aspired at a cognitively equal ranking with the sciences. What was intersubjectively accessible was the material analysis of their objects: texts. This was the positivistic stance that partially survives in the philologies to the present day, in spite of numerous attempts to reveal it as such. A text was (and for some still is) a given, a fact,[50] or at least something that contains facts that only wait to be uncovered. For the philologies of the nineteenth century the ideal of *Wissenschaftlichkeit* really meant proceeding *scientifically* (or getting as close to this as one possibly could). Notions such as *sound laws* make this obvious.[51] If nothing else, "positivistic philology" in the twentieth century has learned from the epistemological discussion that striving for this kind of *Wissenschaftlichkeit* leads to all kinds of cognitive fallacies. And it seems to me that it is due to this lesson that "established philology" often quite vehemently turns against the Medial Approach.

There are—unfortunately—good reasons for this kind of reaction because within the Medial Approach there has, in fact, been the tendency to elevate some observations to the status of laws or (more moderately) rules. An example is that of certain publications from the initial stages of Oral Formulaic Theory. Not only was the observation that "all orally composed narrative poetry is formulaic" reversed into "all formulaic poetry is orally composed"; one even started statistically to prove that certain pieces of poetry must be orally composed because they have a "formula density" of a certain ratio.[52]

Another necessary *caveat* concerns conclusions by analogy, in particular where historical developments are concerned. It may seem particularly tempting, for instance, to discern analogies between medieval and classical philology. Both disciplines analyze cultures with historically increasing literacy. However, the discussions of the group of classical Greek philologists and medievalists who gathered in Washington, D.C., as guests of the Center for Hellenic Studies in June 1994 revealed, among many other valuable insights, that our notion of "transition from orality to literacy" needs a thorough reconsideration for each and every culture and/or period, since the course of such a transition depends on many historically specific intra- as well as extra-medial variables.

A large number of points could be added here, all of which would contribute to an increased awareness that we need to monitor our assumptions and hypotheses. It is the intriguing specificity of the Medial Approach that it should teach us to realize that at least some of our assumptions are conditionally related to the material that we are dealing with. This *is* a *discovery*,[53] yet I dare not decide whether it just *equals* or indeed *is* a scientific one.[54] In any event, this discovery has made us look from a different perspective at familiar things at which generations before us also looked—but now we understand these things differently. Moreover, by assuming this new perspective, we also see things that have gone unnoticed before.

To come to a preliminary close: there certainly is a scholarly community sharing a "constellation of beliefs, values, techniques, and so on"—one of Kuhn's senses of a *paradigm*—working with the hypothesis of the media dependence of human cognition. However, this community does *not* avail itself of any "concrete puzzle-solutions which, employed as models or examples, can replace explicit rules as a basis for the solution of the remaining puzzles of normal science"—as Kuhn paraphrased the second of his notional uses of *paradigm*.

The conference, to which an oral version of this essay was—chronologically speaking—the first contribution, added much to the realization that the Medial Approach does anything but furnish "rules to the solution of remaining puzzles"; however, at the same time it may have contributed to having enlarged the scholarly community of those who consider the Medial Approach to be a road to a new understanding of the objects of our scholarly curiosity, be these scholars just visiting or committed members.[55]

NOTES

INTRODUCTION

1. For a useful survey see Foley 1988.
2. Defined, famously, as "a group of words which is regularly employed under the same metrical conditions to express a given essential idea" (Parry 1971:272, cf. Parry 1971:13).
3. See the bibliographical surveys in Foley 1985, Edwards 1986, 1988. The most recent survey of formula research since Parry is Russo 1997.
4. An important (if perhaps overstated) example is Griffin 1980:xiv. Cf. also Bremer et al., eds. 1987.
5. The phrase is borrowed from Morson and Emerson 1990:127, in a discussion of Mikhail Bakhtin's ideas on "dialogism." "Joint creation of the word" is now a growing interest in linguistics (where such disciplines as pragmatics and sociolinguistics challenge the formalist orthodoxy) as well as in literary criticism (reception theory and reader-response criticism redirecting attention away from author's intention as the sole factor of the communicative process).

1. STORYTELLING IN THE FUTURE

1. For general overviews of this development in folklore studies and anthropology, see Bauman and Briggs 1990; Goodwin and Duranti 1992.
2. On repetition and tradition in epic discourse against the background of ordinary speech, see Bakker 1996.
3. Comrie 1985:9; cf. Fleischman 1990:15.
4. Chafe 1994:195ff.
5. Chafe 1994:207–10; 215–219. On direct discourse as a strategy to effect involvement and vividness in conversational narrative, see also Tannen 1989:98–133; on the historical present, see Wolfson 1982, Fleischman 1990:75–81.

6. See Détienne 1967:9–27. On "social memory" see Fentress and Wickham 1992.

7. See Ford 1992:54–55, 75–76, 125–130; Bakker 1993b:15–18; 1996 Chapter 4.

8. Fleischman 1990:273.

9. An old observation, cf. Munro 1891:65, Chantraine 1963:191.

10. Cf. the earlier discussion in Bakker 1993b:17. On *ara* in general see Grimm 1962.

11. Notice also the use of the "proximal" demonstrative *tode* in *Iliad* 344–345, marking objects of perception right before a speaker's eyes.

12. Basset 1979. The French phrase is from Ruijgh's review of Basset's study (1985:323).

13. Note that *mellein* is frequently used in combination with the "subjective" particle *pou* (e.g., *Iliad* 2.116; 9.23=14.69; 10.326; 13.225–226; 18.326; 21.83; 24.46), which underlines the necessarily "subjective" nature of this verb: *mellein* is the verbalization of what is evident to a consciousness.

14. See Martin 1989. During the final revision of this paper the discussion in Crotty 1994 came to my attention. Crotty's insisting on the importance of commiseration and supplication as performed by characters for Homeric poetics at large is especially relevant for the analysis of Patroklos' speech presented later.

15. See Nagy 1979:94–117, Crotty 1994:15–16.

16. See also Kahane's paper in this volume.

17. See, e.g., Hymes 1981, Zumthor 1990b:49.

18. See Schechner 1985.

19. As far as the performer is concerned, this point centers on the degree to which the experience of "self" is displaced by other mental states, a question with neurobiological interest; see, e.g., d'Aquili et al. 1979.

20. On apostrophes of characters as a regular strategy in other performance traditions, see the article of Martin in this volume.

21. Another example is the way (also often involving *ara*) in which *similes* are rounded off, characterizing the image as evidence experienced "here and now."

22. See Foley's 1991 ideas on the tradition as referent ("traditional referentiality"); see his contribution to this volume. Communicative aspects of the formula are discussed in Schaefer 1992:59–87, and in

this volume. On formulas and "old information" see also Bakker 1993a.

23. Cf. Chantraine 1958:479, van Leeuwen [2]1918:257–258; a useful overview of this older discussion is offered by Basset 1989:11–13.

24. E.g. Meillet [8]1937:243; Lehmann 1993:165, 178–180.

25. See Lehmann 1993:176–181.

26. Lehmann 1993:180.

27. Cf. also West 1989b.

28. The difference between similes and narratives in terms of discourse mode fits in with the differentiation in terms of performance genre offered by Martin in this volume.

29. On the basis of this observation Basset 1989 suggests that the distribution of the augment in Homer can be explained on the basis of Benveniste's distinction between "discours" (subjective, evaluative) and "récit" (the 'objective' discourse of the narrator).

30. Note that *mellein* almost always has the augment, as befits a sign of the "near."

31. On this question, see Schein 1984:62–63, Janko 1992:4–7.

32. Nagy 1979:134–135; 265–268.

33. *Iliad* 20.336. Poseidon's intervention takes the form of a narrative moment articulated as "And now Aineias would have perished *if not* Poseidon . . ." (*Iliad* 20.290–291). Last-minute rescues against all odds are a favorite way for Homeric narrative to (re-)assert its own tradition. See Bakker 1996 Chapter 7.

34. Cf. also *Iliad* 3.352–354; 6.357–358; 22.304–305.

35. Segal 1983.

36. Ruijgh 1985:332n11.

37. One might further think of *melos,* "song," as being related as well. In the discussion following the presentation of this paper, Richard Martin also mentioned possible connection with *melēsigenēs,* the traditional "name" of Homer (see Lesky 1967:4). Parallels for *melein* in the sense proposed here include the epithet *pasimelousa* (in the mind of all people, *Odyssey* 12.70) and *Theognis* 245–246, a remarkable passage involving also *kleos* (245) and the future (251).

38. Edmunds 1990.

39. In connection with the relation between *nēpios* and poetic truth, note that in Hes. *Theog.* 236 its alleged etymological counterpart *(ēpios)* occurs in combination with qualifications for "truth" for

Nereus. Cf. Détienne 1967:29ff. One also wonders whether, by way of folk etymology, a relation between *nēpios* and *epos* (word, poetic speech) would not be possible in the implicit poetics of the epic tradition, the *nēpios* being the "non-poet" *par excellence*. Note in this connection that Patroklos, the quintessential *nēpios* in the *Iliad*, is characterized by his *silence*, cf. Kahane 1994:139.

40. E.g., Hdt. i,32; Soph. *Trach.* 1–3; *OT* 1528–1530.

2. WRITING THE EMPEROR'S CLOTHES ON

The research for this paper was to a large extent done during the 1991–92 fellowship year at the Netherlands Institute for Advanced Study at Wassenaar. I am greatly indebted to NIAS for the opportunity to work on this and other projects.

1. Iser specifically refers to "literary texts," which he distinguishes from "non-literary texts" by the manner in which the text's mimetic function, however minimal, is perceived to be broken, rendering it "indeterminate" at the break, and leading the perceiver to participate in establishing its significance according to prevailing conventions. However, any text has a mimetic function, however minimal, which can be shown to be broken. I therefore take the statement to refer to all texts.

2. I am indebted to Professor Oesterreicher for this suggestion.

3. I am grateful to Professors Deborah Lyons and Wulf Oesterreicher for this observation.

4. The "official" character of the *Annales Regni Francorum* is now generally accepted. It was first convincingly demonstrated by Ranke 1888:115; see also Wattenbach, Levisohn, Löwe 1953:II.246–247. Among contemporaneous users of the *Annales* were Charles's biographer Einhard, Nithard in his *Histories*, the Poeta Saxo, the biographers of Louis the Pious, and the other annals of the ninth century. Its use in court circles is therefore evident.

5. A similar process of prefabrication, by means of traditional formulism and thematic patterns, occurs in the oral tradition, where, however, it is embedded in narrative. For the role of lexical and thematic stereotypes in the "Weitergabe von bereits kollektiv Bekanntem," see, above all, Ursula Schaefer [1992:passim].

6. One cannot, of course, speak of a systematic collection of data in

connection with Carolingian record-keeping, but the production of the *Annals* is itself evidence of such record-keeping. Undoubtedly it is true, as McKitterick (1977:20) observes, that there is "little evidence to suggest in fact that the Frankish king possessed the bureaucratic structure necessary for rule and administration on a large scale by means of the written word." However, the capitulary of Aachen (802) alone makes it obvious that Charlemagne's efforts were aimed at establishing just such a structure. By 813 archives were certainly kept at the palace, where, according to the *Annals*, copies of the canons of the councils of Tours, Mainz, Rheims, Chalons, and Arles were deposited (see the *Annals* under the year 813). But the constant movement of the imperial court inevitably led to losses. In 829, for instance, Louis the Pious had to refer to the private collection of capitularies of Abbot Ansegis of St. Wandrille, who in any case had only succeeded in gathering fewer than a third of the capitularies known to have been issued by 827 (Mühlbacher 1896:263–264; Bresslau 1912:164–165). McKitterick (1989:35; 1983:126) suggests that Ansegis's collection may represent a contemporaneous selection of those capitularies deemed most important. If so, it presupposes a process of selection from a mass of documents that itself was available somewhere. If, however, her earlier surmise is correct, that Ansegis's collection represents all the capitularies on which he could lay hands [McKitterick 1977:21], then this indeed "speaks volumes for the general availability of Capitularies and the resources of the palace archives." In any case, he must have seen some point in making such a collection, which itself argues for the usefulness of its contents. For a lucid and critical survey of Carolingian literacy as social practice, see Nelson (1990: 258–296).

7. The same, of course, applies to the early medieval oral tradition, in comparison to which the written data are quantitatively insignificant. The "items" of knowledge transmitted by the oral tradition are embedded in narrative to be told as "truth"; see also note 5 above. I am grateful to Professor Ursula Schaefer for a thorough discussion of this issue.

8. Chronicles, of course, are not annals; as narratives of events, they served a more general memorial function than annalistic listings. Nevertheless, the countless instances of forgery and falsification in

chronicles indicate that they were also viewed as records in the same sense as annals. To the extent that a chronicle is a narrative, it can be performed and assume "presence." An embedded genealogy, therefore, would have the same possibilities as the catalogue of ships in the *Iliad:* in the context of the chronicle it could be performed; lifted out of that context, it would be a series of "facts." Their performance would foreground the performer rather than the matter performed. I am grateful to Professor J. Clay for raising the issue of genealogies in chronicles and oral narratives in the discussion following the oral presentation of this paper.

9. "Swer nû welle bewaeren,/daz Dieterîch Ezzelen saehe,/der haize daz buoch vur tragen" (14,176–14,178), and "Do der chunic Ezzele ze Ovene wart begraben,/dar nâch stuont iz vur wâr/driu unde fierzech jâr,/daz Dieterîch wart geborn" (14,179–14,182) (Schröder 1892:337–338).

3. TRADITIONAL SIGNS AND HOMERIC ART

This paper represents a prolegomenon to a more extensive study of Homeric poetics, tentatively entitled *Reading Between the Signs: Homer and Oral Tradition.*

1. *Tradition* is of course a notoriously difficult concept that has received many definitions; see espec. Dan Ben-Amos's comments on the "seven strands" of tradition (1984). I use the term in this essay to refer to at least three of his seven possible (and interlocking) senses: as process, as canon, and as *langue.* For further specification, see Foley 1990, 1991, 1992.

2. For a thorough discussion of metonymy in traditional oral art, see Foley 1991: espec. chs. 1, 2, 5. Let me explicitly acknowledge two recent studies of *sēmata* that have been of assistance in my own thinking about this resonant poetic term. The first (Nagy 1990b:202–222) focuses on showing that "the semantics of *sēma* are indeed connected with the semantics of thinking" (202), while the second (Ford 1992:131–171) concentrates on the fixity of signs, especially in the *Iliad,* but also notes very helpfully that "the oral tradition is the necessary supplement to the durable, provocative, but unreadable sign" (144).

3. Compare Martin 1989: espec. 12–18 on the distinction between *muthos* and *epos,* metonymic tags that identify speech-acts according to their illocutionary force; also compare Kahane, elsewhere in this volume, on the metonymic semantics of *oios* and *mounos.*

4. For a bibliography and history of this rediscovery, see respectively Foley 1985 (with updates in the journal *Oral Tradition*) and 1988; on ancient Greek in particular, see Edwards 1986, 1988, 1992. I will hold citation of other scholarship to a minimum, referring the reader to these sources for that purpose.

5. See espec. Murko 1929 (trans. 1990) and 1951; Radlov 1885 (trans. 1990).

6. Of particular importance here is Lord's later work, which continued to evolve and to extend his and Parry's "theory"; see espec. Lord 1991, 1995.

7. Exemplified in Lord 1960 (espec. 99–123 and 242–265); defined and described explicitly in Lord 1969. See also Foley 1990:359–387 and 1991: chs. 3–4. Compare the distinction, discussed by Oesterreicher and Schaefer elsewhere in this volume, between *Wiedergebrauchs-Rede* (reusable discourse), to which category the units of Oral Theory would belong, and *Verbrauchs-Rede* (self-consuming discourse).

8. It is noteworthy that no less a group of authorities than the South Slavic epic singers themselves seemed to support this explanation of units of utterance by observing that, for them, a "word" *(reč)* was never the lexical and textual byte we list in dictionaries but at minimum a line or scene and at maximum an entire performance. See further Foley 1990: espec. 44–50.

9. Compare the welcome problematization of reading, writing, and texts in ancient Greece apparent in Bakker 1993a and Thomas 1989; more generally in Boyarin 1993.

10. Perhaps the strongest version of this quantitative, categorical approach is that of Duggan (1973), who established a percentage threshold for the orality or literacy of various Old French *chansons de geste.* Compare also Oesterreicher's and Schaefer's essays elsewhere in this volume.

11. But see Lord 1986a (espec. 478–481), in which he accepts the notion of the "transitional text" and modifies the concept of "formulaic

density." In 1986b he describes three quite different encounters between oral tradition and literacy in the former Yugoslavia.

12. See espec. Foley 1990:11–15.

13. See, e.g., Foley 1983, 1991: ch. 4 on Christian epic; 1995a: ch. 4 on charms.

14. Scholarship on Old English verbal art has been particularly forward-looking in this regard; see espec. O'Brien O'Keeffe 1990 and Doane 1991, 1994. Also of importance for the understanding of "vocality" in medieval vernacular texts are Zumthor 1990a and, particularly, Schaefer 1992; see, elsewhere in this volume, Schaefer's important remarks on how vocality links narrator and audience in a joint context of meaning. The ongoing discussion between Dell Hymes and Dennis Tedlock on oral traditions and textuality in Native American languages (summary in Foley 1995a: ch. 3) is also very instructive in this regard, as is the history of how oral traditions have been editorially memorialized as texts (see espec. Fine 1984, Foley 1995b).

15. "Way of speaking" is a term and concept developed by Hymes (see espec. 1989; also 1981, 1994).

16. Compare Foley 1990 on the rules that inform traditional idioms in ancient Greek (ch. 4), South Slavic (ch. 5), and Anglo-Saxon (ch. 6); also Nagy 1974; espec. 140–149 and 1990a: espec. 4–5, 50–51 on the symbiosis of meter and phraseology.

17. For the structure of typical scenes (also called "themes"), see Foley 1990: ch. 7 (ancient Greek), ch. 8 (South Slavic), and ch. 9 (Old English); on story-patterns, see note 7 above. Edwards (1992) provides an excellent summary of research on typical scenes in Homer. Cf. Foley 1991 on the traditional meaning associated with narrative units in South Slavic (chs. 3–4), ancient Greek (ch. 5), and Old English (ch. 6).

18. As a suggestion of the reported diversity worldwide, see Finnegan 1977. A great deal of the evidence has come from African traditions; on this area, see espec. Finnegan 1970, Okpewho 1992.

19. On the traditional poetics of Middle English texts, relatively far removed from actual oral tradition, see espec. Parks 1986 and Amodio 1994.

20. See Foley 1991: espec. chs. 1–2. Cf. the complementary findings of Kahane 1994 and Russo 1994, as well as Biebuyck (1971:14) on African epic and DuBois (1994:177) on Finnish oral poetry. Else-

where in this volume, Bakker demonstrates how within Homeric narrative the grammatical signal of tense inherently involves the "cumulative mass of the tradition" in what he calls an act of "commemoration."

21. Foley 1991:155. Compare Martin 1989:38.

22. See further Foley 1991:168–174.

23. See Foley 1990:361–363, 1991:64–68, 100–106, 118–120; Coote 1981.

24. Simple lines of introduction do their job in signaling a speech, for example, by providing a deep and resonant context for noun-epithet phrases, but it is a different kind of job than that allotted by convention to the phrases *pukinon epos* and *hupodra idōn* mentioned above.

25. Thus, *pace* Kullmann 1984, there exists a significant and defining difference between the perspective from metonymy (as an extension of oral poetry theory) and that from Neoanalysis, the latter of which always posits another singular and *textual* situation as the referent for any situation in the source work.

26. Compare the section on "Background: Opportunities and Limitations."

27. This "way of speaking" was of course the thrust of Parry 1932, which took the crucial step of showing how Homer's language was a highly refined, multidialectal linguistic instrument. See also Foley 1996.

28. Parry no. *6699,* recorded in the region of Stolac and quoted from the acoustic recording in the Milman Parry Collection at Harvard University. I am preparing the Stolac material for publication in *Serbocroatian Heroic Songs.* For further description of the Moslem epic *Kunstsprache,* see Foley 1990: ch. 5.

29. See espec. Foley 1995a: ch. 4; and compare Feld 1990 on Kaluli weeping.

30. This is to say nothing of the "transitional reading" well documented for the Old English period, wherein, as O'Brien O'Keeffe (1990:41) puts it, "reception . . ., conditioned by formulaic conventions, produces variants which are metrically, syntactically, and semantically appropriate. In such a process, reading and copying have actually become conflated with composing." Also of paramount importance are the limitations imposed by the technology of writing in the ancient and medieval worlds (see espec. Thomas 1989 and Harris

1989, as well as Stock 1983, 1990), which should not be simplistically assimilated to the modern scenario of mass market paperbacks.

31. See Foley 1990: chs. 5–6.

32. Let me again acknowledge the work of Nagy (1990b), who remarks that "the Greek poem is a *sēma* that requires the *nóēsis* of those who hear it" (222) and Ford (1992), who concentrates on the Iliadic instances and the issues of fixity and text. While I agree with much of what they have to say, here I focus specifically on the identity of *sēmata* as metonyms, that is, as both instances of and a name for traditional referentiality. Compare also Bakker's contribution to the present volume.

33. Burial mounds, like noun-epithet phrases that also serve as metonymic signs, mark a traditional heroic identity via a preapproved traditional sign, again with an arbitrary but institutionalized encoding. As do other *sēmata,* burial mounds symbolically open onto a reality beyond the present time and place of the narrative. It is as if the character's traditional identity were "interred" in the *sēma,* in the sense of both burial mound and metonym. The paradigm case may be the grave of Elpenor (*Odyssey* 11.75), which acquires an immanent significance: Elpenor cannot rest without establishment of this *sēma* and all that it implies. Compare the *sēma* prescribed by Hektor for the Achaean champion he may vanquish (*Iliad* 7.89) and Hektor's own properly constituted burial mound (24.799, 801) only a few lines from the culminating funeral feast that closes the *Iliad* (on the latter, see Foley 1991: ch. 5).

34. On which, see espec. Hansen 1990 and Nagy 1990b:214.

35. Compare the Serbian magical charms (see Foley 1995a: ch. 4) for an example of an extremely densely coded—and superficially opaque—medium.

36. Quotations from the *Odyssey* are drawn from Monro and Allen 1969; translations, with occasional slight emendations for emphasis, from Lattimore 1965.

37. Compare the similar conclusions of Lateiner (1989:20).

38. Note also the two uses of this phrase in the *Iliad,* in both of which Odysseus, well recognized for his wisdom and cunning, chides the impulsive Agamemnon. In one case (4.350) Odysseus is responding to the Achaean leader's wrongfully accusing him and Peteos of cowardice or slackness in battle; in the other (14.83) he seeks to contest

Agamemnon's retreat from Troy. In both cases, the frame helps us to read the incident more clearly: the Greek leader should indeed know better, and his rashness certainly does cry out for remedy.

39. Indeed, this feature of the leg-wound also identifies the hero in some South Slavic return songs, where it is called a *beleg* (sign, mark).

40. On the primacy of the metonymic over the literal in South Slavic and Native American narrative, compare Foley 1994.

41. In addition to *Odyssey* 23.205, this metonymic phrase also glosses passages in which Lukaon realizes his death at Achilleus' hands is imminent (*Iliad* 21.114), Aphrodite is struck down by Athena (21.425), Penelope learns of the suitors' intended ambush of Telemakhos (*Odyssey* 4.703), Odysseus fears the life-threatening storm stirred up by Poseidon (5.297), the exhausted Odysseus can find no landing spot on Scheria (5.406), Eurumakhos realizes his death at the hands of Odysseus is imminent (22.68), Odysseus learns the suitors are being covertly armed by Melanthios (22.147), and Laertes—in a close parallel to Penelope a book earlier—reads the *sēma* of the scar and recognizes his son (24.345).

42. Two essays elsewhere in this volume offer examples of different sites for traditional signification: Martin discusses similes as metanarrative and metaperformance signals, whereas Nagy shows how ellipses of various kinds can key enactment and reenactment.

4. THE INLAND SHIP

1. E.g., the contributions of Kahane, Martin. Bakker discusses the shift of interest toward performance and reception as against production and composition.

2. Compare Blackburn et al. (1989:11) on Indian epics, some of which would take over a hundred hours to recite in full: "even when an epic story is well known to the audience, the complete story, from beginning to end, is rarely presented in performance—or even in a series of performances."

3. Foley 1991:7, emphasis mine. Foley's contribution to this volume applies his view.

4. Lutgendorf 1991:33–41, 53–112 richly documents the various ways of performing the *Rāmcaritmānas*, a sixteenth-century vernacular retelling of the *Rāmāyana* in some 12,800 lines. As a liturgical text,

the *Rāmcaritmānas* offers benefits when performed in full. Ways of doing this range from solitary chanting of five or ten stanzas daily at home to formalized temple recitations by professionals in relays lasting from nine days to a month (with the audience coming and going, nodding off and waking). Finally, the "unbroken path"—the rapid mechanical recitation of the entire *Mānas* in a twenty-four hour period—is sometimes employed as a way of learning the text.

5. Valuable essays toward the archaic reception of Homer are Burkert 1987 (with reference to works of reception theory at n2) and Richardson (1975) for the fifth century.

6. Names of episodes (not always perfectly congruent with the contents of our books) figure regularly in early references to Homeric poetry, from Xenophanes and Heraclitus on, and among painters like Sophilus when they identify heroic scenes: Stanley 1993:282–284.

7. On the ascription of this fragment (to Simonides rather than Semonides) and Pap. Oxy. 3965, see West 1993.

8. The early poet Tyrtaeus converted a hexametric oracle into elegiacs by interleaving his own pentameters (4 *IEG*), and a certain Pigres transformed the *Iliad* into elegiacs in a similar way *(IEG)*.

9. *Certamen* 228.84–229.89 Allen V. The speech is also excerpted to be censured by Plato, a cunning player of poetic games: *Rep.* 390a–b.

10. *Allophroneōn* is indeed found in our Homer (as in *Iliad* 23.698) but never of Hektor who comes closest in being called *oligodraneōn* in 22.337.

11. On hermeneutics and literacy, see Schaefer in this volume.

12. Plut. *Cimon* 7; a slightly different version in Aeschines *In Ctes.* 185.

13. Lutgendorf 1991:36: "a religious epic like the *Mānas* [*Rāmcaritmānas*] has an 'emergent' quality: it is a means rather than an end, a blueprint rather than an artifact."

14. Antisthenes 51 Caizzi = Gianantoni II.391–2.

5. HEXAMETER PROGRESSION AND THE HOMERIC HERO'S SOLITARY STATE

Translations are based on R. Lattimore. Some license is taken with English word order so as to reflect a word's original position in the verse.

1. Especially Oesterreicher and Schaefer in this volume.

2. I use the term "meter" to refer to the formal framework of sequencing and segmentation, syllabic in the case of Homer. I use the term "rhythm" to refer to a much broader and less formal range of sequential/segmentational phenomena. See Devine & Stephens 1994:99–101.

3. "Literate" hexameter authors (Apollonius, Quintus, etc.) use a meter almost identical to Homer's (O'Neill 1942; Porter 1951), but they do not link their rhythm and their diction in quite the same way as Homer. Use of formulae is a case in point (see Edwards 1988:42–53; Sale 1993).

4. Zumthor 1990a:51, 203.

5. Perhaps a kind of *sphragis* ("seal"). Compare Nagy 1990a:170.

6. Many poststructuralist approaches (hermeneutics, reader-response criticism, deconstruction, etc.) strongly suggest that even the *text* is a *symbol* of fixity.

7. See Daitz 1991; Wyatt 1992; Daitz 1992. I would suggest that this "pause" can be a cognitive entity, rather than an actual silent duration.

8. Ordinary parlance can display "phonological isochrony" (Hogg and McCully 1987:222–225), but not large-scale repetition of formally identical (e.g., 6 beats) units.

9. Unlike, e.g., the sonnet.

10. See Griffin 1980:81–102.

11. On ellipsis in this sense see Nagy, in this volume.

12. Foley 1991:7.

13. Bakker 1995:109.

14. See Kahane 1994:114–141.

15. Siren songs (*Odyssey;* Göethe, *Lorelei*) are deadly exceptions. For drama and epic see Greenwood 1953:124: Greek drama "did not attempt to produce in the spectators' minds any sort of illusion, any feeling, however temporary, that they were seeing and hearing what, in the distant past, actually took place . . . in epic . . . illusion was plainly impossible and was in no way attempted [but epic] could nevertheless cause the hearer to imagine vividly the scene and the various persons acting and speaking, so drama could do this."

16. See Chafe 1994:33 ("Conscious Experiences May Be Factual or Fictional"); Bakker, in this volume ("near," "far"); Schechner

245

1985:117–150 ("Performers and Spectators Transported and Transformed"); Lada 1993–1994.

17. See Devine and Stephens 1994, ch. 3. Our sense of rhythm depends on patterned temporal sequences, in which stimuli occur regularly: "8 to 0.5 events per second." "Slower stimuli tend to be perceived as discrete events not joint to each other in a rhythmic pattern." Estimates vary as to the duration of rhetorically significant pauses (see Deese 1980). Actual duration values do not, however, affect our argument.

18. Chafe 1994:29–30.

19. Caesurae also affect the flow, but verse ends/beginnings are more prominent. For the internal metrics of the hexameter see Ingalls 1970; Kahane 1994:17–42 on relative prominence of pauses.

20. See Daitz 1991; Wyatt 1992; Daitz 1992.

21. See Ingalls 1970.

22. The last full position in the hexameter may be occupied by either a single long or a single short syllable. With a few exceptions in "irrational" hexameters, no other position enjoys such privilege.

23. See e.g. Gimson 1994, ch. 4.

24. Compare codas at the end of narratives, which bring the narrator and listener back to the point at which they entered the narrative (Labov 1972:365).

25. See Toolan 1988:162–163.

26. For speech acts see, e.g., Searle 1968.

27. See Linear-B (PY Ta 641): O–WO–WE, TI–RI–O–WE, QE–TO–RO–WE (*oiwowes, triowes, qetrowes,* one-eared, three-eared vessels, etc.).

28. *Oios* from Indo-European **oi-,* "one"; *mounos* (⟨*μόνϝος⟩) perhaps associated with *manos,* "rare, sparse," and *manu=mikron,* "small." See Chantraine 1968–1980; Frisk 1960–1972; Boisacq 1938; *LSJ* with verbal communications from P. G. Glare. Waanders 1992 (on origin and etymology of numerals) is silent on *mounos.*

29. *Oios* and *mounos* are metrically identical, but the former begins with a vowel, the latter with a consonant, i.e. these two apparent synonyms are metrical variants. See following notes.

30. Oral cultures tend to classify items "situationally" (i.e. by linking them to a situation), while literate cultures stress abstract, decontextualized properties (Ong 1982:49–54; Olson 1994:37–44).

31. Narrative is a description of events along a time axis: "John got up (a), brushed his teeth (b), had breakfast (c), and left (d)" = T^0 . . . a . . . b . . . c . . . d . . . T^n. Although the narrative's presentation of temporal events is not always linear (flashbacks, visions, etc . . .), we can generally separate between "narrative foreground," elements that directly push the plot forward in time, "John got up," "he had breakfast," etc., and "narrative background," elements that do not: "He [i.e. John] was an ornithologist." See Fleischman 1990:15–51. For the narrator's comments in Homer see (S.) Richardson 1990:67, 177; de Jong 1987:19, 44.

32. After which the main, "objective" narrative picks up again *dē ȟa toth' Hermeias* . . . "then did Hermes . . ." (457ff.).

33. *Hoios* is an indirect interrogative pronoun (Chantraine 1963: 238–239), but we cannot paraphrase "Poseidon, what are the contents of what you have said?" (since Zeus has just heard his brother's words). The rest of Zeus' speech makes it clear that he is not seeking an answer and that he has not really asked a question: technically (as in Searle 1968) an *expressive* rather than a *directive* speech act.

34. See Frisk 1960–1972 for comments and bibliography.

35. The alliteration is common. Compare *Odyssey* 17.248: *ō popoi, hoion eeipe kuōn olophōia eidōs* "o my, o, what has the dog said, this thinker of destructive thoughts."

36. The formal antithesis of *Iliad* 5.304 is enhanced by the plural/singular antithesis *hoioi/oios*.

37. See Nagler 1974: 1ff. and his note 1, p. 1; Parry 1971:72. On phonetic/semantic relationships see, e.g., Geiger 1958.

38. Compare *Iliad* 12.379–383, where the stone's size is more modest: *oude ke min rea kheiress' amphoterēis ekhoi anēr* . . . "a man would not easily lift it up in both arms."

39. Comrie 1976:111; also Nagy 1990a:31–34.

40. 17 out of 26 examples (65%). This is not the result of simple metrical tendencies. Disregarding semantic, lexical, grammatical, and context-specific considerations, the tendency for words with metrical values $-\cup$ and $--$ to be localized at the end of the verse is 35.9% and 41.3% respectively *(Iliad)*, 34.3% and 41.7% respectively *(Odyssey)* (data: O'Neill 1942:140).

41. There is no metrical reason to prevent terminal usage in any gram-

matical case. Dat. masc. sing. 4x verse-terminal (*Odyssey* 9.160, 10.524, 11.32, 21.146); acc. masc. sing. 1x terminal (*Iliad* 16.340); gen. and voc. masc. sing. not attested in any position; nom. fem. sing. 1x terminal (*Odyssey* 9.207); dat., acc., and gen. fem. sing. never terminal.

42. Terminal localization of *mounos* is metrically possible and occurs elsewhere in epic (e.g. Apollonius Rhodius, *Argonautica* 1.197, 732; 2.112; Oppian, *Halieutica* 2.571; Eumelus, *Corinthiaca* (in Dio Chrysostom. *Or.* 20.13)), but never in Homer except for a single example *mounē* (feminine) in *Odyssey* 23.227.

43. In *Iliad* 6.403 Hektor is the only hero of Troy (*oios* as the mark of heroic isolation): (*Astuanakt'.*) *oios gar erueto Ilion Hektor.* "(Astuanax—lord of the city;) since Hektor alone (*oios*) saved Ilion." But also in contexts where no heroic element is discernible, as when Tudeus kills everyone except Maion (*Iliad* 4.397) *pantas epephn', hena d' oion hiei oikonde neesthai* "He killed them all, except that he let one man alone (*oion*) get home again."

44. These examples are clearly formulaic. But this "system" is not linked, in formulaic terms, to our earlier *kai oios* examples: localization of *oios* may be related to formulaic composition but is a much broader phenomenon.

45. The examples are not statements, but questions (rhetorical, or otherwise), and hence more specifically expressive elements of direct speech.

46. The shrieking Hecuba *kōkusen* (24.200. Pucci 1993:258: *kōkuein* normally in mourning for a *dead* husband) says to Priam: "Where has your mind gone?" (24.201–202). Achilles, in saying "ah, wretch . . ." (24.518) implies that Priam has lost his senses through suffering. Agamemnon says "I fear terribly for the Danaans, my heart is unsettled, I wander, my heart flutters outside my breast, my limbs tremble . . ." (10.91–95). Dolon's first words of reply are "Hektor caused me to lose my senses" (10.391). Priam explains that his motivation is divine (compare 24.220–224) and thus possibly a variety of madness. In his reply to Achilles Priam totally ignores everything in his interlocutor's words (553–558).

47. The choice of *mounos* in verse-initial position rather than *oios* or the accusative *oion* is not affected by meter.

48. (Rhetorical) anaphora in Homer is often localized at the line's ex-

tremities, and particularly its beginning, as for example in 14–15 in our example, //oute . . . //oute . . .; Iliad 2.671–673, //Nireus . . . //Nireus . . .; Iliad 10.227–231, hoi d' ethelon . . . //etheletēn . . . //ethele . . . //ethele . . . //ethele . . . Compare the rhyme in later poetry.

49. For example, TLG (#D) lists total 370 attestations of nominative masculine singular: Eustathius' commentaries on Homer (81); Iliad and Odyssey (66); scholia to Homer (64); remaining 159 attestations are dispersed among 57 authors/collections.

50. The variant form monos is virtually universal. The forms mounos/ mounon are found mainly in hexametric contexts (incl. scholia), but usage is far less markedly Homeric. For example, TLG lists total 340 attestations of the nominative masculine singular mounos: Nonnus (60); Greek Anthology (26); Herodotus (26); Gregory Nazianzenus (19); scholia to Homer (18); Eustathius (15); only 14 in Homer.

51. Comrie 1976:111; also Nagy 1990a:31–34.

52. Even in death Antinoos' rowdy "feasting" continues: he casts away his cup, kicks the table, blood, bread, and meat gush out (17–21). Confusion here is part of the wider matrix of Odyssean disguises and late recognitions. As Antinoos collapses, the suitors rush about in disarray (21ff.), and their thoughts are described in a highly unusual manner (Griffin 1986:45, on Odyssey 20.31ff.).

53. Some elements of this speech may be comparable to Hecuba's address to Priam (see earlier), where oios is used.

54. Kahane 1994.

55. On nēpios see also Bakker, in this volume.

56. The semantic functions of rhythm as described in this article may be more difficult to trace in later, "literate" heroic epic. But this requires separate study.

57. On the magnitude of the Homeric epics, see Ford in this volume.

6. SIMILES AND PERFORMANCE

1. See Meillet 1966:440–453.

2. Parry 1971:171. Parry cites the 1906 edition.

3. Bréal 1911:107; my translations.

4. On the Peripatetic roots of Hellenistic criticism see Richardson 1992 and Porter 1992; also, G. Nagy's contribution to this volume.

5. Erbse 1988.
6. Erbse 1971:73.
7. Richardson 1980.
8. Erbse 1975:91.
9. Griffin 1976.
10. Richardson 1980:280.
11. Some fine recent accounts include Blackburn, Claus, et al. 1989; Lutgendorf 1991; Mills 1990; Basso 1985; Moyle 1990; Connelly 1986.
12. Scott 1974; Fränkel 1921.
13. On similar lags in modern Homeric criticism, see Martin 1989:1–4 and 1993:222–228.
14. Fränkel 1921:32.
15. Moulton 1977:76–86.
16. Whitman 1958:249–284.
17. On the persistence of this method see de Jong and Sullivan 1994:1–8. The method is still at work in Lonsdale 1990.
18. Wellek and Warren 1962:211. This approach appears even in a theoretically sophisticated book, Nimis 1987, still mainly interested in semantic associations and long-distance thematic bundling.
19. Krischer 1971:36–75.
20. On this phenomenon, see esp. Krischer 1971:91–121.
21. Scheub 1975.
22. Stone 1988:12–61.
23. Ibid. 13.
24. Ibid. 27.
25. Ibid. 12–13.
26. Ibid. 21.
27. Often the song features onomatopoetic portions as a rhythmic device, and these are most subject to contemporary influences: at one point in the story, the narrator imitates an airplane noise while describing how Woi's house will go up into the sky. An onomatopoetic formula for ending episodes is the singer's "Dried millet" *wese* (sound of breaking), and the chorus response, "Wese."
28. Azuonye 1990:53–60.
29. Martin 1989:234–236.
30. Reichl 1992:47–49.
31. Phillips 1981:1–6.

32. Ibid. 116 (transcript B lines 428ff.).
33. Blackburn 1986.
34. The existence of such performance-discourse particles is perhaps not irrelevant to the problems of augmented verbs in Homeric and Vedic narrative.
35. Wadley 1991:201.
36. Ibid. 220.
37. Ibid. 217.
38. Shipp 1972: esp. 208–222.
39. Ibid. 215–218.
40. Webster 1964:223–238; Kirk 1965:144.
41. Hainsworth 1989:22.
42. Bakhtin 1981.
43. On Pindaric dialect, see Forssman 1966.
44. On the forms: Shipp 1972:193 and Risch 1974:18, 80.
45. Mss. C and E have the more common genitive *galaktos*.
46. Risch 1974:330; Shipp 1972:98.
47. On this interpretation of the line see Kirkwood 1982:58. It could be that the metaphor is more striking in Pindar: the horizontal axis—what is farthest—is pictured as a vertical ascent—what stands tall like a mountain.
48. Compare *Iliad* 4.495, 2.273.
49. Shipp 1972:196. A similar analogical formation and its poetic implications have been analyzed in Nagy 1979:349–354.
50. Of course, Pindar can on occasion make use of recognizable Homeric phrases for conscious effects: Forssman 1966:86–100.
51. Shipp 1972:197.
52. Commentators on the lines, since von Leutsch in 1871 have read them as dialogue: see Garzya 1958:224; Harrison 1902:196–197; West 1974:156 assumes it is one poem, but not a dialogue; van Groningen 1966:228–230 goes so far as to see two unrelated poems. The emendation by West 1989a:201 (changing the participle to masculine accusative in line 580) destroys the ironic effect that Garzya had detected.
53. A good example of such *mandinadha* duelling is analyzed by Herzfeld 1985:144–146. See also the extensive collection of Droudakis 1982, esp. 123–130.
54. On the topos of poet as bird see Gow 1965:143 on *Theocritus* 7.47.

Note that the *makhana* of Pindar, synonymous with his poetry, is elsewhere styled "winged" (*Pythian* 8.34), and that Pindar can refer to rivals (his or the victor's) as birds (*Olympian* 2.87).

55. Risch 1974:116.
56. Young 1971:61 sharpens the contrast by placing in quotation marks lines 1003–1006 (except *sophoi*), citing Tyrtaeus 9.13ff. and 7.29ff.
57. On such *hupothēkai* poetry, see Martin 1984.
58. Chantraine 1968–1980.
59. See especially Nagy 1985.
60. Shipp 1972:195.
61. For recent discussion see Janko 1992:365 and Schmidt 1986: 109–110.
62. The same phenomenon underlies other Hesiodic lines: see Martin 1984.
63. Against possible objections that such small details cannot evoke such large themes, I offer the evidence gathered from actual field work with living traditional poetics, as summarized by J. M. Foley 1991:1–60.
64. Nagy 1990a offers persuasive metrical and dictional details to support this argument. To my knowledge, his account has not been challenged.
65. West 1983:110.
66. Risch 1974:54.
67. Shipp 1972:245.
68. West 1983:120 notes points of contact with regard to theogonic material.
69. Petropoulos 1994:82. For different comparative evidence tending towards the same conclusion concerning Hesiodic poetry, see Martin 1992.
70. Shipp 1972:12. Kirk 1985:284 accepts the linguistic lateness of the feature but attributes it to "the most developed phase of the language of oral epic; that is, it is likely to be by Homer himself."
71. An older phrase without synizesis, **dendrewōi ephezomenos,* would form a choriambic dimeter, the lyric meter attested in e.g. Anacreon 349 PMG.
72. Shipp 1972:9.

73. ⟨Ἀο⟩σψόρος with synizesis is Bergk's emendation (ἑωσ-, ἀωσ- codd.), necessary for meter.
74. This was suggested in a note by Bury 1892:68, although he prints Bergk's emendation in the text.
75. Leaf 1900:372 notes that one class of mss reads Attic *Borras* here.
76. Shipp 1972:199. Compare *Iliad* 13.334.
77. Martin 1989 passim.
78. Nagy 1990a:199–214, 414–437.
79. Ibid. 375–381 on the multiple personifications involved in *h. Ap.* 156–168.

7. ELLIPSIS IN HOMER

1. LSJ 535–536.
2. Compare Nagy 1990a:177–178.
3. Ibid.
4. Compare Nagy 1990a:155 and 192 (with n195) on *Peisistratidai* in the sense of "Peisistratos + *his* son + *his* son + *his* son . . ."
5. Compare Nagy 1990a:218n23 and 220–221n34.
6. Watkins 1979:270 = 1994:645.
7. Ibid.
8. The α of accusative plural −ας in archaic (versus innovative) situations is consistently long in Homeric diction: see Janko 1982:58–62, especially p. 61 (". . . the large number of older formulae with long endings that it [= the *Odyssey*] retained"); compare Nagy 1990b:61–63.
9. Nagy 1990a:459n108. I take this opportunity to correct three typographical errors in that note: at line 2 (two times) and at line 6 (the second time), read —uu—uu—x . . . not —uu—uux . . .
10. We may note the wording in Plato, *Menexenus* 237b on Mother Earth as being τῆς τεκούσης καὶ θρεψάσης καὶ ὑποδεξαμένης "the one who gave birth, nourished, and accepted [them] into her care," with reference to the Athenians as her autochthonous children (compare Loraux 1993:84n71; also pp. 58–59). I infer from this kind of phrasing that Athena in *Iliad* 2 was really pictured as nursing Erekhtheus.
11. Kirk 1985:206: the phrasing "suggests an annual festival; there may

or may not be some idea of an early form of the Panathenaia, which was held in the month of Hekatombaion."

12. On the homology between Erekhtheus and Phaethon, see Nagy 1979:191–192.
13. Nilsson 1921.
14. Compare Schwyzer 1939:638.
15. Ibid.
16. Ibid.
17. Pylos tablet Cn 3.1; see Nagy 1970:148n187. On the basis of the forms *Mukēnē* and *Messēnē,* I suspect that even the suffix *-ēnē* is endowed with an elliptic function. Also, the element *messo-* of *Messēnē* implies the semantics of ellipsis, in that the idea of the middle is highlighted while that of the periphery is shaded over.
18. Schwyzer 1939:638.
19. Schwyzer/Debrunner 1950:43.
20. Compare *Odyssey* 1.1–2.
21. Muellner 1976:70.
22. Page 1959.
23. Footnotes within the quotations contain my own comments on Page's reasoning.
24. Page 1959:238.
25. Ibid.
26. Page 1959:300.
27. Compare Nagy 1992b:321–325.
28. The involvement of heralds in the narrative containing the Aiante problem, I suggest, is relevant to the involvement of heralds in the "Embassy" scene of *Iliad* 9, containing the problem of the dual-for-plural usage.
29. I offer an objection at this point: we have no indication in the scholia to *Iliad* 13.203, discussed by Page in the quotation earlier, that Aristarchus objected to that verse! The addition here of a third role—earlier in the narrative we saw only two roles—is comparable with the layering of two versus three ambassadors in the "Embassy" scene of *Iliad* 9.
30. Page 1959:272–273.
31. Nagy 1995:174.
32. E.g. Hainsworth 1993:355 (and, earlier, p. 346).

33. Puhvel 1977:399–400.
34. Janko 1982:228–231.
35. Nagy 1990b:29.
36. Page 1959:299.
37. Rengakos 1993:76–77; compare Nagy 1996a:138.
38. Rengakos p. 9; compare Nagy 1996a; ch. 5.
39. Bakker, in this volume.
40. Nagy 1992b:321–325, 1996b:138–145.
41. Ibid. Compare Nagy 1990a:5–6: when an older and a newer form compete for the same meaning, one of the things that can happen is that the older form, ousted from its old meaning, develops a newer meaning that becomes a specialized version of the older meaning now held by the newer form.
42. Lord 1960:100. Underlines mine.
43. Nagy 1995, appearing in a Festschrift for Emily Vermeule entitled, appropriately, *The Ages of Homer* instead of *The Age of Homer.*
44. Nagy 1996a:110.
45. Kirk 1985:1–16.
46. Janko 1992:20–38, with reference to Janko 1982:228–231.
47. Underlines in the quotes from both authors will indicate my highlightings.
48. Kirk 1985:201.
49. Ibid.
50. Ibid.
51. Kirk p. 359.
52. Janko 1992:48.
53. Ibid.
54. Janko p. 69.
55. Janko p. 132.
56. Janko pp. 218–219.
57. Again, underlines will indicate my highlightings.
58. Page 1959:237.
59. Zumthor 1972:507 ("le caractère de l'oeuvre qui, comme telle, avant l'âge du livre, ressort d'une quasi-abstraction, les textes concrets qui la réalisent présentant, par le jeu des variantes et remaniements, comme une incessante vibration et une instabilité fondamentale"). Compare Zumthor pp. 43–47, 65–75.

60. Nagy 1996a, chapter 1.
61. Detailed discussion in Nagy 1990a:42–44, 373–375.
62. Ibid.
63. Ibid.
64. Ibid.
65. Nagy 1985:33.
66. On *sophos* "skilled" as a programmatic word used by poetry to designate the "skill" of a poet in encoding the message of the poetry, see Nagy 1990a:148. See also Nagy 1990a:374n190: "A successful encoder, that is, poet, is by necessity a successful decoder, that is, someone who has understood the inherited message and can therefore pass it on. Not all decoders, however, are necessarily encoders: both poet and audience are decoders, but only the poet has the authority of the encoder."
67. In this and related contexts, *astoi* "townspeople" seems to be the programmatic designation of local audiences, associated with the special interests of their own here and now. The anonymous referee draws my attention to Archilochus fr. 13 West, where the emotional state of the *astoi* seems to be contrasted with the stance of the poet: as I interpret this poem, the poet too is represented as feeling the same emotions of grief as felt by the rest of the community, but he urges all to transcend those emotions—as does the poem.
68. This theme of the alienated poet is examined at length in Nagy 1985:30 and following.
69. The "doing," of course, may amount simply to the performative level of "saying" *by way of poetry.*
70. For a fuller discussion, see Nagy 1996a:221–223.
71. Nagy 1990a:202. For a fuller discussion, see Nagy 1996a:71–73.
72. It can also be argued that Patroklos as the solo audience of Achilles becomes interchangeable with the general audience of the *Iliad.* See Nagy 1996a:72n37 for further discussion and bibliography on the Homeric device of creating an effect of interchangeability between characters of epic and members of an audience.
73. Nagy 1996a:73 with n38.
74. At *Odyssey* 1.10, the expression τῶν ἁμόθεν γε "from *one* point among these" seems to me pertinent to the idea of vertical succession in εἰπὲ καὶ ἡμῖν "narrate to us too!" (addressed to the Muse).

75. Perhaps the expression κλέος οἶον at *Iliad* 2.486 is pertinent: the singer hears the *kleos* or song "alone," as if he heard nothing else. Perhaps also pertinent is the singularity of the Muse invoked at *Iliad* 1.1—and at *Odyssey* 1.1.

76. Bakker, in this volume.

77. Bakker, in this volume.

78. Bakker, in this volume.

79. For subjunctive + potential particle ἄν in the apodosis and εἰ + optative in the protasis, Kirk 1985:167 compares *Iliad* 11.386–387: "Your bow and arrows could not save you, if you did attack me face-to-face with your weapons." It seems to me that both constructions are contrary-to-fact: *if the Muses did not remind me (but they did)* and *if you did attack me face-to-face (but you did not).*

8. TYPES OF ORALITY IN TEXT

1. Compare Söll 1985:17–25.

2. Compare Ochs 1979; Tannen 1980 and 1982b; Chafe 1982 and 1985; Halliday 1987. See also De Mauro 1970; Olson 1977; Horowitz/Samuels 1987; Chafe/Danielewicz 1987; Biber 1988; Olson/Torrance 1991; Downing et al. 1992; Günther/Ludwig 1994; Raible 1994.

3. Compare Bernstein 1960/61.

4. Compare e.g. Schlieben-Lange 1983:81: "Traditionen des *Schreibens im Duktus der Mündlichkeit* und des *Sprechens im Duktus der Schriftlichkeit*"; Bäuml 1993 entitled "Verschriftlichte Mündlichkeit und vermündlichte Schriftlichkeit."

5. Compare Nencioni 1976.

6. Compare Akinnaso 1985.

7. Compare Koch/Oesterreicher 1985:17–19; 1990:5–12.

8. Compare Ong 1982:11.

9. This field of reference is primarily covered by works like Havelock 1976; Ong 1977 and 1982; Goody 1977 and 1987; Le Goff 1977; Stock 1983; Graff 1987; Finnegan 1988; Burns 1989.

10. Compare e.g. Chiche 1989; especially Houis 1989. See also Schlieben-Lange 1983:77–80.

11. Compare Koch/Oesterreicher 1985 and 1990.

12. Compare Koch/Oesterreicher 1985:19–21; 1990:8–10.

13. Compare Koch/Oesterreicher 1985:21–23; 1990:10–12. Compare

also certain categories in De Beaugrande 1980 and 1984; Eigler 1995.

14. Compare Schlieben-Lange 1983:138–148.
15. See also Koch/Oesterreicher 1985:17–24.
16. Compare Koch/Oesterreicher 1990:6.
17. See for example Pulgram 1950; Tagliavini 1972; §§ 45 and 46; Coseriu 1978; Hofmann 1986. Compare also Iliescu/Slusanski 1991.
18. Compare the excellent presentation in Banniard 1992.
19. Compare e.g. Lüdtke 1964; Wunderli 1965; Zumthor 1985; Koch 1990 and 1993; Selig et al. 1993; Selig 1993.
20. A good example here is the history of the Italian language where this problem is discussed under the heading of the *questione della lingua;* compare Vitale 1971; Durante 1981; Bruni 1984; Koch/ Oesterreicher 1990:166–176.
21. Compare Oesterreicher 1988; Koch/Oesterreicher 1990:12–16; Koch/Oesterreicher 1994; Oesterreicher 1995.
22. Compare Watzlawick et al. 1967, ch. 2.5.
23. These two types of phenomena are explained in Oesterreicher 1988:370–378; Koch/Oesterreicher 1985:27–29. For a detailed illustration of these concepts, compare Koch/Oesterreicher 1990:50–126, 142–165, 178–198, 209–233.
24. See for example Löfstedt 1911; Väänänen 1959. For this type of writing compare also Spitzer 1976; Bruni 1984:401–433; Oesterreicher 1994a and 1994b.
25. Compare Fishman 1967.
26. See for example Pighi 1964; Adams 1977; Cugusi 1981; Durante 1981:53–64. Compare also examples of this type in 16th century Spanish America, compare e.g. Rivarola 1994.
27. In this context the Ciceronian *Epistulae ad familiares,* especially *ad Atticum* (Bailly 1937) are usually mentioned; but we should account for Cicero's intent to publish later on the collected epistulae. In this perspective the Ciceronian *epistulae* deviate somewhat from the type *relaxed writing.*
28. See for example Herman 1990; Koch 1993:46, 62–63. See also certain examples given in the *Rhetorica ad Herennium* 4.62–66 (Achard 1989).
29. It is not at all surprising that we have difficulties finding evidence for this type.

30. Compare e.g. Mohrmann 1961.
31. Compare Tagliavini 1972, § 46.
32. Compare Callebat 1992; an excellent description of the domain of technical language in late Latin is given in Svennung 1935.
33. Compare Lausberg 1990, § 1244, elocutio VI; Curtius 1993:602. See also Quadlbauer 1962; Murphy 1974; Bader 1994.
34. Compare the convincing analyses of French literary texts in Stempel 1993 and 1994.
35. Compare Gauger 1986 and Bader 1990; they discuss the plain style concept with respect to Castiglione's *Cortegiano* (Italy), Juan de Valdés' *Diálogo de la lengua* (Spain) and French authors of the 17th century.
36. Compare Goetsch 1987.
37. See for example Stefenelli 1962; Happ 1967; Petersmann 1977.
38. Compare with regard to this problem the fundamental article of Warning 1981.
39. General aspects of oral poetry are discussed in Lord 1960; Bowra 1964; Finnegan 1977; Voorwinden et al. 1979; Zumthor 1983a and 1983b; Bäuml 1984/85 and 1987; Foley 1985, 1988, 1990, and 1991; Boedeker 1988; Ungern-Sternberg et al. 1988. For a discussion of Greek epic poems compare Parry 1971; Bowra 1972; Schadewaldt 1975; Kirk 1976; Latacz 1979 and 1988; Nagy 1979, 1990a, esp. chs. 1–3, and 1992a; Hatto, ed. 1980; Hainsworth, ed. 1989; Kullmann 1984, 1988, and 1993; Edwards 1986/1988/1992; Heubeck 1988; Kullmann/Reichel 1990; Stein 1990; Usener 1990; Ford 1992; Reichel 1994; Kullmann/Althoff 1993; Reichel 1994. For the Germanic area compare Baesecke 1945; Curschmann 1979; Busse 1987; Diller 1988; Renoir 1988; Wolf 1991; Kellogg 1991; Schaefer 1992. The traditions of Romance epic poetry are discussed for example in Rychner 1955; Montgomery 1977; Duggan 1985; Smith 1993; but see esp. the outstanding volumes edited by Lejeune et al. 1981–1987.
40. Zumthor 1983b:52–53.
41. The aspects mentioned are treated in detail by Foley 1977 and 1995a; Zumthor 1983a, 1983b, and 1987; Schaefer 1992; Bakker 1993a and 1993b; Ford 1992.
42. Compare e.g. Nystrand 1982 and 1987; Koch/Oesterreicher 1994. For different types of contextualization see Koch/Oesterreicher 1990:10–12.

43. Zumthor 1983b:52. See also Chailley 1950; Schmitt 1981; Schaefer 1992.

44. Compare Zumthor 1983a:229–234.

45. Lausberg 1969, § 1.

46. Compare e.g. Martin 1989; Kahane in the present volume.

47. Compare e.g. Stolz/Shannon 1976; Miletich 1986.

48. Compare Bühler 1965, Part II, §§ 7 and 8.

49. Compare Bakker in the present volume. Compare Fleischman 1990; see also Weinrich 1984.

50. Compare Martin in the present volume.

51. Compare e.g. Martin 1989.

52. Compare esp. Stempel 1972:596–601. Fundamental aspects of medieval culture and literacy are discussed in Balogh 1927; Crosby 1936; Chaytor 1945; Grundmann 1958; Mölk 1969; Clanchy 1979; Saenger 1982; Cerri 1986; Zumthor 1987; Illich/Sander 1988; McKitterick 1990; Illich 1991; Doane/Pasternack 1991; Keller et al. 1992; Banniard 1992; Curtius 1993; Oesterreicher 1993; Irvine 1994.

53. Compare Balibar 1985:19–56; McKitterick 1989; Bäuml in the present volume.

54. Compare Smith 1993, esp. 25–46; Montgomery 1977; Duggan 1989. See also Quint 1993.

55. Compare e.g. Duggan 1985 and 1986.

56. Compare esp. Curschmann 1979; Bäuml 1993a:262. This phenomenon can be related to Zumthor's concept of *oralité seconde;* compare for example Zumthor 1983b:56.

9. THE MEDIAL APPROACH

1. "Das neue Paradigma 'Kommunikation und die Medien'" (Assmann/Assmann 1990:3).

2. Assmann/Assmann 1990:1; *Vom Mythos zum Logos* is the title of a 1941 book by the classical scholar W. Nestle.

3. "Der neue Gedanke, den Havelock in sämtlichen seiner Werke elaboriert und variiert hat, ist der von der Medienabhängigkeit des Denkens. Sinn, Erfahrung, Wirklichkeit—all das sind abhängige Variablen der Medien, deren wir uns bedienen. Alles, was über die Welt gewusst, gedacht und gesagt werden kann, ist nur in Ab-

hängigkeit von den Medien wissbar, denkbar und sagbar, die dieses Wissen kommunizieren" (Assmann/Assmann 1990:2).

4. "Nicht die Sprache, in der wir denken, sondern die Medien, in denen wir kommunizieren, modellieren unsere Welt. Medienrevolutionen sind Sinnrevolutionen, sie re-modellieren die Wirklichkeit und schaffen eine neue Welt" (Assmann/Assmann 1990:2–3).

5. Kuhn [2]1969:175.

6. Compare Oesterreicher 1977 who discusses this question from the point of view of linguistics.

7. For a detailed discussion of Dilthey's contribution to this differentiation see Gadamer 1972:205–228, and Habermas 1968/71:178–203.

8. "Gegebene Ereignisse können wir mit Hilfe von Gesetzeshypothesen aus erschlossenen Ausgangsbedingungen *erklären,* während symbolische Zusammenhänge durch explizierenden Nachvollzug *verstanden* werden" (Habermas 1968/71:184). Karlheinz Stierle has described the activity of the literary historian as follows: "Comprehensio, Zusammenfassung, ist im Lateinischen mit Verstehen gleichbedeutend. Das Werk selbst ist als eine Struktur der Verständlichkeit eine Struktur der comprehensio. Doch kann die Zusammenfassung da erst ihre höchste Bewusstheit erreichen, wo sie in Entfaltung, explicatio, übergeht" (Stierle 1990:16).

9. Olson 1986:113.

10. Ibid.

11. Ibid.

12. Olson 1986:115.

13. "Verstehen wird zum Verstehen dessen, dass das Verstehen keinen Boden und kein Subjekt mehr hat" (Stierle 1990:20). The only "medially conditioned" subjects Deconstruction seems to allow for are those people who need to realize that there is no such thing as conditions created by the (oral or script) "medium."

14. Derrida 1967:227; 1976:158.

15. Olson 1986:109.

16. Bloch 1990:38.

17. Kuhn [2]1969:111.

18. For the methodical differentiation between *medium* and *concept* compare Koch/Oesterreicher 1985 and Oesterreicher 1993 as well as in this volume.

19. For excellently informed surveys see Foley 1988, 1990, and 1991.
20. Bäuml 1968/79, 1978, 1980, 1984–85, and 1987.
21. Compare in particular Foley 1990, 1991.
22. Schaefer 1992.
23. Foley 1991:7.
24. Bäuml 1987:39.
25. Ibid.
26. Derrida 1976:13.
27. Gnomic diction, maxims, etc., may be regarded as a special form of idiomaticity, as a special kind of *phraseological units;* these are systematically opposed e.g. by Uriel Weinrich to *free construction;* see Weinrich 1969.
28. Spiegel 1990:74.
29. Compare the survey in Culler 1983:110–126.
30. Bakker 1993a:8–9.
31. Tannen 1982a:1–2.
32. Compare my discussion of various such definitions in Schaefer 1992:178–182.
33. "Allgemein liesse sich die Funktion der Sprichwörter in ihrer konkreten Verwendung in Texten und Situationen als *Kommentierung* kennzeichnen. Die Sprichwörter fügen sich nicht wie gewöhnliche Textsegmente in die Beschreibung oder Darstellung ein, sie unterbrechen vielmehr den Deskriptionsstrom durch eine Meta-Aussage, eben durch einen Kommentar" (Thun 1978:244).
34. Compare my discussion of gnomic diction in *Beowulf* in Schaefer 1992:183–210.
35. Compare for instance Tolkien 1936/63; for more critical appreciation of the "Christian Excursus" see references in Schaefer 1992:193–194.
36. The *Beowulf* quotes are taken from the Klaeber edition, punctuation and capitalizations are Klaeber's. The translations are taken from Chickering's edition.
37. It needs to be added here that this "distance" must not be conceived of as having an "alienating" effect. On the contrary, the use of gnomic diction here indicates that what the Danes went through is still pertinent for the audience that the narrator addresses. In Schaefer 1992 I have discussed this problem at some length (compare in particular p. 187). My argument is based on the observation that an

epic such as *Beowulf* was considered as an historical tale, and that we are grossly mistaken if we project our concept of historicity = pastness on the (earlier) Middle Ages; compare Eisenstein 1966 and Hans Ulrich Gumbrecht 1983, esp. pp. 164–165.

38. "Le formulisme embrasse le discours [poétique] comme tel, plus encore que son organisation langagière, et, dans sa mise en pratique, concerne la performance plutôt que la composition: telle est la fonction des *lieux* ou *topoi,* originellement partie de la *memoria* et de l'*actio* rhétoriques . . . Le *lieu commun* a pour fonction de rapproacher de l'auditeur la *materia remota* du discours, de concrétiser un contenu, en évitant néanmoins toute particularisation . . ." (Zumthor 1987:218–219).

39. I quote from Mackie's 1934 E.E.T.S. edition; this edition has no capitalization and no punctuation; the Modern English translations are taken from the same edition.

40. Quoted from the same edition as *Wulf and Eadwacer.*

41. In the manuscript these poems (as all other versified Old English material) appear "in prose," i.e., the arrangement in lines is that of modern editors. However, with *Wife's Lament,* the last metrical line is also the last line of that poem in the manuscript.

42. Note that, besides *Wife's Lament and Wulf and Eadwacer,* four other Old English Elegies (*Wanderer, Resignation, Riming Poem,* and *Deor*) have a gnomic ending. This is a ratio of six out of seven! For a more extensive discussion of gnomic diction in the Elegies see Schaefer 1992:211–230.

43. In German I have suggested to speak of *Sinnvermittlung* and *Sinnermittlung.*

44. Compare Olson 1977 who has argued that with (oral) utterances "the meaning is in the context," while with (written) texts "the meaning is in the text."

45. Compare my discussion of these explicational attempts in Schaefer 1986.

46. This is the title of Stierle's *Antrittsvorlesung* at Konstanz in 1989, where he succeeded Hans Robert Jauss.

47. "Man kann das Werk immer nur verstehen, aber nie es verstanden haben" (Stierle 1990:16; italics added).

48. Compare Oesterreicher pp. 210–211 in the present volume.

49. For the rise of fictionality in Ancient Greece compare Rösler 1980

and 1983; for the Middle Ages compare Jauss 1982 and Schaefer 1996.

50. For a discussion of the status of facts from the medial point of view compare Bäuml's contribution in the present volume.

51. For an excellent survey of the history especially of Romance philology see Gauger/Oesterreicher/Windisch 1981:45–94.

52. For a survey and a critical appreciation of such endeavors see Foley 1988:57–93.

53. Compare the chapter "The Modern Discovery of Orality" in Havelock 1986:24–29.

54. Only a few years ago I was more—and now I think *too*—daring in making a decision; see Schaefer 1993:191.

55. On its way to the printed version, the paper I gave at this conference has undergone substantial changes as a result of the discussion that immediately followed this paper, as well as the discussions of other papers and the many fruitful conversations at the fringe of this conference for which I want to thank all the participants and in particular the organizers.

Achard, Guy, ed. 1989. *Rhétorique à Herennius.* Paris: Les Belles Lettres.

Adams, James N. 1977. *The vulgar Latin of the letters of Claudius Terentianus.* Manchester: Manchester U.P.

Akinnaso, F. Niyi. 1985. "On the Similarities between Spoken and Written Language." *Language and Speech* 28. 323–359.

Amodio, Mark C., ed. 1994. *Oral Poetics in Middle English Poetry.* New York: Garland.

Assmann, Aleida, and Jan Assmann. 1990. "Schrift—Kognition—Evolution. Eric A. Havelock und die Technologie kultureller Kommunikation." In: *Schriftlichkeit: Das griechische Alphabet als kulturelle Revolution,* Eric A. Havelock, ed., 1–35. Weinheim.

Assmann, Aleida, Jan Assmann, and Chr. Hardmeier, eds. 1983. *Schrift und Gedächtnis: Beiträge zur Archäologie der literarischen Kommunikation I.* Munich: Fink.

Azuonye, C. 1990. "Kaalu Igirigiri: An Ohafia Igbo Singer of Tales." In: *The Oral Performance in Africa,* I. Okpewho, ed., 42–79. Ibadan: Spectrum.

Bader, Eugen. 1990. "Celare artem: Kontext und Bedeutung der stilistischen Anweisung 'Schreibe, wie du redest!' im 16./17. Jahrhundert (Italien, Spanien, Frankreich)." In: Raible, ed. 1990, 197–217.

———. 1994. *Schreib-Rhetorik, Rede-Rhetorik, Konversationsrhetorik.* Tübingen: Narr (= ScriptOralia, 69).

Baesecke, Georg. 1945. *Das Hildebrandlied: Eine geschichtliche Einleitung für Laien.* Halle: Niemeyer.

Bailly, Edouard. 1937. *Cicéron—Lettres à Atticus, Vol. I–III.* Paris: Garnier.

Bakhtin, Mikhail M. 1981. "Discourse in the Novel." In: *The Dialogic Imagination: Four Essays,* trans. C. Emerson and M. Holquist, 259–422. Austin: University of Texas Press.

Bakker, Egbert J. 1993a. "Activation and Preservation: The Interdependence of Text and Performance in an Oral Tradition." *Oral Tradition* 8. 5–20.

———. 1993b. "Discourse and Performance: Involvement, Visualization, and 'Presence' in Homeric Poetry." *Classical Antiquity* 12. 1–29.

———. 1995. "Noun-Epithet Formulas, Milman Parry, and the Grammar of Poetry." In: *Homeric Questions*, J. P. Crielaard, ed. 97–125. Amsterdam: Gieben.

———. 1996. *Poetry in Speech: Orality and Homeric Discourse*. Ithaca and London: Cornell University Press *(Myth and Poetics)*.

Balibar, Renée. 1985. *L'institution du français: Essai sur le colinguisme des Carolingiens à la République*. Paris: Presses Universitaires de France.

Balogh, Joseph. 1927. "'Voces paginarum.' Beiträge zur Geschichte des lauten Lesens und Schreibens." *Philologus* 82. 84–109, 202–240.

Banniard, Michel. 1992. *Viva Voce: Communication écrite et communication orale du IVe au IXe siècle en Occident latin*. Paris: Institut des études augustiniennes (= Collection des études augustiniennes; Série Moyen-Age et Temps Modernes, 255).

Basset, Louis. 1979. *Les emplois périphrastiques du verbe grec μέλλειν: Étude de linguistique grecque et essai de linguistique générale*. Lyon: Maison de l'Orient.

———. 1989. "L'augment et la distinction discours/récit dans l'*Iliade* et l'*Odyssée*." In: *Études homériques*. Travaux de la maison de l'Orient 17. 9–16. Lyon: Maison de l'Orient.

Basso, E. 1985. *A Musical View of the Universe*. Philadelphia: University of Pennsylvania Press.

Bauman, Richard. 1977. *Verbal Art as Performance*. Prospect Heights: Waveland Press.

Bauman, Richard, and Charles L. Briggs. 1990. "Poetics and Performance as Critical Perspectives on Language and Social Life." *Annual Review of Anthropology* 19. 59–88.

Bäuml, Franz H. 1979. "Der Übergang mündlicher zur *artes*-bestimmten Literatur des Mittelalters: Gedanken und Bedenken." In: Voorwinden and De Haan, eds., 237–262.

———. 1978. "Medieval Literacy and Illiteracy: An Essay toward the Construction of a Model." In: *Germanic Studies in Honor of Otto Springer*, Stephen J. Kaplowitt, ed., 41–54. Pittsburgh: K&S Enterprises.

———. 1980. "Varieties and Consequences of Medieval Literacy and Illiteracy." *Speculum* 55. 237–265.

———. 1984–1985. "Medieval Texts and the Two Theories of Oral-Formulaic Composition: A Proposal for a Third Theory." *New Literary History* 16. 31–49.

———. 1987. "The Theory of Oral-Formulaic Composition and the Written Medieval Text." In: *Comparative Research on Oral Traditions: A Memorial for Milman Parry*, John Miles Foley, ed., 29–45. Columbus, Oh: Slavica Publishers.

———. 1993. "Verschriftlichte Mündlichkeit und vermündlichte Schriftlichkeit: Begriffsprüfungen an den Fällen *Heliand* und *Liber Evangeliorum*." In: Schaefer, ed. 1993, 254–266.

Ben-Amos, Dan. 1984. "The Seven Strands of *Tradition:* Varieties in Its Meaning in American Folklore Studies." *Journal of Folklore Research* 21. 97–131.

Berger, Peter L., and Thomas Luckmann. 1980. *The Social Construction of Reality.* New York: Irvington Publishers.

Bernstein, Basil. 1960/61. "Social structure, language, and learning." *Education Research* 3. 163–176.

Biber, Douglas. 1988. *Variation across Speech and Writing.* Cambridge: Cambridge University Press.

Biebuyck, Daniel, ed. 1971. *The Mwindo Epic from the Banyanga.* Berkeley: University of California Press.

Blackburn, Stuart. 1986. "Performance Markers in an Indian Story-Type." In: *Another Harmony: New Essays on the Folklore of India*, S. Blackburn and A. Ramanujan, eds., 167–194. Berkeley and Los Angeles: University of California Press.

Blackburn, Stuart, P. Claus, et al., eds. 1989. *Oral Epics in India.* Berkeley and Los Angeles: University of California Press.

Blackburn, Stuart, and J. B. Flueckiger. 1989. "Introduction." In: Blackburn, Claus et al., eds., 1–11.

Bloch, R. Howard. 1990. "New Philology and Old French." *Speculum* 65. 38–58.

Blumenberg, H. 1969. "Wirklichkeitsbegriff und Möglichkeiten des Romans." In: *Nachahmung und Illusion. (Poetik und Hermeneutik I)*, Hans Robert Jauss, ed. Munich: Fink.

Boedeker, Deborah. 1988. "Amerikanische Oral-Tradition-Forschung:

Eine Einführung." In: Ungern-Sternberg and Reinau, eds. 1988, 34–53.

Boisacq, E. 1938. *Dictionnaire étymologique de la langue grecque.* 3rd ed. Heidelberg: Winter.

Bowra, Cecil Maurice. 1964. *Heldendichtung—Eine vergleichende Phänomenologie der heroischen Poesie aller Völker und Zeiten.* Stuttgart: Metzler.

———. 1972. *Homer.* London: Duckworth.

Boyarin, Jonathan, ed. 1993. *The Ethnography of Reading.* Berkeley and Los Angeles: University of California Press.

Bréal, M. 1911. *Pour mieux connaître Homère.* 2nd ed. Paris: Hachette.

Bremer, J.-M., I. J. F. de Jong, and J. Kalff, eds. 1987. *Homer. Beyond Oral Poetry: Recent Trends in Homeric Interpretation.* Amsterdam: Grüner.

Bresslau, Harry. 1912. *Handbuch der Urkundenlehre für Deutschland und Italien,* vol. 1. Leipzig: Veit & Co.

Bruni, Francesco. 1984. *L'italiano. Elementi di storia della lingua e della cultura: Testi e documenti.* Turin: UTET.

Bühler, Karl. 1965. *Sprachtheorie: Die Darstellungsfunktion der Sprache.* 2nd ed. Stuttgart: Fischer.

Burkert, Walter. 1987. "The Making of Homer in the Sixth Century: Rhapsodes versus Stesichoros." In: *Papers on the Amasis Painter and his World,* 43–62. Malibu, Calif.: Getty Museum.

Burns, Alfred. 1989. *The Power of the Written Word: The Role of Literacy in the History of Western Civilization.* New York: Peter Lang (= Studia Classica, 1).

Bury, J. B. ed. 1892. *The Isthmian Odes of Pindar.* London; repr. 1965. Amsterdam: Hakkert.

Busse, Wilhelm. 1987. *Altenglische Literatur und ihre Geschichte: Zur Kritik des gegenwärtigen Deutungssystems.* Düsseldorf: Droste (= Studia humaniora, 7).

Caizzi, Fernanda Decleva. 1966. *Antisthenis Fragmenta.* Milan: A. Nicola.

Callebat, Louis. 1992. "Problèmes formels de la vulgarisation scientifique et technique." In: Iliescu and Marxgut, eds., 63–73.

Cerri, Giovanni, ed. 1986. *Scrivere e recitare: Modelli di trasmissione del testo poetico nell'antichità e nel medioevo. Atti di una ricerca in-*

terdisciplinare svolta presso l'Istituto Universitario Orientale di Napoli. Rome: Edizioni dell'Ateneo.

Chafe, Wallace. 1982. "Integration and Involvement in Speaking, Writing, and Oral Literature." In: *Spoken and Written Language: Exploring Orality and Literacy,* D. Tannen, ed., 35–53. Norwood, N.J.: Ablex (= Advances in Discourse Processes, 9).

———. 1985. "Linguistic Differences Produced by Differences between Speaking and Writing." In: *Literacy, Language, and Learning: The Nature and Consequences of Reading and Writing,* D. R. Olson, et al., eds., 105–123. Cambridge: Cambridge University Press.

———. 1994. *Consciousness, Discourse, and Time: The Flow and Displacement of Conscious Experience in Speaking and Writing.* Chicago and London: The University of Chicago Press.

Chafe, Wallace, and Jane Danielewicz. 1987. "Properties of Spoken and Written Language." In: Horowitz and Samuels, eds., 83–113.

Chailley, Jacques. 1950. *Histoire de la musique du moyen âge.* Paris: Presses Universitaires de France.

Chantraine, Pierre. 1958. *Grammaire homérique, vol. I: Phonétique et morphologie.* Paris: Klincksieck.

———. 1963. *Grammaire homérique, vol. II: Syntaxe.* Paris: Klincksieck.

———. 1968–1980. *Dictionnaire étymologique de la langue grecque.* Paris: Klincksieck.

Chaytor, Henry John. 1945. *From Script to Print: An Introduction to Medieval Literature.* Cambridge: Cambridge University Press.

Chiche, Michèle et al., eds. 1989. *Graines de parole: Puissance du verbe et traditions orales. Textes offerts à Geneviève Calame-Griaule.* Paris: Éditions du C.N.R.S.

Chickering, Howell D. Jr., ed. 1977. *Beowulf: A Dual-Language Edition.* Garden City, N.Y.: Anchor Press.

Clanchy, Michael Thomas. 1979. *From Memory to Written Record: England 1066–1307.* London: Arnold.

Comrie, Bernard. 1976. *Aspect.* Cambridge: Cambridge University Press.

———. 1985. *Tense.* Cambridge: Cambridge University Press.

Connelly, B. 1986. *Arab Folk Epic and Identity.* Berkeley and Los Angeles: University of California Press.

Coote, Mary P. 1981. "Lying in Passages." *Canadian-American Slavic Studies* 15. 5–23.

Coseriu, Eugenio. 1978. "Das sogenannte 'Vulgärlatein' und die ersten Differenzierungen in der Romania." In: *Zur Entstehung der romanischen Sprachen,* R. Kontzi, ed., 257–291. Darmstadt: Wissenschaftliche Buchgesellschaft.

Crosby, Ruth. 1936. "Oral Delivery in the Middle Ages." *Speculum* 11. 88–110.

Crotty, Kevin. 1994. *The Poetics of Supplication: Homer's Iliad and Odyssey.* Ithaca and London: Cornell University Press *(Myth and Poetics).*

Cugusi, Paolo. 1981. "Gli ostraka latini dello Wâdi Fawâkhir: Per la storia del latino." In: *Letterature comperate: Problemi e metodo. Studi in onore di E. Paratore,* Vol. 2, 719–753. Bologna: Pàtron.

Culler, Jonathan. 1975. *Structuralist Poetics.* Ithaca: Cornell University Press.

————. 1983. *On Deconstruction: Theory and Criticism after Structuralism.* London: Routledge.

Curschmann, Michael. 1979. "'Nibelungenlied' und 'Nibelungenklage.' Über Mündlichkeit und Schriftlichkeit im Prozess der Episierung." In: *Deutsche Literatur im Mittelalter—Kontakte und Perspektiven. Hugo Kuhn zum Gedenken,* Christoph Cormeau, ed., 85–119. Stuttgart: Metzler.

Curtius, Ernst Robert. 1993. *Europäische Literatur und lateinisches Mittelalter.* 8th ed. Tübingen: Francke.

d'Aquili, Eugene, and Charles D. Laughlin, Jr. 1979. "The Neurobiology of Myth and Ritual." In: *The Spectrum of Ritual,* E. d'Aquili, C. D. Laughlin, and J. McManus, eds. New York: Columbia University Press.

Daitz, S. 1991. "On Reading Homer Aloud: To Pause or not to Pause." *American Journal of Philology* 112. 149–160.

————. 1992. In response to Wyatt 1991. *Bryn Mawr Classical Review* 3. 1.16.

Davison, J. A. 1962. "The Transmission of the Text." In: Wace and Stubbings, eds., 215–233.

————. 1965. "Thucydides, Homer, and the 'Achaean Wall.'" *Greek, Roman and Byzantine Studies* 6. 5–28.

————. 1968. *From Archilochus to Pindar.* London: MacMillan.

De Beaugrande, Robert. 1980. *Text, Discourse, and Process: Towards a Multidisciplinary Science of Texts.* Norwood, N.J.: Ablex.

———. 1984. *Text Production.* Norwood, N.J.: Ablex.

Deese, J. 1980. "Pause, Prosody, and the Demands of Production in Language." In: *Temporal Variables in Speech: Studies in Honour of Frieda Goldman-Eisler,* H. W. Dechert and M. Raupach, eds., 67–84. The Hague: Mouton (*Janua Linguarum* series maior 86).

De Mauro, Tullio. 1970. "Tra Thamus e Teuth: Note sulla norma parlata e scritta, formale e informale nella produzione e realizzazione dei segni linguistici." In: *Lingua parlata e lingua scritta. Convegno di Studi 9–11 nov. 1967,* 167–179. Palermo: Centro di studi filologici e linguistici siciliani.

Derrida, Jacques. 1967. *De la grammatologie.* Paris: Minuit.

———. 1976. *Of Grammatology.* Trans. Gayatri Chakravorty Spivak. Baltimore and London: Johns Hopkins University Press.

Détienne, Marcel. 1967. *Les maîtres de vérité dans la Grèce archaïque.* Paris: Maspéro.

Devine, A. M., and D. Stephens. 1994. *The Prosody of Greek Speech.* Oxford: Oxford University Press.

Diller, Hans-Jürgen. 1988. "Literacy and Orality in Beowulf: The Problem of Reference." In: *Mündlichkeit und Schriftlichkeit im englischen Mittelalter,* W. Erzgräber, S. Volk, eds., 15–25. Tübingen: Narr (= ScriptOralia, 5).

DK = H. Diels and W. Kranz. 1952. *Die Fragmente der Vorsokratiker.* 6th ed., 3 vols. Berlin: Weidmann.

Doane, Alger N. 1991. "Oral Texts, Intertexts, and Intratexts: Editing Old English." In: *Influence and Intertextuality in Literary History,* Jay Clayton and Eric Rothstein, eds., 75–113. Madison: University of Wisconsin Press.

———. 1994. "Performance as a Constitutive Category in the Editing of Anglo-Saxon Poetic Texts." *Oral Tradition* 9. 420–439.

Doane, Alger N., and Carol Braun Pasternack, eds. 1991. *Vox Intexta: Orality and Textuality in the Middle Ages.* Madison: University of Wisconsin Press.

Downing, Pamela, Susan C. Lima, and Michael Noonan, eds. 1992. *The Linguistics of Literacy.* Amsterdam and Philadelphia: Benjamins (= Typological Studies in Language, 21).

Droudakis, A. 1982. *Mantinades tse Kretes.* Khania.

DuBois, Thomas. 1994. "An Ethnopoetic Approach to Finnish Folk Poetry: Arhippa Perttunen's Nativity." In: *Songs Beyond the Kalevala: Transformations of Oral Poetry*, Anna-Leena Siikala and Sinikka Vakimo, eds., 138–179. Helsinki: Suomalaisen Kirjallisuuden Seura (*Studia Fennica Folkloristica*, 2).

Duggan, Joseph J. 1973. *The Song of Roland: Formulaic Style and Poetic Craft.* Berkeley and Los Angeles: University of California Press.

―――. 1985. "Die zwei 'Epochen' der Chanson de geste." In: *Epochenschwellen und Epochenstrukturen im Diskurs der Literatur- und Sprachhistorie,* H. U. Gumbrecht, U. Link-Heer, eds., 389–408. Frankfurt a.M.: Suhrkamp.

―――. 1986. "Medieval Epic as Popular Historiography: Appropriation of the Historical Knowledge in the Vernacular Epic." In: *La littérature historiographique des origines à 1500,* H. U. Gumbrecht et al., eds., 285–311. Heidelberg: Winter (= Grundriss der romanischen Literaturen des Mittelalters, Vol. XI/1).

―――. 1989. *The Cantar de Mio Cid: Poetic Creation in Its Economic and Social Contexts.* Cambridge: Cambridge University Press.

Durante, Marcello. 1981. *Dal latino all'italiano moderno.* Bologna: Zanichelli.

Edmunds, Susan T. 1990. *Homeric Nēpios.* New York and London: Garland.

Edwards, Mark W. 1986. "Homer and Oral Tradition: The Formula, Part I." *Oral Tradition* 1. 171–230.

―――. 1988. "Homer and Oral Tradition: The Formula, Part II." *Oral Tradition* 3. 11–60.

―――. 1991. *The Iliad: A Commentary: Volume V: books 17–20.* Cambridge: Cambridge University Press.

―――. 1992. "Homer and Oral Tradition: The Type-Scene." *Oral Tradition* 7. 284–330.

Eigler, Gunther. 1995. "Textproduzieren als konstruktiver Prozeß." In: *Enzyklopädie der Psychologie, vol. III,* F. E. Weinert, ed. Göttingen: Hofgrebe.

Eisenstein, Elizabeth E. 1966. "Clio and Chronos: An Essay on the Making and Breaking of History-Book Time." *History and Theory* 6. 36–64.

Erbse, Hartmut, ed. 1971. *Scholia Graeca in Homeri Iliadem (scholia vetera), vol. 2.* Berlin: De Gruyter.

————. 1975. *Scholia Graeca in Homeri Iliadem (scholia vetera), vol. 4.* Berlin: De Gruyter.

————. 1988. *Scholia Graeca in Homeri Iliadem (scholia vetera), vol. 7.* Berlin: De Gruyter.

Fehling, Detlev. 1965. "Zwei Untersuchungen zur griechischen Sprachphilosophie." *Rheinisches Museum* 108. 212–217.

Feld, Stephen. 1990. *Sound and Sentiment: Weeping, Poetics, and Song in Kaluli Expression,* 2nd ed. Philadelphia: University of Pennsylvania Press.

Fentress, James, and Chris Wickham. 1992. *Social Memory.* Oxford: Blackwell.

Ferguson, Charles. 1959. "Diglossia." *Word* 15. 325–340.

Fine, Elizabeth C. 1984. *The Folklore Text: From Performance to Print.* Bloomington: Indiana University Press.

Finnegan, Ruth. 1970. *Oral Literature in Africa.* Oxford: Clarendon Press.

————. 1977. *Oral Poetry: Its Nature, Significance, and Social Context.* Cambridge: Cambridge University Press.

————. 1988. *Literacy and Orality: Studies in the Technology of Communication.* Oxford: Blackwell.

Fishman, Joshua A. 1967. "Bilingualism with and without Diglossia: Diglossia with and without Bilingualism." *Journal of Social Issues* 23. 29–38.

Fleischman, Suzanne. 1990. *Tense and Narrativity: From Medieval Performance to Modern Fiction.* Austin: University of Texas Press.

Foley, John Miles. 1977. "The Traditional Oral Audience." *Balkan Studies* 18. 145–153.

————. 1983. "Literary Art and Oral Tradition in Old English and Serbian Poetry." *Anglo-Saxon England* 12. 183–214.

————. 1985. *Oral-Formulaic Theory and Research: An Introduction and Annotated Bibliography.* New York: Garland. Rpt. 1988, 1992.

————. 1988. *The Theory of Oral Composition: History and Methodology.* Bloomington: Indiana University Press. Rpt. 1992.

————. 1990. *Traditional Oral Epic: The Odyssey, Beowulf, and the Serbo-Croatian Return Song.* Berkeley: University of California Press. Rpt. 1993.

————. 1991. *Immanent Art: From Structure to Meaning in Traditional Oral Epic.* Bloomington: Indiana University Press.

————. 1992. "Word-Power, Performance, and Tradition." *Journal of American Folklore* 105. 275–301.

————. 1994. "Explaining a Joke: Pelt Kid and Tale of Orašac." *Western Folklore* 53. 51–68.

————. 1995a. *The Singer of Tales in Performance.* Bloomington: Indiana University Press.

————. 1995b. "Folk Literature." In: *Scholarly Editing: An Introductory Guide to Research,* David C. Greetham, ed. New York: Modern Language Association.

————. 1996. "*Guslar* and *Goidos:* Traditional Register in South Slavic and Homeric Epic." TAPA 126. 11–41.

Ford, Andrew. 1991. "Unity in Greek Criticism and Poetry." *Arion* 3rd series 1. 125–154.

————. 1992. *Homer: The Poetry of the Past.* Ithaca and London: Cornell University Press.

Forssman, B. 1966. *Untersuchungen zur Sprache Pindars.* Wiesbaden: Harrasowitz.

Fowler, R. L. 1987. *The Nature of Early Greek Lyric.* Toronto: University of Toronto Press.

Fränkel, Hermann. 1921. *Die homerischen Gleichnisse.* Göttingen: Vandenhoeck & Ruprecht.

Frisk, H. 1960–1972. *Griechisches etymologisches Wörterbuch.* Heidelberg: Winter.

Gadamer, Hans-Georg. 1972. *Wahrheit und Methode: Grundzüge einer philosophischen Hermeneutik.* 3rd rev. ed. Tübingen: Mohr (1st ed. 1962).

————. 1989. *Truth and Method.* Rev. trans. by Joel Weinsheimer and Donald Marshall, 2nd rev. ed. New York: Crossroad.

Garzya, A. 1958. *Teognide Elegie Libri I-II.* Florence.

Gauger, Hans-Martin. 1986. "'Schreibe, wie du redest!' Zu einer stilistischen Norm." In: *Sprachnormen in der Diskussion: Beiträge vorgelegt von Sprachfreunden,* 21–40. Berlin and New York: de Gruyter.

Gauger, Hans-Martin, Wulf Oesterreicher, and Rudolf Windisch. 1981. *Einführung in die romanische Sprachwissenschaft.* Darmstadt: Wissenschaftliche Buchgesellschaft.

Geiger, D. 1958. *The Sound, Sense, and Performance of Literature.* Chicago: Scott, Foresman.

Gimson, A. C. 1994. *An Introduction to the Pronunciation of English.* 5th ed. New York and London: E. Arnold.

Givón, Talmy. 1979. *On Understanding Grammar.* New York: Academic Press.

Glasersfeld, Ernst von. 1989. "Facts and the Self from a Constructivist Point of View." *Poetics* 18. 435–448.

Goetsch, Paul. 1987. "Orality and Literacy Events in English Fiction." *Komparatistische Hefte* 15/16. 147–161.

Goetz, Hans-Werner. 1993. "Verschriftlichung von Geschichtskenntnissen." In: Schaefer, ed. 1993, 229–253.

Goodwin, Charles, and Alessandro Duranti. 1992. "Rethinking Context: An Introduction." In: *Rethinking Context: Language as an Interactive Phenomenon,* Alessandro Duranti and Charles Goodwin, eds., 1–42. Cambridge: Cambridge University Press.

Goody, Jack. 1977. *The Domestication of the Savage Mind.* Cambridge: Cambridge University Press.

———. 1987. *The Logic of Writing and the Organization of Society.* Cambridge: Cambridge University Press.

Goold, G. P. 1977. "The Nature of Homeric Composition." *Illinois Classical Studies* 2. 1–34.

Gow, A. S. F., ed. 1965. *Theocritus, vol. 2.* Cambridge: Cambridge University Press.

Graff, Harvey J. 1987. *The Legacies of Literacy: Continuities and Contradictions in Western Culture and Society.* Bloomington: Indiana University Press.

Greenwood, Leonard H. G. 1953. *Aspects of Euripidean Tragedy.* Cambridge: Cambridge University Press.

Griffin, Jasper. 1976. "Homeric Pathos and Objectivity." *Classical Quarterly* 26. 161–187.

———. 1980. *Homer on Life and Death.* Oxford: Oxford Univ. Press.

———. 1986. "Homeric Words and Speakers." *Journal of Hellenic Studies* 102. 736–757.

Grimm, Jürgen. 1962. "Die Partikel ἄρα im frühen griechischen Epos." *Glotta* 40. 3–41.

Groningen, B. A. van. 1966. *Théognis: Le premier livre.* Amsterdam: *Verhandelingen der Koninklijke Nederlandse Akademie van Wetenschappen* 72.

Grundmann, Herbert. 1958. "Litteratus-illitteratus. Der Wandel einer

Bildungsnorm vom Altertum zum Mittelalter." *Archiv für Kultur-geschichte* 40. 1–65.

Gumbrecht, Hans Ulrich. 1983. "Schriftlichkeit in mündlicher Kultur." In: Assman, Assmann, and Hardmeier, eds. 1983, 158–174. Munich: Fink.

Günther, Hartmut, and Otto Ludwig, eds. 1994. *Schrift und Schriftlichkeit/Writing and Its Use: Ein interdisziplinäres Handbuch internationaler Forschung/An Interdisciplinary Handbook of International Research, Vol. 1.* Berlin and New York: de Gruyter (= Handbücher zur Sprach-und Kommunikationswissenschaft, 11).

Habermas, Jürgen. 1968. *Erkenntnis und Interesse.* Frankfurt a.M.: Suhrkamp.

Hainsworth, Bryan. 1969. *Homer. Greece and Rome. New Surveys in the Classics 3.* Oxford: Clarendon Press.

———, ed. 1989. *Traditions of Heroic and Epic Poetry. Vol. 2: Characteristics and Techniques.* London: Modern Humanities Research Association.

———. 1993. *The Iliad: A Commentary, vol. III. Books 9–12.* Cambridge: Cambridge University Press.

Halliday, Michael A. K. 1987. "Spoken and Written Modes of Meaning." In: Horowitz and Samuels, eds. 1987, 55–82.

Hansen, William F. 1990. "Odysseus and the Oar: A Folkloric Approach." In: *Approaches to Greek Myth,* Lowell Edmunds, ed., 241–272. Baltimore: Johns Hopkins University Press.

Hanson, Norwood Russell. 1965. *Patterns of Discovery.* Cambridge: Cambridge University Press.

Happ, Heinz. 1967. "Die lateinische Umgangssprache und die Kunstsprache des Plautus." *Glotta* 45. 60–104.

Harris, William V. 1989. *Ancient Literacy.* Cambridge, Mass.: Harvard University Press.

Harrison, E. 1902. *Studies in Theognis.* Cambridge: Cambridge University Press.

Hatto, A. T., ed. 1980. *Traditions of Heroic and Epic Poetry. Vol. I: The Traditions.* London: The Modern Humanities Research Association.

Havelock, Eric A. 1976. *Origins of Western Literacy.* Toronto: Ontario Institute for Studies in Education (= Ontario Institute for Studies in Education; Monograph Series, 14).

————. 1986. *The Muse Learns to Write: Reflections on Orality and Literacy from Antiquity to the Present.* New Haven and London: Yale University Press.

Herman, Joseph. 1990. "Sur un exemple de la langue parlée à Rome au VIe siècle." In: *Latin vulgaire—latin tardif, II. Actes du IIe Colloque international sur le latin vulgaire et tardif,* G. Calboli, ed., 145–157. Tübingen: Niemeyer.

Herzfeld, M. 1985. *The Poetics of Manhood: Contest and Identity in a Cretan Mountain Village.* Princeton: Princeton University Press.

Heubeck, Alfred. 1988. *Die homerische Frage.* 2nd ed. Darmstadt: Wiss. Buchgesellschaft (= Erträge der Forschung, 27).

Heubeck, Alfred, S. R. West, and J. B. Hainsworth. 1988. *A Commentary on Homer's Odyssey vol. i.* Oxford: Oxford University Press.

Hoffmann, Karl. 1967. *Der Injunktiv im Veda.* Heidelberg: Winter.

Hofmann, Johann Baptist. 1986. *La lingua d'uso latina: Introduzione, traduzione italiana e note a cura di L. Rocottili.* 2nd ed. Bologna: Pàtron.

Hogg, R., and C. B. McCully. 1987. *Metrical Phonology: A Coursebook.* Cambridge: Cambridge University Press.

Holoka, James P. 1983. "'Looking Darkly' (ΥΠΟΔΡΑ ΙΔΩΝ): Reflections on Status and Decorum in Homer." *Transactions of the American Philological Association* 113. 1–16.

Horowitz, Rosalind, and S. Jay Samuels, eds. 1987. *Comprehending Oral and Written Language.* New York: Academic Press.

Houis, Maurice. 1989. "Pour une taxinomie des textes en oralité." In: Chiche et al., eds. 1989, 167–184.

Householder, F. W., and G. Nagy. 1972. *Greek: A Survey of Recent Work.* The Hague: Mouton.

Hymes, Dell. 1981. *"In Vain I Tried to Tell You." Essays in Native American Ethnopoetics.* Philadelphia: University of Pennsylvania Press.

————. 1989. "Ways of Speaking." In: *Explorations in the Ethnography of Speaking.* 2nd ed. Richard Bauman and Joel Sherzer, eds., 433–451; 473–474. Cambridge: Cambridge University Press.

————. 1994. "Ethnopoetics, Oral-Formulaic Theory, and Editing Texts." *Oral Tradition* 9. 330–370.

IEG = M. L. West, ed. 1989/1992. *Iambi et Elegi Graeci.* 2nd ed., 2 vols. Oxford: Clarendon Press.

Iliescu, Maria, and Werner Marxgut, eds. 1992. *Latin vulgaire—latin tardif III. Actes du IIIe Colloque international sur le latin vulgaire et tardif.* Tübingen: Niemeyer.

Iliescu, Maria, and Dan Slusanski, eds. 1991. *Du latin aux langues romanes: Choix de textes traduits et commentés (du IIe siècle avant J.C. jusqu'au Xe siècle après J.C.)* Wilhelmsfeld: Egert.

Illich, Ivan. 1991. "A Plea for Research on Lay Literacy." In: Olson and Torrance, eds. 1991, 28–46.

Illich, Ivan, and Barry Sanders. 1988. *ABC: The Alphabetization of the Popular Mind.* San Francisco: North Point Press.

Ingalls, W. 1970. "The Structure of the Homeric Hexameter: A Review." *Phoenix* 24. 1–24.

Irvine, Martin. 1994. *The Making of Textual Culture: "Grammatica" and Literary Theory, 350–1100.* Cambridge: Cambridge University Press.

Iser, Wolfgang. 1978. *The Act of Reading.* Baltimore and London: Johns Hopkins University Press.

Jaffé, Philipp, ed. 1867. *Monachus Sangallensis de Carolo Magno. Bibliotheca rerum Germanicarum.* Vol. IV. *Monumenta Carolina.* Berlin; repr. 1964 Aalen: Scientia.

Janko, Richard. 1982. *Homer, Hesiod, and the Hymns: Diachronic Development in Epic Diction.* Cambridge: Cambridge University Press.

———. 1992. *The Iliad: A Commentary. Vol IV: books 13–16.* Cambridge: Cambridge University Press.

Jauss, Hans Robert. 1969. "Paradigmawechsel in der Literaturwissenschaft." *Linguistische Berichte* 3. 44–56.

———. 1982. "Zur historischen Genese der Scheidung von Fiktion und Realität." In: *Funktionen des Fiktiven,* D. Henrich and W. Iser, eds., 423–431. Munich: Fink (= Poetik und Hermeneutik X).

Jensen, Minna Skafte. 1980. *The Homeric Question and the Oral-Formulaic Theory.* Copenhagen: Museum Tusculanum.

Jong, Irene J. F. de. 1987. *Narrators and Focalizers: The Presentation of the Story in the Iliad.* Amsterdam: Grüner.

Jong, Irene J. F. de, and John P. Sullivan, eds. 1994. *Modern Critical Theory and Classical Literature.* Leiden: Brill (= *Mnemosyne* supp. 130).

Kahane, Ahuvia. 1994. *The Interpretation of Order: A Study in the Poetics of Homeric Repetition.* Oxford: Clarendon Press.

Keller, Hagen, Klaus Grubmüller, and Nikolaus Staubach, eds. 1992. *Pragmatische Schriftlichkeit im Mittelalter: Erscheinungsformen und Entwicklungsstufen.* Munich: Fink (= Münstersche Mittelalter-Schriften, 65).

Kellogg, Robert. 1991. "Literacy and Orality in the Poetic Edda." In: Doane and Pasternack, eds. 1991, 89–101.

Kinsella, T. Trans. 1970. *The Táin.* Oxford: Oxford University Press.

Kirk, G. S. 1962. *The Songs of Homer.* Cambridge: Cambridge University Press.

———. 1965. *Homer and the Epic.* Cambridge: Cambridge University Press.

———. 1976. *Homer and the Oral Tradition.* Cambridge: Cambridge University Press.

———. 1985. *The Iliad: A Commentary. Volume I: books 1–4.* Cambridge: Cambridge University Press.

Kirkwood, G., ed. 1982. *Selections from Pindar.* Chico, Calif.: Scholars Press.

Klaeber, Frederick, ed. 1936. *"Beowulf" and "The Battle at Finnsburg."* 3rd ed. Boston and New York: D. C. Heath and Company.

Koch, Peter. 1990. "Von Frater Semeno zum Bojaren Neacsu: Listen als Domäne frühverschrifteter Volkssprache in der Romania." In: Raible, ed. 1990, 121–165.

———. 1993. "Pour une typologie conceptionnelle et médiale des plus anciens documents/monuments des langues romanes." In: Selig et al., eds. 1993, 39–81.

Koch, Peter, and Wulf Oesterreicher. 1985. "Sprache der Nähe—Sprache der Distanz: Mündlichkeit und Schriftlichkeit im Spannungsfeld von Sprachtheorie und Sprachgeschichte." *Romanistisches Jahrbuch* 36. 15–43.

———. 1990. *Gesprochene Sprache in der Romania: Französisch, Italienisch, Spanisch.* Tübingen: Niemeyer.

———. 1994. "Schriftlichkeit und Sprache." In: Günther and Ludwig, eds. 1994, 587–604.

Krischer, Tilman. 1971. *Formale Konventionen der homerischen Epik.* Munich: Beck (= Zetemata, 56).

Kuhn, Thomas S. 1962. *The Structure of Scientific Revolutions.* 2nd enl. ed. 1970. Chicago: The University of Chicago Press.

Kullmann, Wolfgang. 1984. "Oral Poetry Theory and Neoanalysis in

Homeric Research." *Greek, Roman and Byzantine Studies* 25. 307–323.

———. 1988. "'Oral Tradition/Oral History' und die frühgriechische Epik." In: Ungern-Sternberg and Reinau, eds. 1988, 184–196.

———. 1993. "Festgehaltene Kenntnisse im Schiffskatalog und im Tro-erkatalog der *Ilias.*" In: Kullmann and Althoff, eds. 1993, 129–147.

Kullmann, Wolfgang, and Jochen Althoff, eds. 1993. *Vermittlung und Tradierung von Wissen in der griechischen Kultur.* Tübingen: Narr (= ScriptOralia, 61).

Kullmann, Wolfgang, and Michael Reichel, eds. 1990. *Der Übergang von der Mündlichkeit zur Literatur bei den Griechen.* Tübingen: Narr (= ScriptOralia, 30).

Labov, William. 1972. *Language of the Inner City.* Philadelphia: University of Pennsylvania Press.

Lada, I. 1993–1994. "Empathic Understanding: Emotion and Cognition in Classical Dramatic Audience Response." *Proceedings of the Cambridge Philological Society* 39. 94–140.

Latacz, Joachim, ed. 1979. *Homer—Tradition und Neuerung.* Darmstadt: Wissenschaftliche Buchgesellschaft (= Wege der Forschung, 463).

———. 1988. "Zum Umfang und Art der Vergangenheitsbewahrung in der mündlichen Überlieferungsphase des griechischen Heldenepos." In: Ungern-Sternberg and Reinau, eds. 1988, 153–183.

Lateiner, Donald. 1989. "Teeth in Homer." *Liverpool Classical Monthly* 14. 18–23.

Lattimore, Richmond. 1965. Trans. *The Odyssey of Homer.* New York: Harper.

Lausberg, Heinrich. 1969. *Romanische Sprachwissenschaft* Vol. 1. 3rd ed. Berlin: De Gruyter.

———. 1990. *Handbuch der literarischen Rhetorik: Eine Grundlegung der Literaturwissenschaft.* 3rd ed. Munich: Hueber.

Leaf, Walter, ed. 1900–1902. *The Iliad* 2 vols. London; repr. 1971 Amsterdam: Hakkert.

Leeuwen, J. van. 1918. *Enchiridium dictionis epicae.* Leiden.

Le Goff, Jacques. 1977. *Storia e memoria.* Turin: Einaudi (French edition: *Histoire et mémoire,* Paris 1986: Gallimard).

Lehmann, Winfred P. 1993. *The Theoretical Bases of Indo-European Linguistics.* London and New York: Routledge.

Lejeune, Rita, Jeanne Wathelet-Willem, and Henning Krauss, eds. 1981/1985/1986/1987. *Les épopées romanes*. Heidelberg: Winter (= Grundriss der romanischen Literaturen des Mittelalters, III, 4 Vol.).

Lesky, Albin. 1967. *Homeros*. Sonderausgaben der Paulyschen Realencyclopädie, Suppl. XI. Stuttgart: Druckenmüller Verlag.

Lloyd, A. B. 1988. *Herodotus Book II: Commentary 99–182*. Leiden: Brill.

Löfstedt, Einar. 1911. *Philologischer Kommentar zur Peregrinatio Aetheriae*. Uppsala: Almqvist and Wiksell.

Lonsdale, S. 1990. *Creatures of Speech: Lion, Herding, and Hunting Similes in the Iliad*. Stuttgart: Teubner.

Loraux, N. 1993. *The Children of Athena: Athenian Ideas about Citizenship and the Division between the Sexes*, transl. C. Levine. Princeton: Princeton University Press.

Lord, Albert B. 1960. *The Singer of Tales*. Cambridge, Mass.: Harvard University Press.

———. 1962. "Homer and Other Epic Poetry." In: Wace and Stubbings, eds. 1962, 179–214.

———. 1969. "The Theme of the Withdrawn Hero in Serbo-Croatian Oral Epic." *Prilozi za knjizevnost, jezik, istoriju i folklor* 35. 18–30.

———. 1986a. "Perspectives on Recent Work on the Oral Traditional Formula." *Oral Tradition* 1. 467–503.

———. 1986b. "The Merging of Two Worlds: Oral and Written Poetry as Carriers of Ancient Values." In: *Oral Tradition in Literature: Interpretation in Context*, J. M. Foley, ed., 19–64. Columbia: University of Missouri Press.

———. 1991. *Epic Singers and Oral Tradition*. Ithaca: Cornell University Press.

———. 1995. *The Singer Resumes the Tale*. Ithaca: Cornell University Press.

LSJ = Liddell, H. R., R. Scott, and H. S. Jones. 1940. *A Greek English Lexicon*. 9th ed. Oxford: Oxford University Press.

Lüdtke, Helmut. 1964. "Zur Entstehung romanischer Schriftsprachen." *Vox Romanica* 23. 3–21.

Lüdtke, Jens, ed. 1994. *El español de América en el siglo XVI*. Frankfurt a.M.: Vervuert.

Luhmann, Niklas. 1970. *Soziologische Aufklärung.* Cologne: Westdeutscher Verlag.

Lutgendorf, Philip. 1991. *The Life of a Text: Performing the Râmcaritmânas of Tulsidas.* Berkeley and Los Angeles: University of California Press.

Lyons, John. 1981. *Language and Linguistics.* Cambridge: Cambridge University Press.

Mackie, W. S., ed. 1934. *The Exeter Book. Part II: Poems IX–XXXII,* E.E.T.S., O.S., vol. 194. Oxford: Oxford University Press.

Martin, Richard P. 1984. "Hesiod, Odysseus, and the Instruction of Princes." *Transactions of the American Philological Association* 114. 29–48.

———. 1989. *The Language of Heroes: Speech and Performance in the Iliad.* Ithaca: Cornell University Press.

———. 1992. "Hesiod's Metanastic Poetics." *Ramus* 21. 11–33.

———. 1993. "Telemachus and the Last Hero Song." *Colby Quarterly* 29. 222–240.

McKitterick, Rosamund. 1977. *The Frankish Church and the Carolingian Reforms, 789–895.* London: Royal Historical Society.

———. 1983. *The Frankish Kingdoms under the Carolingians 751–987.* London, New York: Longman.

———. 1989. *The Carolingians and the Written Word.* Cambridge: Cambridge University Press.

———, ed. 1990. *The Uses of Literacy in Early Mediaeval Europe.* Cambridge: Cambridge University Press.

McNeill, David. 1992. *Hand and Mind.* Chicago and London: The University of Chicago Press.

Meillet, Antoine. 1937. *Introduction à l'étude comparative des langues indo-européennes.* 8th ed. Repr. 1964 University, Al.: University of Alabama Press.

———. 1966. "Michel Bréal et la grammaire comparée au Collège de France." In: *Portraits of Linguists: A Biographical Source Book for the History of Western Linguistics 1746–1963, vol. 1,* T. Sebeok, ed., 440–453. Bloomington: Indiana University Press.

Merkelbach, Reinhold. 1952. "Die pisistratische Redaktion der homerischen Gedichte." *Rheinisches Museum* 95. 23–47.

Miletich, John S. 1986. "Oral Aesthetics and Written Aesthetics: The South Slavic Case and the Poema de Mio Cid." In: *Hispanic Studies*

Deyermond: A North American Tribute, 183–204. Madison: Hispanic Seminary of Medieval Studies.

Mills, M. 1990. *Oral Narrative in Afghanistan: The Individual in Tradition.* New York: Garland.

Mohrmann, Christine. 1961. *Études sur le latin des chrétiens.* 2nd ed. Rome: Edizioni di storia e letteratura.

Mölk, Ulrich. 1969. *Französische Literaturästhetik des 12. und 13. Jahrhunderts.* Tübingen: Niemeyer.

Monro, David B., and Thomas W. Allen, eds. 1969. *Homeri opera.* 3rd ed., 4 vols. Oxford: Clarendon Press.

Montgomery, Thomas. 1977. "The 'Poema de Mio Cid': Oral Art in Transition." In: *"Mio Cid" Studies,* A.D. Deyermond, ed., 91–112. London: Tamesis Books.

Morson, Gary Saul, and Caryl Emerson. 1990. *Mikhail Bakhtin: Creation of a Prosaics.* Stanford: Stanford University Press.

Moulton, C. 1977. *Similes in the Homeric Poems.* Göttingen: Vandenhoeck & Ruprecht (= *Hypomnemata,* 49).

Moyle, N. 1990. *The Turkish Minstrel Tale Tradition.* New York: Garland.

Muellner, Leonard C. 1976. *The Meaning of Homeric EYXOMAI through Its Formulas.* Innsbruck: Innsbrucker Beiträge zur Sprachwissenschaft.

Mühlbacher, H. 1896. *Deutsche Geschichte unter den Karolingern.* Stuttgart: Cotta.

Munro, D. B. 1891. *A Grammar of the Homeric Dialect.* Oxford: Clarendon Press.

Murko, Matija. 1929. *La poésie populaire épique en Yougoslavie au début du XXe siècle.* Paris: Librairie ancienne Honoré Champion. Part I trans. J. M. Foley, *Oral Tradition* 5 (1990), 107–130.

———. 1951. *Tragom srpsko-hrvatske narodne epike: Putovanja u godinama 1930–32,* 2 vols. Zagreb: Jugoslavenska Akademija Znanosti i Umjetnosti.

Murphy, James Jerome. 1974. *Rhetoric in the Middle Ages: A History of Rhetorical Theory from St. Augustine to the Renaissance.* Berkeley and Los Angeles: University of California Press.

Murray, Gilbert. 1934. *The Rise of the Greek Epic.* 4th ed. Oxford: Oxford University Press.

Nagler, Michael. 1974. *Spontaneity and Tradition.* Berkeley and Los Angeles: University of California Press.

Nagy, Gregory. 1970. *Greek Dialects and the Transformation of an Indo-European Process.* Cambridge, Mass.: Harvard University Press.

———. 1974. *Comparative Studies in Greek and Indic Meter.* Cambridge, Mass.: Harvard University Press.

———. 1979. *The Best of the Achaeans: Concepts of the Hero in Archaic Greek Poetry.* Baltimore and London: Johns Hopkins University Press.

———. 1985. "Theognis and Megara: A Poet's Vision of His City." In: *Theognis of Megara: Poetry and the Polis,* G. Nagy and T. Figueira, eds., 22–81. Baltimore: Johns Hopkins University Press.

———. 1990a. *Pindar's Homer: The Lyric Possession of an Epic Past.* Baltimore: Johns Hopkins University Press.

———. 1990b. *Greek Mythology and Poetics.* Ithaca: Cornell University Press (Myth and Poetics).

———. 1992a. "Homeric Questions." *Transactions of the American Philological Association* 122. 17–60.

———. 1992b. "Mythological Exemplum in Homer." In: *Innovations of Antiquity,* R. Hexter and D. Shelden, eds., 311–331. New York and London: Routledge.

———. 1995. "An Evolutionary Model for the Making of Homeric Poetry: Comparative Perspectives." In: *The Ages of Homer: A Tribute to Emily Townsend Vermeule,* J. B. Carter and S. P. Morris, eds., 163–179. Austin: University of Texas Press.

———. 1996a. *Poetry as Performance: Homer and Beyond.* Cambridge: Cambridge University Press.

———. 1996b. *Homeric Questions.* Austin: University of Texas Press.

Nelson, Janet. 1990. "Literacy in Carolingian Government." In: McKitterick, ed. 1990, 258–296.

Nencioni, Giovanni. 1976. "Parlato-parlato, parlato-scritto, parlato-recitato." *Strumenti Critici* 10. 1–56.

Nestle, W. 1941. *Vom Mythos zum Logos.* Leipzig.

Nilsson, M. P. 1921. *Die Anfänge der Göttin Athene.* Copenhagen: Det Kongelige Danske Videnskabermes Selskab.

Nimis, S. 1987. *Narrative Semiotics in the Epic Tradition: The Simile.* Bloomington: Indiana University Press.

Notopoulos, J. A. 1964. "Studies in Early Greek Oral Poetry." *Harvard Studies in Classical Philology* 68. 1–77.

Nystrand, Martin, ed. 1982. *What Writers Know: The Language, Process, and Structure of Written Discourse.* New York: Academic Press.

———. 1987. "The Role of Context in Written Communication." In: Horowitz and Samuels, eds. 1987, 197–214.

O'Brien O'Keeffe, Katherine. 1990. *Visible Song: Transitional Literacy in Old English Verse.* Cambridge: Cambridge University Press.

O'Neill, Jr., Eugene. 1942. "The Localization of Metrical Word-Types in the Greek Hexameter." *Yale Classical Studies* 8. 105–178.

Ochs, Elinor. 1979. "Planned and Unplanned Discourse." In: *Discourse and Syntax,* T. Givón, ed., 51–80. New York: Academic Press (= Syntax and Semantics, 12).

Oesterreicher, Wulf. 1977. "Paradigma und Paradigmawechsel—Thomas S. Kuhn und die Linguistik." *Osnabrücker Beiträge zur Sprachtheorie* 3. 241–284.

———. 1988. "Sprechtätigkeit, Einzelsprache, Diskurs und vier Dimensionen der Sprachvarietät." In: *Energeia und Ergon: Sprachliche Variation, Sprachgeschichte, Sprachtypologie. Studia in honorem Eugenio Coseriu, Vol. 2,* J. Albrecht et al., eds., 355–386. Tübingen: Narr.

———. 1993. "*Verschriftung* und *Verschriftlichung* im Kontext medialer und konzeptioneller Schriftlichkeit." In: Schaefer, ed. 1993, 267–292.

———. 1994a. "Kein sprachlicher Alltag—Der Konquistador Alonso Borregán schreibt eine Chronik." In: *Sprachlicher Alltag: Linguistik—Rhetorik—Literaturwissenschaft. Festschrift für Wolf-Dieter Stempel.* A. Sabban, and Chr. Schmitt, eds., 379–418. Tübingen: Niemeyer.

———. 1994b. "El español en textos escritos por semicultos: Competencia escrita de impronta oral en la historiografía indiana (s. XVI)." In: Lüdtke, ed. 1994, 155–190.

———. 1995. "Die Architektur romanischer Sprachen im Vergleich." In: *Konvergenz und Divergenz in den romanischen Sprachen,* W. Dahmen et al., eds., 3–21. Tübingen: Narr.

ÓhUiginn, R. 1992. "The Background and Development of *Táin Bó Cúailnge.*" In: *Aspects of the Táin,* J. P. Mallory, ed., 29–67. Belfast: December Publications.

Okpewho, Isidore. 1992. *African Oral Literature: Backgrounds, Character, and Continuity.* Bloomington: Indiana University Press.

Olson, David R. 1977. "From Utterance to Text: the Bias of Language in Speech and Writing." *Harvard Educational Review* 47. 257–281.

———. 1986. "The Cognitive Consequences of Literacy." *Canadian Psychology* 27. 109–121.

———. 1991. "Literacy as Metalinguistic Activity." In: Olson and Torrance, eds. 1991, 251–270.

———. 1994. *The World on Paper.* Cambridge: Cambridge University Press.

Olson, David R., and Nancy Torrance, eds. 1991. *Literacy and Orality.* Cambridge: Cambridge University Press.

Ong, Walter J. 1977. *Interfaces of the Word: Studies in the Evolution of Consciousness and Culture.* Ithaca: Cornell University Press.

———. 1982. *Orality and Literacy: The Technologizing of the Word.* London and New York: Methuen.

———. 1986. "Writing Is a Technology That Restructures Thought." In: *The Written Word: Literacy in Transition,* Gerd Baumann, ed., 23–50. Oxford: Clarendon Press.

Page, D. 1959. *History and the Historic Iliad.* Berkeley and Los Angeles: University of California Press.

Parks, Ward. 1986. "The Oral-Formulaic Theory in Middle English Studies." *Oral Tradition* 1. 636–694.

Parry, Milman. 1925. "A Comparative Study of Diction as One of the Elements of Style in Early Greek Epic Poetry." In: Parry 1971, 421–436.

———. 1928a. "The Traditional Epithet in Homer." Transl. Adam Parry. In: Parry 1971, 1–190.

———. 1928b. "Homeric Formulae and Homeric Metre." Transl. Adam Parry. In: Parry 1971, 191–239.

———. 1932. "Studies in the Epic Technique of Oral Verse-Making. II. The Homeric Language as the Language of an Oral Poetry." Repr. in Parry 1971, 325–364.

———. 1971. *The Making of Homeric Verse: The Collected Papers of Milman Parry,* ed. Adam Parry. Oxford: Clarendon Press.

Petersmann, Hubert. 1977. *Petrons urbane Prosa: Untersuchungen zu Sprache und Text (Syntax).* Vienna: Verlag der Österreichischen Akademie der Wissenschaften.

Petropoulos, J. C. B. 1994. *Heat and Lust: Hesiod's Midsummer Festival Scene Revisited.* Lanham, Md: Rowman and Littlefield.

Pfeiffer, Rudolf. 1968. *A History of Classical Scholarship I: From the Beginnings to the End of the Hellenistic Age.* Oxford: Clarendon Press.

Phillips, N. 1981. *Sijobang: Sung Narrative Poetry of West Sumatra.* Cambridge: Cambridge University Press.

Pighi, Giovanni Battista. 1964. *Lettere latine d'un soldato di Traiano.* Bologna: Zanichelli.

PMG = Denys Page, ed. 1962. *Poetae Melici Graeci.* Oxford: Clarendon Press.

Porter, H. N. 1951. "The Early Greek Hexameter." *Yale Classical Studies* 12. 3–63.

Porter, J. 1992. "Hermeneutic Lines and Circles: Aristarchus and Crates on the Exegesis of Homer." In: *Homer's Ancient Readers,* R. Lamberton and J. Keaney, eds., 67–114.

Pucci, Pietro. 1987. *Odysseus Polutropos: Intertextual Readings in the Odyssey and the Iliad.* Ithaca and London: Cornell University Press.

———. 1993. "Antiphonal Lament Between Achilles and Briseis." *Colby Quarterly* 29. 258–272.

Puhvel, Jaan. 1977. "Devatâ-Dvandva in Hittite, Greek, and Latin." *American Journal of Philology* 98. 396–405.

Pulgram, Ernst. 1950. "Spoken and Written Latin." *Language* 26. 458–466.

Quadlbauer, Franz. 1962. *Die antike Theorie der genera dicendi im lateinischen Mittelalter.* Graz and Cologne: Böhlau (= Sitzungsberichte der Österreichischen Akademie der Wissenschaften. Philosophisch-historische Klasse, 241/2).

Quint, David. 1993. *Epic and Empire: Politics and Generic Form from Virgil to Milton.* Princeton: Princeton University Press.

Radlov, Vasilii V. 1885. *Proben der Volksliteratur der nördlichen türkischen Stämme.* Vol. 5: *Der Dialect der Kara-Kirgisen.* St. Petersburg: Commissionäre der Kaiserlichen Akademie der Wissenschaften ("Preface" transl. by Gudrun Böttcher Sherman with Adam Brooke Davis in *Oral Tradition* 5 (1990), 73–90).

Raible, Wolfgang, ed. 1990. *Erscheinungsformen kultureller Prozesse. Jahrbuch 1988 des Sonderforschungsbereichs "Übergänge und Spannungsfelder zwischen Mündlichkeit und Schriftlichkeit."* Tübingen: Narr (= ScriptOralia, 13).

———, ed. 1991. *Symbolische Formen—Medien—Identität. Jahrbuch 1989/90 des Sonderforschungsbereichs "Übergänge und Spannungsfelder zwischen Mündlichkeit und Schriftlichkeit."* Tübingen: Narr (= ScriptOralia, 37).

———. 1994. "Orality and Literacy." In: Günther and Ludwig, eds. 1994, 1–17.

Ranke, Leopold von. 1888. "Zur Kritik fränkisch-deutscher Reichsannalisten." *Sämtliche Werke,* vol. 51. 95–121. Leipzig: Duncker and Humblot.

Reichel, Michael. 1994. *Fernbeziehungen in der Ilias.* Tübingen: Narr (= ScriptOralia, 62).

Reichl, Karl. 1992. *Turkic Oral Epic Poetry: Traditions, Forms, Poetic Structure.* New York: Garland (= The Albert Bates Lord Studies in Oral Tradition, 7).

Rengakos, A. 1993. *Der Homertext und die hellenistische Dichter.* Stuttgart: Franz Steiner Verlag (Hermes Einzelschriften, 64).

Renoir, Alain. 1988. *A Key to Old Poems: The Oral-Formulaic Approach to the Interpretation of West-Germanic Verse.* University Park and London: The Pennsylvania State University Press.

Richardson, Nicholas. 1975. "Homeric Professors in the Age of the Sophists." *Proceedings of the Cambridge Philological Society* 21. 65–81.

———. 1980. "Literary Criticism in the Exegetical Scholia to the Iliad: A Sketch." *Classical Quarterly* 30. 265–287.

———. 1992. "Aristotle's Reading of Homer and Its Background." In: R. Lamberton and J. Keaney, eds., 30–40. Princeton: Princeton University Press.

———. 1993. *The Iliad: A Commentary. Volume VI: books 21–24.* Cambridge: Cambridge University Press.

Richardson, Scott. 1990. *The Homeric Narrator.* Nashville: Vanderbilt University Press.

Rijk, L. M. de. 1977. *Middeleeuwse wijsbegeerte.* Assen and Amsterdam: Van Gorcum.

Risch, Ernst. 1974. *Wortbildung der homerischen Sprache.* 2nd ed. Berlin: De Gruyter.

Rivarola, José Luis. 1994. "Escrituras marginales: sobre textos de bilingües en el Perú." In: Lüdtke, ed. 1994, 191–209.

Rösler, Wolfgang. 1980. "Die Entdeckung der Fiktionalität in der Antike." *Poetica* 12. 283–319.

———. 1983. "Schriftkultur und Fiktionalität: Zum Funktionswandel der griechischen Literatur von Homer bis Aristoteles." In: Assmann, Assmann, and Hardmeier, eds. 1983, 109–122.

Ruijgh, C. J. 1971. *Autour de τε épique: Études sur la syntaxe grecque.* Amsterdam: Hakkert.

———. 1985. Review of Basset 1979. *Lingua* 65. 323–333.

Russo, Joseph. 1994. "Homer's Style: Nonformulaic Features of an Oral Aesthetic." *Oral Tradition* 9. 371–389.

———. 1997. "The Formula." In: *Homeric Questions: A New Companion to Homer,* I. Morris and B. Powell, eds. Leiden: Brill.

Rychner, Jean. 1955. *La chanson de geste: Essai sur l'art épique des Jongleurs.* Geneva/Lille: Droz/Giard (= Société de publications romanes et françaises, 53).

Saenger, Paul. 1982. "Silent Reading: Its Impact on Late Medieval Script and Society." *Viator* 13. 367–414.

Sale, William M. 1993. "Homer and the *Roland:* The Shared Formular Technique, Part I." *Oral Tradition* 8.87–142; 381–412.

Schadewaldt, Wolfgang. 1975. *Der Aufbau der Ilias—Strukturen und Konzeptionen.* Frankfurt a.M.: Insel Verlag.

Schaefer, Ursula. 1986. "Two Women in Need of a Friend: A Comparison of *The Wife's Lament* and Eangyth's Letter to Boniface." In: *Germanic Dialects: Linguistic and Philological Investigations.* Bela Brogyanyi and Th. Krömmelbein, eds., 491–524. Amsterdam: Benjamins.

———. 1992. *Vokalität: Altenglische Dichtung zwischen Mündlichkeit und Schriftlichkeit.* Tübingen: Narr (= ScriptOralia, 39).

———. 1993. "Alterities: On Methodology in Medieval Literary Studies." *Oral Tradition* 8. 187–214.

———. 1995. "Individualität und Fiktionalität: Zu einem mediengeschichtlichen und mentalitätsgeschichtlichen Wandel im 12. Jahrhundert." In *Mündlichkeit—Schriftlichkeit—Weltbildwandel: Literarische Kommunikation und Deutungsschemata von Wirklichkeit in der Literatur des Mittelalters und der frühen Neuzeit,* Werner Röcke and Ursula Schaefer, eds. Tübingen: Gunter Narr.

————, ed. 1993. *Schriftlichkeit im frühen Mittelalter.* Tübingen: Narr (= ScriptOralia, 53).

Schechner, Richard. 1985. *Between Theater and Anthropology.* Philadelphia: University of Pennsylvania Press.

Schein, Seth L. 1984. *The Mortal Hero: An Introduction to Homer's Iliad.* Berkeley and Los Angeles: University of California Press.

Scheub, H. 1975. *The Xhosa Ntsomi.* Oxford: Oxford University Press.

Schlieben-Lange, Brigitte. 1983. *Traditionen des Sprechens: Elemente einer pragmatischen Sprachgeschichtsschreibung.* Stuttgart: Kohlhammer.

Schmidt, J.-U. 1986. *Adressat und Paraineseform.* Göttingen: Vandenhoeck & Ruprecht.

Schmitt, Jean-Claude. 1981. "Gestus—gesticulation." In: *Lexicologie du latin médiéval,* 377–390. Paris: C.N.R.S.

Scholz, Bernhard F. 1993. "Marginalia bij het Boek der Natuur." *Feit & Fictie* 1. 52–74.

Scholz, Bernhard Walter, and Barbara Rogers. 1972. *Carolingian Chronicles.* Ann Arbor: University of Michigan Press.

Schröder, Edward, ed. 1892. *Die Kaiserchronik eines Regensburger Geistlichen: Monumenta Germaniae Historica. Scriptorum qui vernacula lingua usi sunt.* Hannover: Hahn.

Schwyzer, E. 1939. *Griechische Grammatik, vol. I.* Munich: Beck.

Schwyzer, E., and A. Debrunner. 1950. *Griechische Grammatik, vol. II.* Munich: Beck.

Scott, W. 1974. *The Oral Nature of the Homeric Simile.* Leiden: Brill.

Sealy, Raphael. 1957. "From Phemius to Ion." *Revue des études grecques* 70. 312–355.

Searle, John. 1968. *Speech Acts.* Oxford: Oxford University Press.

Segal, Charles. 1983. "Kleos and Its Ironies in the *Odyssey*." *L'Antiquité Classique* 52. 22–47. Repr. in *Singers, Heroes, and Gods in the Odyssey.* Ithaca and London 1994: Cornell University Press.

Selig, Maria. 1993. "Parodie et protocole—l'importance de la 'citation' pour les premiers documents des langues romanes." In: Selig et al., eds. 1993, 91–108.

Selig, Maria, Barbara Frank, and Jörg Hartmann, eds. 1993. *Le passage à l'écrit des langues romanes.* Tübingen: Narr (= ScriptOralia, 46).

Shipp, G. P. 1972. *Studies in the Language of Homer.* 2nd ed. Cambridge: Cambridge University Press.

Slatkin, Laura M. 1991. *The Power of Thetis: Allusion and Interpretation in the Iliad.* Berkeley and Los Angeles: University of California Press.

SM = Snell, B., and H. Maehler, eds. 1975. *Pindarus: Fragmenta.* Leipzig: Teubner.

Smith, Colin. 1993. *Poema de Mio Cid.* 18th ed. Madrid: Cátedra.

Smith, Dorothy E. 1978. "The Social Construction of Documentary Reality." *Sociological Inquiry* 44. 257–268.

Söll, Ludwig. 1985. *Gesprochenes und geschriebenes Französisch.* 3rd ed. Berlin: Schmidt.

Spiegel, Gabrielle. 1990. "History, Historicism, and the Social Logic of the Text in the Middle Ages." *Speculum* 65. 59–86.

Spitzer, Leo. 1976. *Lettere di prigionieri di guerra italiani 1915–1918.* 2nd ed. Turin: Boringhieri.

Stanley, Keith. 1993. *The Shield of Homer: Narrative Structure in the Iliad.* Princeton: Princeton University Press.

Stefenelli, Arnulf. 1962. *Die Volkssprache im Werk des Petron im Hinblick auf die romanischen Sprachen.* Passau: Wissenschaftlicher Verlag Rothe.

Stein, Elisabeth. 1990. *Autorbewußtsein in der frühen griechischen Literatur.* Tübingen: Narr (= ScriptOralia, 17).

Stempel, Wolf-Dieter. 1972. "Die Anfänge der romanischen Prosa im XIII. Jahrhundert." In: *Généralités,* M. Delbouille, ed., 585–601. Heidelberg: Winter (= Grundriss der romanischen Literaturen des Mittelalters, Vol. 1).

———. 1993. "La 'modernité' des débuts: la rhétorique de l'oralité chez Chrétien de Troyes." In: Selig et al., eds. 1993, 275–298.

———. 1994. "Ceci n'est pas un conte, la rhétorique du conversationnel." *Littérature N° 93 (Le partage de la parole),* 66–79.

Stierle, Karlheinz. 1990. *Dimensionen des Verstehens: Der Ort der Literaturwissenschaft.* Konstanz: Universitätsverlag Konstanz.

Stock, Brian. 1983. *The Implications of Literacy: Written Language and Models of Interpretation in the Eleventh and Twelfth Centuries.* Princeton: Princeton University Press.

———. 1990. *Listening for the Text: On the Uses of the Past.* Baltimore: Johns Hopkins University Press.

Stolz, Benjamin A., and Richard S. Shannon, eds. 1976. *Oral Literature and the Formula.* Ann Arbor: Center for the Coordination of Ancient and Modern Studies.

Stone, R. 1988. *Dried Millet Breaking: Time, Words, and Song in the Woi Epic of the Kpelle.* Bloomington: Indiana University Press.

Svennung, Joseph. 1935. *Untersuchungen zu Palladius und zur lateinischen Fach- und Volkssprache.* Leipzig/Uppsala/The Hague/Paris: Otto Harrassowitz/Almqvist & Wiksell/Martinus Nijhoff/Champion.

Tagliavini, Carlo. 1972. *Le origini delle lingue neolatine.* 6th ed. Bologna: Pàtron.

Tannen, Deborah. 1980. "Spoken/Written Language and the Oral/Literate Continuum." In: *Proceedings of the Sixth Annual Meeting of the Berkeley Linguistic Society,* E. B. Caron et al., eds., 207–218. Berkeley: Berkeley Linguistic Society.

————. 1982a. "The Oral/Literate Continuum in Discourse." In: *Spoken and Written Language: Exploiting Orality and Literacy,* D. Tannen, ed., 1–16. Norwood, N.J.: Ablex.

————. 1982b. "Oral and literate strategies in spoken and written narratives." *Language* 58. 1–21.

————. 1989. *Talking Voices: Repetition, Dialogue, and Imagery in Conversational Discourse.* Cambridge: Cambridge University Press.

Taplin, Oliver. 1992. *Homeric Soundings: The Shaping of the Iliad.* Oxford: Clarendon Press.

Thomas, Rosalind. 1989. *Oral Tradition and Written Record in Classical Athens.* Cambridge: Cambridge University Press.

Thornton, Agathe. 1984. *Homer's Iliad: Its Composition and the Motif of Supplication.* Göttingen: Vandenhoeck & Ruprecht (Hypomnemata, 81).

Thorpe, Lewis. 1971. *Einhard and Notker the Stammerer: Two Lives of Charlemagne.* Harmondsworth: Penguin Books.

Thun, Harald. 1978. *Probleme der Phraseologie: Untersuchungen zur wiederholten Rede mit Beispielen aus dem Französischen, Italienischen, Spanischen und Rumänischen.* Tübingen: Niemeyer.

Todorov, Tzvetan. 1968. "Introduction: Le Vraisemblable." *Communications* 11. 2–3.

Tolkien, J. R. R. 1936/63. "Beowulf: The Monster and the Critics." In: *An Anthology of "Beowulf"-Criticism,* Lewis E. Nicholson, ed., 51–103. Notre Dame, Ind.: University of Notre Dame Press.

Toolan, Michael J. 1988. *Narrative: A Critical Linguistic Introduction.* London and New York: Longman.

Ungern-Sternberg, Jürgen von, and Hansjörg Reinau, eds. 1988. *Ver-*

gangenheit in mündlicher Überlieferung. Stuttgart: Teubner (= Colloquium Rauricum, 1).

Usener, Knut. 1990. *Beobachtungen zum Verhältnis der Odyssee zur Ilias.* Tübingen: Narr (= ScriptOralia, 21).

Väänänen, Veikko. 1959. *Le latin vulgaire des inscriptions pompéiennes.* 2nd ed. Berlin: Akademie-Verlag.

Vitale, Maurizio. 1971. *La questione della lingua.* 5th ed. Palermo: Palumbo.

Voorwinden, Norbert, and Max de Haan, eds. 1979. *Oral Poetry: Das Problem der Mündlichkeit mittelalterlicher epischer Dichtung.* Darmstadt: Wissenschaftliche Buchgesellschaft.

Waanders, F. M. J. 1992. "Greek." In: *Indo-European Numerals,* J. Gvozdanovic, ed. Berlin and New York: Mouton de Gruyter.

Wace, A. J., and F. H. Stubbings. 1962. *A Companion to Homer.* London: Macmillan.

Wade-Gery, H. T. 1952. *The Poet of the Iliad.* Cambridge: Cambridge University Press.

Wadley, S. 1991. "Why Does Ram Swarup Sing? Song and Speech in the North Indian Epic Dhola." In: *Gender, Genre, and Power in South Asian Expressive Traditions,* A. Appadurai, F. Korom, and M. Mills, eds., 201–223. Philadelphia: University of Pennsylvania Press.

Warning, Rainer. 1981. "Staged Discourse: Remarks on the Pragmatics of Fiction." *Dispositio* 5. 35–54.

Watkins, Calvert. 1979. "NAM.RA GUD UDU in Hittite: Indo-European poetic language and the folk Taxonomy of Wealth." In: *Hethitisch und Indogermanisch: Vergleichende Studien zur historischen Grammatik und zur dialektgeographischen Stellung der indogermanischen Sprachgruppe Altkleinasiens,* W. Meid and E. Neu, eds., 269–287. Innsbruck: *Innsbrucker Beiträge zur Sprachwissenschaft,* 25. Repr. in C. Watkins, *Selected Writings, vol. II,* 644–662. Innsbruck 1994.

Wattenbach, W., W. Levisohn, and H. Löwe. 1953. *Deutschlands Geschichtsquellen im Mittelalter: Vorzeit und Karolinger.* Weimar: H. Boehlaus Nachf.

Watzlawick, Paul, Janet H. Beavin, and Don D. Jackson. 1967. *Pragmatics of Human Communication: A Study of Interactional Patterns, Pathologies, and Paradoxes.* New York: Norton.

Webster, T. B. L. 1964. *From Mycenae to Homer.* New York: Norton.

Wehrli, Max. 1972. "'Die Klage' und der Untergang der Nibelungen." In: *Zeiten und Formen in Sprache und Dichtung. Festschrift für Fritz Tschirch zum 70. Geburtstag*, Karl-Heinz Schirmer and Bernhard Sowinski, eds., 96–112. Cologne and Vienna: Boehlau.

Weinreich, Harald. 1984. *Tempus: Besprochene und erzählte Welt*. 4th ed. Stuttgart: Kohlhammer.

Weinrich, Uriel. 1969. "Problems in the Analysis of Idioms." In: *Substance and Structure of Language*. J. Puhvel, ed., 23–81. Berkeley and Los Angeles: University of California Press.

Wellek, René, and Austin Warren. 1962. *Theory of Literature*. 3rd ed. New York: Harcourt, Brace & World.

West, Martin L. 1974. *Studies in Greek Elegy and Iambus*. Berlin: De Gruyter.

———. 1983. *The Orphic Poems*. Oxford: Oxford University Press.

———. 1988. "The Rise of Greek Epic." *Journal of Hellenic Studies* 108. 151–172.

———. 1989a. *Iambi et Elegi Graeci, vol. 1*. Oxford: Oxford University Press.

———. 1989b. "An Unrecognized Injunctive Usage in Greek." *Glotta* 67. 135–138.

———. 1993. "Simonides Redivivus." *Zeitschrift für Papyrologie und Epigraphik* 98. 1–14.

West, Stephanie. 1967. *The Ptolemaic Papyri of Homer*, Papyrologica Coloniensia 3. Cologne and Opladen: Westdeutscher.

———. 1988. "The Transmission of the Text." In: Heubeck et al., 1988, 33–48.

Whitman, C. 1958. *Homer and the Heroic Tradition*. Cambridge, Mass.: Harvard University Press.

Wolf, Alois. 1991. "Medieval Heroic Traditions and Their Transitions from Orality to Literacy." In: Doane and Braun Pasternack, eds. 1991, 67–89.

Wolf, Friedrich August. 1795. *Prolegomena ad Homerum*. R. Peppermüller, ed. Halle: Waisenhaus, 1884. Repr. 1963 Hildesheim: G. Olms. (English translation by A. Grafton, G. W. Most, and J. G. Zetzel, *Prolegomena to Homer*, Princeton 1985: Princeton University Press).

Wolfson, Nessa. 1982. *The Conversational Historical Present in American English Narrative*. Dordrecht: Foris.

Wunderli, Peter. 1965. "Die ältesten romanischen Texte unter dem Gesichtspunkt von Protokoll und Vorlesen." *Vox Romanica* 24. 44–64.

Wyatt, William W. 1992. Response to Daitz 1991. *Bryn Mawr Classical Review* 2.7.9.

Young, D., ed. 1971. *Theognis.* Leipzig: Teubner.

Zumthor, Paul. 1972. *Essai de poétique médiévale.* Paris: Seuil.

——. 1983a. *Introduction à la poésie orale.* Paris: Seuil.

——. 1983b. "L'intertexte performanciel." *Texte. Revue de critique et de théorie littéraire* 2. 49–59.

——. 1985. "Archaïsme et fiction: les plus anciens documents de langue 'romane.'" In: *La linguistique fantastique,* S. Auroux et al., eds., 285–299. Paris: Joseph Clims/Denoël.

——. 1987. *La lettre et la voix: De la "littérature" médiévale.* Paris: Seuil.

——. 1990a. *Oral Poetry: An Introduction.* Trans. Kathryn Murphy-Judy. Minneapolis: University of Minnesota Press.

——. 1990b. *Performance, réception, lecture.* Québec: Les Éditions du Préambule.

ঔ

CONTRIBUTORS

EGBERT BAKKER (Université de Montréal). Areas of interest: Homeric philology, linguistics, and discourse analysis; semiotics of speech and writing. Main publications: *Linguistics and Formulas in Homer* (Amsterdam, Benjamins, 1988); *Poetry in Speech: Orality and Homeric Discourse* (Cornell University Press, 1996); *Grammar as Interpretation: Ancient Greek Literature in its Linguistic Contexts* (Leiden, Brill).

FRANZ H. BÄUML (University of California, Los Angeles). Areas of interest: Medieval German literature; orality and literacy. Main publications: *Rhetorical Devices and Structure in the "Ackermann aus Böhmen"* (University of California Press, 1960); *Kudrun. Die Handschrift* (Berlin 1969); *Medieval Civilization in Germany: 800–1273* (London and New York, 1969); *A Dictionary of Gestures* (Metuchen, N.J., 1975, with Betty J. Bäuml); *A Concordance to the Nibelungenlied* (Leeds, 1976, with Eva-Maria Fallone).

JOHN MILES FOLEY (Center for Studies in Oral Tradition, University of Missouri, Columbia). Areas of interest: comparative oral traditions (Ancient Greek, Anglo-Saxon, South Slavic). Main publications: *Oral-Formulaic Theory and Research* (Garland, 1985); *The Theory of Oral Composition* (Indiana University Press, 1988, repr. 1992); *Traditional Oral Epic* (Univ. of California Press, 1990, repr. 1993); *Immanent Art* (Indiana University Press, 1991); *The Singer of Tales in Performance* (Indiana University Press, 1995).

ANDREW FORD (Princeton University). Areas of interest: Homeric studies; ancient literary criticism. Author of *Homer, The Poetry of the Past* (Cornell University Press, 1992).

AHUVIA KAHANE (Northwestern University). Areas of interest: Homer and oral poetics; literary criticism. Author of *The Interpretation of Order: A Study in the Poetics of Homeric Repetition* (Oxford University Press, 1994); editor of *The Oxford English-Hebrew Dictionary*

297

(Oxford University Press, 1996) and *A Companion to the Prologue to Apuleius' 'Metamorphoses'*, with A. J. W. Laird (Oxford University Press, forthcoming). He is co-author (with M. Mueller) of *The Chicago Komer* (University of Chicago Press, forthcoming).

RICHARD P. MARTIN (Princeton University). Areas of interest: Homer, early Greek poetry. Main publications: *Healing, Sacrifice, and Battle: Amēchania and Related Concepts in Early Greek Poetry* (Innsbruck, 1983) and *The Language of Heroes: Speech and Performance in the Iliad* (Cornell University Press, 1989).

GREGORY NAGY (Harvard University). Areas of interest: historical and Indo-European linguistics, comparative metrics, oral poetics, Archaic Greek poetry. Main publications: *Comparative Studies in Greek and Indic Meter* (Harvard University Press, 1974); *The Best of the Achaeans. Concepts of the Hero in Archaic Greek Poetry* (John Hopkins University Press, 1979); *Pindar's Homer. The Lyric Possession of an Epic Past* (Johns Hopkins University Press, 1990); *Greek Mythology and Poetics* (Cornell University Press, 1990); *Poetry as Performance. Homer and Beyond* (Cambridge University Press, 1996); *Homeric Questions* (Austin, University of Texas Press, 1996).

WULF OESTERREICHER (Ludwig-Maximilians-Universität, Munich). Areas of interest: language theory and methodological aspects of linguistics, language typology, and comparative syntax of the Romance languages. Main publications: *Sprachtheorie und Theorie der Sprachwissenschaft* (Heidelberg, Winter, 1979); *Einführung in die romanische Sprachwissenschaft,* with H.-M. Gauger and R. Windisch (Darmstadt, Wissenschaftliche Buchgesellschaft, 1981); *Gesprochene Sprache in der Romania: Französisch, Italienisch, Spanisch,* with P. Koch (Tübingen, Niemeyer, 1990).

URSULA SCHAEFER (Humboldt-Universität, Berlin). Areas of interest: Medieval English poetry, orality and literacy, literary theory. Main publications: *Höfisch-ritterliche Dichtung und sozialhistorische Realität. Literatursoziologische Studien zum Verhältnis von Adelstruktur, Ritterideal und Dichtung bei Geoffrey Chaucer* (Frankfurt, Lang, 1977); *Vokalität. Altenglische Dichtung zwischen Mündlichkeit und Schriftlichkeit* (Tübingen, Narr, 1992).

Cretan *mandinandhes,* 157
Cypria, 103

Decoding. *See* Encoding/decoding
Deconstruction, 218–219, 223,
    228–229
Deictic: element, 22, 26, 29; func-
    tions, 150; scenarios, 211; shifts
    and fluctuations, 115, 116–117,
    119, 125, 129, 135
Description versus narration, 16
Destiny in past, 22, 31. *See also* Fate
Dhola epic, 151, 159
Diachronic viewpoint. *See* Ellipsis
Diglossia, 201
Discourse: direct, 14, 26, 29–30; plan-
    ning, 194; traditions, 194–195,
    203–204. *See also* Writing
Distance, language of *(Sprache der
    Distanz),* 9, 194–195, 207, 211.
    See also Immediacy: language of
    (Sprache der Nähe); Near versus
    distant
Distancing device (hexameter as), 7,
    113, 115. *See also* Deictic: shifts
    and fluctuations
Document time, 44–46
Dual forms, 8–9, Chapter 7; Aiante,
    175–183; citation of, 179–180; in
    Embassy scene, 179–180; versus
    plural forms, 178, 179

Eeion inscription, 100
Elegies, Old English, 224, 226–228.
    See also Anglo-Saxon poetry
Ellipsis, 8, Chapter 7; definition of,
    167–169; diachronic viewpoint of,
    175, 179; dual versus plural, 178;
    functional, 170; I/we, 188; and met-
    rical position, 171; by poetry about
    poetry, 186; and representations,
    113; synchronic viewpoint of,
    175–177, 178, 180
Embassy *(Iliad* 9). *See* Dual forms: in
    Embassy scene
Enactment, 50, 118, 207

Enargeia. See Vividness
Encoding/decoding: of epic, 85, 185;
    linguistic, 220–221, 222, 228
Epic. *See* Allegoresis of epic; Cinema
    and epic; Dhola epic; Encoding/de-
    coding: of epic; Igbo epic; Igno-
    rance of epic character; Indian ep-
    ics; *Kleos: klea andrōn;* Non-epic
    genres; Old French epic; Perform-
    ance; Praise poetry, and epic;
    South Slavic epic; Sumatran epic;
    Supergenre, epic as; Text/texts; Woi
    epic; Xhosa ntsomi
Epos, 5, 35–36
Evidence, linguistic markers of,
    17–23. *See also* Deictic
Evolutionary model, of Homer, 9,
    180–181, 183
Exeter Book, 224
Eyewitness, 15

Face-to-face interaction, 209
Fact ("fact"), 6, 32, 37–55, 229, Chap-
    ter 2; and context, 41–42; and per-
    formed discourse, 42; and power,
    40–41; and reality, 12, 39–40; ver-
    sus truth, 4, 6. *See also* Truth
Fate, 31–33
Fiction, 7, 9, 11, 13
Finnish, 240n20
Five ages of Homer. *See* Evolutionary
    model
Fixity, 107–108, 177; and flexibility,
    112, 136–137; semblances of, 112;
    symbols of, 111–112. *See also* Fluid-
    ity; *Mouvance*
Fleischman, Suzanne, 16
Fluidity, 180–181
Formal spoken versus formal written
    language, 195
Formula, 1, 4, 27, 58–59, 66, 74, 81,
    113–114, 211, 213, 221, 223–224,
    226, 230, 234–235n22; definitions
    of, 1–2, 4; density of, 221, 230,
    239n11; formulaic diction,
    223–224; and gestures, 50, 51;

hoion eeipes, 121; *hupodra idōn,*
65, 71, 241n24; and involvement,
27; and localization, 114–121;
mechanisms versus poetic content,
1–2, 3, 5, 27, 60, 67, 113–114; *pukinon epos,* 65, 71, 241n24; symbols
of fixity, 113–114; *ton d' apameibomenos,* 114, 117; and truth, 50
Functional elliptic constructions. *See*
Ellipsis
Functionally conditioned performance shifts. *See* Performance: shifts
Future, Chapter 1; as *kleos,* 33; in the
past, 22, 31–32; as temporal situation of epic performance, 17, 23,
34–36; tense, 21. *See also* Fate;
Tense

Gestures, and formulae. *See* Formula
Gnomic diction, 222–229

Habermas, Jürgen, 217–218
Heisenberg's uncertainty principle, 39
Heraclitus, 94–95
Hermeneutics, 9, 216, 219
Hero: Achilleus, 18–19, 111–119;
Agamemnon, 124–125; Aiante,
175–183; Diomedes, 20, 120; Hec-
tor, 120–121; Odysseus, 123,
130–132; pairs of heroes, 132–134;
Patroklos, 21–23, 23–26; Patroklos,
name of, 187–188; situational
definitions of, 120, 122, 127–128,
246n30; solitary state of, 118; Tele-
machos, 126–128
Heroic traditions, 32, 147
Hesiod, and Homeric diction, 153,
161, 162, 163, 164
Historical present, 14, 16. *See also*
Tense
Historicization, 52
Hittite, 169
Hoios, 121, 133–134
Homeric Question, 57
Humanities versus sciences, 216–217,
219, 229

Igbo epic, 149
Ignorance of epic character, 19, 24,
31, 35–36. *See also Nēpios*
Imitation of oral performance, 7,
102–103
Immanent art, 6, 63, 71, 78
Immediacy, 9, 14; language of *(Spra-
che der Nähe),* 193–195, 199; lin-
guistic, 9, 214; pretended, 15–16.
See also Mimesis: of immediacy;
Near versus distant
Indian epics, 243n2
Informal spoken versus informal writ-
ten, 194–195
Integrated time *(temps intégré),*
209–210
Interpretation, 19, 35
Intertextual (metaperformative) poet-
ics, 161
Involvement, 27, 200

Kaiserchronik, 54
Kaluli weeping, 241n29
Klage, 52, 53
Kleos: enactment of, 112, 117–118,
134; "epic fame," 32–34; *klea an-
drōn,* 187–188
Kuhn, Thomas, 216, 231
Kunstsprache, 153

Lament. *See* Theme
Language of distance. *See* Distance,
language of
Language of/linguistic. *See* Immediacy
Langue parlée versus *langue écrite,*
191
Latinity, 46
Linear B, 173, 174, 246n27, 254n17
Linguistic conception versus linguis-
tic medium, 9, 191–193
Linguistic medium. *See* Linguistic
conception versus linguistic me-
dium
Literate cultures, 220; and literacy,
37, 41, 47, 49, 52–53, 55, 217,
221; perspective of, 6, 9, 10, 37,

INDEX

Literate cultures *(continued)* 42–43, 54–55, 135–137, 220, 228, 229. *See also* Text/texts; Oral: versus literate
Localization, 114–115, 119, 122, 127, 134
Lord, Albert Bates, 58–59
Lyric poetry and epic, 166, Chapter 6

Marked/unmarked discourse, 123, 128–129
Maxims I, II (Old English), 224
Mechanisms versus aesthetics. *See* Formula
Medial approach, 215–220, 229–231, Chapter 9
Medium: and media, 215–220; transferability, 195–196; written/spoken, 9
Mellein, 5, 17–23, 30–31, 33–34
Memory: and meter, 111; and remembering, 12–16, 19, 24, 29, 32, 35
Merism (figure of), 169
Meter and rhythm, 3, 7–8, 111–113, 245n2, Chapter 5
Metonymy, 6, 63–65, 66, 81, 238n2, Chapter 3
Middle English, 240n19
Milman Parry Collection, 241n14, 243n40
Mimesis: of immediacy, 205, 212; as re-enactment, 184–186
Monologue, 208–209
Monumental *Iliad,* 83–84, 152; and "big bang" theory, 7, 181–183; and Herodotus, 102–103; and Thucydides, 103–104; as whole, 84–89, Chapter 4
Mounos (and *oios*), 8, 118, 123, 126–127, 133–134, Chapter 5
Mouvance, 111, 183–184, 210–211
Murko, Matija, 58, 239n5
Native American, 240n14, 243n40

Near versus distant, 5, 7, 9, 12, 17, 25, 29–30. *See also* Reality/Realities

Neoanalysis, 241n25
Nēpios, 19, 21, 31, 35–36, 114, 135, 235n39
New Philology, 219
Nibelungenlied, 52–53
Notker Balbulus, 47–49
Non-epic genres, 139, 166
Non-hexameter motifs, 166
Non-textual aspects, of Homer, 110, 119, 137
Nostos. See Story-pattern

Oios, Chapter 5; and *hoios,* 121, 123; and *mounos,* 8, 118–126, 128–129, 133–134
Old English poetry. *See* Anglo-Saxon poetry
Old French epic, 16, 239n10. *See also Chanson de Roland*
Onset versus coda, in hexameter, 7, 116
Oral: composition, 27, 221; culture, 220–221; culture's perspective of, 37; poetry, 2, 207–214; poetry, and similes, 8, 142–143; primary oral cultures, 193; texts, 9, Chapter 8; versus literate, 7, 37, 59, 61–62, 68, 82–83, 110, 191, 220–221, 230, 239n9; versus written, 59–60
Oral-formulaic style. *See* Formula; Oral-formulaic theory; Parry-Lord theory
Oral-formulaic theory, 2, 60, 221, 230. *See also* Parry-Lord theory
Orality, 37, 41, 47–49, 53–54, 220; orality/literacy debate, 191; spectrum of, 61–62; in text, typology of, 9, 190, 194, 200–206, Chapter 8
Oral tradition, 1–2, 48, 110; history of studies in, 57–62, 239n4; as language, 61; varieties of, 60–61
Ordinary discourse versus literary discourse, 3
Originality, 11, 36